Praise for Created

"Clever and action-packed."
~Cindy Anderson, reviewer

"Hogan's best work yet. Full of surprises, twists and turns. Fascinating main character. For danger, excitement, and a bite into a world most will never get the chance to try in real life, this story will take you there."
~Kathleen Brebes, reviewer

"Created keeps you on your toes, rooting for spy-in-training Ari Agave when she's sent on a deadly mission to Spain."
~Susan Tietjen, reviewer

"I loved it! I anxiously await the further spy adventures of Ari/Christy."
~Michelle Fredericks

"I thoroughly enjoyed it. I loved the last line."
~Donna Weaver, reviewer

"Really great plot. I love how Christy's character developed throughout the story. I hope this isn't the end."
~Nicole Keller, reviewer

"Created is an exciting ride full of surprises at every turn. It was thrilling, and sometimes terrifying to watch Christy's transformation as she was further introduced into the world of espionage, and decides how far she is willing to go to fulfill her first real assignment."
~Jenny Moore, reviewer

"Amazing! Unpredictable. What a talented author!"
~Amanda Suddeth, author of *Remember*

"Hogan has the ability to tap into the fantasies of those who crave change in their lives and satisfy the desire for a more exciting alternate identity."
~Liz Sears, reviewer

CREATED

Also by Cindy M. Hogan

Watched
Protected

CREATED

Cindy M. Hogan

Watched
Series:
Book 3

Copyright ©Cindy M. Hogan
O'neal Publishing Layton, UT.
First Edition: October 2012
Library of Congress Number
2012914450

ISBN- 978-0-9851318-2-1

Cover Design by Josh Winward
Photo by ADBug Photography ©
Edited by Charity West
Typesetting by Heather Justesen

Printed in the United States of America

To teenagers and adults alike

who are trying to decide who to become.

Chapter One

My steps echoed off the gray stone walls, and I felt like I'd come home. I'd always fantasized about living in a castle. What teenage girl doesn't? And I even had a chance to win over a prince. I stopped and stood in the doorway to my room, one small piece of luggage—its mystery contents packed for me by government agents—hanging at my side. I wondered if it would be too weird to be happy about this.

I tried to hold back my excitement, but the total awesomeness of this place took over, and I jumped over the threshold into my room, letting go of my luggage and throwing my hands into the air. My shriek of delight bounced off the stone walls, making me want to yell out some more.

"Hello!" Summer's high-pitched-cheerleader voice pierced the air. "You gonna get your crap outta my way?"

Back to earth, Ari. This isn't a fairy tale.

Taking a quick look around the room, I noticed not one, but four beds and dressers. I turned to see Summer, who I now had to remember to call Sasha, her tiny frame filling only a small sliver of the doorway. She could have walked around my suitcase, but then she'd have nothing to harass me about. Ever since we'd met in Washington, DC, almost

1

a year ago, she'd had something against me. I thought I'd never see her again but now, an ocean away in Belgium, she was going to be my roommate? *Ughh!*

Pressing my lips into a thin line, I grabbed my luggage and hurried over to the bed in the furthest corner of the room next to a massive window. It was no surprise when Sasha went in the opposite direction. Kira, another of the original DC group who now had a new life and identity as Kylie, danced in next and took the bed next to Sasha's. The bright light from the gargantuan antique chandeliers made her already gorgeous auburn hair even more striking. Melanie, my dear friend I could no longer call Marybeth, took the bed nearest me. At least both Melanie's and Kylie's beds would be a buffer between Sasha and me. My head spun for a moment, thinking of the girls' new aliases. Would I ever be able to stop thinking of them with their real names? Maybe I should just start calling them double M, double S, and double K, just to make my life easier.

The administrator who had been assigned to us at check-in stalked in only seconds later. "Dinner will be in about a half hour. I'll take you down. Please stay in your room until then." She stared at each of us, expectant.

"Yes, ma'am," Melanie said.

The lady waited until we had all agreed verbally and then left.

I looked out the picture window onto the sprawling grounds two stories below us. The lush green lawns and leafy trees appeared a bit dark in the twilight. My bed, on the other hand, looked like a soft ray of sunshine caught up in a cloud. I'd never seen such a fluffy blanket before. Daisies dotted three of the six pillows stacked against the ancient-looking, mahogany headboard. I resisted the urge to leap onto the bed and instead made my way over to

Melanie.

She had already de-fluffed a small section of her bed by sitting on it. Her shoulders slumped, and she looked at her feet. I sat next to her, and, as I put my arm around her, the watch they'd placed on my wrist during check-in caught on her shirt. After unsnagging it, I gave her a squeeze. My throat constricted, knowing I had played a role in her desperate sadness.

"What's going to happen to us, Christy?" she asked. I wanted to remind her that I was Ari and she was Melanie now, but it just seemed wrong to say at that moment.

It felt weird to even be called Christy. If anything, I still felt like Michele. I'd only taken on the alias of Ari a few short days ago. I gave Melanie another gentle squeeze. "I don't know how, but everything will work out. You'll see." For her sake, I tried to suppress the excitement inside me that threatened to bubble over.

She turned to me, sliding away from me as she did, and I brought my hands to my lap.

"I don't want a new life," she said. "I want to go back home." Her eyes brimmed with tears, and I felt mine burn. My excitement faded. I knew exactly what she was feeling. Just under a year ago, I had to leave my family and start over in the Witness Protection Program. It had been hard, extremely hard, and a tiny portion of me still longed for my old, predictable life. But I'd come to accept that my past was my past, and I'd never get it back.

"I know," I said. "I know. I'm so sorry." And I was. It was at my insistence that she had watched someone's head get chopped off. Sure, I didn't know that was going to happen, but if I hadn't made her look, we wouldn't be here, in Belgium, hiding from an unknown number of the most renowned terrorists in the FBI's files.

Tears streamed down her face, leaving trails of glitter like a snail in a garden, filling me with an overwhelming agony. My mind suddenly felt like bees were buzzing around in it. If only I hadn't made her look. I reached out and held her. I'm not sure how long we stayed like that, but the arrival of Eugene, AKA Elmer, brought us back to reality.

"Wow!" he said, announcing his arrival, pushing the bridge of his glasses hard against his nose. "Cool room. It's all soft, colorful, and round. Our room is more, uh... plain, straight, and angular...Anyway, it's time for dinner. That administrator asked me to show you the way." He looked at Sasha, who had apparently collapsed on her bed and was snoring softly. "Didn't they tell you not to sleep? You'll end up having terrible jet lag if you do." He walked over to her and shook her foot.

Melanie and I gawked at him. Didn't he know better than to upset the Queen Bee? After giving her foot a final big shake, still unable to rouse her, he walked back to the door and waited. Melanie and I looked at each other. She used her hand to signal to me that my makeup was a mess. I reached up and wiped under my eyes. We snort-laughed, and I called over to Kylie, "Come on." Leaving sleeping beauty to her own devices, we followed Elmer down the hall, listening while he spouted off the instructions the administrator had given him.

"Just a minute, Eug...Elmer," I said, stumbling over his new name as we girls walked into the bathroom. "We need to clean up." I tugged at my black hair, making sure it was nice and spikey and twirled the stud in my nose, wishing I could take it out before seeing Rick in the lunch room. We then hurried down to eat.

Dinner was served cafeteria-style. We got to choose

between two main courses as well as six or seven sides. Even though I wasn't really hungry, I loaded my plate knowing I'd feel it later if I didn't eat. We were surrounded by lots of kids of various ages as well as lots of adults. I could have sworn I heard all kinds of languages as we passed several round tables to get to our own in a corner of the room, where we'd been instructed to sit, but it was so loud, with everyone talking, that I couldn't be sure. I also noticed a pattern, one adult sat at every table with eight kids. I don't know why, but it gave me a strange, hollow feeling in my gut. These men and women who sat with these kids must act as their quasi parents. It made me miss mine. We sat at the only table with empty seats.

"Pretty rad," Elmer said, looking around the room before taking a knife to his spaghetti noodles, cutting them into tiny pieces.

"Yeah," Melanie said, ignoring his out-dated expression. "What is this place, anyway?"

"Looks like some kind of a training facility to me," Elmer said before stuffing a huge forkful of noodles into his mouth.

"Where's Reese?" I asked Elmer. It hurt to call him Reese. He would always be Rick to me.

Elmer chewed for what seemed forever before answering. "He said he wasn't hungry. I think he'll regret it later. Statistics show that jetlag is harder on the body if you don't do something to keep yourself awake. I hope he doesn't fall asleep."

"Yeah," I said, looking at my food and forcing myself to eat it, wondering if I was the reason he wasn't here. Melanie ate like a bird, stabbing the noodles and then barely getting one or two to her mouth with each bite. Kylie looked around like a wild cat.

5

I desperately wanted to ask Melanie about being kidnapped by the terrorists right before we left DC a year ago, but hadn't gotten the chance. We'd been forbidden to talk about it on the plane ride over here, and I didn't want to bring it up with everyone around in the limo. Now, I was afraid of making her cry again. I'd have to find the perfect time. I wished things could have been different, that when I'd looked through the vent, the only life I'd changed had been my own. I was a completely different person now, and I liked who I'd become. But Melanie truly loved her old life. She loved who she'd been.

To stay sane, I had to believe she would end up loving the new her, too. I had hated who I had been and had even prayed to be different. Although the change had been painful, I'd discovered who I really wanted to be. I had to hope the same would happen for Melanie. It was the only way I could deal with this happening to her.

We headed back to our rooms, and I couldn't help but stop by the boys' room. I told Melanie that I wanted to check it out. But really, I just wanted to see Reese—the boy I hoped would be my prince. Their dorm was a tad bit bigger than ours and held six beds. Each one was a different color, like ours, minus the flowers. They all sported some sort of straight-line, masculine pattern, just like Elmer had described it, although his description had been a bit odd.

Reese sat at a desk by a window. It looked like he was writing. I brushed my fingers over the majestic, oak door jamb as I walked over to him. He seemed not to even notice my presence. I really wanted to see what he was writing, but I resisted the urge to peek and instead walked to his side and looked at an antique painting of a regal-looking man sitting on a throne.

"Whatcha doing?" I asked, still looking at the picture.

He shuffled the papers, and I couldn't help but see out of the corner of my eye that he slipped a blank sheet over the one he'd written on. I looked down at him, and our eyes met. I felt a small fire light in my chest and butterflies flitting around in my stomach. I sucked in a small breath. I had to talk to him, to explain.

"Ah, nothing," he said, his arm now resting on the blank page, his insanely blue eyes calling out to me.

"You wanna go explore?" I asked, repeating over and over in my head, *oh, please, please, please.*

"Uh…could you give me fifteen or so?" He asked, raising one hand to his blondish brown hair and stroking it. I wanted to run my own fingers through his hair.

"Sure," I said, forcing myself to back away from him and letting him have his privacy. I bumped into Melanie. I'd forgotten she was there. I looped my arm through hers. "Meet ya back here in fifteen." My heart pounded against my ribs as I tried to hold back my excitement.

"'Kay," he said, already writing again.

Once in the hall, I said, "What do you think he was writing?"

"No clue," Melanie said. "Maybe a letter to his family?"

"Maybe. But why all the secrecy then? I don't think he'd want to blow his cover, get in trouble, or get killed just to write to his family."

"I know you don't want to hear this, but maybe he has a girlfriend. It has been a year."

I thought about what he'd said at the country club about having said goodbye to me and having moved on with his life after thinking I'd been killed in that car crash. A car crash that had been faked as a way for the FBI to get Alex and me into witness protection. The memory of my infatuation with Alex reared its ugly head.

I thought about "fake dying" with him and felt stupid for ever liking him—thinking I was in love with him even. I'd seen a charm dangle from Reese's neck at the country club in DC, and now that image popped up in my mind and haunted me. Maybe he did have a girlfriend back home. I shook it off and tried to hold on to the memory of those first few moments when Reese had held me close after finding out I was alive.

With fifteen minutes to kill, Melanie and I walked around the castle, admiring the pictures of serene landscapes as well as austere men and women dressed in old-fashioned finery. We made our way out to the gardens in back of the castle. The wide open expanse of well-manicured grassy land seemed to spread out right before our eyes. Trees and hedges lined the walkways and drives. It was a truly beautiful sight. A large fountain stood to the left of the gardens and benches, and hedges helped make the area more intimate. A few buildings were scattered around about a half mile away. Many benches graced the walkways making me want to take a stroll and sit down. We made our way back into the main building and up the stairs. I wanted to freshen up a bit before going to meet Reese.

We walked into our room and found a woman standing in the middle of it. Her dark, tiny goose eyes peered at us over too small glasses. Her black hair stretched tightly over her head into a slick bun and her nose seemed to point right at us. She reminded me of a female version of Mr. Miyagi in the movie, *The Karate Kid*. She held a computer tablet of some sort. I noticed Sasha sitting in a chair by her bed, her puffy eyes staring grimly at the woman. Both Reese and Elmer sat in chairs next to her. Reese's eyes skirted mine and I felt a stab of hurt. Why wouldn't he really look at me?

"Come on in," she said, consulting her computer screen. "Uh, Melanie and Ari, is it?"

We nodded, neither of us wanting to move closer. Just then, Kylie ran into the room and said, "I couldn't find them...Oh, they're already here."

"I need to go over a few things. Please take a seat." The woman paused until we sat in the chairs by the others. I glumly resigned myself to the idea that I would not be able to explore the castle with Reese, at least not tonight. She moved to a more optimal position for talking to all of us.

"I am Ms. Mackley. I apologize for not being available when you arrived. I had pressing business. Welcome to Bresen Academy. Young people from all over the U.S. come here to study the art of espionage."

Something delicious stirred in my soul. A spy school? Lucky me. I glanced at Melanie, who looked at me with a "what-the-heck?" look.

"We usually hand-select young people between the ages of five and ten to be a part of this program. Your group is an exception. We will be studying you and discovering your talents over the next few days and then placing you in groups that can most benefit from your particular strengths and skills. Do you have any questions?"

Only a zillion.

"So," Sasha interrupted my thought. "Are you saying that I have no choice about staying here and have no hope of ever going back home?"

Melanie perked up.

9

"At this time you do not have a choice. However, you have a very good chance of returning home if you choose to. But, if you stay, we would like for you to look at this as an adventurous new beginning." She smiled, her painted on eyebrows raised into two oddly comical arches.

Sasha swallowed so hard that I heard it. Her eyes shot daggers at me. I sat up a bit straighter, unwilling to let her get to me, but knowing that if we ended up having to stay, she would do whatever she could to make my life horrible.

"Any others?"

"I was wondering," said Elmer, pushing his glasses hard against his nose. "Why did the FBI send us here instead of to a safe house? It seems a bit illogical considering we will only be here for a short period of time."

"Actually, the FBI has done a thorough study of each of you since the Washington, DC incident. I have read your files also, and it's easy to see why they chose to hide you here. This is an independent spy school. Each of you has a particular skill set that makes you ideal candidates for a future in the world of espionage, if you choose. Assuming you work hard while here, this school will provide you with an excellent initiation into the covert arts."

"Can we at least write our families?" The hope that ringed Melanie's words made my stomach burn.

"*That* is not possible. At least not at this time. Just know that all your families have been moved into witness protection as a precautionary measure for the time being and they know you are safe. You are separated from them for several reasons. Number one, your presence puts your families in greater danger. Two, you yourselves are in grave danger, and the skills you learn here will equip you to protect yourselves in the future. Three, you may decide what we do here appeals to you and you want to stay."

Melanie kept her eyes on the short Asian woman, concentrating hard, tears looming again.

"Now, I will give you some instruction on the watches you received when you arrived as well as the basics of this Academy. Welcome to Orientation 101."

I looked at the large black pliable watch on my wrist and wondered what it was made of—I'd never felt material like this before—and why did we have to have an overview on a watch?

"Your watch is programmed for you and you alone. You should never take it off, including when you shower or swim. It is waterproof, so you don't have to worry about hurting it. It contains your schedule and will help you get where you need to go, and when. The screen will tell you the information you need. If you will all push the top right button on the side of your watch, now, please."

We all did. My watch vibrated and buzzed, and then the big screen lit up. It was a good two and a half inches long and two inches wide. I felt a bit like Batman wearing it. I couldn't help myself, I wanted to see what the screen would do if I bent it. With my thumb and index finger, I tried to squish it together. It gave a little, but it turned out not to be as pliable as I'd thought. Even the band seemed harder now that we'd turned it on.

"Your new name should be displayed on the screen. Does anyone's watch not show their new name?" Ms. Mackley asked.

No one spoke up. Why were they calling this device a watch? It was nothing like a watch. It was more like a mini computer. Or was it a tracker? The idea sent a jolt through my spine. There were only two reasons to attach a tracker to us—to catch us if we tried to get away or find us if we were captured.

Ms. Mackley seemed to be reading my mind. "In a sense, this watch is a sophisticated tracker. It tracks your whereabouts, your health, your scores, basically everything about you and this school. It will keep you safe and help you do all that is required of you here at the Academy. Let's go over the GPS function in this watch, first. Please tap the screen."

I tapped it, and four options lit up the screen.

NUTRITION

SCHEDULE

MAP

INSTRUCTION MANUAL

"You should have four choices at this time. Please tap MAP. You should see an interactive map on the screen. Tap RESTROOM. It should now tell you there are twenty bathrooms in the Academy and ask you which floor you'd like. Tap THIRD. It should now display the location of the four bathrooms on this floor. The yellow dot indicates your location now. Tap the restroom that looks the closest to the dot."

When I tapped it, the screen zoomed in and a pink line was visible along the corridor leading to the restroom.

"If you tap directly on the restroom, it will give you written instructions in case you don't understand the map."

Sure enough. When I tapped on the restroom, written directions popped up. Way cool. I tapped on a couple of the other rooms and lists of students names popped up. It seemed six students were in each room. Something about it didn't sit right with me, however. It spurred a question I had. "How many students are here?"

"At the moment we are completely full with 197. But, we have two sections about to graduate. So our numbers will diminish over the summer. Then we'll get a fresh batch of recruits in September. Good question."

This place created a minimum of sixteen spies a year. That didn't seem like very many. Were there other spy schools somewhere?

Then Ms. Mackley went into a long winded speech about the nutrition tab on our watches and how vital it was to eat properly to improve our mental and physical acuity. If we used the watch correctly, within a year, we would have the knowledge we needed to eat for our maximum benefit even without the watch. It would be like taking an in-depth nutrition course tailored just for each of us. I'd start utilizing it. I guessed it somehow integrated information on our physical fitness with our intake of food and created an optimal nutrition plan for us.

She showed us how to access our schedules, the Internet, and the library here at the Academy. She went over the rules of using the computer, and the consequences of breaking them. Our privileges would be suspended if we ever hacked into any social media sites or any blogs. That meant no Internet, no free time, and sleeping in the 'hole,' a very small room, all by yourself, for an entire week. We also had email privileges within the Academy. The school had its own server and security.

Everyone followed along, tapping their screens when prompted, and *oohing* and *ahhing*. On top of giving us directions and locating us, it kept track of how much exercise we got, what exercise we got and when, without us even having to input anything. It suggested what activities worked the best to reach our individual optimal fitness.

"It also has its own built-in alarm to signal us if you are in trouble or somewhere you shouldn't be. If you don't make curfew you will find yourself immobilized. This makes it easy for us to find you and help you get where you should be as quickly as possible."

Immobilized? Was she kidding?

"My strong suggestion to you is to be where you're supposed to be at the times you're supposed to be there."

"Yes, but how exactly does it do that?" Elmer pressed.

"We won't be going into the specifics of how the watch works, Elmer, only how you should best utilize it."

He nodded.

"As soon as I label you as educated, the smart fabric on your watch will start bonding. In fact, by morning, you will no longer be able to remove it from your wrist."

"No way," Elmer said, looking closely at the fabric. "That's impossible."

"Actually, this fabric was developed here in our labs over five years ago. We are working on speeding up the fusion process. What we develop in our labs rarely makes it out in the "real" world. We use it for our own purposes only. You will find many things that seem impossible in the normal world and yet are very real here in the spy world."

"I love it here," Elmer said.

Ms. Mackley then went into the history of the school and its traditions. I noted several interesting things about this school. It focused on languages and international training. Apparently there were other spy schools.

"Tomorrow, you will all be tested in many different areas. We expect you to do your best, but it is nothing to stress about. It will take most of you the whole day to complete the battery of tests, but some of you may have the evening or even the afternoon to yourself. After your tests have been analyzed, you will all be placed into the group that will best enhance your abilities. Your group mentor will thoroughly orient you to the school, the program you will be in, and how to maximize the use of your watch in your particular program."

"What kind of tests?" Kylie asked.

"Intelligence, reasoning, psychological, physical, dexterity, common sense, agility…and many more. It is nothing you could study for. It's just a measurement and is nothing to worry about."

Nothing to worry about? *Was she crazy?*

"Also, I know you received your name assignments before you arrived. Please take caution only to use that name here, even when no one else is around. Everyone here is assigned a new name when they come here. You are not the only ones. True identities are precious. Never give yours away. I suggest you rigorously practice using your new names over the next few days. Make sure you start *thinking* your friends' new names, too. Erase the old by replacing it with the new. Don't allow your friends even the tiniest of slip-ups. Help each other."

I guessed I didn't need a new name since Ari already was an alias. Christy was the name I needed to protect.

"Now if you'll each step forward, I will place your ankle bands on you. These tell us you've been educated."

We all got to our feet and waited in a line to get our ankle bracelets. I hated the idea. When it was my turn, I said, "Any way, you could just mark me in the computer as educated? I think I'll go crazy having that thing attached to me."

"Sorry, Ari," she said. "Everyone gets the ankle bands. Please, do what you must in order to stay awake for the next hour." She looked right at Sasha. "You need to have your wits about you tomorrow, so you must get the proper amount of rest. Lights out is ten p.m. Curfew is strictly observed here. I saw the four of you in the cafeteria." She motioned to Melanie, Kylie, Elmer, and me. "Please make sure Sasha and Reese can find it. Otherwise, use the map on your watch to find what you need."

I nodded. How had she seen us? Was she at a table I hadn't seen? Or were there cameras hidden around the castle, watching our every move?

"Remember, I am Ms. Mackley, the coordinator of this facility. I am the one that you come to with questions or concerns until you are given a mentor. My office is just left of the cafeteria. See you in the morning. Your watches will act as your alarm clocks. No need to set them. Your schedule will be programmed in as you sleep. Do yourself a favor and stay up until curfew. Boys, I need you for a few minutes. Please follow me." With that, she touched something on the handheld computer screen and left the room. The boys followed.

I looked at Melanie, who appeared to be on the verge of crying once again and urged her to play around with the watch.

We sat and played with the new toy attached to our wrists and then fiddled with the ankle band for a while. It bugged me already. "Why don't we go explore this place?" I suggested, trying to ward off another flood. "Come on, let's go." I stood up, pulling Melanie with me and beckoning Sasha and Kylie to join us.

Chapter Two

I made a point of walking in the direction of the boys' room, though I knew they most likely wouldn't be there. As we walked, I admired the old woodwork and paintings, and I wondered how the FBI had commandeered this castle. I would have thought it'd have to be the CIA running this place, especially since it was outside the U.S. Ms. Mackley hadn't said anything about the FBI had she? She'd just said it was a spy school. Didn't the CIA run spy schools? I'd have to ask Ms. Mackley the next time I saw her.

"Should we ask the boys to join us?" I asked, peering into their room once we reached it.

"Heck yeah," Kylie said, pushing past me into the room, leaving her sullenness behind. She hadn't changed one bit—as boy-crazy as ever. But after a quick look around, she slumped, visibly disappointed. "No one's here."

I stepped in, making sure she was right. The six beds sat empty, perfectly made.

"Hmm," I said. "I wonder where Ms. Mackley took them."

"They're probably already exploring the castle, too," Kylie said. "Let's see if we can find them." She bounded out of their room.

It was probably good the boys weren't there. I couldn't have talked to Reese with Kylie around.

When we'd first arrived at the castle, the receptionist had shown me the way to our room on a map of the entire castle. It was filed away in my mind, and I knew how unlikely it would be to find the guys. This floor alone had fifty rooms. Sure, a good forty were dorm rooms, but there were two other rooms that interested me. One was called the Strategy Room and one the Viewing Room.

We were nearest the Strategy Room, so I steered us there. On the way, we checked out all the rooms on our floor. The doors stood open, revealing immaculate living quarters with nothing out of place. Not even a scrap of paper. What amazed me was the dorm rooms all appeared quite different, unique even, with varying color schemes and themes, and it was so clean, but not medicinal. It was a happy clean. I found myself drawn to the large windows in each room that looked out on the sprawling lawns and gardens. I couldn't wait to get out there and feel the grass under my feet and smell the budding flowers.

Two gigantic, thick wood doors stood as sentinels revealing the huge Strategy Room. The ceilings had to be at least three times my height, probably eighteen feet or more. They seemed to have kept the original structure of the castle, only changing it when absolutely necessary. It was reminiscent of the rec room in DC, multiplied by a thousand, creating a massive game room. Pool, foosball, air hockey, and ping pong tables dominated one side of the room. A whole wall with hundreds of board and other types of games faced us, and varying sizes of tables and chairs were scattered about the center of the room.

To the left, five large screens were set up with varying

game consoles and computers in front of them. Leather chairs, sofas, and gaming chairs dotted that section of the room. I had to resist the urge to go lay down on a comfy looking sofa. I shouldn't be tired. I'd slept the whole six hours on the plane and two of the three on the limo ride from the airport to the castle. I wondered if they'd somehow given us all sleeping pills in our drinks on the plane. I kept telling myself that it was irrational to be tired, and I pushed on. One foot in front of the other.

We made our way to the Viewing Room, tucked into the opposite corner of the third floor. It contained three separate, small theaters, each with a seating capacity of about forty.

We trudged down the stairs to the second floor, opting out of backtracking to one of the two elevators. From the map, I knew this floor held mostly classrooms and offices, but it also had the mess hall, testing center, and some labs. The number two on the door fuzzed in front of my eyes, my desire for sleep taking over. Jet lag hit me hard. We made our way to the mess hall first, to make sure Sasha knew how to get there. Just as we walked into it, our watches simultaneously beeped. We pushed the buttons as instructed and looked at the screen.

BED CHECK IN 10 MINUTES.

We gaped at each other.

"Guess we'd better get back," Melanie said. "I don't want to find out what happens if we're late. Besides, I can't wait to climb into bed. I'm so tired."

"Me, too," I said, walking back to the stairway door and holding it for the girls.

We hurried up, wondering if we could even make it through the maze of rooms in time.

"Are we going the right way?" Kylie asked, flipping

19

her auburn hair over her shoulder. "I have no idea where we even are."

"Yeah," I said. "Just follow me. Or you could always use your watch to find your way."

"How do you remember the way?"

"I'm just good with directions," I said, not wanting to tell her I had a photographic memory.

"More like good at everything," Melanie said, smiling. "You're amazing, really."

I could always count on Melanie to make me feel good.

We made it with two minutes to spare. I started to look in the drawers under my bed for some PJs. My watch vibrated and the screen read, BED CHECK. Immediately, all the lights went out. Other than a few tiny nightlights, there was no light in our room. All movement in the room stopped. Since the moon was only a sliver, it was dark.

"Get the lights," Sasha said.

"Okay," Melanie said. I heard her shuffle over to the door. "I can't find a switch."

"Ugh!" Sasha said. "Do I have to do everything myself?" Her feet thudded across the room toward the door.

"I think everything is automated here," I said. "The lights automatically turn off at ten."

"How ridiculous is that?" Sasha asked in a loud, frustrated voice. "How am I supposed to clean my face and get ready for bed if I can't see?"

"I guess we'll have to be sure to get back before bed check so we can do those things," Kylie said. "I'm too tired to worry about it today, though. I'm going to bed as I am."

I agreed with Kylie, and then added, "Maybe the lights in the bathroom stay on. Why don't you go check?" Then, I climbed in bed, hearing Sasha leave the room.

I thought about Reese for a few sweet moments until I noticed how much the watch was bugging me. I took it off and put it on the nightstand. I couldn't, however, remove the ankle band no matter what I tried. I couldn't stand the thought of never being able to remove the watch, and I shoved it a bit farther away from me.

They'd never know, and I was too tired to worry about it.

Chapter Three

I popped awake to a glow on my nightstand. Everything else was pitch black. I reached for the glowing thing and remembered it was my watch. I pushed the button. It must have been malfunctioning. No one else was moving. I picked it up and gave a feeble attempt at reading the screen. It hurt my eyes, so I closed them, falling back to sleep. What seemed only seconds later, my hand vibrated. Really, it was the watch. I pushed the button and tried harder to see the screen. I squinted and made out the number 20. I had to be up in twenty minutes? My watch must be broken. Why was it waking me so early? No one else stirred in the room. The watch vibrated again. There was no snooze. I picked it back up and shook it. It vibrated again. Wide awake now, I looked hard at the screen.

GOOD MORNING. REPORT TO THE MESS HALL IN 10 MINUTES.

In the bottom corner, I saw the time, 4:50. Reality hit me. *10 minutes?* I jumped out of bed, securing the watch to my wrist. Why wasn't anyone else getting up? Was I the only one who had to get going already? I used the glow of the watch to find my way out of the room and get to the bathroom. The lights popped on as I entered. I didn't have time to change, so I stayed in the clothes I'd worn yesterday and never changed out of. I splashed water on my face, wiped off errant mascara, checked my piercings, rubbed on some deodorant, and spiked my hair. Then I ran down the hall, dropped off my bag just inside the room and hurried to the stairs, skipping down them to the second floor. As I pulled the door open to the mess hall, my watch buzzed.

YOU HAVE ARRIVED.

I scowled, looking around the room and finding Ms. Mackley, standing next to the buffet table. We were completely alone and moved toward each other. Her heeled shoes clacked on the stone floor, and she tapped the screen with her fingers. "I was starting to wonder if you were going to make it." She pressed her lips together in a thin line, accentuating her strange look. I imagined her turning into a wedge to split wood.

"Sorry. I didn't know I'd have to be here so early, and no one else was getting up."

"Yes. We anticipate your testing will take longer than the others.' Just know that you most likely will not be on the same schedule as your roommates. Today's tests will determine each of your schedules from today forward. Please eat a good breakfast. Your watch will give you suggestions. Follow them."

I stared at my watch. "Do I need to push a button?"

"Just touch the word NUTRITION."

I did, but nothing came up.

She must have noticed my confusion. "Let me see."

I held out my hand to her and she touched the screen. "I don't understand that."

"Maybe with all the confusion yesterday, they didn't have time to load mine."

"No. Your watch should have sampled your blood last night and prepared your optimal meal plan while you slept."

A tiny "ah" escaped my lips, and I rocked back on my heels.

She clicked her tongue. "Any reason you can think of that would have interfered with that process, Ari?"

"Well, I kinda took the watch off last night."

"Didn't I tell you to wear it at all times?"

"Yes, but it was bugging me and we were just sleeping—"

Her beady eyes stared down at me. "Don't ever take your watch off." She enunciated every word.

"Okay," I said, my voice tiny."

"Just make sure you load up on foods full of vitamins, minerals, and fiber and have some protein."

"I will, but did you say it will take my blood every night?"

"Yes. The needle that samples your blood is so tiny, you'd never feel it, even if you were awake."

That was a bit disturbing.

"Your test administrator will collect you at five-thirty. Your watch will warn you when it's time." I looked at the watch. "Oh, and Ari," she said, turning back to me. "You are not to discuss your tests with anyone." She looked me up and down, as if analyzing me.

"Okay." I ran my hands down my shirt, trying to iron out the wrinkles that had formed during the night and then grabbed a plate, filling it with fruits, whole wheat toast, and eggs. I looked around the empty room and counted the tables. Twenty-five. Twenty-five tables with nine chairs around each one. Enough room for over 200 students plus twenty-five leaders. I scanned the room for cameras, but couldn't see any. I suspected a spy school would be able to conceal the cameras so no one would notice them. I would have to look up information on the Internet about surveillance cameras the next chance I got.

My watch beeped, letting me know I would be collected in five minutes. I cleaned up and walked to the door. The man that met me was pallid, like he hadn't been outside in years. His dark black eyes studied me. "Ari?"

"That would be me." I smiled.

He cocked his head to the left and said in a flat tone, "Oh." And he continued to stare.

As we walked down the hallway, he said, "I'm sure Ms. Mackley informed you about the secret nature of the testing today."

"Yes."

"I want to emphasize the importance of that idea." He turned and looked down at me over his glasses and gave me a pressed smile. "We can't have tainted results, you know. If you were to discuss even one question with anyone, that person would have time to think about the answer, and the test results would be skewed."

"I've got it." I nodded my head, trying to assure him.

He pushed open a door, and we walked into a room full of computers. It seemed weird to have all that technology in a room with stone walls and ancient chandeliers. "These tests will help us determine how to help you reach your potential so you can be who you were meant to be."

They could tell me who I was meant to be?

"Please sit at desk number one." He gestured with his hand to the left. The computers were spaced far apart at large tables.

I spotted a monitor labeled #1 and took a seat.

He walked up to me and took some things from the back of my chair. "I need you to attach these leads to your body in order for us to monitor you during the testing." He handed them to me one by one and showed me where to put them. They were cold, and it freaked me out a bit. What exactly would they be monitoring?

"Each of your answers on this test determines the next. It's impossible to predict how long the test will last. Each one is different. There are intellectual questions, psychological, spatial, etcetera. I can't go into the specifics. Just answer to the best of your ability."

It had been a long time since I'd been challenged in school, and I wondered if I'd be slow today. A quick thrill went through me, thinking about having a chance to prove myself. It was abnormal, I knew, but it was typical of me, through and through. Was Christy making an appearance?

The first question threw me off for a split second.

WHAT IS YOUR NAME?

Then it gave me four choices,

CHRISTY, ARI, SAMANTHA, OR MICHELE.

My brief moment of hesitation ended with a quick click on ARI. I would not blow my cover ever again. But, obviously my real identity was not a secret to them. After about twenty questions about my cover, it moved on to questions where I had to pick one of two answers. One question stopped me cold.

IF YOU HAD TO KILL ONE OF YOUR PARENTS, WHO WOULD IT BE?

A. YOUR MOTHER

B. YOUR FATHER

Neither, I thought. I wouldn't kill either. I loved them both too much. My thoughts turned to my last birthday and how my dad had worked an extra shift in order to buy my favorite foods for the whole family for my birthday dinner—steak, finger potatoes, asparagus, and cheesecake—and how my mom had worked really hard to prepare the meal perfectly and in secret.

But, I had to choose, I couldn't skip any questions. I pondered the question for what seemed a long time, weighing the reasoning behind each one. On the one hand, children needed their mother. Who would care for them? A mother was a teacher, a guide, a comforter, a helper. On the other, children needed their father for financial support, a different love, a different caring.

Why, why would I be killing them? I wanted to know. I tried to skip the question. It wouldn't let me. Finally, I clicked on Father. Not sure why. Just did.

The question, this time altered to use my parents' first names, showed up again after a little while.

IF YOU HAD TO CHOOSE ONE OR THE OTHER, WHO WOULD YOU KILL?

A. MARTHA

B. JAMES

I knew immediately what to do. I clicked on MARTHA. That would even it out. The questions got progressively more difficult to morally negotiate.

IS IT OKAY TO KILL TO SAVE ANOTHER?

WHAT WOULD YOUR SISTER HAVE TO DO TO MAKE YOU KILL HER? CLICK ALL THAT APPLY.

Questions about hypothetical missions popped up. I answered as quickly as I could process the information, feeling like they were asking me the impossible. If I thought too much, it was harder. I had to let instinct take over.

IF YOU HAD MEAT, A GUN, AND A KNIFE WITH YOU AND WERE ATTACKED BY A TRAINED ATTACK DOG, WHICH ITEM WOULD BE MOST EFFECTIVE TO DEFEAT IT?

As suddenly as it had started, I reached the end of the

section.

PLEASE STAND AND STRETCH. IF YOU NEED TO USE THE RESTROOM, PLEASE ALERT YOUR TEST ADMINISTRATOR. YOU HAVE FIVE MINUTES. PLEASE HELP YOURSELF TO AN ENERGY BAR IN THE DESK DRAWER.

I stood, stretching, and looked at the clock on the wall. It'd been three hours. Three hours! Unbelievable. I shook my legs and arms and rolled my neck around in a big circle before reaching my arms in the air and stretching to the ceiling again. I asked to use the restroom. And the test administrator escorted me after I removed the leads. When I got back, I helped myself to an energy bar before replacing the leads.

The screen lit up.

PLEASE TAKE YOUR SEAT.

I sat down and a picture of a girl appeared on the screen for about ten seconds. She looked sad, and my first impulse was to comfort her. The picture disappeared, and then a set of questions appeared. It was free-response, no multiple choice or true-false.

WHAT COLOR WAS HER HAIR? HER EYES? WAS SHE SCARED? WHAT WAS SHE DOING BEFORE THIS PICTURE WAS TAKEN?

Such odd questions.

They forced me to make conclusions without having all the facts.

One picture after another popped up. I must have looked at and then dissected a thousand different people on the screen.

Then diagrams appeared on the screen, and I was directed to draw them on the electronic writer's pad next to the keyboard. The diagrams got more and more complicated. They threw in colors, and I had to select the right colors for each line, each symbol. One thing was sure. I needed to take a drawing class.

PLEASE STAND AND TAKE A FIVE MINUTE BREAK, EAT AN APPLE, AND DRINK A BOTTLED WATER FROM THE DRAWER.

I snagged the apple and took a bite, then looked around the room as I stood. My tester sat at a desk in the front of the room again, working at a computer. I glanced at the blind-covered windows beside me and reached over to take a look outside. There was no outside. Through the window I saw a lab, where people were working. I let the blinds fall, disappointed. I stretched and the com-puter beeped.

PLEASE TAKE A SEAT.

The next section of testing gave me a situation and then asked what I would do given the circumstances. Then lists of about fifteen suggestions showed up. The differences that separated the answers were miniscule. I had to concentrate. Next, I had to copy handwriting, draw pictures of people and animals, and copy codes.

New scenarios popped up, crazy strange ones about being attacked by bugs, books, and other things. I was getting tired and had to smile when the computer told me to stand and take a forty minute lunch break.

By the time I stood, the test administrator was by my side asking me to remove the monitoring leads I'd reattached after my bathroom break. I headed for the door.

"Uh, lunch is this way," he said.

I turned to see him motioning to the back of the room.

"Oh, we're not going to the mess hall?"

"Not when you're testing."

Okay. Weird. We went through a back door into a small

eating area. A boy who looked about fifteen sat chowing on a large piece of lasagna. A piece of garlic bread sat on a smaller plate to his right, and a bowl of green beans on his left.

"Have a seat," my tester said. "They'll bring your lunch shortly." He smiled at me. A genuine smile, like he somehow had decided he liked me. He started to move toward the door, and I called out to him.

"I never caught your name."

"I'm Jeff."

"Jeff," I said as he walked out the door.

"Wow! You're lucky ya know," the boy said.

"I am? Why's that?"

"Jeff never tells people his name. He has a thing about it."

"A thing?"

"Yeah. I didn't get the privilege until my eighth year here."

I looked back at the door Jeff had gone through.

"He must be impressed with you. It seems he only talks to people who impress him in some way...I'm Tyler, by the way."

"Hi Tyler. I'm Ari."

"Nice hair."

"Thanks," I said, reaching up to touch my black spikes.

The door opened, and a woman brought in a covered lunch tray.

She glanced at Tyler and his almost empty plates, then she looked at me and said, "Ari?"

I nodded my head and started to stand.

"It's okay. I'll bring it to you."

She lifted the cover and set down the identical food Tyler had, with the addition of a small piece of chocolate cake, in front of me.

Created

"Enjoy," she said as she left the room.

Tyler eyed me, and I figured it was the cake that interested him. I lifted the plate of cake and said, "You want this?

He laughed. "We're not allowed to share food here. No one told you that?"

I shook my head. "But I don't mind. You can have it. Really."

"Really," he said, a serious tone lacing his words. "You're not allowed to share food."

"But you didn't get any cake. That's not right."

"Your watch monitor tells the kitchen what your body needs and that's what you get. At least when you're in the mess hall you get a variety of choices to get what you need."

I remembered what Ms. Mackley had said about the watch taking my blood at night. Again, the watch. Why didn't they teach a class on nutrition instead?

"Who oriented you? They sure didn't do a good job," he said.

"I just got here last night." I touched the watch all over, examining it. How did it take my blood? There was no such technology available, was there?

"It's all a bit crazy," he said.

"Yep."

"They already have you testing?"

"Yeah."

"Huh." He took the last bite of his garlic bread and chuckled. "Just wait until you get put into your group. Your group leader will teach you all the finer aspects of that watch. It will blow your mind."

It already had. "But how—"

I heard a slight vibration on the table, and Tyler looked at his watch.

"Ah, gotta go," he said. "They'll explain it all. Don't sweat it."

I kept messing with the watch.

"Good luck," he said, standing and stacking his empty dishes on the counter.

"Thanks."

"Make sure you follow your watch." He winked at me.

Watch? Hardly. This was more than a watch, and even more than a sophisticated tracker. I eyed it while I ate, pushing buttons to see what would happen.

When I finished my food, I tried to open the door to go back to the testing room, but it was locked. I sat back down and removed the watch/tracker, giving it a good once over. I know Ms. Mackley said to never remove it, but I had to check it out. It vibrated in my hands and I looked at the screen.

PLEASE ENTER THE TESTING AREA.

The door was now unlocked, and I entered the testing area.

Jeff stood in the aisle next to the desk by my computer.

"I realize you don't know everything about your watch, yet. Be patient. You will know it all shortly," he said.

Had he been listening in on my conversation with Tyler? Would I have any hope of privacy here?

"Also, remember, you have a watch instruction booklet as an icon on your screen."

I remembered seeing that icon when Ms. Mackley gave us the ultra-quick orientation in our room.

"Why didn't Ms. Mackley just tell us everything yesterday?"

"It would be too much information too fast for most kids. Besides, students here love this watch. It does everything. It's cool. They play around with it and figure it all out really quickly. You're the exception. She should have known from your file that you would need, even demand more than what she gave you."

He was right. I couldn't wait to find out more about this thing. I realized with a jolt what he'd said—there was a file on me? She'd said it before, but its meaning just sunk in.

"One thing's for certain. It is vital that you never take it off. Ms. Mackley told me you removed it last night. That upset the bonding mechanism. The watches on your friends have already bonded and are no longer removable. You need to keep it on for a minimum of twelve hours to complete the seal. Once it's joined together, there are serious consequences for breaking the rules. Also, by tomorrow you will be unable to remove it without special tools, and even then you wouldn't like the screech that comes from removing it."

"But, I can't sleep with things around my wrist." All thoughts of files disappeared at the thought of the watch always being attached to my wrist.

"You'll have to learn. Don't worry. You'll get used to it and forget it's there. Give it a chance. Oh, and if you feel a slight pressure on your wrist, don't worry, it's taking your vitals. It lets us know where you are, what you're doing, and what you need."

I felt a bit claustrophobic and ran my finger under the band. I had been ready to seize the day and run with this spy training, but I wasn't so sure now. I didn't like the idea of being watched all the time. *Creepy.*

"Anytime you feel the watch buzz or it beeps," he continued, "read the instructions and follow them. It's as simple as that."

"Simple and yet so complex."

He snorted. "You said it. Anyway, those are the basics. Your mentor will teach you all the nuances for your particular training field."

I thought of Elmer and how much he loved the watch already.

"Wait. How does it take my blood without me knowing it? And how does this little thing analyze it?"

"I don't have time to go into the technology right now. We need to get you back to testing. Just know this. At this academy and as a spy, you will see and experience things you thought impossible. And in the civilian world, they are impossible."

I thought about diabetics and the elderly and how this technology could revolutionize their care. I had to find out why it wasn't available mainstream.

"All right. Let's get back to work," Jeff said.

Chapter Four

He led me out of the computer testing center and down the hall to another room. "There will be a bag with your name on it in that changing area." He indicated a door marked 15. "Go ahead and put the clothes on."

Short shorts and a tank top. Lovely. What would we be doing? Once back in the open room, a woman joined us and pasted more of those sensors all over me. My feet, calves, knees, thighs, rear-end, hips, tummy, upper chest, arms, hands, and head. I could only think of a few spots she'd left uncovered. She left the room.

"Okay," Jeff said as he placed a pair of goggles over my eyes. "You are about to be in a computer simulation. It will feel real, but it is not. I need you to close your eyes and keep them closed until I tell you it's okay to open them. Got it?"

"Yes."

"I'll lead you."

I heard a door open, and after I was led inside, I heard it shut. Jeff put some kind of a belt on me, and I heard little clicking sounds and occasionally felt a tug on one of the wires. I figured he was plugging me in to a computer of sorts. "Okay, I'm leaving the room, but I will talk to you through the intercom system. Just keep your eyes closed. It

35

will help you get right into the computer simulation."

I heard him leave and felt a bit silly, standing wherever it was I was standing, certain that I looked like a total idiot, the wires poking out all around me. After what seemed like a long time, he spoke, "Your task is to get the five people by the river safely to the blue cabin while evading your pursuers. Your pursuers have orders to kill on sight. The cabin is past the river and over a gorge. It will seem real. It is not. Count to five slowly and then open your eyes."

At the count of five, I opened my eyes. I stood in a forest next to a river. Melanie, Sasha, and Elmer were trying to move a large log into the water about fifty yards away. This place seemed so real. I could smell the pine and feel the spray of the water on my skin. My skin. It was dark brown. I held out my hands and moved them, palm up, palm down over and over. My short, black spikes had been replaced by long, midnight-black hair that fluttered across my face. I tugged at it. It wasn't a wig. I was dressed in jeans, hiking boots, a long sleeved t-shirt, and a jacket. I pulled the jacket close, trying to squeeze out some warmth against the cool breeze.

Out of the corner of my eye, I saw Kylie and Reese come out of the woods, walking toward the others. On closer inspection, I could see that Reese was helping Kylie walk. She held her right leg in the air and hopped along. What had happened to her? I almost ran to them, but then remembered that I did not look like me.

I would have to save them without them knowing who I was. Tricky. Were they trying to cross with that log? It didn't even seem long enough. There had to be a better way. I looked the river over, hoping to find spots where the water wasn't so deep or where it didn't move so swiftly, or maybe a row of rocks to spring across. I walked along the tree line, searching.

This was a computer generated simulation. There had to be a way across. About a hundred more yards away, there it was—a row of rocks. It seemed to pop out at me, like a fluorescent green map across the river. Sure, the rocks zigzagged and you even had to backtrack a bit, but they got you across. I grabbed some driftwood from the river and marked the spot before making my way over to the others. I scanned the area for signs of enemies but found none.

Melanie was the first to notice me. She let go of the log and screamed.

I held my hands out in front of me. "No. No," I tried to say. "I'm here to help you." But a language I didn't recognize came out of my mouth. It could have been gibberish for all I knew. By now, they were all standing, staring at me with suspicious eyes.

I had to convince them I was their friend and wanted to help, but how? We stared at each other for a few precious moments, my mind whirring. Finally, I patted my chest and drew a heart with my fingers and then pointed to them and motioned for them to come with me.

Reese shook his head and said, "No. We have to get across the river. People are after us."

It was hard to hear over the rush of the river, and I thought it curious I could understand him when I didn't seem to be able to speak English.

Nodding, I moved back, motioning for them to follow and then pointing across the river. I bowed again and again and kept motioning as I moved back, hoping I looked submissive rather than threatening.

Reese's arm was tied up against his chest, a blood spot seeping through the cloth near his shoulder. He shook his head emphatically, pointing to the log.

Pointing to the log, I shook my head and then pointed down the river and nodded, backing up all the while.

"She's trying to tell us there's a better way across," Elmer said. "At least I hope she is. Even if we got this log into the river, which is doubtful, it's not long enough to get us all the way across, and who's to say it won't just float down the river? I say we follow her. What do we have to lose?"

"She probably lives around here," Reese said. "Haven't you noticed that she looks like the guys following us? Shooting at us? What if it's a trap and she's working with those men?"

"Yeah, really," Sasha protested. "Why should we trust her?"

"What do we have to lose?" Melanie said. "If we don't, we'll most likely be captured, or killed, anyway."

The silence sat on me like a hundred pound weight.

"She better know what she's talking about. It took us hours to get that log as far as we have." Sasha glared at me.

"How far away do you think it is?" Reese said. "I don't know how much farther I can carry Kylie."

"We'll help," Melanie said. "Come on, Elmer."

They took Kylie from Reese, and he grabbed his hurt arm, lifting it slightly, and they ambled along after me.

I pointed out the path to the others when we reached it, but they couldn't seem to see what I saw. I stepped out onto the first rock and to the next and beckoned to them. Elmer followed first. I slipped on one of the rocks and reached down to clean off as much of the moss as I could, but without a knife, my efforts were futile.

Sasha complained when we had to zigzag back a bit before going forward again, but had nothing to say when we were all safely on the other side, our shoes and boots sopping wet. When we turned from the river, we were about fifty feet from a deep gorge. Dense trees and bushes hid most of it from our view, but a rope hanging from one side of the gorge to the other was unmistakable.

I looked back to the river and off in the distance, where the log lay, and I could see some people walking out of the trees. The pursuers. It wouldn't take them long to find a way across. I wished I'd covered our path to the river somehow. Sweat beaded on my forehead.

I motioned for them to follow me into the trees. I couldn't make it easy for the bad guys to see us. All eyes fell on the rope that traversed the wide gorge in a large shallow 'U'.

"Can we shimmy across?" Kylie asked.

I knew I could. It was only twenty-five yards across, and I'd been training hard the last six months and was in top physical condition, but looking at the other girls—and Reese with his injured arm—I knew it would be suicide. They wouldn't have the strength. Reese looked at the others and must've come to the same conclusion because he said, "We can't all make it across with that."

Since they couldn't understand me, I took a stick and drew my plan in the dirt. I drew a picture of a seat looped under the rope.

We searched around in the woods, for anything that might help us. We collected rocks, sticks and twigs. It didn't look good. Then I thought of our clothes. I took off my jacket and motioned for the rest to give me what they could, pointing at the most obvious items.

"Good idea," Reese said. "Let's see what we have." We all gathered together under a canopy of pine and aspen trees and removed whatever we felt we could go without. We took four sturdy leather belts and quickly made a seat of sorts. A couple of jackets cushioned the belts. For this to work, we had to move fast. Getting six of us across would be more than lucky. Especially if we were to do it before our guests arrived and before the belts gave out.

Looking down into the gorge made me dizzy and my knees weak. I couldn't see the bottom. I kept telling myself it wasn't real. No one would die, even if someone fell. It wasn't real.

"We need something to put between the belt and the rope," Reese said, "to help it not wear out and to help it slide along."

"You're right," I said, or tried to, but again produced only foreign sounds. The others looked at me suspiciously. I was frustrated not being able to communicate with them.

I used a sharp rock to cut my pant leg and wrapped it around the leather.

No one wanted to be first to slide across, but I thought it would be best to send the heaviest person first. That was Reese. I motioned to him, insistent.

"I need to be here to help if there are problems," he said.

"And how exactly are you going to help with a bullet in your arm?" Kylie shot back at him.

"Okay. Okay," he said climbing into the harness.

Just as we were going to push him across a thought occurred to me. I cried out, slightly panicked. I grabbed hold of the chair just in time. I quickly motioned to the other side of the gorge and then to the chair and raised my shoulders to indicate confusion.

Everyone stared at me with blank expressions.

I pointed to the chair and then the other side of the gorge and then raised my hands in the air, palms up and eyes wide. Then, I motioned with my hands like I was pulling on a rope.

That finally got them.

"Ah!" Melanie said. "We need a way to get the chair back after we send someone over."

I looked at everyone's clothes and took off my top. It wasn't *my* body they were seeing, right? I still had on a bra. I grabbed a sharp rock and made a tear in my shirt and then ripped it the rest of the way and then another and tied them together. Elmer took off his shirt, trying the same thing. We made the strips thin and we cut up everyone's shirts except Reese's —it would take too much effort to get around his makeshift sling, and it would probably further aggravate his wound. We'd have to do without the extra length. Reese kept watch for the bad guys.

We tied the cloth rope to the chair and then sent Reese flying. He jerked to a halt about ten feet from the opposite side. Sasha cursed. We hadn't made our return rope long enough. I turned to try to communicate to the others that we needed more rope, but Elmer had already taken off his jeans and was handing them to me to cut. He stood in his Spiderman briefs. Good man. We added the pant strips to the cloth rope, but it still needed more. Kylie volunteered her pants and I cut them up, giving her back shorts. She huddled with Sasha and Melanie to stay warm.

Finally, the cloth rope was long enough, and Reese slid the final few feet and jumped out. The jean material seemed to be holding up well. I checked it after each run. Once it was down to Sasha and me, I heard something from the direction of the river. Shouting. Great. They were getting closer. I hurried Sasha into the chair, noting that I really should have replaced the jean material between the leather belt and the rope, but there wasn't time. I hoped the groove in the leather wouldn't give way. I indicated to

41

Sasha to be ready to grab the rope if it gave way. I pushed her hard and she sailed across until she hit the middle, then the sailing stopped. Keeping one hand on the rope at all times, she used the other to pull herself across.

I thought about staying put, cutting the rope, and then hiding so the bad guys couldn't follow, but then I remembered my task was to see them safely to the blue cabin. I snuck back into the woods to see if I could gather some more information about our pursuers. The three men, guns in their hands examined the spot across the river where we had crossed.

It appeared they were trying to figure out if we had crossed there, and how. I didn't know how long they'd been there, studying the site, but I had to assume that within a short amount of time they would figure it out. Hopefully, the little jog back we'd made in the middle of the river, toward the starting shore would cause them enough trouble, giving me ten minutes or so. It had been good the trail across was not straight. With no one to give me a starting push, I would have to drag myself across the rope. I would never make it across without them seeing me and shooting me. I needed to place another obstacle between the forest and the gorge.

I looked at the pile of sticks we'd found and only one idea flashed in my head. I grabbed two rocks and started striking them together. Sparks flew and hope filled me. This could work! I thanked my camp leaders back home for always insisting we know so many survival skills. I quickly built a log cabin formation out of dry sticks, and stuffed in dry leaves. I struck the rocks together feverishly. One of the sparks caught, and I blew gently to encourage the flame. The dry fuel burned fast and hot and quickly grew. I looked around regretfully at my surroundings.

The forest was dry, but it was beautiful. I hated to destroy it even if it was computer generated. But I needed to buy myself some time. I took a bunch of twigs and dry bark from all over the ground and lit them using the fire I'd already started and placed them on dry mounds of fallen leaves. I rapidly lit a dozen small fires and watched them grow hot. The piles quickly raged and lit anything dry near them. When I couldn't bear the heat on my face any longer, I ran to the gorge.

I climbed into the harness and it broke straightaway. I gasped as my back hit the hard ground, and I breathed a sigh of relief that I hadn't already been over the gorge. I looked back at the fires I'd started—each tiny fire spread and joined with the others forming a wall of flames and thick black smoke. If the men didn't get me, the fire just might. Right then, I saw body shapes behind the fire. I had no time to spare. I grabbed hold of the rope, threw my legs above it, ankles crossed, and started shimmying across. *Don't look down. Don't look down.*

With only a quarter of the way to go, the clear voices of the men hit me. They'd made it through the fire. *How?* I leaned my head back and looked at them. They burst out of the burning trees and moved toward the rope, then grabbed it and started swinging it.

One of my hands, slick with sweat, slipped. My heart seemed to fall into the gorge. Luckily, I was able to grab the rope again and continued to cross. I heard them yelling and screaming, and then shots flew past me. I tightened my legs and held on for dear life as I quickly shimmied the rest of the way, bullets whizzing past me. Only one hit its mark. Pain seared through my thigh, but my fear and adrenaline quashed it, and I was able to make it. It was getting harder and harder to make myself believe this was all fake.

As soon as my feet hit the ground, Melanie rushed forward with a sharp stick and started sawing the rope. I pulled her away, wrapped my arm around Elmer's shoulder and ran as best I could, hoping the others would follow. It was a risk, leaving the rope for the men to use, but they hadn't started crossing, and I took the gamble that the blue cabin was not very far away. Cutting the rope would take too long, especially with such primitive tools, but if we ran, we could make it to the safe-zone before they got across. I tried to ignore the fire that licked my thigh.

We ran as fast as possible with our injuries toward a clearing. No blue cabin. I pointed to the opposite side of the clearing and urged Elmer to run there and seek the cabin. Once he got there, he waved us to him. With Melanie's help, we walked quickly to the crest. There it was! I felt sweet relief—my gamble had paid off. Sasha and Elmer broke into a sprint. The rest of us hobbled our way down the hill. Once we reached the cabin, we would find help. Gasping, Sasha pounded on the door. When no one came, she yanked at the door handle. Still, no response. "They said to get to the blue cabin. We're here. Why can't we go in?"

Kylie screamed out, "They're here. Run!" Melanie, Kylie, Reese, and I were still twenty yards from the cabin and the men were gaining on us.

I knew if we ran, we'd never conquer. I pointed to Sasha to keep trying the door. Pushing the pain away, I ran out to the others, waving my hands and shaking my head, just as the five men started down the hill. I made a motion like a mother grabbing up her children and holding them to her as I ran.

Everyone froze, wondering what to do.

Reese understood. "She's right. We need to stick

44

together to have the best chance of taking these guys."

Everyone turned in unison to the approaching men.

The simulation ended as abruptly as it began, and the room I'd been in for the last two hours came into view. I stood on a huge mat in the middle of the glass flanked room. The wires all fed into a belt around my waist. I tipped to the side, and it felt like I was losing my balance, and the room started to spin.

Chapter Five

"Close your eyes," I heard over the intercom.

I did and soon after, I got my bearings and the dizziness left me. I still felt weird. Was that real? Were my friends in that simulation with me? Did they have wires all over their bodies, too?

The woman who had plastered me with leads earlier said, "Coming out of a simulation can be disorienting. Keep your eyes shut until I remove all the leads and you should be okay." I felt the leads pull away from my body and gladly did as she suggested.

"Okay," she said. "I'm done."

I opened my eyes, and Jeff came in the room as the woman left. "Good job," was all he said. Relief slid over me being out of the simulation. It had made me feel so strange, so out of myself. He had me go back in the changing room and put on a yoga-looking outfit. The whole time, I was thinking about the simulation and my friends. Had they been with me in that simulation? Jeff brought me to a room where I had to take on an opponent with hand to hand combat. All thoughts of the simulation were shelved while I fought. I rocked it, bringing seven of the eight opponents I had to fight into submission. The one that beat me wasn't a youth like the rest of them, he was a bulky, tall man. Thank heaven for all my training. I wouldn't have been able to beat even the first girl two years ago.

I also had to do some spatial tests with putting blocks into patterns and solving physical puzzles in front of a camera. My mind ached from the testing. I wanted to go see my friends and make sure they were okay. It was a bit overwhelming.

I'd just finished my last puzzle when someone opened the door. A hand curled around it when I heard someone call his name. It was Jeff. He shut the door behind him, only it didn't really shut. It sort of bounced back, the dead latch clicking out of the hole in the strike plate and resting on it. It looked closed, but it wasn't. Apparently, that was all that was needed to break the room's sound proofing.

I heard low voices.

"...doesn't belong here...too advanced."

Definitely not Jeff. It was a woman's voice.

"Yes, she does," Jeff said.

The woman's voice said, "She's a *natural*. We haven't seen that in over 25 years...simulation?"

"She's a child...keeping her...a few years," Jeff said.

"...sending her, Jeff...need her. ...perfect...is ready."

"Well, ...be right. ...know how..." Jeff said.

Her voice raised in pitch. "Don't...dare... I am ...director now."

"Marie, be reasonable. ... not psychologically..."

"...test scores. ...ready."

"She's a child." Jeff's voice was plaintive.

"Enough....no more a child .... tests." I heard the clackety-clack of shoes hitting the stone floors of the castle. Was that Ms. Mackley walking away? The door scraped open, and I whipped around, pretending to be watching something else.

"Done?" he asked, looking at me.

"Yep," I said, turning to see him inspect the strike plate and dead latch. He looked at me. I smiled at him, trying not to look as guilty as I felt. My mind was reeling. Where did she want to send me?

"Well," he said, shutting the door hard. "It's time for dinner. How would you like to go to go into town with some of the kids after you eat?"

"Sure, what are we doing?"

"You'll be having a night out with the kids near your same level."

"Oh, not with the ones I came with?"

"No. After dinner, get dressed up like you are going on a date and meet in the front lobby at six sharp."

I realized he wasn't really asking me. He was telling me. Was this another test?

Dinner was a bit awkward. Even though I knew my experience in the computer simulation had been fake, I still let out a huge breath of air when I saw my friends, safe and uninjured. Reese's arm no longer had a bullet hole in it, and Kylie walked effortlessly around the cafeteria. I wanted to grab them and tell them how glad I was they were safe. They wouldn't know what I was talking about, or would they? Had they been in that simulation with me?

None of us knew what to talk about because we were forbidden to talk about the tests. We couldn't even talk about our past together. Others were too close and could overhear. So, our conversation always reverted back to the cool castle, how many people there were, and the crazy test administrators. We did discover that by our age, students who'd been here since they were five already knew five to six languages and they spoke one of them at all meals, rotating every day.

I was dying to know what the others had done all day. It didn't take me long to figure it out, though. All I had to do was watch my friends. Reese kept feeling his arm where the wound should have been, a bothered look crossing his face each time. Melanie asked me if my leg hurt and when I said, "What?" she seemed to realize she'd said something she shouldn't have and changed the subject. She had been there. They all had been. Sasha kept smelling her clothes as if there was a smell there that bugged her. Could it have been smoke? They had been in the simulation with me. Incredible.

Back in our room, Kylie and Sasha were green with envy when they found out I was going to town.

"That's not fair," Kylie said, plopping down onto her bed. "We should all get to go."

Sasha glared at me.

"Just stay here with me," Melanie whined. "Don't leave me here alone."

"Hello! We're right here!" Kylie said.

Melanie lay back on her bed, "I know, but…." She let the statement hang out there, not finishing it and choosing to watch me pick clothes from the closet instead.

"You know I'd stay if I could." I pulled out jeans, a belt with a large black buckle, a black top and black, sparkly boots. I loved this place. Free food, free clothes, and a continuous sleep-over. Who could ask for more? I took the clothes, boots, and my overnight bag to the bathroom to get ready. Melanie followed me. She sat on a couch in the outer powder room of the bathroom and waited for me. After showering, I quickly dried my hair and spiked it, putting a few bobby pins here and there. They could come in handy.

Melanie sat on a couch reading some magazine when I walked into the area she was in. "You've come a long way, Chr—, I mean, Ari."

I smiled at her.

"There was a time you couldn't have pulled together an outfit like that in a million years."

"I had an amazing teacher." I knew she thought I meant her, and I wanted her to keep thinking that. The fashion classes John, one of my FBI trainers in Florida, had sent me to had taught me more than Melanie ever had, but I had still learned from her.

"Why'd you cut your hair?"

She'd asked me about my hair. Was this the opportunity I'd been waiting for. Should I ask her about hers? "I had to pretty much change everything about myself to get away from the terrorists." I told her all about Florida and what had happened and then paused, before gently asking, "What happened when the terrorists kidnapped you from the gala?" I couldn't have asked for a more perfect opening to get the information.

A shadow passed over her face.

"Never mind. You don't have to tell me."

"No," she said, grabbing my hands and looking around the room. "I want to tell you. I want to tell someone. I told the FBI, but they told me I couldn't tell anyone else."

"Maybe you shouldn't."

"It was so long ago. I need someone to know."

I waited.

"They hurt me, Chri-Ari. Really bad. First, they shaved my head." She tugged on her shoulder-length locks. "Then, they broke my arm and ribs. I was a mass of bruises when they finished with me."

I gasped. "It makes me crazy to think they hurt you."

She squeezed my hand. "If the FBI hadn't shown up when they did, I'd probably be dead...They hit me so many times, I don't know what I said to them. I don't know if I betrayed everyone or not." Tears filled her eyes and spilled over onto her cheeks.

I pulled her into a hug. "It doesn't matter anymore. It doesn't matter."

"But, what if I gave it all away?"

"They knew who we all were anyway. Even if you told them everything, nothing would have changed."

"No, you don't get it. They didn't care about you and our group. They wanted names and descriptions of FBI agents and other FBI stuff. I only knew one. I just know I gave him away."

I'd never suspected they would want information on the FBI.

"They wanted to know how we got into the FBI building and all that."

Scary. My watch beeped. I looked up, knowing I should leave, but I didn't want to abandon Melanie after opening such a raw wound.

"Go," she told me.

I hesitated, but finally agreed. These people and their schedules—who knew what they'd do if I disobeyed a directive?

"We'll talk about this later." I gave her a sympathetic smile. "But don't worry. I won't tell anyone what you told me. It's our secret."

Chapter Six

I was the last to arrive in the lobby. It was full of other kids. Jeff and another man were talking to the receptionist and turned when the door shut behind me.

"Nice of you to join us, Ari." Jeff said.

"Am I late?" I looked at my watch. It was exactly six o'clock.

"No. Just perfectly on time."

I made a mental note to be early next time.

"Go load up," Jeff said, turning to the receptionist. He signed some papers on a clipboard and gave it back to her. I waited for him to come with us, but he never turned around. Instead, he started tapping his computer tablet and asked the receptionist some questions. I realized the rest of the group had already left, so I hurried out of the door, climbing into the waiting van and sitting on the front row next to a young man.

"Hi!" I said as I buckled my seatbelt.

The man from the lobby turned to us and said, "Who can tell me who is sitting next to Craig?"

Those next to me raised their hands. I assumed everyone else did, too.

"Tell your neighbor."

I heard my name ring throughout the van interior. "Ari."

"Who didn't pay attention?" he continued.

No one spoke.

"I heard a different name. Fess up."

"It was me, chief." The girl next to me with wide set eyes and a tiny nose said.

"And how do you explain that away, Tabetha?"

"I was not in touch with my surroundings as we waited in the lobby."

"And can you tell Ari why that is a big mistake?"

"Because our surroundings, no matter the occasion, can tell us all we need to know about possible danger." The way she spoke like a robot sent a chill through me. I hoped he wouldn't quiz me on who was in the lobby. I hadn't paid anyone but Jeff any attention.

"Good. Don't let it happen again. When we get back to the school, you will spend your next four days of free time working in the museum. Be prepared to give me the layout and every fine detail about the works in section 9B."

"Yes, sir!" Her voice sounded enthusiastic, but her face showed horror.

My eyes drifted back to the man in the front passenger seat.

He gave me a pressed smile. "I'm Todd." He held out his hand to me, and I took it. "Even though this is a night out on the town, it's important to stay alert and focused. Even leisure moments can hold extreme danger."

"I'll remember that, sir."

Once in town, we went to a carnival that was set up all along the open spaces in one district just outside the city center, the Grand Place. I guess there wasn't enough open space in the city to set the rides up in one place. It sprawled out all along a long roadway called the Ring. Some rides and food vendors stood on a grassy strip between two directions of traffic. More lay along the sides of the streets in the narrow walkways and grassy side sections of the area.

Everyone split up the second they were out of the van. I watched the backs of several girls and boys walk away from me. Others just looked at me sideways. Luckily, two girls and one boy came and introduced themselves to me. I knew one of them, Tabetha. The other two were Sandra and Craig. We rode some of the rides, and every time I sat in one of the seats, it took all I had to convince myself I was safe. There didn't seem to be much supervision, so I wondered if any care had been taken when setting them up. My insides were a terrible mess the whole time.

Relief filled me when the carnival started shutting down. We walked along the sidewalk to a man selling what Belgium was famous for, waffles, and I mused that it was only nine at night. Why would a carnival close at nine? In the U.S., that's when they seemed to pick up. I'd read that everything but restaurants and bars closed at about five here, so I guessed I should have felt lucky there was a carnival we could go to.

I admired the red tiled roofs, the immaculate porches and the charm and quiet of old times that graced the city as I ate my waffle. It was spectacular. Crunchy, and ultra-sweet, with three gooey strips of chocolate in the center. I sat on a bench at a bus stop. The waffle was so rich, I was on a sugar high when I finished eating it. Despite the growing ache in my gut, I looked back at the small building where the waffles were sold and contemplated getting another.

As I stood to act on my desire, adding the justification

that I would buy some for my roommates, someone stepped in front of me.

"Hey."

I looked up and sat back down. A tall boy, stared down at me. His pecks bulged through his T-shirt and his armholes strained to keep his muscles in check. He was so hot, I had to look away and try hard to stop the blush I felt spreading across my cheeks. Sure, Reese was my guy, but pure beauty stood before me, and I felt obligated to worship him.

"You must be the new girl, Ari."

"Yep." I kept my eyes on the ground beside me. Someone had talked to me. Did it have to be Adonis?

"I'm Kevin." He put his hand out for me to take.

I dared a look up. I shook his hand, my face burning.

"Where did you come from?" he asked.

I must've looked confused, because he followed up with, "I mean, I haven't seen you around the school. I would've remembered and no one, I mean no one, ever comes here so old."

Not knowing exactly what to say, I said, "How old do you think I am?"

Without a second's pause, he said, "Eighteen."

I gave an exaggerated frown and nodded. "Not bad. How old are you?" Ari was eighteen, after all. It didn't matter that Christy was only seventeen.

"Eighteen."

I was still nodding and then added, "And when did you get here?"

"I was five."

"You're eighteen, and you've been here since you were five?"

He was nodding now.

"Does anyone ever leave this place?"

"Actually, the nine of us are accelerated. Usually,

recruits stay here another two years. We've only got about three months to go."

An exaggerated push of air escaped my lips—almost a hmmh. "What usually happens when you're twenty?"

"It depends on how you test. Some leave to be field ready spies, others go for specialization training or something else. I'm going for instructor. I'll have to go in the field for a few years—get some missions under my belt, but then I'll come back here or to another training facility to finish up."

"Hmm," I said. I hadn't thought about being an instructor.

"What training facility did you come from?" he asked.

Cort's voice came to my mind, "Don't trust anyone with the truth, ever." He'd been my very own FBI agent before I'd flown to Belgium.

"None, really," I blurted, probably not the best answer ever. "I've taken karate classes, tumbling, stuff like that, but nothing big."

"I'm just surprised they didn't find you when you were five or even a bit later through testing. You're old to end up here—and be with us. I don't get it."

"I lived in a small town. It probably wasn't involved in the testing."

"Believe me, they test everyone."

"How do you know?"

"I'm on a track to be an instructor, remember?"

"Oh, yeah. I guess I just didn't test right."

"How did they find you then?"

"I got into a bit of trouble and they came and took me."

"What kind of trouble?" His eyes fell on my hair and piercings with a quick sweep.

"I'm just going to leave it at that."

He raised his hands in the air, palms out to me. "Okay. Okay. I get it. No threat here."

I smiled and looked at my feet.

"You're an interesting girl. There are stories of other Secondaries coming in—"

"Secondaries?"

"People who show up after ten years old. I know of a couple who came in at thirteen, but they are a bit behind. It's almost like their abilities somehow manifested themselves when they hit puberty or something. It's rare, but these kids are agile, super-smart...but behind, none-the-less. None have ever ended up at this training Academy, according to my instructors."

"Are there any tricks I should know?" I asked.

With a dead serious look, he said, "Whatever you do, don't ever break your cover."

I gave him a half smile. It was like I'd heard that so many times here it was like listening to a parent repeat the same things over and over again.

"So, where are you from?" Kevin asked.

I gave him my cover story in a matter of fact way and he laughed.

"Yeah, I'm from..." I could tell he was just giving me his cover story by the bored way he told it to me.

He made me laugh. A part of me wished I were someone else. Michele, maybe—good to look at. Maybe then I'd be less self-conscious with my spiky hair.

Another trainee came and sat by us on the bench and suddenly, I was nothing. She was everything. Her porcelain skin, midnight black hair, big kid eyes, and pouty lips were only part of the package. She had a figure that popped guys' eyes out.

I reached up and twisted my ball earrings, a nervous habit I'd picked up. I peeled my eyes away from the girl.

"Thanks for waiting for me," she said, turning and laughing.

"Ari," he said. "This is Kendra." He stared at her a few seconds too long. There was something between them for sure. I noticed an intense curiosity rise in her eyes as she looked at me.

"What training center did they transfer you from?" she asked.

"I—" I began, only to be interrupted by Kevin.

"She's *brand* new. No training."

The curiosity in her eyes went up about ten levels. "Really," she said, drawing out all the vowel sounds. "That's interesting. So, what's your story?"

"I've already tried that, Kendra. You'll only get the company line from her."

"Then she must've had *some* training." The tone in her voice was menacing. She saw me as a threat. "Well, we'll have to let time tell."

Our watches vibrated and we all looked at them.

TRANSPORTATION HAS ARRIVED

I took a seat on the front bench again, but behind the driver. Kevin and Kendra sat in the back with someone else. A guy named Henry sat next to me. We made idle chitchat as we drove away. Elaina, who sat on the seat behind us, pulled herself forward holding onto our van's seatback and joined our conversation. I could tell that she liked him. She would stare at him until he turned her way, and then she'd look away. I complimented her on her hair, her nails, anything I could do to help the situation. As we talked, I felt a burning cold shiver at the base of my neck, and I turned forward. Everything went in slow motion from there.

The van screeched to a halt, sliding sideways across the street. There was no crunch. No *real* collision, but it played before my eyes, ever so slowly. The driver's head hit the windshield. Crack. Where were the airbags? His head lolled forward, and Todd slammed into the dash and was slumped over, a trickle of blood coming from his nose. I flew forward, my forehead banging into the seat in front of me, my seat belt digging into my hips. In a flash, I saw two things at once, a big, black truck only inches from the side of the car with its side doors flying open, our van doors opening, and men in black reaching into our van.

The other students were fighting, kicking, and screaming. I climbed under the bench, getting into a ball. I covered myself with a blanket. I wouldn't let myself be kidnapped again. I wouldn't let them hurt me like they had Melanie.

I continued to hear the fighting, clawing, and screaming, but it didn't last long. Silence fell over the van. Was I safe? Had they left? That's when I felt him.

Chapter Seven

I knew this person knew I was there. I realized suddenly that I was holding my breath and that realization caused my lungs to ache desperately. I knew if I did breathe, it would be jagged and loud. It was silly to hold it, knowing he knew I was there. Why was this person waiting? I was about to freak out. I needed air. I was a bird, cornered, ready for flight.

I took a tiny breath in through my nose and opened my lips, desperate for more. Little tiny bursts of sweet oxygen. Why was I hiding like this? Was I crazy? I was powerful. But I'd remembered that too late. Now I was truly vulnerable.

He grabbed me, pulling me across the carpeted floor. I'd been found at spy school. That could only mean one thing—there were still moles—still terrorists after me. It was too much, and they were everywhere. I tried to kick him but caught only air. I felt a prick in my upper arm, the blanket that covered me vanished, and I felt a bag clamp down over my head. He tied my hands behind my back, and bound my feet before the meds took effect. The world went black.

When I woke, I was sitting in a chair, my arms tied together and then to the chair behind me. I was in a room like the FBI interrogation room I'd been in DC, but minus the table. I heard someone shuffle his feet behind me.

"Who are you?" an American voice asked. He couldn't be a member of one of the terrorists groups that were after me, could he?

Who was I? That was easy.

"Ari," I said

"Who are you, and who do you work for?"

I had to get out of here. Whether he was a terrorist or not, it was clear he was my enemy. I had to escape.

He put his hands on my shoulders.

How could I get out of this? What had I learned that would save me? I didn't listen to him. I focused. I prayed. That always seemed to help. My feet were free, so there was a way to escape. I was getting out of here. Was I sure there was only one man in the room? I sent out my feelers trying to discover the room's secrets. One man. I had to wait for just the right moment.

He kept repeating, "Who are you? Just tell me, and you're free."

"Ari," I said. I appreciated that he got right to the point, but I knew he was lying. It couldn't be all he wanted. Were they just trying to verify which of the girls in the group was Christy? I wouldn't tell them.

"Stop it. We both know that's only your cover. Who are you really?"

"Ari."

His grip lessened. I had a better chance now.

"We know Ari is only a made-up name. Who are you?'

Ari *was* who I was, except a little dot at the center of

61

my soul that remained Christy.

He patted me on the head and leaned down.

That was his mistake.

"You know," he whispered in my ear.

I hit him hard with the side of my head. I knew it hurt him, because it hurt me, but I had been ready for it. I pushed off the ground with my feet concentrating all my strength there, not knowing if I could pull it off. I used all of my will, my concentration, to flip back and kick, hoping to make a connection with the guy as he stumbled from my head butt. I'd practiced this move a thousand times in Tai Chi, but had never been tied to a chair when trying to do it. I'd become quite good at it, flying through the air, but having no hands took away a lot of my momentum. I focused on getting out of there.

I got air, but didn't quite get all the way around. The chair hit something behind me. The man? I turned my head to the side right before my face hit the ground and the chair broke. I sprawled out and didn't hear any sound from my captor anymore.

Once out of my daze, I undid my hands from the chair pieces. After being tied up in Montana by the terrorists, I had practiced with Katy, my undercover FBI nanny in Florida, on freeing them. I had to hurry. My knees crunched up. In one quick movement, I slid my hands under my butt, just like I'd practiced a thousand times after the cabin. Never again would I be caught unprepared. I stood up and undid the ropes in no time.

I covered my mouth with my hand to prevent the scream that welled up inside me. The man's body was splayed out on the floor, drips of blood spattered around it. I had been too busy trying to get myself free and hadn't noticed him lying there.

I had to escape. I could do this. Eyeing the rope that had fallen from my arms, I considered tying him up, but thought better of it. What if touching him roused him? Through the sidelight on the door, I saw there was no one in the hall. I tried the knob. It turned. Taking a deep breath, I slid out and ran.

Unfortunately, I ran the wrong way.

I found myself at a dead end. When I turned, a man was standing between me and my escape route. I was like a cornered raccoon. I'd have to fight my way out. I would not be re-captured.

"Let's see," the man said. "Ari, right?"

I didn't nod or shake my head. I had to find a way past him.

"Don't worry. This is just a live simulation. It's okay. We're with the school. It was just a test to see if you'd give away your cover. We had no idea you were so good."

Was he for real? Was this part of the test today?

I crouched slightly. I couldn't let him distract me. I had to be ready. I'd kick and claw my way past him if I had to. It would be best if I were not on the offensive, though. For me to beat a man of his size and training, I'd have to be on the defensive, use his strength against him.

His fists clenched and unclenched, contradicting his previous words. The muscles in his neck bulged. He was so big. Did I really have a chance? I'd have to use his strength against him, but I wasn't sure how I could if he didn't attack. Why had I run the wrong way? Why?

"Ari. I don't want you to get hurt."

Another guy showed up. Two against one. At least the newcomer was considerably smaller. I should have acted sooner, but he hadn't made a move against me. Maybe this *was* just a test. The air was stale, and I couldn't seem to get enough oxygen to breathe.

"Who was she with?"

"Guess."

"Sam?"

"You got it."

"But he's good."

"And green."

I stared at them, trying to focus. *He's lying. He has to be lying.*

"Go check on him," the big man said. "Would ya? She's a fighter. He might be hurt."

"Are you sure?" The other man said.

"I'm sure. Ari and I are about to be friends."

The smaller man walked away, keeping his eyes fixed on me until he disappeared into the room I'd so hastily exited.

"See, Ari," the big man said. "We're not ganging up on you. You're making me nervous. I'd like to relax."

I could no longer be caged. I had to go on the offense. More men would come, and I wouldn't have a hope of escape.

He took a step forward, hands out, shaking them. "Okay, really. Look. Wait." He held out his hand for me to take. "I'm Bill."

I couldn't shake the thought that it was a trap. Why else would I have been tied to that chair? Who were these people?

"Really, there's no reason to be afraid." He took a step closer. He was almost within attacking distance. Then, another step.

Turning once again to my legs, my most powerful weapon, I kicked. I had no room in the narrow hallway to kick him properly, but it was the only chance I had. I could get lucky. My foot caught him on the chin, but he was ready. It was like hitting a brick wall. He had me by the legs, my head dangling near the floor. I grabbed his legs and tried to unsteady him, but like a boulder, he wouldn't budge.

"Nice move," he said, huffing a bit trying to control my legs. "Who taught you that?"

It was a stupid move. It didn't work. I tried to kick again, but he held my shins, so I bit him, hard, on the thigh.

"Ouch!" he yelled and cursed, his hold on me faltering for a mere second. "Cut it out. I'm not kidding. Crap! This is only a simulation. I don't want to hurt you."

I heard footfalls. Reinforcements. I tried to bite him again, but he'd pulled me hard out in front of him.

"This is Ari," Bill said, huffing. "Sam's."

I could see four new sets of legs move around Bill toward me, and I swung out with my arms trying to hit whatever I could.

"She's hard to convince. Good grief. Help me get her restrained. If she bites me again, I might have to drop her."

One man restrained my arms while the other helped Bill with my legs. Then they righted me, and handcuffed my hands.

I stood there panting, but couldn't fight because they held my arms, tight. Bill stepped away and said, "Ari. You're the most fun we've had in a long time. We can tell you've not been trained here. You're unique, but girl, you have to believe me. We are the good guys. This was a test…Crap! She bit through my pants."

I could still taste his blood. I shivered. The fight was leaving me for some reason. I was starting to believe they weren't terrorists.

They stared at me like I was a lab rat. "Go get Ms. Mackley on the phone. She may be able to convince her," one of the guys restraining me said.

At the mention of Ms. Mackley's name, I relaxed even more, but only a bit—it could still be a trick. If they were bad guys they would probably know who she was. This was too ridiculous to be a terrorist kidnapping. This place was too clinical. Too FBI or CIA or something. When the terrorists had grabbed me in Montana, they'd taken me to a pit. Then again, maybe these were neat-freak terrorists. I went back and forth in my mind until I heard footsteps coming down the hall and started really listening to the banter between these men.

"I can't wait to see the footage on that one," the other guy restraining me said.

"Me either," said a guy walking up the hallway. "Sam was out cold on the floor, the chair broken and everything."

That convinced me. I gave in. These people didn't want to hurt me. It was just a simulation.

They took me to what appeared to be a break room, undoing the handcuffs, and pouring me some orange juice. They told me to clean up, pointing to a restroom on the left wall of the room. I washed my hands and face, a headache threatening. I breathed deeply and rolled my head in a big circle, hoping to relax.

When I came out, Sam walked in and the guys razzed him. "She really got you, man." He walked over to the sink and splashed water on his face, drying it vigorously with a paper towel.

"Sorry," I said. "I thought it was real."

"It was my mistake. I underestimated you. You should

patent that move. Get it down. Just think if you'd made it all the way around."

A strange feeling fell over me, and Cort's words echoed in my mind about not trusting anyone. They were still trying to get me to blow my cover. Was that what this was all about? Did they give me to the greenie, thinking it would be easy to get my identity from me because I was so new to all this?

"Who are you again?" Sam asked. "I'll never live it down if you don't tell me."

I felt sorry for him, and I really wanted to help him, but I focused on my orange juice instead.

"Ari," I finally said.

"I know that's your cover, but what's your real name?" He whispered to me. All the other guys were chatting loudly amongst themselves seeming to pay us no attention.

I turned and started in on a muffin someone had set before me.

The other guys suddenly burst out laughing and one said, "Not to worry, Sam, we have records. We can check it after."

"What is your real name?" He said it through gritted teeth. Moments later he whispered, "Ari, did you hear me? Please, you could make it so I don't look like such a fool."

I had to physically bite on my tongue in order to prevent myself from spilling the beans. I hated it when people were taunted and teased. He finally sat back and sighed. Were they ever going to let me talk to Ms. Mackley?

The men came and went, telling stories about their lives and asking me about mine. I told more lies than I could count. I would not break cover. Sometimes I sat, and sometimes I paced. One guy even turned the TV on for a while. It was a nice diversion because I was starting to get really tired. Then the picture on the screen changed to a room just like the one I'd been imprisoned in. A man wearing a mask stood behind someone in a chair. I recognized the flirty skirt and sandals immediately. It was Sandra.

I moved forward with a jerk. "What is this? Is that Sandra?" No one in the room said anything. She had wires coming out from her hands and feet.

A gravelly voice came out of the TV. "Tell us her real name."

Sandra didn't respond. They weren't asking for her name, but someone else's.

The man spoke again, "We'd get it from her ourselves, but unfortunately, she's unable to speak at the moment. It's not a difficult thing I'm asking for. What is Ari Agave's real name?"

No response.

"For each ten seconds that pass without you telling me what I need to know, I will give you a little shock. They will get a bit stronger as time passes. Save yourself some pain and agony." He started a countdown.

I was only inches from the TV now and turned to look at the men in the room. They all sat in their chairs, leaning back slightly as if nothing was about to happen.

"You can't let her get hurt because of me!" I looked at blank stares. I turned back to the TV as I heard Sandra scream out. "I don't know! I don't know!"

He started to count again.

"Please," I pleaded to the men in the room. "Please."

Sam spoke up, "We will let her go if you give us the information we require."

I turned, ready to fight my way out of the room and find

hers and rescue her. Like he could read my mind, Sam stood and moved toward the door. He no longer looked weak or defeated. He crossed his arms in front of his chest and put a completely unreadable face on. I looked from him to the other six in the room. It seemed they were all smirking at me. Just as I figured a way to take out three of them, a shrill cry from the TV filled the room.

My hands shook, and I felt sweat drip down my back. I grasped my legs to prevent the shaking and tried to concentrate on an exit plan. I had to talk them down. I glanced at the TV and saw Sandra's head loll to the side as the man started with the count again.

I prayed. Should I give myself up for this girl that I barely knew, that had been kind to me when others had not? A big portion of me wanted to be that selfless girl, but something in my gut told me I should not. But I could end her suffering, I reasoned. It's the right thing to do. I was about to spill my real name when a terrible feeling came over me. I reversed my decision and immediately a peaceful feeling filled me. I tried to tell myself I was crazy, but couldn't. I should not break my cover. I would not break my cover.

In my mind, I distanced myself from the screams on the TV. Songs I'd learned as a child in church filled my mind, and I let myself return to that time and become a child, singing songs of hope and happiness. Somehow I found my way into a seat. I have no idea how long I remained in those memories.

I was shaken out of my stupor when a skinny guy with a closely cut goatee brought in a sheet of paper and set it down in front of me. "Time to go home," he said. "We just need you to read it through and then sign it at the bottom.

I couldn't help myself. I turned and looked at the TV. Some soccer game was on, and the guys were all talking about the last play. There wasn't even an echo of Sandra there. I almost felt like I'd dreamed it. Was she okay? Certainly she wasn't dead. Was she? I grabbed the paper and quickly read; it asked for me to sign at the bottom. I was to print my alias name and sign it and then do the same for my real name. Just as I was about to fill it in, I got that tingly feeling that I shouldn't. I moved the pen tip from the alias line and wrote, *Ari Agave* on both lines under *real name*.

"Look, you guys," I shouted. "I'm Ari. I'm tired of you asking me who I am when I've already told you. I am Ari Agave. It's the last time I'm going to say it."

Several of the men chuckled.

How long were they going to keep me here?

"She's not going to break you guys," Bill said. "Let her go get some sleep." He handed me another glass of orange juice, and I drank it down, hoping it would help me stay alert. I was bushed.

Sam stood and pulled out a hood from his back pocket, dangling it in front of me. "I'll have to put this on you. You can't know where this facility is." He moved to set it over me, and I slouched away.

"Whoa," the skinny, goatee guy said.

"Is it totally necessary?" I asked feeling suddenly very tired. "I could just close my eyes and promise to keep them that way."

"Not a chance. It's policy, so please don't karate chop me again." He moved toward me.

I stepped back, my hips hitting the counter. "You're not putting that on me." I said, trying to sound deadly serious, but thinking I sounded funny instead.

"You don't have a choice." Determination slid across his eyes. A fierceness. A challenge.

"What if you put it on yourself?" Bill said, his eyes conciliatory.

He read me much better than Sam. I needed to be in control of the hood or they would have no control over me. At least I think that's what I thought. I tried to snatch the hood from Sam's hands without answering Bill, but for some reason I missed, swiping only air and then snorting.

Everyone started to laugh, including me. It was all suddenly very funny. I held out my hand in hopes Sam would give me the mask. My hand looked so strange, hanging out there in front of me, I moved it in front of my eyes and laughed some more. The room filled with roaring laughter as I felt myself tip forward.

Chapter Eight

My alarm sounded, and I almost fell out of bed in shock. My eyes seemed sewn shut. I was so tired. I fumbled around for my watch, which I'd forgotten was on my wrist. I turned it off then tried to remove it, but it had sealed. I couldn't break the bond. I hadn't been this tired in a long time. I brushed sleep from my eyes and glanced at the hated watch. Eleven o'clock. Then I started, a horrible memory of yesterday coming to the forefront of my mind. Sandra. The hood. I reached up and felt my head. I looked frantically around. There were no men. I wasn't in a staff lunch room. I was back in the castle in my bed. Had it been a nightmare? My aching body told me otherwise. How had I gotten here? The memory of my uncontrollable laughter filled my mind, and I remembered falling toward the ground. Then I woke up, here, safe in my bed in the same dirty clothes as yesterday.

I was alone in the room and it was full of light. My stomach rumbled. I shook my head, trying to make sense of it all. I hurried to take a much needed shower and get ready.

I blindly followed the watch's instruction to meet Ms. Mackley in the mess hall, the whole time my mind struggled to put the pieces together and understand what had happened.

The mess was empty except for Ms. Mackley, but I still looked for Sandra. Everyone must be in class. "What...Where...How?" sputtered from my mouth as I noticed Ms. Mackley.

"You must have a lot of questions. Let's get you some food, and then maybe we'll both get some answers."

I grabbed a plate and started to load it up with food. It occurred to me that everyone was already assigned to their new groups. Ms. Mackley must want to tell me which group I was going to be in. Why didn't she just tell me this morning with everyone else? Was it because I'd been drugged? Then I remembered the conversation I'd overheard between Ms. Mackley and Jeff. I'd been mulling it over every chance I got. She was going to tell me she was sending me away.

I felt her watching me and looked back at her. She tapped her thumb absently on the side of the computer tablet she held. She looked at me with her goose eyes over her glasses, her dark skin looked a bit pasty in the fluorescent lighting.

"Have you already checked your watch for the best choices for you today?"

"Oh," I said, my mouth remaining in the shape of an 'O' for a few seconds too long. She raised her eyebrows, and I had to suppress an irrational desire to giggle even though laughing was the last thing on my mind. I pressed the nutrition tab on the screen and looked over the suggestions, complying with most of them, but I had to choose the chocolate cake over its suggestion of peach cobbler. I could tell it had too much spice, the sauce too brown.

Ms. Mackley led the way to her office and I trailed behind, carrying my tray of food. Nerves made it shake a bit. I didn't want to leave. Her office was large with two separate seating areas as well as an area with a big rectangular mahogany desk. Books lined one wall and framed certificates filled a second. I sat on a chair that had a side table next to it, where I could set the tray. I dug in, not wanting her to hear the loud rumbles that had taken over my belly.

"So, tell me about last night."

I stopped chewing mid-chew. Was she not going to tell me about my placement? Suddenly, I didn't want to talk about last night. My shame at letting a comrade get tortured pushed itself forward. A burn started in my gut and radiated out.

"I would like to know what you were thinking during the abduction and escape. What was going through your mind?"

"I'd like to know how I ended up in my bed. The last thing I remember is...is...I was about to fall on my face...laughing."

She pushed a puff of air through her nose and then said, "Well, you drank the orange juice."

The orange juice. Great! I'd been had by the orange juice once again. "They drugged me." I said, resigned.

"Yep. Once they figured you weren't going to give up your identity, they had to get you out of there without compromising their position."

At least this time it didn't make me sick. "How'd I end up in bed?"

"They delivered you to us, and we tucked you away." She gave me a hard smile. "Never eat what the enemy offers."

"I think I should fear the good guys. They're the only ones who have ever drugged me."

"Now you know." She tapped her finger on the table next to her.

"Now I know."

"So, you were about to tell me what you were thinking when you woke up in that interrogation room with Sam."

I swallowed hard. My head hurt. "There's not much to tell. I've been abducted before and didn't want to be abducted again. I had to act. That's all."

"Hmm," she said. "You did exceptionally well. We've had others escape before, but no one has ever gotten away without giving up their cover. No one. No tricks worked on you. I've seen the footage."

I drew my eyebrows together.

"You're wondering why I asked you about last night when I've already seen the footage?"

"Yeah."

"I can't read your mind. I can only see the physical reaction you had. I wanted to dig a bit deeper into your motivation."

"I was taught never to break cover."

"A result of being taught and trained by John, I'm sure." She looked down on the computer tablet and added, "And your secondary training by Cort. Both are excellent at what they do. Bravo."

She knew both John and Cort? Maybe they'd all trained together.

She stared at me, through me.

"Go ahead and ask," she said.

"Ask what?" I said.

"Sandra?"

I felt a buzzing in my brain.

"Where did you get the grit to withstand the pressure? A girl you knew was being tortured. Hurt. And you didn't give in." She shook her head.

"I just knew somehow that I couldn't reveal my identity. That the most important thing for me to do was to protect myself, no matter the cost. I felt horrible, but I couldn't go against what I knew was the right course of action."

"Interesting. Very interesting. I've never heard that before."

"Is Sandra okay?" I asked.

"Of course she is. Nothing was really happening to her. It was a show, put on for you.

While I felt better knowing that, I still had big questions. I stared at her, recalling the conversation I'd heard between her and Jeff outside the testing room. My insides twisted. "Can we discuss the elephant in the room?" I asked, trying to change the subject.

"The elephant? What elephant?"

I looked her directly in those strange eyes and said, "What group am I in?"

"Well, I don't think it's an elephant, but I'm glad you're curious."

I raised my eyebrows this time, and she raised one eyebrow and smirked at me like I was a tasty piece of meat.

"Yes, yes. The thing is, Ari, we are not sure you're a good fit for this school. Your skills are just as advanced as our graduating classes."

The elephant came charging past. I held my breath.

"Yeah, but certainly I don't know all I need to know. I

just got lucky."

"No, you didn't just get lucky. You scored a perfect score on the computerized tests. No one has ever done that before. Never. You also tested near expert on the physical tests, and on the psychological tests you were impeccable. You are a beautiful anomaly."

She stared at me, smiling, but somehow it wasn't genuine.

"What does that mean exactly?" I shifted in my seat and felt sweat pool in my palms.

"That's what we were wondering. While others disagree, I believe it means you are ready to move on. You definitely do not belong here."

"Please don't send me away. Not yet." I had things I needed to clear up.

"Where would we put you? You simply don't have a place here."

"How can I possibly know everything I need to know? That's crazy."

"I believe it has to do with your photographic memory." Her eyes glinted and her mouth pressed into a tight smile.

"You know?"

"Yes, of course. I figure it would only take you four weeks or so to go through all fifteen years of instruction we give at this school. Of course, you wouldn't need all of it, considering who has been training you."

I saw my opportunity. "I would like that a lot." I knew she wasn't really offering, but I figured I'd let her know what I needed. Reprieve before my eyes, my heart raced. I'd have four weeks to sort it all out. To get closure.

"Well, I wasn't offering…"

"Please. I need to be confident in my knowledge, and

this would give me the confidence I need. It would make me believe in me as much as you do."

"Uh…" She looked at me with doubt all over her face.

"If you let me out now, I'd be so nervous, I'd totally screw up and embarrass you." I would play on her fears that I'd heard in the hallway with Jeff.

"Sometimes you have to put your belief in the people who believe in you, and your belief in yourself will manifest itself in time."

"It's only four weeks. Please." I had to resort to begging. I just couldn't leave my friends. I knew I'd be ok, but I had to fix things with Reese and Melanie. I had this massive need and desire for closure. I couldn't let her take it away from me.

"I realize that your desire to stay has nothing to do with your perceived lack of abilities. I can imagine you must be a tad emotionally confused. What confuses me is that your profile indicated you to be a go-getter, ready to move on at a moment's notice."

"I am. I mean, I will be. I just need a couple of weeks."

"Well, good, because that is all you will be getting. Take care of what you need to. You were meant for greater things. I want you to know this goes against my better judgment. You will not get a second request."

"I understand. Thanks." I was thrilled. I'd gotten what I wanted. "So, what group should I join for the two weeks?" I tried with all my might to send out vibes to her that I should be with Reese.

"None."

"None?"

"Actually, I'll put you in a self-study that I'll direct. With your photographic memory, you should be able to get through most of the information our teachers take thirteen to fifteen years to disseminate. It will be a good challenge for you. Maybe I'll have you skip years five through ten and start you on eleven just to be sure you get the most vital information. I'll put you in the vault with the curriculum and have you go through it. When you need more information on a subject, just jot that down, and I'll get someone to teach you. Move through it all as fast as you can."

"What if it takes longer than two weeks?"

"See that it doesn't."

I'd lost interest in my food as it turned cold and unappetizing.

"Let's get you going."

I lifted my tray.

"Leave that. I'll have the custodians take care of it."

She stood. "Let's get you in the vault."

Chapter Nine

I didn't dare ask what the vault was. I felt completely and utterly happy knowing I had a chance to make things right with Reese and Melanie. We went into the basement, and she led me into a room with a secretary, who looked a bit like a female version of the Rock, a muscle-bound wrestler, sitting at a desk right inside the door.

"Ms. Mackley?" the Rock asked, standing.

"Yes, Renae. This is Ari." She pointed to me. "She will be needing access to the vault every day from five a.m. to ten p.m. She is free to go to the mess hall for meals, but should be here for all other times." She looked pointedly at me.

"Yes, Ma'am," she said. "I'll see to it."

Did this woman ever leave her post? I felt bad for her for some reason. "Do I get any breaks?" I asked.

"Yes. I think two hours a day should be plenty."

"Thank you," I said as calm as possible but wishing I could scream out, Yahoo!

"Could you please provide her access now?"

The Rock went over to one of the five vaults and pressed some buttons, putting her eye up to some sort of scanner and setting her hand onto a hand scanner that lit up when she touched it. One green light appeared. Ms. Mackley did the same thing the Rock—Renae—had done and then two green lights appeared and the vault door swung open.

"Ari," Ms. Mackley said. "I need you to come to my office first thing after dinner to get you set up on the security of this vault. It will take both you and Renae to grant you access each time you enter and exit."

"Okay."

"Good." She motioned for me to enter.

What I thought was going to be a small room turned out to be quite spacious. Three walls were lined with row after row of built in file cabinets, and the other had a large screen on it.

"Please start here," she brought me over to a file cabinet marked Module 13.1. "It will be interesting to see what you think of it. Please do not skip a single page."

"It's all on paper?"

"Yes. All but the video demos, which are on this side." She swept her arm through the air to the other side of the room.

"Why isn't it all computerized?"

"While we feel our computer systems are safe, we still take the extra precaution of not storing our curriculum digitally. There is a computer over there," she pointed to a computer on the other side of the room, "to use if you want to find more information on something you read about in the training modules."

In other words, she didn't feel they were safe at all. "All right," I said, not sure I was going to like being in a room with no windows for twelve hours a day.

"Well, we'll leave you to it."

I checked my watch. Five hours until dinner. I couldn't

wait to see Reese and the others. I opened the file cabinet and was shocked at how far back it went. The good thing was that there weren't loose papers in files. One behind another, in a long row, sat thick white binders. I pulled the first out. I grabbed it and sat down at the long table in the center of the room. I looked around, suddenly feeling quite claustrophobic.

I closed my eyes and breathed deeply through my nose, in and out, until I calmed my racing heart and found that happy place I needed to be in to survive this room, this closed off vault. I forced myself to keep my eyes on the binder and not look around again so I could forget where I was. I let my curiosity take over, and pored carefully over each of the first few pages, soaking in all the details.

After that, I quickly fell into a one-second glance at each page. I had to fiddle with holding the page and flipping it in just the right way to make it fast enough. I didn't have time to really think about each page—I just looked and my mind automatically filed it away into the correct file in the vault in my brain. I found I already knew a lot of the information I was scanning.

Occasionally, I would pause on an interesting tidbit, but by the time the Rock called me over the intercom, I had filed 17,000 pages in my file brain cabinet and had reached Module 16.16. When I stood up and went to the door, Ms. Mackley was back and the door to the vault swung open.

"As soon as you've eaten, Ari, come to my office, and we will set you up to get into the vaults without me."

"Okay," I said, anxious to get up to the mess hall to talk to everyone and see Sandra.

"How did it go?" Ms. Mackley asked.

I was afraid to tell her exactly how fast I was going through the information, so I just said, "Fine," and inched my way to the door that led to the hallway.

"See you after dinner, then."

With that, I ran to the elevator and punched the button, if the elevator was there, I'd use it. If not, I'd take the stairs. It was there, and I rode to the second floor and bounded down the hall to the mess hall. It was already ten after. I had wanted to be early to make sure I got to talk to everyone, but getting me out of the vault had delayed me.

Scanning the room, I quickly found Reese. He sat at a table next to Sasha. Sasha. She was in his group? The table looked extra crowded with eleven squished in around it. I frowned. No room for me. After I stared at Reese for several more moments, Sandra walked past him to her table. She didn't even look injured. Quickly, after sitting, she laughed. I guess she really was okay. It had been fake. Had she known she was acting for me? Kylie came right at me carrying a tray full of food, and before I could even say anything, she started in on me.

"Should I kill you now or allow you a slow death by poison?"

"Huh?"

"Just guess where I was placed." Her eyes darted to a table where kids about ten years old sat, all looking at us, smiling and waving us to them.

I let my head fall and chuckled.

"Not funny, Ari. Not funny."

"It's obvious they love you. We've been here only two days and you already have a bunch of fans. Lucky you." I winked at her.

"There's no way I'm sticking around here. Think of how old I'd be when I graduated. I refuse to live with these little squirts forever."

"Sometimes you have to go back to go forward."

"Not me. I'm out of here the second we get the all clear."

"Hopefully it won't be very long."

"It better not be Ari, it better not be." She walked with clipped steps toward her cheering fans.

Even though her words sounded menacing, I saw a slight twinkle in her eye as I brought up the "fan" thing. A part of her loved it, but I knew it wouldn't last long. Kylie needed the attention of teenage boys to help keep her happy.

Turning to go get some food, I noticed Elmer, sitting at a table with all boys and only one girl. He was talking animatedly with his hands, obviously stoked to be in that group. I had no doubt it had to do with computers and technology.

"Hey," I said, seeing Reese and Melanie head toward me. Reese walked by me, but Melanie stopped to chat. Great. There he goes.

She looked at me.

"Just give him some time." We both looked his direction.

Then she beamed at me, her smile a mile wide.

I raised my eyebrows. "Happy, are we?"

"Yes."

She led me to her table and we squished in. We spoke English even though everyone else spoke Italian today. "So, what's the deal? Why are you so happy?"

"Well," she said. "I love my group."

"Don't keep me waiting. What's your specialty?"

"Politics."

"Shut up!" I looked at her with wide eyes.

"I'm going to train to be a senator or at least a representative." Her smile was so big I could see her back teeth.

"That is so cool." I thought about my first reaction to her wanting to be a senator back in Washington, DC, and how I believed she would never be strong enough to do it. Since finding out about what happened when the terrorists abducted her, I felt ashamed for doubting her and wanted to give her my full support now. "You will be so great at that!"

"It's what I've always wanted." Her face actually shined as she spoke. She pulled me to the side of the room, away from everyone else. "I mean I do want to go home, but I never want what happened to us to ever happen again. I am going to be a senator, and I'm going to make some serious changes."

"I'm so happy to hear you say that."

"I just had no idea what was out there. And now that I do, I want to put an end to it, and I'm going to." She nodded her head with surety.

"I'm sorry, Melanie." My eyes wandered to her hair. "I should have called you. I should have and, I don't know—I guess I was just so selfish. I wasn't used to people wanting to be my friend, and I thought you were just being nice to me in DC. I figured you'd call if you really wanted my friendship."

"Are you crazy? You rock! But I did the same thing, waiting for you to call. So, I guess we're both to blame."

"Yeah, but you have good reason not to forgive me. I shouldn't have made you see something terrible."

"It's not your fault we saw what we saw," Melanie said. "We were in the wrong place at the wrong time. That's all. Don't worry about it. You don't need my forgiveness."

"In a strange way, I'm glad it happened," she

continued. "If it hadn't, I don't think I'd ever have really had the courage to try to become a senator. Not that I do now, but before, I didn't have what it took. I know what it will take, now. I will be an amazing senator."

"I know you will." I gave her a big hug. "Do you do all your training here, then?" I tilted my head to the side.

"I leave for my new training center in two weeks. They thought it best if I train two or three years tops, and I will have twice-a-year home visits for a couple of weeks each. It's not like this particular program I'm in requires me to be hidden. I need to be seen. I'm excited, but I'll miss you."

"I'll miss you," I said, choking on the words. We would be leaving the Academy at about the same time.

"But you'll see me again, somewhere in the spy world." She grabbed my arm.

My eyes burned, and my lip quivered.

"You'll see me as a senator." Her smile forced my tears back. "I have a lot of work to do. I need to be more involved in the political world. I've been following my parents all this time. Whatever they liked, I liked. Whatever they hated, I hated. I need to form some opinions of my own. I need to go for it. I know the CIA…did I tell you this is just a spy farming school? They get you ready as a generic spy and then someone claims you as theirs. It's the CIA that wants me. They will give me an agenda, and I'll really only be their puppet for certain things, but I love the idea. Am I crazy?"

"No. It's exciting. So, three years and you're done?"

"Not exactly. After the three years, I will be put out there with more freedom. I'll have to really start going to all the meetings, showing my face as much as possible and doing good like crazy."

"I love it. And you look happy."

"I am. I mean, I hate not being with my family, but I really, really want this. Am I bad?"

"Not at all. You're going to do what you've dreamed of and in a really impactful way. You are anything but bad."

I saw Reese, sitting at a table with kids maybe a year younger than he was. He looked down as he ate.

"What about you?" Leave it to Melanie to take the attention off her and put it back on me.

"It's not important. Tell me more about your group."

"Uh-uh, Ari. You are not getting out of telling me what's up with you. Why weren't you with us when they sorted us? Why did they let you sleep in, and how did you get that bruise on your arm?"

I looked at it. Sure enough, I had a dark black, purplish bruise on my upper arm. I tugged on my shirt sleeve trying to cover it.

"Oh, that's nothing." I had to think fast. How could I explain the bruise away? "I bumped into a pole in town last night. It was stupid, but I was fiddling with this watch, trying to figure it out and whack! I walked right into a pole. Not my finest moment." I felt like the lie was good and almost sold myself on it.

She squinted at me, but then moved on. "What group did they put you in?"

"Uh, that's a bit more complicated."

"Spill it, and tell me the truth this time."

She knew I'd lied about the bruise. I lowered my voice and said, "None."

"None?" she said, louder than I'd wanted.

"Shh!" I said. "I don't want everyone to know."

"Fine," she whispered. "But you have to tell me."

"I'm leaving here in two weeks, too," I whispered.

"What?"

"They couldn't place me here. I don't fit into any of the groups. They are sending me to another training facility for advanced spies."

Her mouth dropped open and a few seconds later, she said, "You're always the exception. I'm not surprised." She sounded totally genuine and smiled.

"What's the deal with Reese and Sasha?" I asked, glancing over my shoulder at them. My whole body seemed to soar thinking about getting a chance to talk to Reese.

"They're in the same group. It's the group that produces the handlers."

"Reese is going to be a handler?"

"Yep, and so is Sasha."

I couldn't keep the shock off my face.

"I know, Ari. Wouldn't you hate having her rule over your every move as an agent?"

I just nodded and stared some more.

Chapter Ten

Getting everything done for security clearance into the vaults took more time than I'd expected, and getting the eye scan actually hurt. We were in one of the computer rooms with Eric, another tech guy at the Academy. A lot of the time was spent waiting for verifications, and we had to do the hand scan three times to get it right. I had a hard time relaxing my hand properly. Once done, we went to the vaults to try it out. It worked.

"Well, it's only eight, why don't you stay and get some scanning done?" Ms. Mackley said.

I wanted to say no, so I could go talk to Reese, but I could tell it wasn't really a question.

"Okay, but can I leave early today? I need to talk to someone."

"All right, but work fast." She walked out of the vault, and the door closed behind her.

My scanning didn't go nearly as fast as it had earlier that day. I was preoccupied, thinking of Reese and Sasha. Finally, at nine p.m., I asked Renae to let me out.

I wondered where Reese might be and thought about our conversations late into the night back in DC. I remembered him saying how he loved to swim. Could he be in the recreation building? I didn't wait for the thought to go cold. I took off toward rec building. It was located behind the main building to the east. I rushed to the reception desk. It was unmanned. I noticed the camera pointing at the desk. It must be manned remotely.

I brushed my watch up against the wall scanner, pushed the swinging doors open, and looked around. Several people were in the pool, but I found him. I recognized the curve of his neck, the length of his hair, and the contours of his shoulders. Reese. His furious yet graceful strokes had him gliding quickly through the water. I watched as his hands and feet cut through the water, barely leaving a ripple in his wake. I wondered what demons he was trying to rid himself of. Perhaps the demons he had were from me. I didn't dare join him. What if he left while I was changing? Instead, I watched him, admiring his push, his determination.

Was he trying to rid himself of me? I'm alive. He thought I was dead, and I'm alive. After many more lengths, he pulled himself out, water cascading off his body, leaving it shimmering in the bright lights. He walked to the bleachers, grabbed his towel, and headed for the men's locker room without a glance in my direction. I watched the door swing shut behind him, then I walked back into the reception area.

I would catch him when he came out. We had to talk. It was time. Ten minutes later, smelling faintly of chlorine, shampoo, and soap, Reese barreled out into the room. I breathed in deeply, causing him to look up. His eyes lit on mine, and he stutter-stepped, ever so slightly, his eyes wide. We only had fifteen minutes to curfew.

I had begun to move toward him, but his hesitation hit me like a slap. A few awkward silent moments passed until I swallowed hard and said, "Reese, please. Can we talk?"

"Uh," he said, looking around and then at his watch. "It's late. Curfew's just around the corner. Maybe we can do this tomorrow?" He made a move toward the exit.

Anger welled up inside me. I stepped in front of him, forcing myself not to touch him, even though I wanted to. I didn't want to wait. I wanted to clear this up now. No more waiting. "No, Reese." I said. "No. We need to talk about this right now. No more delaying. No more hiding. This isn't like you. Since when do you run?"

His head dropped and he looked at his shoes like there was something very interesting there.

"Let's lay everything out on the table. Then we can both go back to living normally, no more avoiding each other. There won't be a reason to. We can fix this right now."

He looked up, his head cocked to the side. "Christy—"

"Ari," I said, correcting him before I could stop myself. Part of me wished I hadn't. It felt so good to hear him call me Christy.

He shook his head. "No! You are Christy. I. Am. Rick. This is ridiculous. Please, can't we, just for the next few moments, be Christy and Rick?" His eyes were soft, pleading. My heart thumped hard.

At that moment, hearing his voice, him looking at me, I would have agreed to anything. I nodded.

He took a step closer to me, a strained expression on his face, eyebrows knitted together and nose scrunched slightly.

Someone came out of the men's locker room behind him and walked through and out of the lobby. Rick took my arm and led me to the side of the room, away from the entryway.

"I'm so sorry," I sputtered.

He reached up and fingered the object dangling from his neck—a ring? Crap! He did have a girlfriend. I looked at him, questions swirling in my mind. *Do I dare?* I had to hear it from him. I needed answers. "What is that?" I pointed at the ring.

He let it fall beneath his shirt. "Nothing."

"If it's nothing, then you won't mind showing it to me."

"I'd rather not."

I stared for a few moments in silence then added, "Well, at least tell me what it is."

"It's uh, um," he stumbled over his words and then changed directions. "Why didn't you call me back?" His eyes flooded with emotion, and his shoulders sagged even more.

"What do you mean, call you back?"

"I called you after DC."

"You did?" My little brother filled my mind. I was about to tell him he must have spoken to my little brother, who was only three, which meant I never got the message, but I stopped myself. If I did that, I'd have to explain that the same thing had happened to Alex, and I wanted to stay away from anything to do with Alex.

"I just kept hoping," he said, "But you never did call. I called and called, trying to catch you. I kept looking for an email. I called every stinking day. I wanted to surprise you on your birthday." He lifted the ring from his shirt, perhaps unconsciously, and fingered it again. I couldn't take my eyes off it. I so wanted to know what it was about. He saw me look at it and tucked it back under his shirt again. I could tell it wouldn't stay there long, the shirt he wore was too loose and low to cage it.

"I thought you'd abandoned me. Then I saw you with Alex, dead. My heart broke in more ways than one that day." His voice pitched. "I didn't think I'd ever recover, and in a way, I haven't. I never thought I'd feel like that."

My heart lay on the floor in a thousand pieces. "I'm sorry. I never got the messages. I'm so sorry." I didn't want to say much. I wanted the floodgates to stay open and have him get it all out. Lay everything before me, but he stopped and kept his eyes intent on me. "I don't know what to say, Rick. If I'd have known, I'd have found a way. I really didn't know. I thought you'd forgotten me, because of that micro-world we'd been living in while in DC."

"I could never forget you. I told you I'd call. I wanted to come and surprise you on your birthday. I had it all arranged—and then you died." He leaned forward and brushed some lint from my pants. A nervous gesture.

"You have to understand how hard it was for me to see you dead. I mourned you. Even though you were with Alex, I still mourned you. I had so many questions. I had to assume the worst. You hadn't called me because of Alex. I figured all along you'd been with Alex, mocking me. You died. It broke my heart." His eyes filled with tears, and mine burned. "I didn't think I'd ever recover. I don't know. Maybe it was stupid, me being so attached to you after such a short time, but it was what it was. It was terrible."

"It was awful for me, too."

"I want to know what happened with Alex when he showed up. I thought you weren't allowed to date until you were sixteen." He stepped back.

"He just showed up on that Friday, and for some reason I still don't understand," I said, "my parents disregarded their own rules and allowed me to show him Helena on my own. We went on a hike after lunch, and that's when Iceman came and abducted us. He wanted to use us to bargain with the FBI, to let Abdul out of prison."

Our watches vibrated. The screen read ten minutes to curfew.

"This," Rick said, "is why I didn't want to start this conversation tonight. We don't have time to finish what we've started."

"I'll give you the short version, then."

"Why would you think I'd want that?" He stepped back, a look of frustration on his face.

"Closure, maybe? The same thing I want." I reached out to him, almost stepping forward.

"I want to hear it all, though... We can finish this tomorrow."

I didn't want to leave him on such shaky terms. I felt a rush of worry slip down my spine and fan out. "Please..." An overwhelming urge to cry took over. Stupid.

"Don't cry. Don't cry on me." His voice was soft, gentle, even. "It will be okay."

"I don't know what to tell you. I can't say anything that will make it better, can I?" Tears welled in my eyes.

He let out a quick puff of air. "I can't believe you didn't even try to get in touch with me after you got home. Email or something. I tried to crack yours, but couldn't. I tried."

I thought about my email address, *archeologist-srule@yahoo.com*. Certainly he'd never have gotten that.

"But my email is not hard to crack," he repeated, "And you're so smart. It's my name. Just my name."

He was really hung up on me not getting ahold of him. I had been caught up on him not calling me, too, until Alex arrived. "I'm sorry. I'm an idiot. I was waiting for you to call me. I thought you'd forgotten about me. You can't hold it against me. I was hurt that you hadn't contacted me." Tears spilled down my cheeks. Why wasn't he holding me? "I'm sorry. A thousand times, I'm sorry."

"I tried everything to get a hold of you, but it was like you didn't exist. And yet Alex found you. You let Alex hold you." Bitterness laced each and every word.

"The government erased us all. At least on the Internet. But you're right. I didn't try to contact you. I was being selfish and having a pity-party." I took a little step forward. "I'm sorry. It just kills me to have you right there and not be able to touch you."

He sighed, long and breathy, and then held out his arms to me. It was all I needed. I blasted into them. My world seemed to stop as I felt his heat, and smelled his distinct smell, the one that hid behind the soap and shampoo. My heart thudded hard against my chest. Too slowly, his arms wrapped around me, his hands gently touching the curve in my back. I cried all the more. Again, I was safe. Christy was safe.

My watch vibrated, and I felt his vibrate, too. I didn't want to look. I didn't care what the watch said.

I felt the pressure of his hand on my back leave for a few seconds and his head move to look.

"Christy, we've got to go. We only have five minutes. We'll be lucky to make it if we run."

"Just one more minute."

"We have to get back." I heard the exasperation in his voice.

"Just one." I breathed, taking in every bit of him I could, controlling the tears now.

Our watches vibrated again and he pulled away. "We've got to run."

"What will happen if we break curfew?"

"I don't know and—"

"We could find out together." I thought it might be advantageous to be in detention with him.

"*And*, I don't want to find out." He turned and started to jog.

I followed. I had to hurry to come up beside him.

His arms were bent, his hands in front of his chest.

Like a needy child, I reached up and grabbed his arm, but he didn't grab my hand. Instead, he looked down at me and said, "I'll race you." And he took off. I ran after him.

The race had the effect he wanted, I'm sure. It softened his rejection somehow. His room was on the side of the building we were already on, just two doors down from the stairs. He had too big of a lead for me to catch him and at the top of the stairs, he raised his hands in the air and yelled, "Victory!" I gave him a small smile as I tried to catch my breath. "You better hurry. You've only got one minute." He turned to go to his room, and I sprinted off.

A couple of feet from the door, my hand outstretched to grab the knob, I fell to my knees, both hands hitting the ground before me. My body was hit with a sharp pain that froze my muscles. I tried to reach the door again and the pain jolted through my body. I lay there, unable to move. I had been immobilized just like Ms. Mackley had said I would be.

Jeff's voice came out of the watch. "I'll be right there. Don't try to move."

Minutes later, he appeared at the end of the hallway, walking quickly in my direction. Once he reached me, he said, "What are you doing out of bed?"

"I was almost there."

"No, you were almost to your room."

"Whatever. I was almost to my room." I was annoyed now. Why wasn't he helping me? He towered above me, shaking his head from side to side.

"Ari. This is a serious violation." His expression was

hard.

I could see I would get nowhere with sarcasm and said, "I'm sorry. Please help me get up."

"Don't let this happen again." His words seared into me. A strange fear filled me. "You won't like what happens if you do." Something about the way he said it made me believe him.

"And do you think I liked this?"

"Maybe I should leave you here until morning to have the seriousness of this sink in."

"No. Please, no. I'm sorry. I won't sass again."

"Just always make curfew."

"Okay. I will." I had every intention of it. "But what if I need to go to the bathroom? Are you saying I'll be paralyzed if I have to pee?"

"Of course not, Ari," he said. "Once you are *checked in*, so to speak, the corridor to the closest bathroom is always open. You just can't go wander around."

I heard him pull out his handheld computer and punch some buttons. I couldn't see, because I couldn't move my head. He gave me his hand and helped me up. No more shock.

"So, this watch and this band around my ankle act as a taser?" I asked, getting to my feet.

"Pretty much."

"And what happens if I am in danger and you paralyze me"

"Did you notice it was a two-way com? You could tell us if you were in danger. It can be disabled remotely. Besides, you are monitored everywhere you go. We would most likely know you were in a dangerous situation before you did."

"You told us in the training that this was a computer. It

is way more than that. What do you mean you would most likely know if I were in danger before even I did? Is someone constantly monitoring my every word? My every action?"

"I did tell you this was a tracker. I did not keep anything from you."

He was holding something back, though. But what? "Except the fact that 50,000 volts would pulse through me if I didn't comply."

"I told you the consequences of breaking curfew were severe. Just be glad it wasn't a real taser. You'd have some nice welts for a week or so if it were. Besides, the pain and immobilization only lasts as long as we let the current flow."

I huffed.

"The intricacies of these watches are many. I will not outline them for you. You know what you need to know. You are a smart girl. Follow the rules, and you will be safe. Why do you feel you need to challenge me?" Jeff cocked his head to the side as if pondering a science project.

"I just want to know the truth."

He chuckled. "The truth? Good luck with that. Now get to bed. Sweet dreams." He walked away.

"Hmpf. You, too," I said, opening my door. I had to find out the truth. I might have access to all the records of this place on the computer in the vault. I would find it. My muscles ached as I climbed into bed. I thought of the terrible pain I'd just felt and was in jeopardy of feeling sorry for myself when the memory of Reese's arms holding me tight only minutes earlier filled my mind. The pain had been worth it. I was glad Reese made it to his room on time. I already felt guilty enough. I would remember the pain, which would in turn remind me of the amazing way

I'd felt in his arms.

Chapter Eleven

I woke gently ten minutes before my alarm went off. I slipped out of the room and after getting ready for the day, hurried to the mess hall. If I knew Reese, and I thought I knew him, he'd be the first one in there, just like he'd been the first one to breakfast every day in DC. I burst through the opening and there he was. Only not alone. He was standing near his table, hugging Sasha. I stopped short. When had she left our room? What could this mean? Had he held me last night just to appease me? I started to retreat back into the hall to catch my breath, but then his eyes lifted to mine. He didn't even flinch in embarrassment. He stayed steady, holding her, and gave me a pressed smile that said, *she needed this*.

I couldn't leave now, but I didn't want to go forward. Sasha pulled back and looked at Reese, rubbing at her eyes. Was she crying? I didn't know she could cry. She was hard as nails and as mean as a moose protecting her young. I moved toward the food line, and without checking my watch, plopped several things onto my plate. The smell of something rotten assaulted me at the end of the table. Today they offered an assortment of European cheeses that filled the air with a less than appetizing odor. I carefully made my way to Reese and Sasha and said, "Hey." It sounded more like a question than a greeting.

Sasha looked the other direction, and Reese gave me a sheepish look.

"Is everything all right?" I asked.

Sasha gave Reese a quick shake of the head. She didn't want me to know.

"It's nothing. Sasha just had a bad night."

She scooted away to the food line, leaving us alone.

I beamed up at him, so happy to get to talk to him.

"Ari, not cool."

I gave him a what-are-you-talking-about expression.

"Couldn't you see that she needed someone to talk to?" He scolded.

I shrunk a tiny bit. "I didn't realize she ever needed anyone." My bitterness from the safe house in DC spilled out.

"Everyone needs someone sometimes. Don't be cruel."

I truly felt bad now. "Sorry, I…"

"It's been three days, and Josh hasn't shown up yet," he whispered.

A heat overtook my middle, and I looked Sasha's way. "You don't think—"

"No. But she does. She spent a lot of the summer with him. They were really close." She started our way, and I looked back to Reese.

"Okay," I said. "I'll let you two talk." Then I walked away, to join Melanie, who had just sat down at her table. I should have been more sensitive to Sasha. Josh could have been killed by the terrorists at the country club. I would be beside myself if I didn't know what had happened to Reese.

After breakfast and a fierce Ju-Jitsu workout, I made

my way to the showers and then to the vault room. I was flying through the pages in the notebooks in hopes of getting some time to use the vault computer to find out about the wrist and ankle bands we had to wear while here. When I finally got on it, I learned some revealing information. Apparently, ten years previous, several teen spies in training had escaped the Academy and leaked sensitive information.

The Academy scientists developed the watch and ankle band to prevent that from happening again. Why didn't Jeff just tell me that? I'm a reasonable person. I could understand security having to be tight. I also saw that the device, because it contained a two way radio, *could* truly help keep me safe if someone tried to abduct me. I thought the information should be common knowledge. Then I read a few more memos on the technology and found what they didn't want me to know. Several students had died from the charge when they tried to escape or remove the bands. And still others had died when they snuck out and swam in a nearby lake after the watch paralyzed them. Their dirty secrets.

Still curious at what I might find, I found a folder titled, Bresen Coordinators. I couldn't resist. It appeared that this position was typically a short lived one. The longest anyone had been a coordinator was six years and that was the last one, right before Ms. Mackley. He died in a car explosion only one year previous. I wondered how long Ms. Mackley would last.

At about two, I realized I'd worked right through lunch. "Ughh!" I said aloud, although it was probably better this way. Reese would think I was being nice and giving Sasha time and space. Maybe I should try a little harder where Sasha was concerned. I got the Rock to let me out early for dinner, and I brought the tray to the vault room, not wanting to meet Reese's disapproving look again. Later, I worked out again, and made my way to my room with fifteen minutes to spare before curfew. Melanie sat in bed reading when I came in. Kylie and Sasha weren't there.

"Hey," I said, grabbing my PJs and overnight bag to head for the bathroom.

"Hey," she said. "I missed you at dinner."

"Sorry, I ate early and worked out with Master Li."

"I don't know why you like him. Master Li scares me."

"Really? I think he's great. He taught me a few new defensive moves this morning and worked me out hard tonight. I worked with a group of six students. One against six."

"I guess I just don't get all that karate stuff."

"I love it," I said, heading for the door to go to the bathroom. "It calms me."

I wanted to tell her about Sasha, but when I got back, Kylie and Sasha had returned, and now sat on Sasha's bed whispering. They looked full of worry.

Melanie looked at me with a great amount of sympathy and mouthed, "Josh," raising her eyebrows. She knew.

I gave a slight nod and slipped into bed, picking up a book from my nightstand and staring at the same page until the lights went out.

The next morning, I woke with my alarm and was shocked to see everyone else climbing out of bed, too. Were they all going to be on the same schedule as me now?

Kylie called out, "It's freaking five-thirty!. I thought we didn't have to get up until six-thirty. What are they trying to do to us?"

"Maybe they're brainwashing us. Sleep deprivation is

one way to do that," Sasha said. "I need my beauty sleep, and it looks like I won't even get a nap later. I'm scheduled solid all day."

"Me, too," Kylie said. "It sucks."

We found Reese and Elmer in the mess hall and joined them, bagels in hand, at the empty table we'd sat at our first day there.

"Do you think they're sending us home soon?" Kylie chirped, flipping her auburn hair over her shoulder.

"It seems too early," Reese said, his eyes filled with worry.

"Statistically speaking," Elmer said, "for them to have rounded up every last terrorist in the last five days is an impossibility. However, the initial estimate of two months is much longer than necessary. I estimate a three to four week stint here."

Everyone just stared at him. He didn't seem to notice and just dug into his oatmeal and fruit. We all ate without speaking after that. I glanced at Reese several times, but he was never looking my way. I shut my eyes against the sadness that threatened to claim me.

Our watches vibrated just as the room started filling up. We all carried our trays to the kitchen and headed for conference room number one. Ms. Mackley, a man, and another woman stood behind a circle of chairs when we entered. The room smelled like fresh pine. The neatly pressed outfits on the three people in front of us made me feel like this was a very formal meeting. The two new people smiled, and Ms. Mackley invited us to sit. We did.

"This is Dr. Houseman," she said, indicating the woman. The doctor nodded her head and smiled. "And this is Dr. Cook." He also nodded, but did not smile.

Did we have to submit to physicals now?

"They are our in-house psychologists. They are here for you if you ever find you need someone to talk to about anything."

They both nodded again, and then all three sat in the empty chairs in the circle.

Were we going to have some kind of bare-your-soul session, now?

"I thought it would be nice if we took this chance this morning for you to get to know them a little before you head off to your classes."

Dr. Houseman started off. "As Ms. Mackley just said, I'm Dr. Houseman. I love helping people. When I'm not working, I like to hike and bike. I spend a lot of time training for races and love the spirit of competition."

Dr. Houseman turned to Dr. Cook, who said, "I'm Dr. Cook and also enjoy helping others. In my spare time I fish and race cars. There's nothing like speeding around a race track at 200 miles an hour."

Elmer's mouth hung open, and Melanie's eyes widened.

"Why don't you each go around and tell these two your names and one or two things you enjoy."

We did. Then we played several team building games with the psychologists which were obviously engineered to help us trust them. After our little two hour pow-wow session with the psychologists, we were instructed to attend our classes, which meant I would be heading for the vault. I caught up with Reese and asked him if we could meet later. We decided to meet in the museum.

Back in the vault, I discovered quickly that I couldn't keep up the pace of 3600 pages per hour. I had to have a break for about half an hour after each hour of scanning or

I'd get a raging headache. But, in my ten hours a day in the vault those first few days, I was able to clear about 24,000 pages, two year's worth of instruction. I was a steam train. In my mind, I'd named my photographic memory my superpower. I never realized how powerful it could be until I came here. It had just always been a part of me. That, along with the idea that the faster I got done, the more time I'd have with Reese, took away a lot of the tedium in the vault. I'd be done before the two weeks were up for sure.

I was amazed at what I'd been learning. The people who had engineered these classes were geniuses. So much information, and good information at that. I was anxious to try some of it out. To do the things I'd been reading about. Practice it. I was also shocked at the technology that was available to spies. More than cutting-edge. This stuff was beyond what was already out there. Some of it was hard for me to believe. At mealtimes and during physical trainings, I found myself thinking through the information, trying to digest it, but Reese seemed to always take over my thoughts, and all I wanted to do was spend time with him.

Ms. Mackley appeared in the vault after I'd only been working about half an hour. "I'd like to send you on a mission with the same group you went into town with last week since you are so far ahead of schedule in your studies."

She was monitoring me. I had no privacy.

"They are going on a practical today that I'd like to see you experience," she continued.

Tension gathered in my back as I thought about the last time I went with this group. "Okay."

"Head up to the lobby. Everyone is already there, waiting on you."

"I love it when people are waiting on me." I couldn't

hide my sarcasm.

"Ari, since you arrived at Bresen, I've been somewhat lenient with your behavior because of the traumatic circumstances that brought you here. But you've had time to adjust. From now on, you will remember that you are a student and will treat the instructors and administrators with the respect they deserve. Do you understand?"

A twitch in her lip made me say, "Yes, ma'am." I now understood why Melanie and Kylie were mildly afraid of her. She could be scary.

"Good. Now, hurry up. You're wasting time."

Chapter Twelve

I didn't even bother with the elevator. I just ran up the stairs and when I burst into the lobby, they all stared at me again. I smiled. "Sorry," I said to Todd, knowing he hated it when people were late. "I just found out I was supposed to be here."

"Let's get out of here," Todd said.

We all climbed into a van like the one that had taken us to town the last time. I couldn't help but notice that they all carried backpacks with them. I sat next to Craig again. I stayed alert, prepared for the unexpected, feeling a bit naked without my own backpack. The group talked and laughed freely as we drove east this time, through a couple small towns. We drove into what looked like the middle of nowhere even though we'd just driven through a town five minutes ago.

"Today starts a competition among all of you," Todd said. "The person who earns the most points over the next four weeks will have one hour of extra free time each week until you graduate and will have his or her name on the plaque in the lobby that showcases the best of the best at the Academy. Each of you will have a mission to complete today. They are not unlike the others you've already been on."

I felt anxious and wanted to raise my hand and inform him I'd never really been on a mission.

"Your directions are specific," he continued. "You will be given points on how well you accomplish each task in your mission. I told you all to bring your go bags. So, you should be prepared."

Go bags? Were these bags the same thing as the backpack John had given me? I didn't have it with me.

"Ari, I have yours," Todd said.

My heart stopped racing, and I felt a sliver of peace.

"Hopefully, you all have them stocked properly. You must commit your mission instructions to memory and then burn them, making sure no one will be able to follow you. Treat this as a real mission and remember that true danger lies in front of you. Be careful and precise and you will be fine. And remember, your watch will record all you do, but it will not be a resource available to you to use. When you leave the Academy at the end of your training, you will not have it at your disposal, nor do you have it at your disposal today."

I tapped the screen on my watch. It appeared to be off. I tapped it again. Nothing. The kids whooped and hollered as they jumped out of the van, carrying their backpacks with them. Todd jumped out, too, and handed each person an envelope with his or her name on it. He gave me mine last and handed me a heavy grey backpack. I wanted to tear right into it, but everyone was already reading their mission assignments. Kendra looked at me and blew me a kiss with a mocking smile on her face. There was no way I'd let her beat me.

I tore open the envelope in my hand and read the

instructions. It was two pages long. One glance, and I had mine memorized. I opened my pack and reached in to get the lighter I hoped was there. My fingers found the familiar shape and I grabbed it, but my instinct told me that I didn't want to show my hand to these kids. Something told me it wouldn't be good if they knew about my superpower. It might be better if I waited until another person burned their mission notes first.

I spent the time discretely going through my backpack and coming up with a plan of action. This was a good thing. I brought up the maps in my mind that I'd seen of Belgium and used the phone in my pack to decide on my first move. I was thrilled that I had Internet service. The pack was eerily similar to the one John had made for me. I had my course mapped out and, still, the others were staring hard at their papers. I couldn't wait any longer. I was antsy. I set my instructions on fire just as Kevin did.

He glanced at me but didn't smile, instead he took off in the direction we'd come. He intended to win. That part of me that always came out on top rushed forward, and I headed out a different way. This was a training practical combined with a competition and nothing more, but a thrill coursed through me, thinking this was my first real—well, sort of real—mission. Contrived or not, I had seven things to accomplish to complete it, and I wasn't going to let anything get in my way.

1-GO TO HOGESCHOOL HIGH SCHOOL AND RETRIEVE A FILE FROM THE PRINCIPAL'S OFFICE LABELED *RAPPORTS DES ETUDIANTS 1969-71*. DO NOT READ THE CONTENTS.

I used my phone to run a search for a cab company as I ran toward the nearest main road and ordered the taxi. I looked up the school, the principal, and the town I was headed to. The driver arrived on the road just after I did. Perfect timing. We were about half an hour away from the school, and I used that time to find all the other resources I'd need for later. I got a little sick as the driver sped along the road. I didn't think I'd ever get used to the narrow European roadways. When a car came from the opposite direction, it seemed like we would have a head-on collision. I tried to ignore it and busied myself with search and social networking sites as I researched this man, the school, and his family.

The picture of the principal on the school's website showed a round, fat face and a bald head. His eyes were like tiny marbles that would soon be swallowed up by the rolls of skin around them. I didn't want to meet that man. I wouldn't have to. I only had to get him out of the school office so that I could get the file.

According to the website, it was a school for the masses and embraced diversity. I wondered if that was the mantra of all the schools in Belgium, considering its divided history. Groups of people were still trying to split the country in half, Flemish speaking and French speaking, and that division was to go right through Brussels. This school would definitely be in the French section. I would get to the administration by targeting that professed love of diversity. If they loved tolerance, I would give them intolerance. What better way to accomplish that than to write racial slurs on lockers? Even though the thought made me feel a bit queasy, I knew it would be effective. They were easy enough to find on the Internet. The admin would have to go investigate once the lockers were discovered.

I had the driver wait for me while I ran into a hardware store to get supplies. Everything I needed fit into a medium sized shopping bag, one that cost me an additional euro. Apparently, I was supposed to bring my own bag. I went next door to a clothing store and bought a button-up shirt, slacks, and dress shoes and wore them out of the store, stuffing my other clothes into the hardware bag. I applauded myself for not having to waste another euro on a plastic bag. I climbed back into the cab.

Once I was within a mile of the school, I had the driver drop me off. I paid with the money I found in my go bag. I braced myself for my next move. I'd found what I knew would be an effective slur using my phone. Even though sixty percent of the country was fluent in English, I would write this slur in French, playing on the area's French heritage. I told myself I was an actor and it didn't matter, that I didn't believe what I wrote. The country's anti-bigotry laws would surely cause the school administration to act quickly.

I walked to the school during the break between classes. I hoped the schedule on the school website was up to date. I tried to look like I belonged, and trolled the halls while kids found their way to their next classes. During that five minute break, I was able to locate the office and the two places I would write the racial slurs. They were far away from the office and off the beaten path, away from cameras.

I spray painted the words, Go home Dutch trash in French on one section of the wall, trying to keep my shaking hands from making it illegible. I took a deep breath and headed for the other spot I would paint on.

By the time I finished the second slur, sweat dripped from my forehead. This spy thing was stressful—real or fabricated by Bresen Academy. I left the school from the nearest exit and then called the school, "My son just called me," I said in a clipped British accent. "He told me the school walls are filled with racial slurs! This is unacceptable!" I knew I sounded convincing as a concerned mother, and my earlier work would validate my claims.

I hurried around to the doors by the office and waited for the admin to leave the office. I watched two men go down the hall, neither of whom looked like the picture of the principal I'd seen on the Internet. Could he have gone on a diet? I hadn't considered that. I waited, hoping what I'd written was bad enough to have the principal go check it out. Finally, the fat, bald man left the office, talking on a walkie-talkie. Apparently, he hadn't been on a diet.

I entered the office and asked to see the principal, this time with an American accent. They directed me to sit outside his office, saying he'd be with me shortly. I sat calmly for a few minutes, until the secretaries got back to work. A phone rang and a student entered the office. My chance had arrived.

I tried the door to his office. I was sure it would be unlocked—the principal had no reason to lock it in the middle of the day, with secretaries there. I turned the knob quietly. It stuck. *No, no, no.* My mind raced through my options—pick the lock? Try to find an open window before he returned? I nearly panicked, and then—the knob slid the rest of the way. Thank Heaven. I let out an inaudible breath of air and slipped into the room. My blood raced through my body, causing a buzzing in my ears that set me on edge.

He had four file cabinets. I went for the first one, hoping it would contain the oldest materials. Bingo. I found the file I needed in the third drawer down and stuffed it into my backpack. I slid the file cabinet closed, took a deep breath, and turned to leave. I watched in horror as the door cracked open. I freaked out for exactly one millisecond, then instinct took over. I raced to a chair in front of the desk and sat down with my head turned toward the door, as if I was supposed to be there and was merely curious about who was entering the room.

"Oh, there you are," the secretary said in a heavy British English accent. "I didn't mean for you to wait in here. I meant for you to wait outside on the chair."

"Oh, I'm so sorry," I said. "I didn't know."

She gave me a disapproving look and directed me to the seat outside the door.

"Is it going to be a long time before he comes?" I asked, keeping up the innocent act.

"Well, we've had a little incident, and I can't say how long he might be tied up."

"I have a bit of shopping to do. Should I come back a little later?" I said this as I made my way past the secretaries' desk toward the exit.

"That might be best," the secretary concluded.

"Okay, I'll be back in an hour or so." I opened the door and walked calmly out.

"That'll be just fine."

My heart didn't stop screaming until I'd put a distance of a whole block between me and the school. I leaned against the side of a building and took several deep breaths. Being a spy was harder than it looked. But hey, I was kinda awesome at it.

Suppressing my urge to look at the file, I called a cab to take me to my next destination: the principal's home.

2-GO TO THE PRINCIPAL'S HOME AND RETRIEVE A KEY TO THE LOCKERS AT LIÈGE-GUILLEMINS TRAIN STATION FROM HIS BEDROOM.

I had the driver stop at a drug store, and I grabbed a receipt book, clipboard, and a nice pen. My earlier searches had told me all I needed to know about the principal's wife. Mrs. Girard loved cats. Every picture she posted to social sites had a cat in it, and eighty percent of her posts had some reference to cats. As a spy, I would need to motivate people to do things. I had to direct them in one direction or another dependent on what I needed. I would entice her with a spiel about donating to a local cat rescue that never killed the animals. I would pull on her heartstrings. She only needed to let me in the house.

I went to the local library and created a flyer and printed it out. In the library's bathroom, I put on a short blonde wig and donned some cool disguise glasses. I'd been hoping for a chance to use them since seeing them in my go bag.

I practiced my spiel in British English as I walked to the target house. Much to my dismay, I didn't even have to use it. I rang the doorbell and when no one came, I peeked around to the back of the house. I found Mrs. Girard with her back to me, digging in her garden. At least, I hoped it was Mrs. Girard. Just to be sure, I went back around to the front of the house and rang again. No answer. I tried the door. Locked. I would have to use the back door. I walked carefully to the back French doors and opened them. She kept digging. I figured if she turned and saw me, I would just give her the planned speech about the shelter.

Once inside, I ran from room to room, looking for the master bedroom. Once I found it, I searched every nook and cranny, careful not to make any noise. No sign of a key. I knew I could be interrupted at any moment. Frustrated, I considered opening the closet and bathroom doors to search some more, then scenes from movies and

TV shows popped into my head. People loved to tape small things under furniture! That would be the perfect place to hide a tiny key.

After checking out the window to make sure Mrs. Girard was still out there, I ran my hand on the underside of all the furniture. Ah-ha! I found it under his nightstand, taped to the wood. I grabbed it and heard movement behind a door to my left. The bathroom? Then, I heard singing. Mrs. Girard! That must not have been her in the garden. Frozen for several seconds, it only took the click of the bathroom door handle to make me move. I ran to the bedroom door, glad I hadn't shut it behind me when I'd come in, and high-tailed it out the front door, running right into Mr. Girard.

He was so shocked, and I was so shocked, we both screamed and stepped away from each other. His eyes had probably never been bigger—no longer marbles, but golf balls. Just as he seemed to get his wits about him, I got mine. He reached for me, I darted to the side and stumbled, almost falling off the porch. My arm flailed in the air and his hand clamped down on it. I hadn't counted on him being an agile fat man, either. I'd pegged him as a slug. My mistake. My pack slid off my other shoulder into the bushes beside his porch, and he dragged me inside. The way he held my arm prevented me from getting any good hits in even though I was able to hit at his hands. And he was fast. This was not any ordinary principal. He had skills. He had been trained somewhere.

He was way stronger than I was, and I couldn't break his grip on me. He picked me up easily and slammed me into a chair in his dining room. His breath smelled of old tuna fish. I gagged. Holding me still with one sweaty, slimy hand, he slid his tie off his neck with the other and then tied my wrists to the chair. His mistake. He spoke to me in French, and I didn't respond. I would not break cover. I had no doubt I could free myself, but I had no idea how I could get around this wall of a guy. I had to find a way.

The Academy had put this operative in my way as a challenge, for sure. I knew I wasn't in any real danger, the Academy had set this up, but I still didn't want to fail. I couldn't fail. I started working on freeing my wrists from the tie while he kept speaking to me in French, pacing back and forth in front of me, his face and neck blotchy with big red patches. I could see sweat beading on his forehead.

"Roland? Roland?" A woman's voice called.

His wife. She called down the stairs to him.

He spoke to her in French, and she responded in French, too. I could hear her coming down the stairs, moving quickly. She turned the corner and gasped, putting her hand over her mouth when she saw me tied up.

The tie gave way, and I grabbed it with one hand preventing it from falling to the floor.

He moved toward her, speaking in a soothing tone. She spoke loudly, her arms flying in the air, her eyes never leaving me. He moved her behind the divider wall.

I couldn't hesitate one second. I had him. I leapt out of the chair and took off for the front door, slamming it behind me. I dove to retrieve my backpack from the bush. As I straightened, he was on the porch, reaching for me. But my feet were steady this time, and I slid under his arms with ease, not underestimating his speed or strength.

I ran flat-out down the sidewalk, not looking back. I could hear him yelling. Was he yelling into his phone? I had to learn French. As quickly as I could, I ducked behind a business and riffled through my go bag, pulled out a brown wig and a different shirt. I ditched the glasses, got dressed, and after dumping the contents of my backpack onto the ground, I turned the backpack inside out and repacked it. It was no longer gray, but green. I made my way to the nearest hotel and jumped into a cab. I chided myself for underestimating my opponent. I would never do that again. I had to move forward, assuming he had discovered his key was missing. I couldn't take my time.

3-ACQUIRE A MEDIUM-SIZED BOX AND A LARGE MANILA ENVELOPE. TAKE THE BOX AND THE KEY TO THE LIÈGE-GUILLEMINS. REMOVE THE CONTENTS FROM THE LOCKER AND PLACE THEM IN THE BOX.

I couldn't relax the entire ten minute drive to the station. I had to keep checking out all the windows for any sign of Mr. Girard. I didn't have time to stop and get a box. I would have to get the contents of the locker and just put it all in my bag. When we drove up to the station, I couldn't believe it was a train station. If I hadn't seen all the signs indicating it was, I would have assumed the driver had taken me to the wrong place. The structure was huge and looked like a suspended turtle made of glass and steel, anchored to the ground like a hot air balloon before take-off.

I quickly located the lockers, but there was a problem, there were no keyed locks. They were all electronic. I had no time to spare, my hands were shaking so hard, I had a hard time punching in his name to the electronic keypad. I didn't think I'd ever get it in there. I tried to tune into my spidey senses, but my nerves were way out of whack, and I couldn't concentrate. His name pulled up nothing. I punched in the numbers on the key and it asked for a password. Crap! I tried the numbers in his address. No go. The screen told me I had two more tries.

I cursed myself for picking such an obvious code. He is a trained agent; he would never use something so obvious. Then, I thought of the cats. Maybe he was a cat lover, too. I spelled it out. No go. One more try. My brain flashed through all the numbers I'd seen in my research of Mr. Girard. Which could it be? The folder that I'd stolen from his office popped into my brain. On the label, beside the dates, there was a series of five numbers.

I didn't hesitate, I punched in the code. All I could think about was getting the contents and getting out of there. The idea of Principal Girard's sweaty, meaty hands touching me again both creeped me out and urged me forward. The locker clicked open. I sighed with relief. Inside, I discovered six thick, sealed plastic bags, more than would fit into my backpack. I looked around for anything to solve my problem. There was nothing.

I had to improvise. After checking for Mr. Girard, I grabbed my pack from off my back and opened it, pulling out a thin windbreaker that was rolled in a tiny column and undid it. I laid it on the floor and put four of the six bags in the middle. I folded the hood and bottom edge up like a taco and then knotted the arms together, making a makeshift bag. The other two fit in my backpack. I shut the locker and headed for the first train I saw. It didn't matter what train I took. I just had to get out of there.

I jumped in and then looked at the display to see when it would be departing. Less than one minute. That would do. My eyes searched for the train system map, and I snapped a mental picture then slunk down in my seat. I studied the map. I was going the exact wrong direction to Liège-Palais station. I didn't care. The stop was not far, and I hoped the conductor did not come through this section of the train to validate tickets. I had none. The train began to move. With a sigh of relief, I pulled up my instructions again.

4-SOMEWHERE PRIVATE, TAKE €10,000 FROM ONE BAG AND PUT IT IN THE ENVELOPE. REPLACE THE BAG IN THE BOX, KEEPING THE ENVELOPE OUT.

I had read these instructions before, but the weight of them fell on me hard this time. I had a lot of money on me. If all of those packages were filled with money, it was a lot more than I thought. What was that principal doing with it?

Once at the next stop, I jumped off and went to an office supply store and bought the envelope and box I needed. From there, I slipped into the bathroom and cut a plastic bundle open with a knife from my bag. Even though the directions I'd received said I would be dealing with money, I was shocked to discover that it was the only thing in that locker. Six bricks of money. There must have been a half million euro in there—five hundred 100 euro bills. Suddenly the thought struck me—this couldn't be real money. It was all just part of this practice mission, so of course it was fake. The thought soothed me I looked at the bills again—they certainly looked and felt like authentic euro. The Academy had gone all out in making this all seem so real.

After the initial shock wore off, I put the blocks of money in the box and then stuffed ten thousand into the manila envelope and threw away the bag that had held it, letting the rest of the money from that bag slip into the cracks around the other bulky bags in the box. I looked at the file and felt a true desire to open it, but I'd been instructed not to. I didn't want to jeopardize my chance at becoming a spy and, more immediately, I wanted to win and thought looking might disqualify me.

They could be watching, after all. I chuckled at the thought. There would be no way they could be watching me run all over the place, especially since the watch was disabled right now. They wouldn't be able to anticipate my every move. It would be impossible. I guessed they could have someone or several someones tailing me. That would make more sense, after all. Still, I would not look. I would always know I'd looked, and I couldn't handle that. My next instructions were even more complex.

5-IN DISGUISE, TAKE THE CONTENTS OF THE BOX AND THE FILE TO AN ATTORNEY. PAY HIM A RETAINER OF 3,000 EURO FROM THE MONEY IN THE ENVELOPE. HAVE THEM DELIVER THE TWO ITEMS TO THE POLICE, AND HAVE THEM OPEN THE CONTENTS IN THE LAWYER'S PRESENCE. THE LAWYER SHOULD DOCUMENT THE AMOUNT OF MONEY CONTAINED IN THE BOX. HAVE THE LAWYER PUT THE POLICE REPORT INTO A FILE IN HIS OFFICE LABELED, *SODA MONEY EMBEZLER.* FOR CONTACT INFOR-MATION, HAVE THEM WRITE, *CONCERNED CITIZEN, CHAUDFONTAINE.*

I replaced the lid on the box and set it aside. I needed a new disguise. I checked the IDs I'd been given in my go bag and chose the one for an alias named, Athail Castel, a young Venezuelan woman.

I left the supply store and found a clothes shop on the same street so I could purchase new clothes to fit the alias. In the dressing room, I ran a quick search for lawyers in the town I was in. I researched the three I thought were candidates and read all the news I could find about them. I narrowed it down to one man in a legal aide firm. Mr.

Henrie.

Another cab ride and I was there. I met with Mr. Henrie. I liked this lawyer, and he was so excited about the 3,000 euro, he couldn't stop thanking me for being so generous. After he told me he'd never met someone from Venezuela, I had fun speaking English with a Spanish accent. I figured I could play with it and he would never know the difference. I instructed him on what he was to do with the box, then I walked out, feeling a weight leave my shoulders. Only two directives left.

6-GO TO KBC BANK IN A NEW DISGUISE AND OPEN AN ACCOUNT UNDER ONE OF YOUR ASSUMED NAMES FROM YOUR GO BAG. DEPOSIT THE REMAINING 7,000 EURO.

I chose the alias Madelyn Marcus and snagged another outfit. I took a taxi to the bank and marched into it to open an account. I liked acting older than I was. I felt powerful when I acted. The terror from earlier was starting to fade.

7-GO TO LIÈGE-GUILLEMINS TRAIN STATION AND REASSUME YOUR ARI IDENTITY BEFORE TAKING THE TRAIN BACK TO GARE DU MIDI TRAIN STATION AND THEN TAKE A TAXI THE REST OF THE WAY TO THE ACADEMY.

I hopped on the train and then got off in the town I'd fled, feeling confident that even if Mr. Girard was there, he would never recognize me. After scouring the train station and not finding him, I went to the bathroom and changed back into Ari and climbed onto the train. I was tired and hungry, but instead of stopping for something, I grabbed some protein bars from my backpack and the bottle of water and ate and drank while I waited for the train to move.

I found myself dozing off on the train. After the first

head bob, I set my alarm on my phone to wake me a few minutes before we were supposed to arrive in Gare Du Midi.

I had already called the taxi to meet me at the train station, exactly three minutes after I arrived. I walked into the lobby of the Academy and the receptionist told me to head to the Viewing Room. I'd already figured I couldn't be the first to arrive with my detour and all. I tried not to feel too badly. When I entered the room, it was filled with the other students, all sitting in the comfy theater seating. Several had sour looks on their faces. They had all beaten me. Figures. Maybe I'd been fooling myself about this spy stuff. Maybe I wasn't cut out to be a spy. I didn't know what I was doing.

"Nice of you to finally join us, Ari," Todd said. "Take a seat. We are about to watch you accomplish your mission."

Had I really been filmed? This was too incredible. There was no way. The faint smell of popcorn lingered in the air. Had they had popcorn? I sat in one of the comfy theater seats on the front row, my heart racing and my face burning. What would they say about what I'd done?

Part of my face popped up on the screen. It was incredibly clear, just not a good shot. How had they taken this video? I was running, using my phone to call the taxi. We could see where I was running, but not me. The picture bounced, like the camera was attached to me.

I looked down at my shirt and subconsciously felt my clothes. It cut to the taxi. Someone had edited the film. I lost interest in finding the camera. It was weird to watch myself. I was using the phone to research. It broke off when I got to the hardware store and then cut back on once I was back in the taxi. Then it shut off, and I was in disguise getting ready to go to the school.

It then showed me at the school during class change time. They filmed me the whole five minutes. It then showed me spray painting the walls and getting the file. A hush grew over the room when they saw what happened at the principal's house and that silence remained until the video ended with me climbing into the taxi to drive back to the Academy.

The lights in the room popped back on.

"What was different in this video than the last three we just watched?" Todd asked.

No one spoke up.

Had they already watched all the others' videos? I wanted to see them, too.

"Someone had better start talking, or I think there might be lines tonight."

Lines? What were lines? Whatever they were, they were the incentive the class needed.

"She executed some tasks almost seamlessly and when she did blow it, she recovered quickly." "She was innovative." "It was fun to watch. Like a real movie." People chuckled at that. They had to, though, it was Kevin who had spoken. "She used all her resources." "She did not hesitate." "She did not show fear." "She played her aliases perfectly."

Pride welled up in me. A smile crept across my face.

"Did she make any mistakes?"

"She underestimated her opponent," Kendra spoke up. "She didn't create the account or find the lawyer in the town she was supposed to."

"It actually didn't specify an exact town, but yes, she made mistakes, like many of you. Do you think she completed her tasks and should be rewarded?"

Silence.

"Come on now. Did she complete her mission?"

I heard a quiet, "yes" and then when Todd didn't blast that person, they all chimed in with a yes.

"Kendra?" Todd asked.

"Well, I guess so."

Todd smiled.

"She absolutely did accomplish her mission. Nowhere did it specify the town she had to do those things in. Sure it didn't say to do these things anywhere. Ideally, she should have done it in Liège, but it did not mandate that." He cocked his head to the side as if he were measuring me, studying me. "What I want to know is, why she accomplished her mission, her first mission, I might add, without any training, while three of you, who have had almost thirteen years, failed."

"To be fair," I spoke up, hoping to deflect my instructors' praise. "I did do one mission before." I was thinking of stealing the bike in Niceville. My words, however, didn't have the effect I'd hoped for. All eyes were on me again. Todd laughed.

"You have all been on how many missions, now? Fifteen? Twenty? No, Twenty-four. Twenty-five counting today's, and you three give me what you did? Why can't you all be like Ari?"

I was transported in a whirlwind back home to Helena, Montana. My parents were asking my siblings why they couldn't be more like me. I was suddenly once again a self-conscious girl, lonely and afraid. My triumph taken away, I shrunk in my seat.

"You all need to be better, but especially you three." He pointed at Tabetha, Elaina, and Henry. "You are falling behind. You may end up staying back a year to play catch up. Do your practicals again. All of you should have

125

succeeded.

As you know, clandestine missions like this, where no one is really working against you, you have to be smarter than the average cat. Innovative thinking on your feet. Like Jashon did when he slipped out the bathroom window when he suspected he'd been made. Like Kevin did when he sensed trouble in the bank and discretely left to go to another one. And like Kendra did when she found another way into the Catholic seminary building when she found all the doors had been electronically bolted. Like Ari when she planned to pose as an animal activist to gain access to a home where the owner loved animals.

"Stop being scared little rabbits and focus. The good thing is we made our goal of retrieving twenty thousand euro. We could have had twenty-five, however." He looked at the three who had failed with a pointed look. "I realize there were extenuating circumstances. No one could've predicted the power to go out in that part of the city causing total chaos for the three of you, but, you should have been more innovative and still completed the mission. No mission is ever without snags or problems. Let's go celebrate our wins for the day with some friendly competition in the Strategy Room." All the others headed out. I hung back, waiting to talk to Todd. "You coming?" he asked.

"Nah," I said. "I don't think they'd want me there. I don't really fit in."

"I don't buy that. You could be anyone you want to be. You proved that today."

I felt a blush slide over my cheeks. "I was just wondering if maybe I could watch the footage from the other missions."

"No. You have better things to do than stroke your own

ego." He turned to go.

"I don't want to stroke my own ego." I felt my face go hot again, but not from embarrassment. I was mad. "I was curious what everyone did and hoped I could learn from them."

He gave me a look that said, *tell me another one*.

"Really," I said, taking a step toward him. "What was it that made them so scared when there wasn't any real danger?"

"What do you mean, no danger?"

"Well, it was just a drill today, a made-up mission."

"Whoa! Is that what made you so bold? So fearless? You thought this wasn't real? That it was just set up by us? Here's a news flash for you, sweetheart. Today was absolutely, one-hundred percent real."

My jaw dropped. It almost hit the ground. I felt a wave of nausea hit me. "But you told me what to find and where."

"Yes, we gather all the intel for you, but that's it. The people involved do not know it's happening to them. By the way, why didn't you read the file?" His eyes darted toward mine.

I shrugged.

"Why? Tell me. Everyone reads the files." He moved close to me, challenging me.

"I wanted to win," I whispered. "I didn't want anything to disqualify me."

"Well, you did win. I'll tell you what you won. That principal was embezzling that money from the school vending machines. It may not seem like you could get a lot of money from that, but a little here, a little there. It all adds up. After twenty years, he'd amassed more than a half a million euro. And we had to stop him. It was time. Yes. It was real." He turned and walked out.

I sat back down. It was real. My hands shook. Would I have behaved differently had I known? Would I have failed due to fear? I was afraid to go on the next mission, now. I knew it was inevitable that I'd be sent on another. Todd had to see if I could perform just as well, knowing it was real. I wondered if it would make a difference. I knew it would.

Chapter Thirteen

After dinner, I made my way to the museum, excited to have some time with Reese and patch things up, but still trying to figure out where I stood as a spy. I realized how powerful the practicals could be, and that I would not be able to do them all in the short time I had left here. Those kids in the graduating class would have about one hundred missions under their belt when they graduated. I might have two. I had so much to learn. Seeing it on paper was one thing; doing it was a completely different matter.

I found Reese on a bench between a statue of Mata Hari, a spy from World War I, who used her womanly wiles to get information, and a picture of Nathan Hale, the first American Spy, according to the plaque underneath it. Reese smiled at me as I sat. He didn't waste a second before cutting straight to it.

"So, they made up this whole Alex thing?" He looked at me, stern and unyielding. I didn't have time to respond before he added, "Why didn't they choose me?"

I shook my head. I didn't want to tell him the whole truth, that Alex had showed up and I had been ecstatic about it. A lie almost crossed my lips, but this was Reese. I couldn't lie to him. I would have to lay the whole ugly mess in front of him. It was now or never. I chose now. There was too much at stake. I would just leave the emotion out of it.

"They didn't send Alex," I whispered, my head hung in shame. "He had the same problem getting ahold of me as you did, so he just showed up one day."

"I knew it." His face looked tight and disgusted. "He came of his own accord. He came for you. He beat me once again."

I decided not to reply to that and to continue with the story. "We went hiking and Ahmed found us." I couldn't tell him that I'd kissed and held Alex and loved every minute of it. I paused, looking deep in his eyes. "I need you to know there is nothing going on between Alex and me. Nothing." I tried to ignore the spasm in my chest.

"Now or then?"

I didn't know what to say. He'd obviously thought a lot about this. "Reese, I was at school, and when I left the building, he was there." I let that hang out there.

"Don't stop on my account."

Did he want all the torrid details? I felt my lip tremble, and I saw him see it.

"What happened after that?" He slid to the side a bit, away from me. "Just tell me."

I absolutely wanted to lie. But, he would know I lied. And, I would know. One day it would come out, just like on soap operas, and it really would be the end of us. No. I couldn't lie. Just the basics, the outline. "We ate dinner together at a lake and went to a party and then he showed up the next day, and we went for a hike. That's when it all went bad."

"Did you kiss him?" His eyes looked scared and yet he didn't lose eye contact with me.

I swallowed hard. "I did."

His shoulders slumped, and he blew out a blast of air through his nose while shaking his head. "I never had a chance against him, did I?"

"Yes! Yes you did. It was all just an infatuation. He was there and you weren't. I thought you didn't want me."

"And now you want me simply because I'm here and he's not?"

I felt a slight quiver in my heart. "No. I do not want him. Not at all. I'm new at this. Remember? I don't know what I'm doing. When I thought you hadn't called, I just figured you'd forgotten me, that you'd gone back to your regular life and didn't want me anymore."

"How can I ever trust you?" He wasn't mad any longer. He truly wanted to trust me.

"I don't know. All I can say is I'm sorry, and I didn't know you wanted to be with me. I just didn't know." I hoped he'd take that leap of faith. I would be true to him.

Then we sat, staring at each other for what seemed a long time before he spoke.

"Do you love him?" He looked me directly in the eye. I knew I couldn't look away. Instead, I squished up my eyes and let out a frustrated sound deep in my throat. "No. Haven't you heard a word I said?"

"Yes. And I can remember the way you looked at Alex in DC and how it must have been thrilling when he showed up at your high school. Once again, he beat me to the punch. How could you not love him?"

"I don't." I said, grabbing his face in my hands. "I don't." Tremors racked my organs.

"How can I be sure?" He did not waver.

"I promise you. There is nothing between us. Nothing. I

want you." My voice faded out when I said 'you' and my hands dropped to my lap. The feeling of Alex kissing me, holding me and caring for me fell further away from my center.

"Look Ari," he grabbed my hand. "I think you want something more than I'm able to give right now."

Despite the searing pain that hit my heart, I said, "Can't you be my friend? Can we start there?" I tried to hold back the mounting hysteria I felt.

He didn't answer for many long moments.

"I want to. But I don't ever want to feel what I felt when I saw you dead with Alex ever again. It still splits me in two remembering."

"Let's take it slow, then." I hoped slow to him meant a couple of days. "Let's take it slow."

"I'll try. But, no promises."

I snatched him up into a hug, unable to control myself. I felt a deep warmth when he didn't hesitate to wrap his arms around me. Pulling away after a few minutes, I allowed my cheek to graze his, and I closed my eyes, relishing the rough feel of his five o'clock shadow. The hug dislodged the ring that hung around his neck.

His hand covered it, and my eyes met his.

"What is that?" I asked, hoping I wasn't pushing it.

"Nothing."

"It's obviously something. Every time we talk, you play with it or try to hide it."

"I do?"

"Yeah, you do. Can I see it?"

His head cocked to the side, like he was contemplating hard, then, in one swift movement, he undid the chain, bringing it in front of me, the ring dangling in the middle, gently swaying back and forth. "Hold out your hand," he said. It made a zipping sound as it slid along the chain into my hand. It was a beautiful ring with a green stone. As I flipped it over and over in my hand, I noticed an inscription, so I picked it up between my thumb and forefinger and read it.

To, Christy - Love, Rick

I gasped. I sat there, dumbfounded, the whisper of a lost kiss on my lips. His hand lingered on mine and his face moved closer. It was what I'd wanted. A small fire started in my toes and slid through to my finger tips and a second fire seemed to start at my heart and burn slowly out through my chest. We sat in silence, staring at the ring in my hand.

"I bought this for you for your birthday right after I got home from DC and was planning to visit you. It is an emerald. Your birthstone. Do you like it?"

"I love it! It's beautiful." I wanted to shove it onto my finger and never take it off, but I'd said we could take it slow.

"I've been wearing it since you died. Something to help me remember you. Remember the good times we had. The times we could have had. At first, I wanted to chuck it into the ocean or drive over it with my car when I found out you'd died with Alex, but something wouldn't let me. I went to your funeral, you know. Your death was all over the news. Your pictures splattered all over the place."

"I saw the footage of the funeral a few weeks ago." I crossed my feet.

"I made my mom go with me. It was awful. I didn't want to say goodbye, so I bought this chain and have kept you by my heart ever since. I'd decided to hold onto only the good things. I know it doesn't seem like it by the way

I've acted. I'm sorry about what happened at the country club. I had suppressed all the bitterness I held about Alex and somehow seeing you, alive, brought it all back in that moment I held you. I guess I'd never dealt with all the pain of that part of your death."

He picked up the ring from my hand and slid it back onto the chain before clasping it around his neck.

"You've been right here." He pointed to his chest. "All this time."

I was an awful person. I had enjoyed every minute I'd had with Alex and the whole time, Reese had been hurting. It was completely my fault. Would I ever be able to forgive myself for this? He took my hands in his, and we sat in silence until our watches vibrated. Ten minutes to curfew. We stood in unison and walked toward our rooms, but this time, he held my hand.

Chapter Fourteen

On the sixth day in the vault, I discovered that I was able to handle longer sessions without getting a headache. I guess my mind was adjusting. I could skip every other break and be okay. That meant I could shave another day or two off my time scanning in the vaults. Maybe I could spend the extra time doing hands-on practicals.

I made certain that I spent my time exercising with Reese, and our whole DC group arranged to meet in the strategy room to play for an hour each night. At first, it was awkward coming together with the echoes of DC haunting us. But as the days passed, some of the kids from other groups joined us, and some of the originals moved on to other groups. Elmer only hung out with us every so often, and Sasha and Kylie were all over the place. But, three of us were a constant, Melanie, Reese and me. Slowly but surely, Reese and I fell into a rhythm together, and I could tell Melanie started to feel like the third wheel. I didn't want her to, but it was inevitable.

I started toward my room to get a sweater one afternoon when I got a message on my watch telling me to go to a meeting room on the first floor. I trotted down there, feeling a mix of emotions. What was this all about?

Walking into the room, I noticed my DC group was all there in a circle with Ms. Mackley and the two psychologists we'd met that third day at the castle. There was a heaviness in the air. It was somehow hard to breathe. I cut my way to the one empty seat.

"Welcome Ari. We're glad you made it. We were just about to discuss how everyone's handling being here at the academy."

Something wasn't right. There was a vibe in the room that set me on edge. She had something super important to say, and she was just easing into it. She started talking about fitting in with the groups we'd been assigned to and asked if anyone needed to talk to anyone about what had been going on. After one round of forced participation—it was like pulling teeth—I finally snapped, "Can you just tell us why we're here? The suspense is killing me."

Everyone gaped at me, including the two doctors who looked at me and then each other.

Ms. Mackley half smirked, half reveled in my outburst. "As Ari has so astutely picked up, there is a reason we brought you all together at this particular time. Although we did truly want to see how you all were adjusting now that you've been here over a week, we do have some unpleasant news. We wanted to remind you that there were people here to help you through it."

We all looked expectantly at her.

"Josh sustained some serious injuries at the country club," she said. "He was shot several times in the abdomen. He's been in a hospital ICU since then, where he received the best care possible. Even with the doctors' best efforts, his injuries were too severe, and he died this morning. I'm sorry."

My heart sunk. This was my fault. Josh was dead because of me. A quick glance around the circle revealed several ashen faces. Sasha stared wide-eyed at Ms. Mackley and said, "What? What does that mean? He's dead? For real?" By the time she asked that final question, her voice was shrill. Her eyes whipped from the doctors to Ms. Mackley and then rested on me.

My eyes involuntarily widened and a harsh fear overtook me as I remembered her words back at the safe house. *If anything happens to him, you're dead.* The look in her eye confirmed her resolve, and I found myself shrinking in the seat even though I could easily take her if she attacked me.

Sasha screamed and flew at me, but Reese stepped in front of her and held her, holding her back. After pounding his back with her fists, then clawing, trying to get away, she seemed to melt in his arms, her face burrowed into his chest. Something horrible burst in mine.

It all came back to my curiosity about voices in a hotel bathroom. He was an innocent casualty. I felt like I'd been slugged, my heart no longer able to beat. Melanie's hand was still at her mouth, and Kylie's eyes were still closed. Elmer turned to Kylie and started spouting the statistics of the survival rates in ambushes.

Sobs wracked Sasha's body as Reese held her tight. Dr. Houseman stood and moved over to Sasha, motioning for Reese to let her go. He slowly turned her over to the doctor, and just as they were leaving the circle, she turned and I saw her hand coming. I could have easily deflected it, but I decided to allow her one slap.

It stung.

Then she pointed at me. "You are responsible for his death. You and you alone. If you hadn't seen that murder,

137

he would be alive."

Then her finger, pointed at me only inches from my face, lifted up and down in a fierce motion. The look she gave me shook every ounce of security I had left inside me out into a heap on the floor, leaving me completely empty and vulnerable. I did not move, but one slap was all she would get.

It took both Ms. Mackley and Dr. Cook to remove her from the room. Ms. Mackley squished her eyebrows together and gave me a pointed look, then flicked her head toward Dr. Cook, who was stepping back into the room without Sasha. I guess I had an appointment with the psychologist. I stood and headed out with Dr. Cook through a different door at the back of the room. Before the door shut, I heard Ms. Mackley order the others to stay seated and wait.

Opposite of my first impression of Dr. Cook, that he was aloof and too professional, I found him compassionate and approachable. The hard part was keeping my cover. How could I do that and bare my soul? I couldn't tell him about my guilt because there was no way to hide my true identity if he knew the story. He kept assuring me that I could tell him anything and the information would be safe, but I couldn't get Cort's warning out of my head. He said not to trust anyone. Sasha, on the other hand, would probably tell Dr. Houseman everything. Would that compromise me? Was I being silly? He was the Academy's shrink, after all. Surely they knew everything about us.

I couldn't tell him, though, and instead I told Dr. Cook everything in a generic sort of way, no specifics of time or places or names—besides Josh's. He did give me some comfort, but my insides still ached when I left his office. Pain tugged at my heart, and I wanted to bring Josh back even though I knew it was impossible. My watch vibrated, and I numbly followed the directions to the vault.

For the next hour, I plunged myself into the files, my mind never wandering. When my watch vibrated for me to go to bed, I considered staying a bit longer. I seriously didn't want to run into Sasha. But, right on schedule, the Rock Renae called over the intercom for me to go through the security sequence to let me out.

I went to our room and noticed one bed was missing: Sasha's. Did they transfer her? My heart both sank and lifted at the thought. I slept, dreamless.

The next morning, I made my way to the mess hall and was shocked to see Sasha sitting there, eating breakfast with Reese's and her group. So, they hadn't transferred her, they'd only removed her from my room. Something hot and terrible rippled down from the base of my neck and out through my body.

I figured my best bet at avoiding Sasha would be to eat elsewhere. Besides, the group I joined for practicals stared at me constantly, whispering and sneering. I knocked on Ms. Mackley's door. When she opened it, she swung her arm out to the side, welcoming me in.

"Didn't want to face Sasha's fury?" Ms. Mackley peered at me, eyebrows raised like upside down v's.

"It doesn't rank high on my list."

"You could have avoided the slap. Why didn't you?" She picked up a pen and started tapping it on her desk.

Her question shocked me into silence. I set my tray down on the same side table I had set my dinner on the other night and took a seat.

"It wasn't a rhetorical question," she said.

I took a bite of my soup, hoping to avoid answering.

"I'm waiting," Ms. Mackley said.

"I guess I figured I deserved some of her wrath."

"How far would you have let it go? Until she really hurt you?"

"I don't know."

"Yes you do, and you'd better be honest with yourself and be intimately aware of your limits before allowing someone to accost you. You could have easily deflected the slap. No harm, no foul."

"It wasn't a big deal."

"But it was. The truth of the matter is that you didn't want your friends to see you in attack mode."

"I should probably avoid eating in your office from now on. Something about it makes me lose my appetite."

"You won't have to worry about Sasha. I've moved her in with the girls in her group. She is under strict orders to stay away from you. In fact, your watch will beep if she comes within fifteen feet of you."

"Great. My own little warning system."

"We didn't do it to protect you. We did it to protect her."

"Why do you see me as a threat?"

"Let's just say I know you. While Sasha doesn't have any qualms with breaking the rules, you do, so I figured you'd wait for her to attack first and then let your fury rage. That way, she would have been the attacker and you could say you were just defending yourself."

I took a sudden interest in my food and ate away, clear to the bottom of the bowl and then took my tray, standing to leave. I wasn't a threat. She didn't know what she was talking about.

"Being in control," she said, "and hiding your abilities are two very different things. You need to be in control in order to hide them. Remember that."

I scowled at her and grabbed the door handle.

"One more thing. Deal with problems as they arise. Don't let them fester until you explode and get out of control. Guilt only leads to death in this business."

"Thanks for the pep talk," I said as I left the room.

I let her words rattle around in my brain until I opened the file cabinet in the vault. Was I a ticking time bomb? Then I deliberately pushed them to the rear of my mind while I worked. I played around with them again on my way to the mess hall for lunch. I was in control, wasn't I?

I finished scanning the training manuals even earlier than I thought possible. I just got faster and faster and by the late afternoon of the tenth day, I'd finished them all and had started watching the practical videos, taking note of the things I needed hands-on practice with. Ms. Mackley arranged for me to learn how to rewire alarms, set explosives, set up cameras, and discover trip wires, none of which took me long to get a handle on. Sure, I'd have to give more time to practicing in order to master them, but I now had a working knowledge of how to do those things. It felt great. I was anxiously awaiting my practicals for the next day: lock picking, hotwiring cars, and safe-cracking.

It seemed Sasha had forgotten about me, or maybe it just seemed that way because I always tried to go the opposite direction she went. Every time I saw her, however, heat spread from my gut to my extremities in a matter of seconds. Reese and I had been spending most of our free time together out on the grounds to avoid her. Everyone else, Melanie included, headed for the Viewing Room or the Strategy Room each evening to be with the new friends they'd made. I still spent every meal with

Melanie, and we always spent time laughing and chatting before bed.

That night, after the lights were out, my thoughts kept me up. My time at the Academy was almost over, and I hadn't told Reese yet. He'd be going to a new school soon, too, but still. A part of me was hoping the FBI would call and say they had finished their clean up, and we could all go home. I didn't hold my breath, however. According to Elmer, that would take at least three weeks, and it would be a miracle if we got to go home that early. I believed in Elmer and his statistics. I'd be long gone by then. Would the CIA or FBI come for me once the terrorists were all rounded up, or would they leave me to be a spy wherever I was without the option to return home even once that was a possibility? I had to tell Reese, but would he give up on me if I did?

My body went cold just thinking about it. My first real mission had been thrilling, but so scary. Did I want to live my life in fear? Finally, exhausted by all the questions without answers, I fell into a fitful sleep.

Chapter Fifteen

I woke the next day, still thinking about Reese's possible reaction to my news, and if I could be a good spy. I walked through the early-morning darkness outside and into the building in which I was supposed to be learning how to hotwire cars. I felt good. Excited. I thought about the last week and a half and all I'd learned. It was incredible. I pushed the fact that I was leaving in a couple of days to the back corner of my mind so that I could focus. The instructor demonstrated how to use a master type key to start some cars and how to hotwire five different types of cars in case the master key didn't work. But before I had a chance to actually try it myself, my watch vibrated.

PLEASE JOIN THE PRACTICAL IN THE LOBBY IMMEDIATELY.

I said, "Sorry, they need me inside. And just when it was getting good." I smiled at him.

He pressed his lips together and waved me out.

When I arrived in the lobby, I was excited to see that I wasn't the last one there until I noticed the few that were there already had their go bags. Crap! I should have known I'd need mine. I took off to my room, returning with it dangling on my shoulder. Everyone had already arrived. As soon as I stepped into the lobby, Todd motioned for everyone to go out. The last one again.

My heart pounded as we drove an hour north, anticipation eating at me. I had a hard time even contributing to the other students' conversations. Most of the eight in the van were chatting about all different things, but I was mesmerized by the fact that I was seeing more of Belgium. The flat green grasses seemed to go on forever until suddenly, a town or city would spring up out of nowhere. It seemed they liked to have large tracts of open space and then cram as many people as possible into towns. The sprawling urbanism of the U.S. was not to be found in good 'ole Belgium. I had to rip my eyes away from the beauty of it as Todd started telling us about today's missions.

"There are only three missions today. That means you will be working in groups of three. The catch is each person in the group will be trying to achieve the same goal. Only one of the three can succeed. Pretend your classmates are your enemies, trying to obtain the same information you need. You must be faster and smarter than your competition. Be creative. By the way, you will not know who is on the same mission with you unless you run into them, which you do not want to do. We are about to arrive at the first of four drop-off points."

We were in Flemish-speaking Antwerp in Northern Belgium, and we pulled into a food market parking lot. Todd barked for Kendra and me to get out of the van and then handed us each an envelope out the window. "Make sure you dispose of the instructions after you memorize them. You don't want them falling into the wrong hands."

The van sped away. I wondered if this mission would

have anything to do with Antwerp being a port city or the city of diamonds. From what I'd seen, it didn't dazzle. It was a typical European city with lots of colored stucco, with brown wood crisscrossed throughout, narrow streets, and the rare very modern building. A token child here and there, tiny fast cars, and cool canals.

As I opened my envelope, I wondered if Kendra would be working on the same mission as I was. I glanced at my instructions and stood there, allowing the maps I'd seen of the area fill my mind. I thought it could be advantageous to use the canals if possible. I tapped the watch, but it didn't respond, so I took out my phone and searched a few things, pulling up more detailed maps and then switching to a site that actually showed pictures of areas. If I'd been dropped off on my own, I would have done this surfing on the go, but I needed to let a bit of time pass before I left, because I definitely didn't want Kendra to know about my superpower. So, I turned away from her and surfed away.

I wondered how I would possibly accomplish all I needed to at top speed without knowing a lick of Flemish or French. I had to somehow retrieve a notebook from the desk of a wealthy businessman, Mr. Courtlandt, who was having a large brunch at his home in less than two hours. Eight armed guards protected the grounds as well as the home. Four in. Four out.

The caterers were from Zilverstrand Catering, who I discovered from the Internet wore bright white uniforms. The home was wired, but it was thought the alarms would be turned off for the fancy brunch. While the home was completely gated, it backed up to the canal. Entertainment would be provided by an orchestra, and the office was located on the main floor near the front door. The last note in the instructions read,

USE EXTREME CAUTION

I had no problem following that advice. I knew this was real, and I wouldn't be taking any chances. My heart pounded hard thinking of the danger. If only I had a clear-cut plan. I hoped when I got to the house my ideas would solidify into something fool-proof. My initial ideas had me looking for a diving store, a hardware store, and a uniform store. I found all three, thanks to the Internet, spread out over several blocks. I hoped the shop owners spoke English. According to my research, sixty percent of the people, especially the youth, spoke English. I took off, heading for the trash container I intended to dispose my mission instructions in and leaving Kendra to her memorizing.

After lighting my instructions on fire and tossing them in the empty trash bin, I headed for the stores I'd located and gathered my supplies, stuffing them into my bag as I continued to work on my plan. I pushed myself to hurry over the cobbled sidewalks, glad I had good cross-trainers on and being amazed that many women were walking just as quickly as I was but with heels. Definitely natives.

I couldn't find any information about Mr. Courtlandt and that sent my spidey senses raging. I didn't want to waste time, but I had to know more. I felt blind. He must be a bad guy, but what made him bad? Goosebumps crawled up my arms. I went to the tourist information office and asked if there were any famous or notorious people who lived in town. When on a vacation, a lot of people like to see the homes of these types of people. I tried to get the attendant to mention Mr. Courtlandt or at least refer to him, but even with prompting in that direction, the attendant didn't mention him. I figured he must be a truly bad dude, one that flew under the radar of the local citizenry or the tourist information host would have given me the scoop.

I took a taxi past the front of the home to check the accuracy of the photographic maps I'd viewed. The picture I had seen was taken last year and a lot could happen in a year. From what I could tell, however, not much had changed. The best way for me to get onto the property would be by the canal in back, but how could I divert the guards? The modules about diversion sorted themselves in my mind.

A tall wrought-iron fence surrounded the yard and a guard shack stood at the entrance of the circular driveway. The 1700s architecture was mesmerizing, especially compared to the two homes on either side that were plain and uninteresting, obviously built after the war. There was nothing in the U.S. that had as much character as Mr Courtlandt's home. How had it stayed standing after the bombing this city had sustained during World War II? It had devastated this key port.

New urban developments that housed a lot of people had been built in the place of all the destroyed buildings. It was my good fortune that his home backed up to the canal and that homes on the other side of the canal also backed up to it. In many areas of town, one or both sides of the water were flanked with streets and sidewalks, making it hard to sneak in. I could use this to my advantage. I didn't see anyone from the Academy. Could I be the first here?

I noticed several more very old homes scattered here and there as I rode around in the cab. I was glad we were on the outskirts of the city and avoided much of the horrendous traffic nearer the city center. It surprised me to find that Mr. Courtlandt's home was not as unique as I'd thought.

Once back, closer to town, it killed me to pay the two-euro fee to use the public bathroom. At least it was clean and smelled good. It was funny to see a building full of rooms with toilets and sinks set up right on the sidewalk in the middle of town. McDonalds loomed in front of me, another place that allowed random people to use their bathrooms, but I didn't want people to see me go in as one person and emerge as another. At least on a sidewalk, the people who saw me enter the bathroom would not be the ones who saw me exit it.

After changing into the wetsuit I'd picked up at the diving store and putting the server's uniform over it, I left the store. Moving in a wetsuit was no fun. I felt like a medieval soldier dressed up in full armor, minus the clanking. I would first find a boat, then float down to the target's property, divert the guards with fireworks, and finally enter the home. Hopefully, it would be that easy and I'd never need to use the wetsuit to get into the water.

The supplies from the hardware store made it easy to build some rudimentary fireworks on timers. I also called a different cab company to pick me up and take me back to the target's neighborhood. The driver dropped me off only a half a mile from the house. Sweat trickled down my back even though it was cool outside.

I found a place to stash my go bag after taking out only the things I thought I would need to complete the mission: binoculars, bobby pins, a knife, rope, fake ID, my phone, and a small mirror. I stuffed those things into the waterproof bag I'd picked up at the diving store.

After hiding my go bag, I went through a large tenement about a block away from the home and grabbed a boat tied to the cement canal wall. Tied up boats lined the canal, but no one rode in any at the moment. I secured the waterproof bag to my waist and climbed into the boat. Some freezing cold water splashed up on my hand. The wetsuit should keep me from freezing in the canal after retrieving the notebook. The water smelled musty but was clear.

With some difficulty, I crouched down in the boat in hopes of not being seen by the nosy guards, and sailed to the opposite edge of Mr. Courtlandt's property. It might have been better to brave the freezing waters of the canal than to wear that wetsuit. It was so restrictive. I tied the boat to a hook behind the neighbor's house. It would serve as my primary way out after I'd gotten the notebook.

I sat behind one of the few bushes near the canal in the neighbor's yard and watched the guards. I surveyed the area, but could only see two of the guards. No other Academy kids. Where were the other two guards? I hoped they were out front, helping out with the arriving guests. These guards moved in a circular pattern around the grassy yard, constantly in motion, from the sparsely wooded area on the right, to the canal, then to the impressive man-made waterfall and stream bed and then finally to the house. Then they started all over again.

I couldn't help but notice that the space behind the house was too open. The online maps had made it seem so small. In reality, it was a large yard. It would be almost impossible to get in without being seen. A new gazebo stood about two-thirds of the way to the house from the canal. Maybe I had chosen the wrong path, entering from the rear of the building. Then again, at least here I had a chance. The Gazebo might just save me. Without speaking Flemish, there was no way I could make it through the front gates that I could think of. But, to make this work, I needed more than just a few fireworks and luck. Time to improvise.

I retreated farther away from the property and called several companies to deliver things to the target address at specific times to act as diversions for the guards in the front of the house. I hoped chaos would help me gain access to the house. The windows were not covered at the back of the house. Using binoculars, I could see the dining hall was on the left side of the building. I hoped that meant the kitchen was on that side, too. I spotted a door on that side and figured it must lead to the kitchen. I would have to get the guards to go to the wooded area on the right of the building. Darn it. I would have to swim upstream.

I put everything back into my bag, shrugged off the uniform and climbed into the canal, using all my strength to swim upstream in the wetsuit to the right side of the property with my hair tied up so that it wouldn't get wet. I could feel the chill of the water, but I was nowhere near chattering. I threw four of the six firework bombs onto the right side of the property and planted two in the neighbor's yard. They were all pretty far away from each other, and I set the timers to go off every fifteen minutes, starting twenty minutes from the time I planted the first one. Two would explode at a time. This coincided with the times of the scheduled deliveries.

I swam back to the left side of the property and dried myself off a bit in the sparse sun and waited, wishing I could ditch the wetsuit, but knowing I might have to get back into the freezing cold canal to escape this place. I got dressed just in time to hear and see the first firework light up the area. Where was the second one? It should have gone off at the same time the first one did. I watched the guards look around and then radio each other.

The guard nearest me, who I'd nicknamed guard #2, stood steadfast until the second went off, and then he took off toward it. What had happened? Why had that one been delayed? I couldn't dwell on it. I ran toward the house, my white uniform blazing in the sun. My speed was my only hope of getting to it. I made it to the gazebo, only forty feet from the kitchen and took cover as another guard, guard #3, came around from the front of the building. I could now see and hear a bustle of activity coming from the open side door to the house. Why did this have to happen in the middle of the day? It was so easy to see me.

Guard #3 was alert and looked in all directions as he made his way to the other guards. I ducked down as far as I could, hoping the white paint of the gazebo would hide me. Once he joined his comrades, his attention was diverted as he talked to the other two guards. I cruised to the open side door and slid into what was obviously a receiving area for deliveries. The air smelled of fish and something sweet. I pushed out a sharp breath and collected myself, glad I hadn't walked directly into the kitchen and relieved I'd made it without being seen.

Much to my chagrin, my perfectly white uniform now had mud stains and hardly looked presentable. I took a deep cleansing breath, and reminded myself that I was prepared to meet the chef. I'd had my taxi driver teach me ten phrases I thought I might need on this mission. I whispered the ten phrases to myself and hoped I wouldn't need more. I hid in the delivery alcove and used my mirror to check on the guards outside and see what the kitchen staff was doing. I watched the guards scramble as the next set of fireworks exploded and then studied a mass of servers enter and exit through a single door on the far side of the room. I also caught sight of a second door on another wall of the kitchen. I would have to go through that door. The cooks moved about the kitchen in a frenzied dance, barking out Flemish words here and there.

I only had about ten minutes to get into the office, retrieve the notebook from Mr. Courtlandt's desk and get out before all the fireworks would be spent. Maybe I should have given myself more time. Sweat pooled underneath my wetsuit, and I took another deep breath before stepping into the kitchen, planting a smile on my face and heading toward the only other door in the room, hoping it would lead me to the office. The servers all seemed to be going in and out the other kitchen door, so I figured I had a pretty good chance of being right. I didn't want to try and use any of the ten sentences I'd learned. Flemish was not an easy language to speak, so I moved slowly, pacing myself and pretending I belonged.

One of the cooks, holding a tray of what looked like open clams, spotted me and called out to me when I was only a few feet from the door I'd planned on exiting. I had anticipated this. I paused and looked back at him. Which Flemish phrase should I use? I had no idea what he was saying to me. I could only assume he wanted me to carry the tray into the dining hall. That's when I remembered the mud on my uniform. I called out two of the phrases I'd learned, "Het ene moment, ik heb het toilet." *One minute. I need the toilet*. I was glad I had learned this little phrase. It would save me today. It went against my sensibilities to call it a toilet, but that was standard in Europe. You went to a bathroom to bathe, not to pee. In homes in Europe, most combine the two and you can actually pee in the same room you bathe. Good upgrade, I think.

"Nee. Nee," he called out to me. "Green tijd."

I had no idea what he was saying besides the 'No. No,' but I had to be more clear on why I couldn't go to the dining hall. I pointed to the mud on my clothes. That seemed to do the trick. He threw his hands in the air. I loved the mud at that moment. I went through the door.

I pulled up short as the door swung shut behind me. This was a tiny, dim, narrow hallway. Servants' corridors, a common part of old houses like this one. They once helped household servants go about their business without being seen, and this one would help me do the same today. Many doors branched off to the sides. Luckily, they were labeled with engraved gold plates. I punched the words into an online translator as I passed them and knew where they led. While my instructions told me the office was on the main floor by the front door, it didn't tell me anything else about the floor plan.

When I got to the door labeled *Kantoor*, *office*, I gave it a tiny shove. It didn't open. I don't know what I expected. I lay on the floor and tried to look under the door, but there wasn't a crack. The last door in the corridor read *Vorinstaap*, *front entry*. Once again, the door allowed for no peeking underneath or on the sides. I put my ear to the office door and heard nothing. I figured I had my best chance going into the office, feigning stupidity if I found anyone there. I pulled a couple bobby pins from my hair, pulled up Module 18.2 from the spy academy on how to pick a lock with bobby pins, and cursed the fact that I still hadn't had hands-on experience with lock-picking. I didn't have much time, so I went full force.

Sweat dripped into my eyes as the seconds ticked by. I kept looking down the dim corridor, expecting to see one of my fellow Academy classmates come running down it, or worse a guard or maid or someone. I heard a bunch of clicks and felt things move while using the bobby pins and each time thought I had gotten it, but I hadn't. The blood pounding in my ears made my task all that much harder.

Surely no one was in the office, or they would have come to investigate who was trying to get into the room. Hot frustration coursed through me, and I jabbed hard at the lock and kicked the door. Much to my glee and utter fright, it popped open. I guess the jab and kick had freed the lock. I froze. For a second, I wondered if I really had opened it or if someone else had and he was about to come through it. After a few more seconds, when no one came, eyes wide, my body ready for anything, I went in. It was empty. I pushed out a long, sharp breath. Lavender scent assaulted me. I hurried to the desk, checking my phone. I had only five minutes until the final fireworks exploded.

I opened all the drawers in the desk and searched them except for one that was locked, but found nothing. I didn't bother trying to pick the lock. I used a letter opener and broke it. No notebook. I wondered if someone had beat me to it. Out of sheer hope and determination, I felt under the drawer and tapped it. A false bottom? Module 6.2 on false bottoms popped up, and I finally figured out where the finger-pull was. Ah-ha! The notebook stared up at me.

I grabbed it and, for good measure, took a picture of it with my phone. I considered leaving the notebook, but my instructions specifically said I was to take it. That's when I heard someone at the door. I could see no viable hiding places besides under the desk, the lamest hiding place of all. But there was nowhere else. I had no time to contemplate, so I scampered under it as fast as I could in the restrictive wetsuit, stuffed the notebook down my wetsuit, pulled the chair up to me and grabbed my knees as tight against me as possible. I also opened my mouth wide in an effort to control my breathing. What if this person tried to sit at the desk? I was a dead duck.

The person did not walk in like someone who belonged there. My neck tensed, hot and sweaty. His feet were light and almost silent. He shut the door behind him with almost no sound. It had to be one of the students on the same mission. Or would a guard, who suspected someone was hiding in there, act the same way? Who could it be? I could not let him find me, but if he did, I had to be ready to fight. How could I fight in this wetsuit?

I held my breath when I saw his legs. He pulled on the drawer. He must have noticed it had been jimmied and broken, because he cursed quietly, and I saw one of his hands make a fist and then release. I heard the drawer shut and felt a breeze of air as he moved away, but heard no footsteps. It had to be a student. He didn't seem to have triggered an alarm. He was good, whoever he was. As quiet as a mouse. I didn't even hear him go out the door.

I waited a few extra seconds, but figured I had no more time to waste and crawled out. I'd be lucky to make it out, now. He hadn't left. Kevin stood there, dressed in musician's garb, in all his glory on the opposite side of the desk. I couldn't help it, I gasped.

He grinned.

I scrambled on my hands and knees for the servants' door, but he caught me by the legs, the wetsuit slowing me down.

"I think you have something I need," he whispered, holding my legs tight.

I tried to kick him, but he had a solid hold on me, a good Ju-Jitsu hold. My only hope was to use my upper body to escape. I twisted, forcing him to adjust his grasp on me. In that second of freedom, I kicked him in the nose. He grabbed for it as it began to bleed, and I slithered away, grabbing the doorknob. He must've been in a lot of pain, but he didn't make any indication of it. No gasp. No shriek.

"Oh, no you don't," he whispered with a growl, grabbing my feet again and pulling me back down. He had my legs again, my best weapons. I had to get him to allow me to stand. I struggled a bit for good measure, and he tightened his hold on me. "Give it up, and it won't get ugly."

I huffed and then said, "Fine. You win. Let me get it for you."

"No, you just hand over your pack, and I'll take the whole thing in with me."

He wrapped his legs around mine and then slid my wet pack away from my waist.

If he wanted my bag, he could have it. It didn't have anything important in it besides my fake ID. He held me there, longer than necessary, and I looked behind me. He gave me a curious look, pausing a few more seconds, his eyes firm on mine. I felt my skin prickle. Why did he have to be so perfect? A huge boom sounded outside and he let go. After standing, he even gave me his hand to help me up. He thought he'd won. Inside, I felt complete joy.

"Yours?" he asked.

Sure he was referring to the sound, I said, "Yep."

"Better hurry then. You got a clean way out?" He rubbed his bloody nose, his eyes piercing me.

"If I go now," I said, wondering why he was being so nice. For some strange reason, it reminded me that we all had a mission to complete, and we couldn't all succeed.

"See ya back at the Academy." He grinned and winked as he went for the door to the front hall.

I grimaced and hurried out of the room, down the corridor and through the kitchen, ignoring the calls of the cooks. I hoped I still had my window to escape. I couldn't see any guards, so I pretended to be on break from my hard work as I walked out the side delivery door. I stretched and walked a bit further onto the grounds. Four guards came out of the woods on the right, sweeping the yard and heading for my exit route, the canal. If all four were in back, who was taking the deliveries? Perhaps no one. Could I just go right out the front gate?

I walked up the side of the house, casually peeking around the corner of the house, to check out what was going on in front. The circular drive was full of cars, but no delivery vehicles. The gate was closed, and I could see two delivery vans lined up outside the gates, a guard speaking to the man in the first van—Craig, my second challenger from the Academy. I scanned for another guard. I couldn't see one, but I'd have to be careful, my neck hairs stood on end.

I followed the fence with my eyes to see where it ended in the front, leaning on the side of the house, trying to look like I belonged during my surveillance. A hand grabbed my arm from behind, and I whipped around. A guard I'd not seen before had spotted me and held my arm. My heart ripped into my ribcage. The CIA had given me shoddy intel. There were more than eight guards. He said something to me in Flemish and in a flash, I looked past him, far enough to see that he was alone and the four other guards were still by the water's edge looking at the dirt and pointing. I thought of two things at once: There were at least six guards outside and probably more. And I needed to smile, and quick.

He smiled, too. I sized him up. A definite Casanova. "I'm sorry," I said, batting my eyelashes and choosing to play the clueless foreigner from Module 12.2. "I don't speak Flemish."

His smile got bigger, if that was possible, and his hand left my arm, but only after he let it slide all the way to my hand.

I was glad for the thick fabric of the uniform that hid the fact that I wore a wetsuit.

"No here," he said, shaking his head. "Back in." His hand only left mine when he pointed back the way I'd come. He held his arm out, as if to guide me back.

"But, I got this mud on my uniform," I said, pointing to the mud near my knee. "And my boss will kill me."

He looked down, where I was pointing and even though I was sure he hadn't understood, he reached for the stain. My chance had arrived. I kneed him hard in the nose, and before he could fly backward, I clasped my hands together and pounded on his back. He fell on his face with a grunt. I figured he had come from the sparse woods to my right, and I headed in that direction, ready to climb the fence once I got to it. It was harder than I'd anticipated. There was nothing to grab hold of, the sign of a great perimeter, so I had to climb a tree that stood near the fence and swing over and down from a branch.

I hurried behind a big, scraggly tree in the neighbor's yard, rubbed the sweat from my forehead and hands and called a cab to pick me up about a mile away. I pulled the notebook out and shoved it into my go bag that I'd retrieved. I tugged and pulled myself out of the wetsuit behind the cover of the tree and put regular clothes from my go bag on. Not fun. As I ran to meet the taxi, I smiled.

Once in the cab, I directed him to take me to a restaurant where I ordered something to go and then used their bathroom to change. I called the first cab company I'd used that day to send a cab.

I kissed the notebook when I pulled it out and wondered when Kevin would discover he didn't have it. When I came out of the bathroom, the server handed me my "take-away" bag full of my order, and I chuckled thinking about them calling it take-away instead of to-go, like we did in the U.S. It wasn't in Flemish, either, it was in English, take-away. I ate while in the taxi, enjoying the new scenery.

I was excited to get back to Brussels, and it occurred to me, as I watched Antwerp disappear behind me, that even though Brussels wasn't very far from Antwerp, it was extremely different. Each street had its own personality and I'd never seen such narrow alleys. It seemed Antwerp had been able to hold onto its roots a bit more, where Brussels was definitely more modern.

I wondered if this notebook I'd retrieved had anything to do with diamonds. Antwerp was the city of diamonds, after all. I wanted to look in that notebook, but I refrained. It was common knowledge that as a spy you weren't supposed to look. Most didn't follow this 'rule,' but I would.

Once back at the Academy, I was instructed to head up to the Viewing Room. I figured I'd be the last one there again. It seemed par for the course. I wasn't the last, however. Four others were missing. I went straight to Todd and handed him the notebook. He shook his head as he took it from me, and I couldn't help but smile. Kevin ambled in shortly after me, scowling. The look he gave me was truly frightening. I wished I could melt into the ground. The lights went down, and the review started.

Chapter Sixteen

I was shocked at how good these kids were at being spies. Talented and amazing, daring and creative. It was fascinating to see and hear them in action. And, on top of it all, they all seemed to speak perfect Flemish and French. I wished there was better film for certain parts of the mission. The watches shot amazingly good pictures, but they were rarely angled favorably. It was nice when the editors cut in some footage from cameras around the city, and we could see the bigger picture. I wondered how long the first group had been back before I got there.

The editors showed what each person in a group was doing at the same times, cutting in and out from each person's point of view. They had to have worked fast. It turned out that Kendra was the first one back. She was a super spy for sure. When group number one's video was almost over, Tabetha and Sandra slouched in, followed by Jashon. I guessed her mission didn't go well. Jashon, smiling, handed Todd something and said, "Here ya go, Chief."

I tried to see what it was, but I'd know soon enough when their film started. Our group was next. After watching the first group's film, I was afraid to let everyone see ours. My fear was justified. I looked clumsy and silly compared to the other group, while both Craig and Kevin acted like real spies, speaking the language and making everything seem so easy.

He turned on the lights after my group's film. My face burned. Comparison time.

Todd asked, "What was the difference between what you saw the first group do and the second?"

No one was shy this time. Hands popped right up.

"Everyone in the first group seemed to act smoothly, doing exactly as they should." "The second group looked messy, made up, not well thought out." "Kendra followed protocol and really made Henry and Elaina work hard."

I shrunk in my seat. The criticism for my group was endless, while the praise for Kendra's group increased in intensity.

"Kendra's group did the logical." "Kendra's group worked seamlessly out there." "Kendra's group did as we've been taught." "Ari's group was lucky, careless."

Just as I thought I couldn't feel any worse, Todd called out, "Do you agree with them, Ari?" His eyes seemed to penetrate mine.

I swallowed hard, hoping to find some moisture in my cottony mouth. "To a point, yes." My voice was gravelly.

"Do you think that *following the book* will save you or hurt you?"

"I think it is engineered to save you."

"Nice dance around that question. What made you think to detonate those fireworks, timing them with deliveries?"

"I just wanted to create chaos so I could make it into the house without being seen. Without being able to speak the language, I wasn't sure how to weasel my way into the band or food service or whatever like Kevin and Craig did.

I knew I didn't have a lot of time and so I did what I knew how to do and what popped into my head at the time."

I heard giggles.

Todd looked everyone over, and I felt a weight fall on the room.

"Sorry, Sir," a male voice spoke up.

"I'm not the one you should be apologizing to."

"Sorry, Ari," Kevin said.

"You should all be moving from doing things you've been taught in your training, to doing things instinctively because of your training. Ari is at a bit of a disadvantage because she hasn't received the training you all have, but she adapted. She used her instinct, which all of you need to learn to do. It is what we are working toward in this last stage of training. You will all hopefully develop that instinct. It appears that Ari comes with a great deal of that natural ability. Why they didn't find her sooner, I'll never know. But now she has a chance to become someone amazing, just as you all do.

"Don't get me wrong. I'm not telling any of you to throw out your training. This instinct should start developing naturally for you. Some of you may already be experiencing this. You know what the Academy would tell you to do, but you think there might be a better way, or you think there might be a flaw in the plan. You may have two trains of thought for a while until they merge together. You'll start analyzing things by asking, 'If I do what the agency would tell me to do, what would be the risks? If I did it this other way, what would be the risks? Which will give me a better outcome?' Ari needs a little bit of ya'll and ya'll need a little bit of Ari." He gave a pointed look to Kevin.

There was a thick silence.

"You both can learn from each other. When the manuals talk about letting spying become a natural part of you, Ari exemplifies this. She may not have all the experience you've had, but she did a great job today. She needs a bit more structure to be more efficient, and you all need a bit more flexibility and creativity." He looked at me, sharp and focused. "She's a natural, and we haven't seen this in a long time."

I could feel all the students' stares. I hated being the example. It never ended up being a good thing.

The last group's mission had been a comedy of errors, with things breaking, car accidents holding them up, and extra security they hadn't planned on, and the Academy had had to step in to save them. I didn't feel like joining everyone in the Strategy Room to play games until dinner, as was tradition with the group. I did, however, want to finish my practical on hot-wiring cars. I went to Ms. Mackley's office to see if I could. She said it was impossible, and she was trying to find time for me to get all three practicals I'd missed today scheduled for the next day.

I made my way to the vault instead and watched a few interesting practicals. There was so much to learn. How could I possibly master it all? How could I be an effective spy if I didn't? Self-doubt swirled around me and then settled on my shoulders through dinner. Once I spotted Reese at his typical table with Sasha, and a deep ache spread through me thinking about having to tell him I would be leaving in two days.

It turned out that everyone's free time got hijacked by Ms. Mackley. She had us all meet on the grounds after dinner to play strategy games. I hoped I'd have a chance to talk to Reese.

The two summer graduating groups, which included the

one I'd gone with on two missions, were the ones leading the games. I'd never played paintball before, and I was excited for the chance. Apparently, most of the students had played this game before, so they didn't belabor the details. I wanted and needed those details.

Kevin's voice boomed over the speakers telling the groups of students where to go to meet their leader one by one. Twenty fortresses of various sizes and shapes littered the grounds. I watched as the groups left the front area of the area and moved to their respective spots they'd been assigned in front of the structure. After all the leaders at the front of the meeting grounds, except Kevin, had gone to meet their teams, he called my name as the leader of a group.

My eyes turned to golf balls, and then I went to him to explain I didn't know what I was doing. The group assigned to me went running to the structure labeled nineteen.

"It's paintball, Ari," he said with a smooth ease.

"But," I said, "I'm supposed to lead my team, and I don't know what I'm doing."

"It's simple. You protect your property and person while trying to destroy other teams. Just be creative."

"Simple enough for you, you've played this game I don't know how many times, but I have no clue."

"Ari, I don't have time to show you everything, but I can show you how to prepare and use the guns, at least."

He gave me a quick demonstration on how to assemble the guns and shoot.

"You need to get them all assembled for your team."

My group had found their gear behind the structure and were getting suited up. I went to the guns and prepared them exactly as he had shown me and thought about a strategy to win. I mentally examined the great leaders of various countries and quickly created a plan.

I told the group of strangers, who were now on my team, the plan as soon as they were all suited up and then I armed them. I hoped I'd developed a good plan. I hoped we wouldn't be the first structure out of the games.

When the cannon to begin the war sounded, our compound was rushed, and we didn't have a chance to execute the plan. We were all forced to run out and start shooting or risk losing our structure in the first few minutes of the war.

We would have had a chance of driving them away, if our guns didn't jam and splatter paint all over us when we tried to fire them. I had assembled them incorrectly. What had I messed up? I looked at the gun in my hand and examined it. I went through all the steps Kevin had showed me. That's when I noticed the problem. He had me put the pin in upside down. I hadn't messed up. Kevin had had me sabotage my own team's guns.

I was mortified, and our structure fell in record time. In fact, it only took thirty seconds. I was responsible for the failure. I, alone. I shouldn't have trusted Kevin. He was my enemy. Lesson learned.

I looked over to Kevin's structure and he stood, with a smug smile just long enough to let me know he had done it on purpose. Then he was off, leading his troops to their next battle.

No one in my group smiled. They looked at me like I was dirt. I felt like dirt. But I would not be taken again.

We had to go and sit in the gathering place where the whole night had started and take our spot of shame watching the war until one team was triumphant. Kevin's. I never had the chance to talk to Reese. When watches warned of curfew, I chose not to run away in shame, but waited for Melanie and walked inside with her. Whispers about a 'stupid' new leader flew all around us. I wouldn't let Kevin or anyone else in that group get the better of me again.

"I still haven't told Reese," I confided to Melanie as I climbed into bed, all showered and free of paint.

"You've got to tell him, Ari. You leave in two days."

"I know. I don't want to tell him though, and I don't want to go."

"The longer you wait, the madder he's gonna get. Get it over with. He'll understand. He knows we don't have a lot of choice here." She paused for several minutes and then added, "I'm sorry about tonight. That must've been embarrassing."

"It was," was all I could say, hatred boiling inside me.

The lights went out.

I did not sleep well.

Chapter Seventeen

The harsh vibration of my watch woke me.

I was to meet Ms. Mackley in one of the rooms in the basement before breakfast. I figured she must have a practical lined up for me and wondered why she chose such a strange time.

The one good thing about my short spiked hair was that it took no time to do each day. It only required a few haphazardly placed bobby pins to complete the look. And, as I'd learned on the latest mission, a bobby pin could be quite handy. My watch directed me to the specified room in the basement. It looked like an interrogation room in the FBI building, with one table in the center and several chairs around it. Two other chairs sat in a corner of the room. It felt sterile, cold. I wrapped my arms around my waist trying to warm up.

"Have a seat, Ari," Ms. Mackley said, smiling and swinging her arm out to the side, directing me. Breakfast stood on the table.

I sat quickly, rubbing my hands back and forth on my pants for warmth.

"You cold?"

"Just a bit."

She touched some things on her computer tablet and shortly thereafter, I could hear the rush of warm air being pushed through the vents in the ceilings as I started to eat.

"I apologize for that. These rooms aren't used very often so the temperature will need to be adjusted." She paused, looking at me for several moments. "I have some exciting news. I've discovered—"

Her phone rang, an insistent buzzing sound vibrating out of her pocket. "One moment." She got up and walked out of the room as she said, "Yes?" and shut the door behind her.

I started eating, expecting Ms. Mackley to walk through the door any moment. I'd finished everything on the plate and still she hadn't returned. I looked at my watch. She'd been gone twenty minutes already. I tried to open the Internet on my watch, but I couldn't connect. In fact, it seemed nothing but the time worked on my watch in this room. After thirty minutes, I really started to get antsy and tried the door. Locked. I knocked on the door, pounding harder with each hit. There were no windows in the room, and my claustrophobia set in. I climbed up on the table and began meditating. It was the only way to ease the panic. Had she forgotten me? What was going on? Was this another test?

It took me longer than expected to ease myself into complete peace. After an hour, I decided I needed to find a way out. This must be a test. I looked at the door, the only viable escape route. I pulled up the diagrams in my brain on door knobs and locks from year fourteen, Module 14.3, cursing once again that I hadn't had a practical on picking locks, and decided I would try to tackle it anyway. I pulled out two trusty bobby pins from my hair and went to work.

No matter what I did, it wouldn't unlock. I threw the pins on the floor and decided to use a chair to break the knob instead. I had to get out of there. I was starting to feel out of control again. I bashed the doorknob with the chair over and over again until finally, with a loud clang and rattle, the broken knob fell to the floor. I had to fiddle with the guts of the lock to get the door to open, but when it did, I sprang out, drawing deeply on the air in the hall. It seemed I couldn't get enough. To my surprise, Ms. Mackley walked toward me and then jumped as the outer knob that still hung on the door, suddenly clattered to the stone floor.

"Oh, Ari," she said, clutching her computer tablet to her chest, "That startled me. I'm so sorry you had to wait, stuck in that room for so long." She eyed the knob on the floor in the hall and then the other just inside the room. "I see you figured a way out?"

"Sorry, I just thought maybe you'd forgotten me or something."

"Well, I didn't. And I don't forget. I just got waylaid. I wanted to be the one to relay the news to you." She cocked her head to the side and looked at the knobless door, muttering, "Hmmm. Let's step inside, shall we?"

I walked back into the room. She followed, leaving the door open. When I turned to look at her, she gestured for me to sit. She pulled a chair across from mine and sat, consulted her tablet, and then looked at me expectantly. "Well, it turns out that they've cleaned things up back home."

"Cleaned things up?"

"Yes. Apparently, Ahmed has been caught and everyone in his organization that was important or had a stake in you kids is either dead or in custody."

I listened for a qualifying word that would allow for a margin of error, but she had said 'everyone.' All the terrorists had been taken care of. An immense feeling of peace overcame me.

I repeated it, just to make sure. "Everyone?"

"The agent at FBI headquarters, Jeremy, I believe, said you'd ask that." She peered at me over her glasses. "Yes. Everyone." Her face looked pinched. Like she was upset about something.

My lips curled into a smile as I thought about Jeremy delivering the news. The danger had passed and my friends and family were now safe. Relief filled me with an exquisite joy. And I savored the moment.

After a minute passed, she continued. "So, you kids are free to return home to your families if you wish." The tone in her voice was off. What was up?

My mind suddenly kicked back into gear, and I wanted to run far away as fast as I could so that I wouldn't have to make the decision. She wouldn't make me go home. But how could I stay? Air wouldn't fill my lungs as I tried to imagine either outcome. Both had their pros and cons. I gasped. How could I choose? Trying to compose myself, I squeaked, "If we wish?"

"Well, yes." Her eyes suddenly sparkled.

I wanted her to continue, but she sat in silence. *Beg me to stay. Please. Beg me to stay. Help me make the decision.* She didn't. She just sat there, looking at me. A deep guilt spread through me for not wanting to go home. Not wanting to be with the people who'd raised me and loved me and most certainly wanted me back. I was a traitor to my family, caught between what I felt I should do and what I thought I might like to do. I couldn't go back and I couldn't stay. Could I?

"So, I can stay?" The words both stung my tongue and teased it with a sweet honey.

"Of course. If that's what you want." I could have sworn her lips turned up in the corners as she spoke.

Come on! Throw me a bone. Tell me you've never seen the likes of me before and can't imagine me throwing my gifts away on anything other than being a spy. Make it easy on me.

Her look turned inquisitive, her eyebrows raised and her mouth pinched together. "I thought this would be an easy decision for you." She looked a bit pale. Or was it my imagination? And she said nothing more, just looked at me with those … eyes ….

"Yes. It is. I mean it should be. I just… my family." If only she could see how desperately I wanted to stay.

She gave me nothing more. This was my decision, and she wouldn't help me make it. That's when Reese filled my mind. If I went home, I could be with him. But I couldn't go home. I needed to talk to Reese. My mind was on overload. "Could I talk to someone before I make my decision?"

"Certainly. But the shuttle leaves for the airport in…" she consulted her watch, "one hour. If you decide to go, you'll need to be on it. So, you'll need to hurry. Just keep in mind that your decision, whatever it is, is permanent."

"I will," I said, jumping up and heading for the door. I ran to the boys' bedroom so fast that my calf cramped just before reaching it. I had to hop the last five feet. The door stood ajar. Empty. Maybe he'd gone to my room to talk to me. The thought thrilled me, and I hopped all the way there.

Kylie hustled about our room, filling the small suitcase with the few items she'd been given. "Christy—"

"Ari," I hissed, sitting down to massage my cramped calf.

"Whatever! I'm so out of here. I can't wait to get home."

171

"You didn't happen to see Reese on your way up here did you?"

"No," she said, throwing a pair of shoes into a small suitcase. "I'd think he'd be in his room packing, though. Don't you?"

I didn't want to tell her I'd already been there.

"You better get started," she said, as if we had a ton to pack.

"I'm staying." My heart flipped at my words, and I knew it was the right decision. A heavy peace filled me. I had to find Reese. I rubbed the muscle harder, urging it to relax, but it seemed bent on staying a hard, solid mass.

"I should've known. With all those brains, they're probably begging you to stay. Where are Sasha and Melanie? Certainly they aren't thinking of staying." She flipped her auburn hair over her shoulder as she fastened the buckle on her suitcase.

I shrugged, wondering if Melanie would stick to her guns and stay. I had no idea about Sasha. We hadn't spoken at all. Her eyes often found mine, however, and she had this way of making them into little slits, like a snake's eyes on the horizontal, when I'd notice her staring. I always looked away in a flash but couldn't help thinking about Josh and wondering if he had suffered terribly when he'd died.

After a few very painful kneads of my calf, the muscle finally relaxed. I stood, testing it. A deep soreness nagged at it, but I could walk. "Well, Kylie. I guess this is it, then?"

She rushed over to me and said, "Yep. I hope you have fun here. I think you're crazy for staying, but…"

"Have fun at home and be safe." We hugged.

"Without you around, it won't be nearly as hard."

We laughed, but inside me, something pinged. I had made life hard for so many people.

I watched her go and then walked back to the boys' room. Like he was trapped in a daze, Reese stood still, his suitcase lying open on his bed. My heart thrummed. Did he want to go home?

"Ari!" He moved toward me and gathered me into a hug.

I pulled away. "Are you leaving?" I glanced at his open suitcase. I wiped my wet palms on my pants.

"I don't know. Are you going home?" His blue eyes pinched.

"I don't know. I mean, do you want to stay?" I reached for his hand.

He didn't need to say it. His whole face seemed to light up, and I'm sure mine did, too. "Yeah. But if you're going home, then I am, too." He cocked his head to the side. "Do you want to stay?"

"More than anything."

"Well, then, we'll stay. It's going to be great." He squeezed my hand.

The 'It's going to be great' part seemed a bit forced. "Are you sure? We *could* go home." Nausea swept over me with those words, but I didn't want Reese to choose to stay for me. He had to stay for himself.

"No, I'm sure. It just freaks me out a bit to think about being away from my family."

I knew that would be a sticky spot for him. He loved being with his family. I frowned sympathetically. This would be hard for him.

"But, I think they'll understand when I explain it to them. Sure, I won't be a senator, or president, but I'll be protecting the country in a way they can be proud of," he said.

"Do you think they'll let you tell your family what you're doing? Wouldn't it put them in danger?" I asked.

"Hmm. I hadn't thought of that." Reese stroked his chin and looked up at the ceiling.

"Are you going to be okay if they don't let you tell your family the truth?" I asked, looking him directly in the eyes.

"I'd have to come up with a big whopper of a lie. And it'll have to be totally believable. I'm not good at lying." His head dropped.

I loved that about him. He was a truth-teller. "You're going to have to learn to be if you want to be a spy." I could tell he was processing all the new information I'd thrown at him and was uncertain.

"I hadn't thought of that, either. Can they teach you to be a good liar?" The corners of his mouth rose.

I nodded and grabbed his other hand. "Yes, if that's what you want." It killed me to put that last part after the statement, 'yes,' but I couldn't handle messing up his life. This was forever. Not only for him, but for me.

"I want to stay," he said at last.

"Awesome!" I said, releasing his hands and put my arms around him.

"I'm so excited about seeing you every day. This will be the best—"

A horrible realization washed over me, and I jerked away from him. I was scheduled to leave to a different training facility tomorrow and he would leave soon, too. We wouldn't even be training together. I moaned.

"What?" He took a step toward me, and I took one back, checking my clock. The shuttle to the airport left in thirty minutes.

"Maybe we *should* go home." I'm sure my voice squeaked, but my head was so full and heavy, I didn't hear it. We wouldn't be together if we stayed. Why hadn't I realized that? I had been dumb to get my hopes up to be a spy. It was silly, really. Being a spy was serious business, and I wasn't sure I was up to the continual stress and danger involved.

"What? Didn't we just decide to stay?"

I nodded in slow motion. I felt like an idiot, bouncing back and forth with the idea of staying, I thought I knew what I wanted. I wanted to be a spy, but being here with Reese made me think about all the variables. I discovered I hadn't really thought it through, and I needed this time to discuss the idea and bounce it off another person. I needed someone to talk it through with. The fact was, I knew I was supposed to stay. I felt it deep in my core—I just didn't like some of the consequences of that decision.

"Come on, Ari, talk to me. What are you thinking?"

"I'm not staying here." I felt awful, like a surgeon was using a scalpel on me, gutting me at that very moment.

"Okay," he said, his face screwed up. "We'll go back home and then go to college together. It's no biggie. We'll have fun—"

"No, I mean, I'm not staying *here*, at this training facility. They won't let me stay. They're moving me to a different facility."

"I don't understand."

"They say I'm too advanced to stay here."

"Then we'll go home—" He looked like he'd been kicked in the gut, but was pretending it didn't knock the wind out of him.

"No," I said. "You don't get it. I want to stay here, and I want to be with you. But it doesn't look like I can do both. If we decide to be spies, the CIA or whoever runs this place, will take me and you away, and we won't be together. I don't know if I can handle that."

"Why don't we just go home then?'

"I can't go back to my old life. I can't live like that anymore. I'm a totally different person, and I don't fit into that box anymore."

He took a deep breath.

"We'll talk to Ms. Mackley and convince her to let you stay at this training facility until I leave. I'm sure you're the best she's ever had here. She won't turn you down."

"She will. She has. I've tried to reason with her already. She won't budge."

"Then I'll just work my tail off and come after you."

I held back a sob. He was only staying for me. I couldn't allow it. "I can't do that to you. Go home, Rick. You don't really want this life, do you?"

"I do want this life. I want to be a spy. I want to be here. These last two weeks have been amazing, and I feel like I belong here. I love it, in fact. But, I want to be with you, too. If we go home, we could go to the same school and be with each other all the time. You wouldn't have to stay in your old town long." He grabbed my hands.

"I'm not eighteen, and my parents would never allow me to go to college before I turned eighteen. Never. And I couldn't go back and then disobey them. It would kill them. Choosing to be a spy is choosing a hard life, Reese. Do we want a hard life—forever?"

"We can do this. It *will* be worth it in the end."

I could see it in his eyes now. He really did love the idea of being a spy.

"It's dangerous. I've been on a few missions, and it's nothing like that spy museum simulation we did back in DC. It's scary and hard and bad things could happen."

"I know," he said. "I choose this life."

He drew a spiral on the back of my hand with his finger, over and over again, sending tingles up my arm. Then, he grabbed my hand, his thumb stroking over my knuckles, soft as a feather. He pulled me up to him. Our breaths mingled, and he moved his lips to mine. Soft and gentle, the kiss was almost a whisper. He pressed his forehead to mine.

Why had he stopped? I wanted, no needed, him to kiss me again. I needed to feel the pressure of his mouth hard against mine. I couldn't stop the moan that escaped my lips. I wanted more. Were we destined to always say goodbye? My watch answered in the affirmative, Ms. Mackley summoning me to her.

Chapter Eighteen

A slow, mournful howl developed inside me as I made my way to see her again. It sat in the pit of my stomach, making me feel sick. Before I descended the stairs to the meeting room, I saw Kylie in the front lobby getting her watch removed. A cold feeling brushed the innermost part of my being. I was letting fear take over. I needed to believe in my decision to stay. I needed to remember the joy, the warmth, the peace, I'd felt in making it. When I walked through the door to the meeting room, Ms. Mackley was sitting at the table writing something.

"Take a seat," she said. "So, I guess you have chosen to stay with us?"

"Yes."

"Good choice. We'll get word to your parents that we need to keep you here for a while longer. Then, when you turn eighteen, your time is yours. I'd like to tell you that you will love it here, but, as you know, you won't be staying here much longer. You were scheduled to move on to a more advanced training center tomorrow, but an opportunity has arisen that I think you will like. You have the chance to go on a mission tomorrow. It will be a baptism by fire considering you haven't completed all the practicals or attended the advanced training courses."

"Tomorrow?" I questioned, hoping by doing so, the date would change.

"Well, I guess technically it starts today. You will be briefed on the assignment in about thirty minutes."

I realized she'd been banking on me staying. She'd intended to tell me this when we'd met earlier. Then she'd gotten the call. She had to hope I'd stay. I had probably given her a heart attack when I hadn't decided immediately, though it didn't show on any part of her body. She was one controlled woman.

"Obviously, you've missed many of the practicals—but at least you got the written instructions for all levels."

How did she know that? I'd never told her.

"I'll let your handler know you need some practical training while in the field because they'll be expecting you to have already practiced opening safes, hot-wiring cars, and other things. It will be a learning experience for both of us as we discover how well your brain processes the practical without experience. I will load your watch with as many video practicals as I can, but I don't think anything translates better than the real hands-on stuff. If our lock specialist is available tonight, I'll have her work with you this evening." Her eyes darted toward the broken door knob.

"Why are you rushing this? Just let me have the time I need to get the practical experience they expect me to have."

"We are in a crunch and don't have time to wait."

"What is so important about this mission that you—"

"When I got wind of this mission, I couldn't believe just how perfect you are for it. Wait until you hear the details. I can't believe our luck."

I didn't miss the fact that she said, *our luck* and not

your luck.

She continued. "Your team will be here soon to fill you in. They are a clandestine section of the government known as Division 57. You are about to meet some truly seasoned spies, and you should treat them with the utmost respect. Don't let me down, Ari." She looked at her computer tablet and then said, "Ah, they're coming down the elevator. Let's move to the next room, where we can actually close the door." She smiled.

Was this about her making up for a past miscalculation? The thing Jeff had talked about in the hall while he tested me? Was I supposed to be her saving grace? Trepidation coursed through my body. I was going on a mission. Tomorrow. What if I failed? Ms. Mackley would surely kill me if the mission didn't. I couldn't fail. They'd probably send me home. I couldn't go home. Christy no longer existed. Not really. She was just a file tucked away deep inside me. I couldn't go back to that life. I couldn't have my family looking me over, not truly seeing me. Would they ever accept who I'd become? A determination pushed through me. I had to do what I had to do.

Blood surged through my body as the door swung open. Three people stepped inside and shook Ms. Mackley's hand. I wanted to impress these people. They were full-fledged spies, like Cort and John. I now knew how cool that was and appreciated spies in a way I never had when I'd been with my mentors. Now that I knew first hand just how hard it was, I was amazed. Just before they shook my hand, I brushed my sweaty palm on my pant leg.

Every notion I'd had about everybody in the FBI being beautiful was collapsing around me. Two very average, though a bit odd looking, people stood before me. One man and one woman. The third, a woman, was stunning, just like all the other FBI agents I'd come in contact with. She had long, flowing hair, big eyes, and pretty skin. She was a good foot taller than the other woman who stood directly before me.

Ms. Mackley introduced me to my handler, the beautiful woman, Claire, and then said, "I've pressing issues to attend to. Come see me later, Ari. You're in good hands."

She left the room. Claire introduced the other two as my new parents. The woman's name was Tracey. She had dull, walnut colored hair and eyes, her skin appeared waxy, and her teeth were an odd shade of yellow. She was so thin, she looked like a drug addict. The man, Cory, came across as a professional wrestler with gargantuan muscles, a square face and jaw sitting atop a huge neck. His tan skin contrasted oddly against his wispy, greasy black hair. He glanced over me with his gray eyes, sizing me up.

I'd seen agents do magic with disguises. All I had to do was think of Cort as a bum that day in Florida, and I had to recognize the idea that these could just be disguises, but how did he make his skin bulge, and how did she make her skin look waxy? Did she go on an extreme diet just to appear emaciated for this 'part?' I doubted it.

Claire set a briefcase on the table in front of us and popped it open, pulling out a file and a computer tablet of sorts. All three of them sat down. I did, too.

Claire opened the file and slid a picture of a girl to me. "This is Sophia. Your job is to befriend her and get inside her father's lab or at the very least get us the intel we need to get inside the lab." The girl had short, mostly purple hair, ample piercings, and a couple of visible tattoos. Her clothes were black with lots of metal attached. Now I understood why Ms. Mackley thought I'd be perfect.

Befriend her? That seemed easy enough. I nodded.

"You have two months to accomplish this."

I nodded again. Two months seemed like more time than I would need.

"Sophia," she continued, "likes to play hard and party harder. She misses her absentee scientist dad, who spends all his time in his lab in his basement, and she longs for positive attention from her mother. She loves her Harley Davidson Nightster more than anything else in the world."

I'd read about that bike in one of the magazines Cort had given me to study at the safe house in Florida. "Nice bike," I whispered.

"Very nice bike," Cory said. "But you're going to have a nicer one, the Night Rod Special."

"Hold on," I said, "I'm going to have my own bike?"

"It will be dangled in front of you at least," Cory said. "But your bad grades and poor behavior keep it from you." I remembered how I'd scoffed at the idea of being average as Michele the cheerleader, only a short time ago. The thought of getting bad grades and having poor behavior for a while now gave me no worries.

"Whew!" I said, before realizing I'd done it.

"You afraid of riding a little bike? You should try the Ultra Classic. Now that's a bike you gotta learn to ride," he said.

"Sorry, I've just never driven a bike before. I've ridden on one, just not been the driver."

"Well, you better get some time on a bike then, so you can talk about it like you really know about it."

"You mean so I can say things like, I see you're riding a soft tail custom with apes and Vance and Hines pipes, but I figured you for a sissy bar, too."

Created

"Good girl!" Cory said. "You know your biker terminology."

Claire piped in, "Sophia has a crew that follows her. They will definitely play a role. She also has a boyfriend, Sven. He's more of a convenience thing. It's obvious she doesn't really care for him. We're not exactly sure why she stays with him. She inherited her temper from her father. She's a master manipulator and gets what she wants when she wants it, except when it comes to her dad. She hasn't discovered the magic pill to get him out of the lab long enough to pay attention to her."

I stared at the picture of Sophia. Even though her face was full of piercings, she somehow looked lost behind that hard mask. I had the feeling she had not chosen this persona because it was innately herself. Her teeth were a brilliant white and her eyes seemed to hold a secret. I felt a kinship with her. She reminded me of Christy, somehow. I picked the picture up and another one fell to the table. A different girl looked up at me. Her lightly tanned skin, black eyes and black, glossy hair gave her the look of someone from somewhere exotic. She looked happy, well adjusted.

"That was Sophia two years ago," Claire said, tapping the picture "She's a different girl now."

I looked closer and said, "You're kidding, right?"

"Nope. That's her," she said, dismissing my disbelief, putting the picture back in the folder and moving on. "Her father, Diego Ramirez, has invented some sort of biological weapon that can be set to target only certain DNA strands, or at least he has the production of it close at hand."

"The implications of which are more than horrendous," Tracey said. "Killing off an entire race with one puff of air,

183

a gender, a family…"

"How is that even possible?" All the data I had in my brain on targeting DNA and chemistry pulled up. I sifted through it. The knowledge I found was basic, and the research far from such a discovery.

"That's what we need to find out. He has never sold a formula without having the antidote figured out also."

"He's done this before?"

"Yes. Many times over. But, our sources feel like the antidote is the sticking point for him now. Apparently, he is having a hard time perfecting it. We must get in to the lab, steal the chemical and erase all the information about the antidote and the chemical from his computer system. We need to put a stop to it and him."

"By we, you mean me?" I said.

"Yes. But we will be there for support," Tracey chimed in, tapping her finger on the table.

I nodded, mulling over all the information in my head.

"No one has been able to get anywhere near the lab. We know it's deep in the ground under his home but, so far, we've been unable to find the entry point. We believe, however, that through his daughter, you will be able to gain access. His wife is adamant about having free reign inside the house, so there are no alarms, only on outside walls, near the lab and perimeter of the estate. We think there might be an entry to the lab from inside the home."

"Lovely." I shifted in my seat and looked at the newest picture of this girl I was to befriend. She was like me. Someone who just wanted to change her life and become a girl people cared about and wanted to befriend.

"It's rumored that Diego Ramirez holds several well-known scientists hostage, working on the project, but it can't be confirmed."

"We have about forty hours of video footage of

Sophia," Claire said. "You need to watch and study it. We leave here at eight p.m. tomorrow. You can continue watching on the plane. Learn her routines, her habits, her schedule."

"We can't tell you how to find the lab, but we believe there is an entrance through the basement." Tracey said.

How hard could it be?

I thought of the things I hadn't practiced yet, but figured I had time to learn. Could I have everything down in less than two months? I wasn't sure, but I had to pretend I thought I could. Ari was perfect for this. Of course, I wasn't like Sophia. I could never take drugs, drink, or be truly wild. I could only pretend. I looked at them and then her picture again.

"Can you do this for us?"

I thought about my home. My predictable, somewhat easy life in Montana, and how far I'd left it all behind. I knew I could do it. I had to.

Chapter Nineteen

It was too early for lunch, so I went to the vault and started watching the video footage of Sophia. I watched her leave her house, drive to school on her Harley, and then dominate the school. She could be scary. She reminded me of Katie Lee, the bully back home, but on steroids. People actually moved out of her way as she walked down the hall. I knew I would have to become like her to be her friend, but I didn't want to be a Katie Lee.

I watched Sophia party with and treat everyone with contempt, even her devout followers. Many did as she said out of fear, but others appeared to revere her. Even I was mesmerized by her. She had this amazing charisma. The one thing that bugged me more than anything was her use of curse words. They spewed from her mouth. Sure, I'd heard these words at school often enough, but never at home and it graded on my nerves. I could tell she was pretty smart, so why did she insist on swearing?

My sophomore year in high school, I had perfected a method to tune out all the horrible words I heard in the halls. Immediately upon hearing the beginnings of them, I replaced them with another word and had my mind shout it, smothering the offending word. The first time I tried it, it seemed to have no effect, the curse words still rattled in my brain, but there was something about practicing it that eventually worked. I made a game of it, substituting ridiculous words for the bad ones. I'd done it so long now, I'd mastered it. I also needed to figure out a way to get around all the drinking and drug taking. I didn't think the opportunity to water a plant nearby would always work with this group.

The Rock Renae, informed me it was time for lunch. As I made my way up the stairs, I thought about my remaining day and a half at the Academy and wondered how I could learn about Sophia and still make time to spend with Reese. What would he think when he found out I was leaving tomorrow?

As I hurried up the steps, my watch vibrated. Ms. Mackley.

She wanted me to grab my food and meet her in her office. Reese hadn't arrived in the lunchroom by the time my plate was loaded, so I hurried off to get the meeting over with.

I sat in my usual spot across from her desk and listened.

"This is quite the opportunity you have here. I suspect you will do an amazing job. It will open a lot of doors for you or close them. You really need to be stellar on this."

"I don't understand completely. Open what doors?" Was I opening doors for her or me?

"It could give you more freedom, more ability to do what you want to do. It will help you get the good assignments and help you get your own place to live."

"I'll have my own place?" I still thought of myself as a child, who needed her family or at least someone like Katy, my nanny in Florida, to care for her. I wasn't an independent grown up, after all. I was barely seventeen.

"Certainly you don't think agents live together in a dorm?" She smirked. "Really, Ari, for your unmatched intelligence, I sometimes wonder."

I felt my cheeks burn. This was the first time she had made me feel small. "I hadn't really thought about it."

"Obviously not. This could be a great opportunity for you if you decide to take hold of it. But if you fail, you could end up at another training center and possibly at a desk job. It also dictates how often you'll be away on assignment, and the assignments you'll get."

Was she just trying to scare me or had she spoken the truth? A stray thought flitted across my mind as I thought about what this all meant. "What was it you wanted to tell me earlier?"

"I was going to tell you about the mission you just accepted." Her eyebrows rose.

"Did I have a choice then?" Could I have refused this mission earlier?

"Not really, Ari. Like I said, I knew you'd be the best for this assignment."

"What if I'd decided to go home?"

"I knew you'd stay."

"How did you know?"

"Your profile indicates it. You were meant to be a spy. And, quite possibly one of the greatest spies ever. If, that is, you live up to your potential. It's unbelievable how perfect this assignment is for you, like it was tailored for you. You are the target age, have the look and attitude, and have been properly prepped. You will be a valuable member of the team. The apex, really. Once you finish this mission successfully, you will be able to live a somewhat normal life. In terms of a spy's life, that is. You'll have a 'normal' life to live when you're not on assignment, at least."

My mind was all awhirl thinking about the possibilities.

Reese and I could be together one day. I had to make sure we would be on the same detail eventually. In my mind, I fast forwarded to us getting married, living in a nice house, and with kids even. Would I choose what Alex's parents had chosen, or would I quit when I had kids? Could I quit?

"People around you," Ms. Mackley said, "will think you lead a normal life. Only you'll know better. It won't be like you have to hide yourself. You will, however, need to create an identity that is you. Your cover. Who you want to be when you aren't on a mission. But you can work on that after you succeed. No need to worry about it now."

Christy jumped into my mind, the spot growing bright in my chest. Ms. Mackley was confirming what Cort had said about remaining Christy at my core. I could be a modified Christy again for Reese...and myself.

"You will live near a field office. You could end up in serious training for a couple of years if you fail, but honestly, I don't think you will. Tap into minor trainings that will be offered you along the way. Pick and choose what you think you need and what interests you. Make this happen." She stared at me and then changed course. "Just out of curiosity..."

I didn't think she'd ever asked anything just out of curiosity and my attention was piqued.

"That memory of yours. If I asked you for page 356 of Module 7 would you be able to pull that up in your brain?"

Before I could think over the consequences of answering her, I said, "Yes." I already had page 356 at the front of my brain.

"Tell me what's on there."

I swallowed hard and then told her. No reason to hide it now. Somehow she knew what was on that page. She shook her head, her eyes wide.

"You will truly be useful."

There it was. *Useful.* I was a thing to be used by this secret division of government. It made me feel uncomfortable, resentful, and a bit suspicious.

"Does it also translate to video and real life situations?" she asked.

I wasn't sure I wanted her to see all my cards and made a split decision to keep some things back from her. "Not exactly. It's not as reliable. It's hard to file stuff like that away."

"Do you remember everything forever?"

"I guess…I'm not sure."

"Well, Ari, you are no longer a part of the FBI, CIA, or the Bresen Academy for spies. You are a spy that works for a secret section of the government of the U.S. in whatever capacity they might need you."

A thrill moved through me, so fast and intense, I even got light-headed. I was a spy.

"And Ari. This is privileged information. You are not to share any details about your assignment with anyone. Understood?"

"Yes, ma'am." As I headed out of her office, a thought came to me out of the blue. "Ms. Mackley."

"Yes." She peered up at me, her eyes scrutinizing my face.

"This girl I'm befriending, she spends a lot of her time partying. Drinking, doing drugs. Stuff like that. I don't drink or do drugs." I couldn't imagine being able to fake smoking a joint.

"Oh, we have stuff for that. We have pills you can take that counteract the effects of drugs and one for alcohol."

"No. You don't get it. I will not drink, do drugs, or

anything like it."

"That will have to change. You'll have those pills. It won't matter. You'll be able to do those things and not suffer the consequences. It's a teenager's dream."

But it wasn't a dream to me. I didn't want that crap in my body, ever. My stomach churned. Then it came to me in a flash, as if an answer to a prayer. I didn't have to take those pills or drink or smoke. The realization settled over me like a warm blanket. I could simply become a master of sleight of hand. By studying magicians, I could become an illusionist. A smile crossed my lips. Leafing through the pages of Sophia's file on my way to our destination in Prague wouldn't take long, and I could watch some of the video on the way. Right now I would become an illusionist. I looked heavenward, smiled and thought, *Thank you. Thank you.* Someone wanted me to be a spy, someone I trusted. Peace washed over me.

"Thanks, Ms. Mackley," I said as I left her office. She nodded at me.

I was so wound up in my desire to become an illusionist, I forgot I'd had wanted to see Reese and went straight for the vault. Magicians focus on the art of distraction and deception, but had years and lifetimes to perfect what they knew. I had to be better, faster. It would be a great advantage to my spy self to be an illusionist. I studied the likes of Houdini, Kole, Martin, and of course Copperfield. Then I got lost in practicing. Even the basics were extremely hard to master. Could I actually do it? I was frustrated but determined. If I were caught faking it with Sophia, it'd be over.

I had fewer than two months to worm my way into Sophia's life. Certainly I'd have one solid week to learn sleight of hand. I knew it took magicians years to master it, but I was special, wasn't I? The videos I was supposed to watch of Sophia fell by the wayside, and I busied myself with magicians' tricks.

The Rock startled me when she called to me over the intercom to tell me that it was time for dinner. I stretched and thought of missing Reese at lunch. I hoped he wasn't too mad. I couldn't wait to tell him all about my magician's training. I didn't want to leave him, but this spy thing was getting really exciting. I hoped he'd be excited for me. I wished I could tell him everything.

Back in the cafeteria, Melanie bumped me and said, "Spill it. I know you're excited to see him, but I think you've looked back at him a thousand times in the last twenty minutes. You haven't even taken a bite of your food, and you're not listening to me."

"Sorry, Melanie. I'm just so stoked to tell him about what I've been doing today. I can't wait."

"Well, are you going to fill me in?" She gave a meaningful pause before looking back over at Reese. "Uh, never mind. Prince Charming just stood up."

I grabbed my tray to drop it off in the kitchen, making sure to bump Reese with the tray's edge as I came up behind him. He turned and his eyes lit up. I'm sure mine did, too. He took my tray and put it on the waste conveyer belt, then grabbed my hand and pulled me out into the hall and down to the gardens. He pulled so fast I was out of breath when I got there. He tugged me into an embrace only he could give, and I purred into his chest with delight. We sat on the edge of the fountain in the waning light, and I was glad for his warmth enveloping me.

"Do you think you can just stare at me all the time?" he said, his lips only inches from mine.

"I feel it's my duty. I know how much it means to you to be adored."

192

"Very funny."

"Guess what?" I said, a rush of adrenaline hitting me.

"What?" he said, pulling back from me.

"I've been having so much fun today. You won't believe it. I'm learning to be a magician."

"A magician?"

"Yep."

"What? Are they going to send you on a mission as an undercover magician?" He snorted.

"Not exactly. I just figured I'd be better at my mission if I learned sleight of hand."

He pulled away, a look of worry crossing his face as his brows pulled together and his lips frowned. "You're going on a mission? For real?"

A cold chill slipped down my spine. I'd totally goofed. I should have told him about leaving and been somber about it instead of letting him discover it through a blunder of mine. This mission meant I was one step closer to being away from him. I looked quickly at my hands. "I'm sorry. I should've told you that first."

"Ya think?" I could feel his stare. "How long have you known?"

"I just found out this morning."

"Where were you at lunch?"

"With Ms. Mackley and then in the vaults." I felt red splotches take shape on my neck.

"They made you work through lunch?"

"No. Actually...Wait. Let me tell you about it." I looked at him, tilting my head to the side and trying to look contrite. "I leave tomorrow night."

Something dark passed over his eyes. "Tomorrow? So soon?"

I nodded, then grabbed his hands. His head was slowly going from one side to the other. "Listen. I'm not excited that I'm leaving. I'm just excited I found a way to accomplish the mission they gave me without compromising myself and my beliefs."

"I'm excited for you." His words fell flat.

"I'm sorry. I didn't mean for you to find out like this. Besides, the sooner I go, the quicker I can get back."

"But you're not coming back, are you?"

It had been a stupid thing for me to say. I wasn't coming back, but my need to pacify him and myself had taken over.

"Sorry, Ari. I don't mean to be a downer. The prospect of being without you again is terrible." He seemed to think about his words, and we fell into silence. How long, I'm not sure, but he finally broke it, looking at the floor.

"Enough of that. We can't be down. We should just look to our futures and enjoy the snatches of time we have together until you leave." Rick looked me straight in the eye. "This will work. I *am* happy for you. I'm excited that you're excited." He was obviously working hard to convince himself. "So, show me the tricks you've learned." His eyes shone again. He would be successful at being a spy. He had tricked even himself into believing he was excited.

"Okay." I took a rock from the path and made it disappear.

"Wait. Where'd it go?"

I produced it. It looked up at him from the palm of my hand.

"Do it again."

I did.

"How did you do that?"

"I diverted your attention and then acted fast."

"Do it slow for me."

I did.

"Let me try." He took the rock and made the same movements I had, fumbling the rock.

I picked it up from the ground and showed him again, adding a few tips I'd learned while practicing. He was doing pretty well.

"So, what mission is this that requires sleight of hand if you aren't a magician or a card dealer?"

"I wish I could tell you. In fact, I'm dying to tell you. But, I can't."

His eyes clouded over, but only for a second. "I guess I need to get used to not knowing what you're doing and just enjoy the time I have with you." He kissed my nose. "What else can you do?"

"Not much. I need practice. I tried a few other moves I saw, but I was terrible at them."

"Let's work on them together, then."

Reese had a spark in his eyes. He liked this, too.

I smiled big, then explained the tricks to him, and we worked on those. He was actually faster at learning the tricks than I was. We laughed and joked. I enjoyed having the good-natured competition.

The lights had come on in the garden because it was very dark outside. We'd played through our exercise time, and he had to get to class. I had to get to the vaults. He kissed me, and we walked back into the main building. I went to the basement and he to a classroom. I practiced and practiced emptying a glass into a cup. The cup sat on the floor behind me or between my legs on my chair. It was hard. I needed lots of practice. I knew this speed I'd been perfecting would not only be for silly drinking parlor tricks, but also for serious spy deception. Tomorrow brought new hope.

After filling Melanie in with the details once we were in bed, I found myself truly exhausted. It was mostly mental but physical as well. I got up at five the next morning and pounded away at my work. Around six, Ms. Mackley came into the vault, which she never did. I was in the middle of making my cup disappear.

"How many tapes have you been able to go through?" Her strange goose eyes bored into me.

"Uh, I'm kinda going in a different direction."

My words were obviously not a surprise to her. She smiled and raised her eyebrows. "Consider this a course correction for you. After your breakfast, I expect you to be watching the video footage."

"Yes, Ms. Mackley." I had to bite my lip to quell my frustration.

By lunch I'd watched some video footage as well as made inroads on a few tricks and felt good about what I'd accomplished and anxious to try them out with Reese.

I wished he would break his unspoken rule about eating with his group and sit with me today. One day. Just one day. I'd be gone tomorrow. He would have years with Sasha since they were in the same program to be handlers. I felt a pang deep inside. Instead, I sat with Melanie, and we chatted about things we'd learned, and I practiced on her. Much to my satisfaction, she was amazed with my trickery. I knew I was leaving her, too, and I felt hot tears in my eyes as I looked at her. I was glad Ms. Mackley would be moving her into a room with the girls in her group once I left. With Kylie gone, we were the only two in ours.

When Reese was finally finished, I ran after him, like a lost puppy. Our bodies melded together in the hall and again in the elevator as we spent our coveted ten minutes together. I memorized him. His smell, his touch, his kisses. Unfortunately, I didn't get enough of those before having to return to the vault.

I watched four hours of video, practicing my voice-over trick, and rewarded myself with an hour of magic practice before dinner. I'd only made a small dent in the footage I had of her. Sophia was definitely hiding something. If I hadn't known better, I'd have thought she was a spy, just acting a part. I wished I could watch her inside her house. See what she was like when she wasn't with everyone at school. Her true person was not in these videos. I was sure of that. Her secret loomed, dark and dangerous. I really didn't want to enter her world, but curiosity lit a fire in me.

I still had to pack, and I needed to say goodbye to Melanie, then every last second was for Reese. I ran upstairs and grabbed Melanie. This would be my last little bit of time I'd have with her. Seeing her tears caused mine to flow freely. We promised to keep in touch and watch each other excel in our new lives. We laughed before parting, talking about how incredible our lives had turned out. I wanted to remember her with that beaming smile, that shiny look of anticipation and happiness.

After a final hug, I sought out Reese in the mess hall. He had just finished loading his plate. I looped my arm through his and whispered, "Let's sit together. I want to spend every last minute with you. I need every last one."

"Ari, what about Sasha? She'll be alone."

"It's one meal. Our last meal together. Besides, she needs to make friends." I raised my eyebrows.

"You have a point."

We sat alone at the table our DC group had first sat at the day we'd arrived at the Academy. A fitting end. It was hard to eat. I just picked at Reese's food since I never got my own. He didn't seem to have any problem finishing his plate, though. We rushed out into the hall, down the elevator and into the gardens. Our respite was short lived. Reese's watch vibrated.

"I have to go work out with Master Li. He didn't like me missing yesterday. We could work out together, though. Besides, I need all the help I can get to catch up with you."

We worked out together, and I didn't hold back. I wanted him to make it back to me one day, and I wanted that day to be as soon as possible. I held him in a head lock several times during our sparring time. It always ended with him murmuring, "I give. I give." Then, Master Li would give him pointers, and we'd run the spar again. He would sometimes dominate after that. After we'd showered and met back up, he said, "I don't know if I can be your boyfriend if you can kick my butt."

We laughed. "I can't wait until you can kick my butt." I kissed him hard and quick and then spun around, trying to catch his hand as I did. Instead, he grabbed me and pushed me against the lobby wall. His lips were hot as they hit mine, and I softened, falling into him. My skin flamed at his touch, and I wanted to disappear with him and forget our decision to be spies. His touch, kiss, and smile transported me away from all my troubles.

My watched buzzed, and Ms. Mackely's voice came through the speaker, "Are you packed, Ari?" I wouldn't miss being watched every moment.

This jolted me back into reality. I hated the idea that she had witnessed that personal moment. The really good thing about leaving the academy would be getting rid of the watch.

"No ma'am. I'm on my way." I dragged Reese to my room and quickly packed before heading for the garden, our last interlude with the fountain at Bresen Academy calling to us.

I kept two jackets out of my luggage and then deposited the bags in the lobby. I wrapped one around my watch.

"Uh, Ari, what's that for?"

"I don't want anyone listening or watching us." I made a tight knot in the jacket.

He chuckled. "Why would they bother?"

"I don't know." I motioned for him to do the same with his watch and the other jacket. "But, think about it; how did Ms. Mackley know I hadn't packed? I don't want her to see our last moments together. For whatever reason, they are listening, constantly listening. Maybe this will at least distort what they hear. This 'watch' is the one thing I won't miss when I leave. Ms. Mackley will be removing it before I leave and giving me a real spy watch."

Sitting on the edge of the fountain, amazing memories hit me. When I looked at him, I longed for him to kiss me. Nostalgia made me want it even more. Why was he waiting? We had such little time together. Our futures right now were not really in our hands. Ms. Mackley wanted me to think I was in control, but my future was being determined by others and so was Reese's. However, I knew my decision to stay and be a spy was the right one. There was no question about that.

"Do you feel it inside you?" Reese asked. "The Pull? The pull for this life?"

"I do," I said, shifting my eyes to my feet. "And I'm excited about it, but the whole idea of being away from you for who knows how long is killing me."

"It's not like we won't be able to communicate. We can video chat and email over the secure servers—right?"

"Right," I said, trying to be optimistic. "But I don't want you to remember me like this. Your memory of me will be with spikey hair and a face littered with metal."

"Yeah. It's beautiful." He looked at my lip ring.

I moved back, squishing up my eyes in disbelief.

"This getup...it's kinda fun," he said, laughing.

That was a shocking revelation.

"It's like you're in a Halloween costume every day."

I laughed.

"I wonder who you'll be when I see you next," Reese said.

"Don't say that." Cort's words came back to me once again. *Remain who you are at your core. Never forget who that person is.* I wrapped his words up and made a new file for them in the front of my brain. I would not forget. I could lose Reese if I did. My heart seemed to spin in my chest. "You won't even miss me. You're gonna be so busy."

"Oh, so are you saying you're going to be so busy you're not going to miss me?" Reese grinned and moved in closer still.

"Very funny."

I wished I had a camera, phone, anything to document these last moments together.

We just looked at each other. There was nothing more to say. We held hands, and he touched my fingers one by one, looking down at them. He picked up my hand and kissed my palm. Then he kissed the back side of it and then my fingers one by one, slowly. He looked at me. My lips ached to press against his. He kissed my palm again. I thought he was going to kiss my lips, but instead, he leaned his forehead on mine. My heart banged on my ribcage.

Read my mind. *Kiss me. Kiss me.*

"You have to promise me something," he whispered.

"Anything." *If you just kiss me.* I opened my eyes and looked at him. He was serious.

"No matter where you are, no matter where they take you. Promise me, once a month you'll find me. I want to say once a day, but I know that's totally not doable."

I knew he was thinking of me not getting in touch with him when I got home from DC so long ago.

"I will."

"No excuses. We are spies. We can do this." He didn't want to feel what he had felt before—betrayal, abandonment, and loss.

I was keenly aware that others milled about the garden, but I didn't care. "I promise."

"I'll do the same."

He brought me into his arms again, the spray of the fountain lightly dusting us. That's when I felt his heart pounding. My heart had become a battering ram, one set with great speed and force. And then he slipped that ring, my birthday ring, on my finger.

"I'm not naïve enough to think you'll be able to wear it all the time. I mean it's probably a *tell,* and they won't let you, but keep it nearby. This seals my promise to you. I will wait for you and will do everything in my power to get back to you."

My whole body seemed to buzz as I looked at the ring. "Thank you," I whispered. "But, I have nothing to give you."

"You are all I need."

I leaned in to his incredible lips and whispered, "This

seals my promise to you." Electricity shot through me. This was the kiss I'd never forget. I kissed him like my life depended on it.

"By the way," I said. "What were you writing that first day here when I asked you to go explore with us?"

He chuckled. "Have you been curious about that ever since that day?"

"Well," I said. "Yes. I thought maybe you were writing your girlfriend."

"I was," he said, matter-of-factly.

"What?" I said, pulling away from him.

He grinned, and I was about to hit him, when he held up his hands and said, "You're that girlfriend."

"What?"

"I was writing a letter asking you to please leave me alone," he said. "That you had broken my heart once and it wouldn't survive the pain and disappointment again."

"I'm so sorry," I said. "I won't ever break it again."

"Good," he said. "Because I trashed the letter."

We laughed.

My watch vibrated and buzzed. Without looking, I slipped a finger under the jacket and pushed the button to turn it off. I never knew I could feel something so deep inside that it hurt and yet felt so good. I heard a beep again.

"I can't tell you how much this is killing me." I felt his sandpaper cheek slide across my smooth one.

"I don't want to go."

"You have to," he said.

"Why? Why can't we just be together?"

"Because we are destined to save the world?" Tears pooled in the bottom of his eyes, threatening to overflow onto his cheeks. "You'll just have a jump on me. I'll be right here working hard to catch up with you." He tried to make his voice cheery. "Go, before it gets any harder to let you." He whipped his head to the side, away from me.

I stood, and he grabbed my hand and squeezed it, rubbing his thumb over the ring.

"Go." His face turned back to me. His cheeks had two wet streaks running down them, and his eyes still glistened.

I couldn't take it. I ran. If I'd have walked, I wouldn't have been able to go. My feet wouldn't have taken me. I stopped at the door and looked back. He stared intently at me. He winked. My eyes burned with tears as they fell in gushes.

I went to embrace my future.

Chapter Twenty

I sat in the back of the classroom of the International English Academy in Prague the very next day. The flight from Brussels in the Gulfstream had been short and sweet. I felt like I'd moved forward a thousand years in the modern building this Academy was housed in. I also felt a huge weight descend on me. My first mission as a true spy. Would I succeed?

The English teacher, Mrs. Lee, who looked like one of those teachers all the kids liked, stylish, bright cheeks and eyes, and a smile that lit up the world, asked the wrong question, "Why don't you tell us about yourself." It was hard not to smile at her cool British accent.

I felt a moment of shame, knowing she didn't deserve what I was about to dish out, but the mission was more important than how I felt about this woman.

"I'm Ari. I love the feel of wind on my face when I ride my Harley, the gentle tug of my lip ring between someone's teeth, and the sting in my hand when I've given a good slap."

"Well," Mrs. Lee began.

I leaned back in my chair, foot propped up against the backside of the chair in front of me. My plaid skirt slid dangerously high up my leg. I had to push hard into the chair to stop my leg from shaking. They were just words, but super powerful words that were engineered to guarantee Sophia would take a second look at me. I stared at Mrs. Wheatley with a bit of a sneer on my face and leaned my head back further as I nodded, my teeth biting my front lip in defiance.

"That was inappropriate on so many levels," she scolded.

I pushed my foot harder into the chair in front of me, glad the large boy that occupied it would prevent it from moving. "Well, you asked me." *This is only a job. It's not really me.*

"Please put your foot down, Ms. Agave."

I did, but I slapped my foot on the floor, making a loud noise. It looked like I was being disruptive, but really, I had to do it because if I moved it slowly, everyone would see it shake.

"Sit up straight. We require more than a modicum of decorum here at IEA"

I slid up in my chair, but only after a ten second pause to drive home the point that she couldn't rule me.

I was supposed to be a super smart girl that was bored in school. Hence, I acted out. I'd made sure I missed every answer on every test, which was a way of saying, *Ha, I know it, but I don't care about your stupid grades.*

When the bell rang, she excused everyone, but asked me to stay.

"Ms. Agave, I will not tolerate you acting out in my class."

My insides squeezed, and I fought to keep my composure on the outside.

"Do we have an understanding?" she continued.

"Yes, ma'am," I said, rolling my eyes and tilting my head to the side. I always hated it when kids were rude to teachers. I hated that I had to be.

"Don't make that mistake again. I will respect you and you will respect me."

"Yeah, whatever," I said, shrugging.

It was a weird sensation to be in my body, but to temporarily be someone totally different than I truly was.

I left class and there was Sophia, all dark leather, metal and makeup, staring at me. Part of me was thrilled, the other part scared spit-less. There was no turning back now. I trembled inside. *I am Ari. I am Ari.* I started to walk past her, but she reached out and grabbed my arm.

"Hey," she said. "I'm Sophia."

I looked pointedly at her hand on my arm, and she released it.

"Nice move in there." Her eyes bored into mine.

Do not look away, I told myself. She had such a cool accent. Why had she moved from Spain to Prague of all places? I made a mental note to learn to speak English with a foreign accent.

"You've got guts. I like that." She nodded her head slowly, calculatingly.

"And, I should care what you think because?" A large earthquake erupted in my gut.

"I rule this school, and I can make your life great or difficult. It's your choice." She leaned into me.

I huffed. I was being bullied again. She was Katie Lee only in another body. I twisted one of the studs in my ear. It calmed me. I felt a sudden urge to break her neck. I breathed deeply. Ms. Mackley's warning churned in my brain. Maybe I was unstable.

"So," she continued. "Stop acting so tough. I'm the tough one around here."

I smirked and pushed out a rush of air through my nose. The bell rang.

"Come in here." She pointed to a bathroom behind her. I noticed a series of white scars on her wrist. "We'll just say we're on our periods. What bike do you ride?"

I took a deep breath, trying to block out images of Katie Lee and her cronies and followed her into the bathroom. She was a good head taller than me and meatier besides. *Pull it together. Pull it together.* I looked at her, then at the floor, took another deep breath and forced myself to be Ari.

"It's a Night Rod Special."

"No freaking way. That's hot. What seat did you choose? Did you get the heated handlebars?"

Her enthusiasm and interest in my bike surprised me. She didn't seem mean at all. After giving her the drawn out story about getting my bike, I said, "You have a bike, I assume."

"I have the Nightster with heated handgrips, custom mirrors, and an awesome seat I designed myself. Look at this picture...." She talked without a break for five minutes. She obviously cherished it. "So, you should totally become a part of my crew."

Something ugly reared in my chest, and I couldn't hold back, "Don't you mean gang?"

One of her dark eyebrows rose. "Does it matter?"

"Of course! I don't want to be a part of your stupid gang." I wanted to make her hurt like she's made others hurt. "I don't even know you."

Her neck got all splotchy red, and she clenched her teeth. "You don't know what you're saying."

Anger boiled in me, "I absolutely do and I don't want to be a part of your juvenile *gang*." I felt spit fly from my mouth. It'd been a long time since I'd been so passionate about something, and that passion almost left way for her fist to smack my head. I dodged it just in time, hitting her in the gut. She bent over but then quickly brought me down with a sweep kick. I pulled my head to my chest to prevent it from smacking into the dirty tiled floor. I had underestimated her.

I rolled under the sink and threw a hard kidney punch. She arched her back and fell to her knees. Taking advantage of this, I grabbed her back into a choke hold, the back of my head resting on the front of the sink. I squeezed harder and harder, anger for all the teasing and taunting making my arms strong. I didn't want to stop, even when I heard a horrible gurgling sound escape her mouth. For a split second all I could think about was making Katie Lee and all the other mean girls pay. A dark feeling passed over me and then seeped into me. I continued to choke her.

This was not Katie Lee, nor was it anyone who had ever tortured me. I had to stop. It took all my effort, but I released her, shoving her away from me. She coughed, grabbing her throat and I turned away from her, not wanting her to see the dark meanness that had enveloped me and caused me to lose complete control. Who was this person? Is this what Ms. Mackley had alluded to back at the Academy? She was right. I was out of control. I had to learn to separate Christy from the character I had to play.

I sensed her attack before it happened. In my time of introspection she had at some point stood and had crooked her arm around my neck and brought me back down to the tile floor. My back pounded with pain, but I quickly and easily rolled, holding her beneath me. Pure hatred pooled in her eyes. I held her tight with my legs and while one hand pushed a shoulder hard into the floor, I pushed the other forearm into her neck. The pressure was light, just enough to let her know I meant business.

"I give! I give!" she sputtered out.

When I drew away, I scooted on my butt to a corner, breathing hard and trying to come to terms with the fact that for a moment I had truly wanted to kill Sophia. She rolled over, coughed several times before coming to a seated position.

I had blown this. How would she ever want me for a friend when I'd tried to kill her? How could I fix this? I had to fix this. There was only one way I could think of, and I wasn't sure even it would work.

"I'm sorry," I whispered. "It's just my parents have taken everything away from me: my bike, my friends, my home. And I can't have you taking away the only thing that's still mine. My dignity. My choices." It was pure instinct that made me say these things. Perhaps she needed to see humility in strength. A sweet peace filled me as the words tumbled from my mouth.

"That's what you don't get, Ari. The second you walked into this school, you lost your choice. I rule this school, and I'm not willing to give it up."

Was she serious? I had just kicked her butt and she was telling me she ruled the school?

"Can't you just leave me out of it?"

"No way. People would notice." I knew from debate that I had to be careful. I could easily lose this battle of words. I would wait on her. "Join me and all will be forgiven."

I had to suppress the chuckle that was slipping up my throat. "Look. I have no desire to take over the little thing you've got going here. I just want to be left alone."

"Impossible. Either you're with me or against me. There is no in between. Join me, and I won't make your life miserable."

"I refuse to be your crony," I said, still unwilling to give in to her but knowing at some point I would have to. "I will not hurt people."

"You've just shown me that's not true."

"That was self-defense," I said.

"Hmpf," she said, swearing colorfully. "You don't have to worry about that. I worked my bony butt off last year to achieve the dominance I enjoy now. It's a smooth running machine. Sure there are small uprisings here and there, but I quash them quickly and definitively. My reputation keeps me where I am. Seriously. It rocks. You'll see."

"What did you do to gain this dominance?" I asked, truly curious but trying not to let it show.

"This isn't a history lesson," she scoffed.

I remained silent, so she continued, "Besides, we can ride together."

Claire, my handler, had been spot on throwing that bike into the mix. I don't know that she would be offering me asylum without it.

I let a grin spread across my face as if that was exactly what I wanted, too, then let it falter, saying, "Did you hear what I said? My parents took my bike away. I can't ride with you." I was hoping to get more traction with some sympathy.

"What do you have to do to get it back?"

"Get all A's."

"What do you have now?"

"D's and F's."

The room filled with curses. "Are you just stupid or something?"

She didn't say it in a mocking tone, she was really

curious. She thought maybe I was stupid. It shocked me how a twinge of anger zoomed through me. I had to crush it. "No, I'm not stupid. I was getting F's and D's at my old school on principle. School's a waste of time for me. I've finished all the credits I needed to graduate, but my parents won't let me until I'm eighteen. It's a ridiculous waste of my time. Getting D's and F's is harder than A's for me. My parents make me do the work, so I do, but I make sure I never answer anything right. It's hard work."

She snickered. "I know a girl who can write your papers for you."

I snorted. I couldn't help it. The idea of someone writing a paper for me was absurd.

"You get someone to do your papers? Are you stupid or something?" I grinned and waggled my eyebrows at her, hoping she'd think back to calling me stupid.

"Touché," she said. "I have other, more important things to *work on* than homework."

I figured she was talking about riding her Harley and let it go.

"How long will that take you? To get all A's, I mean."

"My parents made a deal with the school that they would disregard my F's and D's from my last school if I turned in all my work on time. So, I guess that means I could have all A's pretty quickly."

"Then do it. We need to ride." She grinned.

I nodded.

"Wait a minute. Why don't we just sneak it out?" She cocked her head to the side and opened her eyes wide.

"I don't know."

"You don't know? You have a Night Rod . Your butt must be aching to get on it."

I had to come up with a lie, and fast. "I tried sneaking it out once, and my dad took the front wheel off and put it in a big safe-deposit box at a bank."

She opened her mouth wide and huffed. "You're kidding me, right?" She cursed up a storm.

I shook my head. No words needed. Both of us shook our heads for several beats.

"So, you're in, right?" She looked at me with a powerful, unyielding anxiousness.

"I guess, but just remember. I won't hurt anyone, so don't ask ... no mental torture, either."

We stood up, wiping our butts off and heading to the sink to wash our hands when a student entered the room, took one look at Sophia, let her eyes fall to the floor, turned around and left the same way she came.

"See, I've never met or seen that girl before and yet, she knew when to split. I'm all-powerful here." Her eyes gleamed with satisfaction.

I rolled my eyes and she punched me, but soft. "Now, we've got to get those A's for you so we can ride."

We smiled conspiratorially, and then I finished washing my hands. "If I'm going to accomplish that, we should go to class," I said, turning on the dryer and shoving my hands into the blowing air.

"Meet me at lunch and I'll introduce you to the crew," she said, as we entered the empty hallway.

Chapter Twenty-One

Sophia met me at the door to the cafeteria like she had been waiting for a buddy. We parked ourselves near the exit of the food lines. I watched her smile turn to a scowl all of a sudden. Following her gaze, I noticed a blonde cheerleader type chatting up the boy who must have been her man. "Is that your boyfriend?"

"Yes," she said through clenched teeth. "And it looks like someone needs a lesson in proper etiquette." Her eyes were like lasers, melting into that girl. "Later," she continued, under her breath.

I wondered if she was talking about her boyfriend, or the girl. I didn't dare ask. When her Sven arrived, she acted like nothing had happened, so I looked back at the girl and cringed. As we walked to Sophia's table, her cronies looked at me like I was a piece of meat, and their suspicious eyes seemed to be sending tenderizing blows before I reached them. This was an interesting little group. Complete non-conformity. They were all very different from each other, not like other cliques where everyone in them looks and acts exactly the same. I thought it interesting that she seemed to completely change how she talked when with this group than when she had been with me in the bathroom.

"Everyone, this is Ari. Ari," she said, addressing me. "This is the crew. She'll be joining us from now on. She rocks, so respect her."

Their suspicion seemed to turn to curiosity. I nodded at them, afraid that if I spoke, my voice would quiver. Would none of them challenge me? I sat with confidence and pretended I totally belonged. *You are brave.* Sophia directed all the conversation at the table. "Ari, here, has a Harley Night Rod Special. I can't wait to set my eyes on it." It seemed that was all it took. Bike talk dominated the rest of lunch. It appeared that I'd made it past Sophia's crew.

She and I had physics together after lunch and all her minions followed behind us as we walked. What had she done to inspire such loyalty and fear? No student ever got in her way. It was like the parting of the Red Sea as we walked down the hall to class.

When it came time to pick partners at the end of class for the project Mr. Ferris assigned, Sophia chose me instead of her own boyfriend. I'm sure it was her attempt at helping me get back on my Harley. One thing I knew for sure after watching her take the quiz the teacher gave at the beginning of class, Sophia was a science wiz, just like her dad. From where I sat, I could read every word and see every equation.

Project partners. I had my way into her house. We exchanged cell numbers, too. I wasn't only taking baby steps forward, I was leaping ahead on this mission.

When it came time to go home, Cory came to pick me up in his shiny new BMW. I felt all the embarrassment any high-schooler feels when her dad picks her up from school, but the sting was lessened by the coolness of the car. I'd never felt that before. It was awful. I waited until we were out of sight before I turned to Cory and said, "You'll never believe the progress I made today."

"Could you hold off on that news until we get you home and Tracey can hear it, too? It will save us some time. I wanted to update you as we drive on what we discovered today about the security around Sophia's home."

"Okay." I was all ears. "What did you guys find out?" My sense of euphoria at what I'd accomplished filled me.

He told me about some sort of jamming signal that protected the entire area of the property so that no electronic device besides cell phones, however powerful, could penetrate it. Cory and Tracey had been able to get some infrared images of the house, however, and I would be able to see them when we got home. They would try some other ways to get through the jammer tomorrow. They were also mapping the schedules of everyone who came and went from the house.

When we started down the drive to our house, I said, "Could we spend some time on a few practicals I missed while at the Academy?"

"What practicals?"

"Oh, I made a list of them this morning and put them on the counter."

"Wait a minute. That list was of practicals you haven't done?

"Yes. Why?" I felt my face go hot.

"I had no idea what that list was all about. I thought you were simply listing things you'd learned."

"Didn't Ms. Mackley tell you I had some practicals to make up?"

"She didn't mention it." He seemed peeved. My face now burned. "And so many." He shook his head.

"I'm a quick learner," I jumped in. "I've read all the

manuals. I just need some experience with those things."
What game was Ms. Mackley playing that she didn't tell them I wasn't field ready?

"We'll look at the list when we get home and work out a schedule. If I remember right, some of those things were quite remedial."

"I'm sorry."

"It's not your fault. I just don't understand why they would send you unprepared."

I didn't either.

That night we strategized my practical schedule after I filled them in on my interaction with Sophia at school. They showed reserved excitement at best, telling me only time would reveal the truth of it all.

The next day, Sophia was waiting outside the school for me when I arrived. Once I caught up with her, she immediately started speaking, "Why not tell your dad that you're getting a ride home tonight?"

"Am I?"

"Yes!" She grinned from ear to ear. "With me."

Crap! What if she asked me to drive? "I'm not sure they'll allow it. Especially if they know you own a bike."

"What they don't know, won't hurt them."

I shook my head.

"Go on. Call 'em. Tell 'em you have to stay after for a test or something." She tilted her head to the side. It was a challenge. A test.

I dialed Cory. "Hey, Dad. I just found out there's a game after school. Can I stay? I can get a ride with the girl I met at school yesterday."

"No. Your grades."

"I know, but I thought since I just got here and don't have any homework."

"I will be picking you up right after school. Be ready."

"Fine." I hung up.

"He has to see improvement on my grades before he will allow me to do any extracurricular activities." I said in as disgusted a tone as I could muster.

"Well, I'm having a party next Friday night. You better be able to come."

"Two weeks? No worries."

"So, you can swing all A's by next Friday, then?"

"Without a doubt."

"Make sure it happens."

The first warning bell sent us to class. The day went pretty much the same as the day before. Sophia's crew treated me like one of their own, and I wondered how it was possible. It had been too easy. Was Sophia truly powerful enough to command whatever she wanted?

I got held up in Mrs. Lee's English class for a good half hour after school, talking about the in-class essay I'd written the day before, until she realized she was missing faculty meeting, and she rushed away.

I hurried out of her room and headed for my locker. I pulled out my phone to text Cory and tell him I was on my way out, but before I had the chance, I ran right into Sophia's crew. The halls were completely deserted. I looked around for Sophia and found her at the end of the hall at an intersection to another hall. She waved, and I waved back as I started toward her. The group suddenly fell in, creating a circle around me. I looked back, the way I'd come. Sven stood at the other end of the hall. The base of my neck spasmed, and I knew I was headed for trouble. I made note of where each of the eight were.

Sophia and her crew had only been pretending. I was not a part of them and they were about to try and hurt me. I wouldn't let them. "What's up, you guys?" I asked, hoping to disappear, sprout wings or spontaneously combust, but at the same time allowing kick-butt Ari to emerge. If they were as skilled as Sophia in fighting, I was a dead duck.

"It's time for your initiation," said Davon, a tall guy with muscles the size of machine guns and a yellow Mohawk. He threw a punch, but he was slow. I dodged it easily. I took his feet out from under him with a slide kick, and he hit his head, hard on the floor, and didn't move. One down. I threw my backpack at the second largest guy, his constant scowl made him an easy target. When he ducked, I saw Sophia shaking her head and mouthing, "Let them!"

Was I supposed to let them beat me up, like in some real gang initiation? This was ridiculous. Why didn't they throw a party for me instead of beating me up? That was welcoming. This was torture. But Sophia had created a reputation on torture and fear. Why would this be any different? I should have expected this. They were a gang, after all.

I glanced at Davon who still lay there next to the lockers unmoving and counted my blessings he wouldn't be throwing any of the punches that would jump me into this gang. I dodged a punch from the second largest guy, Max, who I'd previously thought was skinny, but soon found out was thin and buff. He clocked me hard with a punch to the cheek. I turned, seeing the littlest of the group, Passion, come at me.

I became a possum, hitting the floor. They kicked and punched, and I held myself firm in a ball. It seemed like I let them pummel me for hours, and I was just about to

Created

make them stop. I'd had enough, when I heard a loud whistle, then a bunch of running feet—away from me. They must have all scattered.

I peeked out, hoping it wasn't a ruse to expose the rest of my body to their abuse. Only one person stood near me: Sophia. I flinched. Was she here to finish me off?

"Hurry, faculty meeting just let out. Teachers are on their way," she said, putting her hand out for me to take.

My whole body ached as I moved, but I didn't take her hand. "A warning would have been nice," I spit at her. "Stupid initiation. If my whole body didn't feel like it'd been shoved through a meat grinder, I would kick your butt." My crunched brain buzzed, and I spoke low, trying to prevent my busted lip from stinging worse than it already did. I glared at her and turned to go.

"Wait!" she called out after me.

I kept going. I did not look back. I felt her hand on my arm, and I shook it off and kept walking. I turned down the hall that led to the front doors. She ran in front of me, supplicating. I looked past her. I would not give in to her. I would make her fight for me. Something inside me told me this was the best plan and besides, it felt good to show the bully up. I just hoped it wasn't my abhorrence of bullies that made it feel like the right path. My cheekbone throbbed as I walked.

She ran farther ahead of me and spoke, "Everyone is jumped in, Ari. I couldn't very well let you out of that rite of passage."

I caught up with her.

"Is this why you wanted me to 'ride' home with you, so your crew could jump me? Well, Sophia, I'm not here for your crew's enjoyment. I'm a real person. I have real feelings. Do you want me to hate you?" Maybe I could

219

insert some values into her head and turn her away from her path of manipulation and domination.

"Come on, Ari. Let it go. It was just our way of welcoming you into the crew. All gangs require new members to be jumped in."

"I don't want to be a part of your gang." Here we were, alone again, and she'd definitely changed her speech pattern.

"That was it. There's nothing more. You passed. You're in. I swear." Sophia looked at me, pleading.

I could see her weakness. She needed me. She stared at me like a scared child. Her look reminded me of the picture I'd seen of her in the file for this mission.

"Nothing like that had better happen again, or I will really have to hurt you." I shouldered her hard, and then walked out the door and to Cory and the waiting BMW. I had to force myself not to run. As I climbed in, I peeked back at the school. Sophia stood in a doorway and watched me. The rest of the crew joined her, and I shut the door to the car. I looked straight ahead as we drove away. Once out of sight, I let out a large breath of air.

He chuckled. "Still feel like you've made progress?"

"Very funny. And as a matter of fact, yes! I just got jumped into her gang."

"Looks like they got you good."

I reached up and touched my throbbing cheek. "They are thugs. Slow and unskilled. I let them do this to me."

After a debriefing with Cory and Tracey about what had happened at school and having them tell me about what they found out all day about the Ramirez compound, nothing too earth shattering, I ambled into the shower to let the hot water massage my muscles and then finished up my homework.

We spent the rest of the evening cracking safes at a safe

shop in town that closed at seven. I thought it was quite ironic that we were able to break into a safe shop to mess with their safes. All the while, Sophia texted me little things here and there. Each time she did, I was reminded about some part of me that hurt.

At school for the next few days, I spent time between classes, before school, and during lunch with the crew. It seemed they were all a bunch of misfits that fit like a giant puzzle together. I got hints of secrets that Sophia held over their heads. She must have used these secrets in the beginning to manipulate them and must hold them over her crew to keep them in line. They all seemed to be on the brink of discovering themselves.

By the first Friday, the bruises from my beating began to fade, and I started to wear short sleeves again. I also had all A's, and Sophia's crew venerated me. I had to be careful to always defer to Sophia to keep her at the top of the pack, though. I wanted her to know that I was going out of my way to keep her where she was, too. It felt good to have the option to be at the top of the food chain if I chose it. I thought I could maybe slowly change the way they bullied and somehow teach them to lead others rather than intimidate them.

"Way to go," Sophia said, looking at my grade report. "You really are a smart little idiot. The party next Friday will be awesome. Don't blow it next week. By the way, was that your mom who picked you up yesterday?"

"Yeah. Why?"

"I was just wondering what was wrong with her. Not to be rude, but she looks sick."

Before I could stop myself, I blurted out, "She's a recovering drug addict." Had I just said that?

"Oh man. That sucks. My uncle was a meth addict and

221

ended up in prison and died there. She paused, her face showing surprise, as if she was surprised she was sharing this with me, then blurted, "He was my favorite uncle, too. I can't imagine what it is like to have the addict be your mom."

I was flustered that I'd said it, but at the same time, I thought it brought us closer together. She had sympathy for me now.

"It's not fun, and every day's a struggle."

"What I don't get is why your parents are so overprotective. They are such hypocrites."

"Maybe. Or maybe they just don't want me to end up like her. And I don't want to end up like her." It just occurred to me that not only was I garnering sympathy from Sophia, the drug addict angle just might save me from having to pretend to take drugs at the parties she threw. Could it excuse me from drinking alcohol, too? I wouldn't hold my breath. I had to make sure and give Cory and Tracey a heads up on this development. I hoped Tracey wouldn't be offended. Did she know she looked like a drug addict?

Sven walked up and gave Sophia a kiss. It was the first time I'd seen any type of physical affection besides handholding between them. He looked adoringly at her, but she didn't return the same look.

Chapter Twenty-Two

It turned out to be a very good thing that I had those two weeks before the party to do practicals with Cory and Tracey. I also learned a ton from Claire, my handler, each morning when I checked in with her. Tracey and I practiced lip-reading and the tricks that made you silent when breaking and entering. I was a pro at stealing cars after two long sessions at several different dealerships. I was also pretty good at wiring, surveillance tactics, and riding that Harley. It wasn't as easy as it appeared. It was a good thing I was as strong as I was, because picking those things up was extremely tough. I wasn't sure I would be able to do it, but Cory was a great teacher, and patient besides.

It was fun seeing more of Prague even though a lot of it was at night. The Cathedrals and churches were illuminated with outdoor lighting making them look magnificent. I'd visited one already and couldn't wait to attend services. I'd become comfortable with the night. Dark alleys and streets no longer scared me. I also worked on my sleight of hand. I even used it on my parents and kids at school without them knowing it. I felt strong and ready. I only had a few practicals left on my original list, but I'd actually discovered a few things I wanted some instruction on that I added to the list: computer hacking and explosives wiring.

When the Friday of the party rolled around, Sophia and the crew waited anxiously outside my eighth period class to look at my grade report. I walked out, with a sullen look on my face, and Sophia snatched the report from my hand and said, "No way." There was a bit of desperation in her voice. When she saw a column of A's she punched me and everyone high-fived or knuckled me. You'd have thought I'd won the lottery or something. I was a part of their team, and it felt good.

Once home, my parents and I went over the plan for that evening. We all discussed our amazement that Diego Ramirez was allowing a party in his house. It seemed it would be too large of a security risk, but it was what it was. I got to use all the cool gadgets they had given me to take pictures, get audio, confirm the layout of the building, and discover if guards roamed the house. My necklace and watch took pictures, my earrings took amazing audio and my rings plotted the home. I couldn't transmit anything out of the house, but I could record it within all the devices they gave me. My hair accessories would act as jump drives if I got access to any computers, which was deemed doubtful. Oh, and my buttons had poison in them that knocked a person out for ten minutes. I was a walking spy gadget.

When I proposed that I just plant a bunch of bugs around the house, I was shot down. They were sure the house was swept for bugs regularly and definitely after a party. They didn't want to leave any trace that we were gathering information about the Ramirez family. If they got tipped off, they could change their security procedures and check into everyone at the party. It could give me away.

My most important goal was to make sure I got invited to her house again. I was to "do what it takes." A knife was secreted into my shoe in case I needed it. Tracey gave me the pills I'd need to counteract the effects of alcohol and drugs, and I slipped them into my pocket. I decided it would be to my benefit to learn as much about alcohol as I possibly could before I had to leave. I downloaded *The Definitive Guide to Alcohol* by T.S. Miller and glanced quickly at each page. I then asked Tracey and Cory about popular teen drinks. I was now half an hour late, but before I felt completely ready, I found myself walking into her house with a few other stragglers.

A guard at the door took my invitation and scanned it with a hand-held scanner, then consulted the computer screen attached to it. Whoa. They were taking every precaution with this event. I was glad I didn't forget the invite. The guard then pointed for me to go through a doorway on my right even though I could see the party was through a large entryway to the left. With the music so loud, I figured I wouldn't even try to ask why. The guard wouldn't have heard me anyway. I walked into the designated room, and the French doors shut behind me.

A man with dark, bushy eyebrows sat at his desk behind a computer monitor looking me over. "You are no in school records. Why?" His thick Spanish accent made him a bit hard to understand.

"Uh." I wasn't expecting this. They had acquired the school's records? How? "Uh," I said again, buying time to think. *Duh!* I was just a seventeen-year-old student. I should act like it. "Maybe because I just started there a few weeks ago?" Why wasn't I in the school records already?

He looked me up and down again. "This will have to be

verified." He reached up by his ear and spoke in Spanish. At first, I thought he was talking to me, but then I saw a com pressed against his cheek and wrapped around his ear. "We are updating our records, now," he said.

I nodded, glad that his information was out of date and that Division 57 hadn't dropped the ball.

"Please stand on the black star in front of the wall just to your left."

I moved into position, and he pushed a button on his desk. A camera flashed. He had just taken my picture. Was that okay? He looked at his computer screen. I tried to think of a clever way to get my jump drive into that computer but came up short.

"Now, step to this side of my desk and stand on the black moon." He motioned to his right. Another picture? I blinked several times trying to get rid of the echo of the flash in my eyes. Once there, he asked for my hand. Reluctantly, I gave it to him. "Relax your hand please. I need your finger prints." I pulled away just as Sophia flew into the room.

"I was about to give up on you. You're late!" She had a huge, dumb grin on her face, already a bit tipsy, I thought. "Come on," she said, motioning for me to follow her.

"One moment, Miss," said bushy-eyebrow guy to Sophia. "You know this girl?"

"Of course! This is Ari. She's my new best friend so keep your hairy paws off her."

I was?

"Miss, she is no in the system. I must fingerprint her."

"No. I've verified her identity. The party's already started. What do you think, that she's a spy? She's seventeen," and then her mouth raced off, speaking Spanish, at what I thought was a mile a minute. I never wanted to be chewed out in Spanish and especially not by Sophia. Her finger flashed up and down and her body leaned forward.

The man was now standing between us and the door. "It *is* protocol, miss."

I would be fingerprinted. That was for sure.

Then Sophia yelled out, "Screw your protocol and get out of my way, Fernando, or you'll regret it."

He didn't move, but when Sophia shoved past him, dragging me along behind, he didn't stop us.

What the heck? They had taken a picture of me, and had tried to get my fingerprints. What if Fernando had been successful? What if Sophia hadn't come in just then? What would my fingerprints reveal? I needed to tell Cory and Tracey ASAP. The security here was incredible. I would have to code my texts in case security was intercepting them.

I was once again in the booming foyer, but this time I was being led about by Sophia. I pulled hard on her arm, and she spun around to look at me.

"What?" she yelled into my ear over the noise.

This was the perfect opportunity for me to get her to tell me about her dad's lab—anyone would be curious about such heavy security, so I wouldn't call any attention to myself by asking about it. I pulled her close to me so that I could talk loudly into her ear. "What was that all about?"

She turned her head and spoke directly into my ear. "My dad. His lab. He's paranoid."

"Lab?" I asked, determined to get more out of her. She had already started pulling me toward the party again. I held her firm.

"A science lab. You know. Science experiments?"

"No way!" I yelled. "Really?"

"You're weird!"

"You should have had the party in there," I yelled. "Drinks in beakers. Food in Petri dishes. Food on scales and equipment. It would rock. Dress like mad scientists. Frankenstein party!"

"Forget it, Ari! My dad would never allow it." She pulled me into the main party room, not stopping until we were in the middle of the see-through dance floor. Colorful lights zoomed around in it. The room pulsed with energy, and the dance floor rocked. It seemed the whole senior class was there. Some danced, others grouped along the edges of the room playing video games, pool, and karaoke while still others hung in small groups chatting.

Many of the kids dancing had drinks in hand and a sheen of sweat over their bodies despite the cool air blowing on us. It seemed so weird to have parents supply the alcohol for a teen party. I had to remind myself that this was the norm in Europe and wasn't even illegal. The sound coming from the band seemed to shake all my internal organs out of place. The air was filled with electricity, and strange smells kept assaulting me. Sweat, fermentation, and an awful sweetness. My head started to pound after only a few minutes.

I had to be fun and exciting, so I would garner another invitation. So, I faked it. There were loads of people there. Sophia could really dance. I tried to copy her Latina moves. I would have loved to be able to dance like she danced. Thirty minutes later, Sophia's boyfriend snagged her away from me for a slow song, and I headed for the foyer to decompress, lie down, and get rid of my headache. I wished I had some ibuprofen, or better yet, my migraine meds. I fingered the anti alcohol and drug pills in my pocket. I wouldn't need them tonight. I would be Houdini instead.

Two girls from Sophia's group, Mendi, from India, whose thousands of piercing glimmered in the dim lighting, and Bashan, from Croatia, whose short platinum blonde hair, ultra white skin, and small frame made her look like a pixie, grabbed me before I could get there, and I ended up being playfully dragged to a table near the bar. As we neared it, Mendi said directly into my ear, "Stefan wants to challenge you to a game of beer pong. You are so lucky." She raised her eyebrows at me. She obviously thought this was quite the honor.

"Who's Stefan?" I asked. I refrained from asking the obvious question, *what's beer pong?*

Before she could answer, we had arrived at the beer pong table, and it was surrounded by anxious spectators. I assumed the tall, dark, and ruggedly handsome guy at the other end was Stefan. He made me ache for Reese. He wore a crooked smile, and his eyes flashed a bright green. His tousled midnight black hair was the frosting on the cake. He wore his confidence on his sleeve. I tried to look self-assured, too, hiding the terror I truly felt. I had no idea what beer pong was, and Bashan had just handed me a ping pong ball. I looked around, trying to neutralize the acid that burned my gut.

I am calm. My head feels light and clear. I can do this.

I scanned the crowd for social clues to help me at least start the game. I started to see colors swirl in front of me, the smoke, lights, and stress exacerbating my migraine. On the table in front of me sat some plastic cups. The same cups looked back at me from Stefan's side. Beer pooled inside them. The teens were pointing at specific cups and arguing about which one the ball would land in or whether it would at all. I took aim and tossed the ball. The spectators cheered. Unfortunately, each glass seemed to turn into two. The ball didn't get anywhere near any cups.

The crowd roared their drunken roar. New bets were cast and realization dawned. If Stefan got his ball into one of my cups, I would be expected to drink it. I casually felt around me with my foot and found a discarded cup. I pulled it toward me, placing it right next to me and then using my foot to make it stand.

I thought about how stupid the game was. It gave everyone the excuse they needed to drink themselves silly and pretend like they hadn't chosen to. They were trying to give their responsibility away, whether consciously or unconsciously.

Mendi laughed in my face, and her strong breath threw me for a loop. I almost offered up the contents of my stomach to her. The smoke swirled around the room, adding to my nausea. With a small splash, Stefan's ball hit its target, and everyone cheered. I reached for the cup, but my fingers just grazed it instead. This caused a greater cackle of laughter.

My chance to use my illusionist training had arrived. I should have been excited, but worry settled in. I couldn't even grab the cup.

"She's already soused." "She's all yours Stefan." "Someone hand it to her." A mingled mix of English with varying accents filled the space.

These kids were acting like animals. Couldn't they see I wasn't feeling well? Besides, if they thought I was drunk already, why would they push more alcohol on me? To think I would get out of taking drugs or drinking alcohol just because my mom was a supposed addict was totally naïve. I would have to do one of my abracadabra moves to get rid of the drink. I was quite an expert at this scenario. Sure, I didn't feel very hot, but I'd done this so many times, I was sure I could pull it off. There were a lot of people watching. I'd have to be really good at distracting them all. It would have to be a huge diversion since I was not totally in control. I couldn't have them looking directly at what I was doing. Sure, they were a bunch of drunk teens, and it shouldn't be hard, but I wasn't feeling well. I'd have to make them look away.

I could just take the pills in my pocket. No harm. No foul. But that seemed like such a copout. I had practiced this. I was a pro. A sick pro today, but it was time to do it for real. I closed my eyes tight, shook my head and tried to ignore the pounding and the nausea drumming through me for just the few seconds it would require to create the illusion of me drinking the beer.

"Ladies and Gentlemen," I said in my best performance voice. "It is time to witness the complete and total over-sousing of Ari Agave." I laughed. "If you will give me your attention, you will witness the great event." I waited for all eyes to be on me and my cup. I held it out in front of me. I intended to distract them, dump the cup while everyone looked away, and when their eyes returned to me, I'd have the empty cup at my lips. Normally, I'd do the illusion right in front of them, but I didn't dare. I didn't feel well enough. "Hold on everyone, I believe that gentleman there wants to say something." They all looked where I was pointing, including me, and I tried to pour the drink into the cup I'd placed at my feet. I was just about to congratulate myself on my speed, when Mendi screeched and everyone looked back.

"She dumped her drink on me." "Ah, she's trying to get out of drinking it." "Nice try." "Give her a different one."

Shouts from all around.

Stefan stared at me with a non-judgmental look in his eye, and I said, "Excuse me," tossing the cup to the side and heading for the front door. The guard didn't want to let me pass, until I heaved, and he must have figured out it was the bush, the floor, or him who would get the liquid bursting from my mouth. After I heaved my guts out into the bushes on the side of the porch, I stumbled out to the lawn and lay down, eyes closed, sweat beading from my forehead. I had blown it. Sophia would never invite me back. I was no fun. I hadn't even lasted an hour.

Next thing I knew, someone lay down next to me. The shock of it made me turn quickly. Stefan, the boy who wanted to play beer pong with me, smiled that crooked smile. I had to admit, even with my headache, he was endearing. I sat up, trying to listen to the voice that told me to get vertical. The pounding in my head made me lay right back down.

"Had a little too much?" He didn't appear to be the least bit drunk.

"Actually, I think I'm getting sick from a migraine." I covered my mouth, hoping to keep my barf-breath to myself. If I'd been in my right mind, I might have used the situation to my advantage and played up the drunk angle.

"That's what too much alcohol does to a body."

I tried to laugh, but it made my head ache worse, so I groaned instead, grabbing my head. He didn't believe my migraine story anyway. What did it matter what he believed? This person he knew was not me anyway.

"Let's go get you something for that *headache*," he said, standing and offering me his hand. I took it. It felt strong in mine. He pulled me to him, he smelled like peppermint and musk, and I gladly leaned on him, the world still spinning around me. He led me into the kitchen where he asked the staff that bustled about if they could direct us to some headache meds. A stout, jolly looking woman, who reminded me of Santa Claus's wife, opened a cupboard and pulled out a large plastic container. I greedily stuffed the pills into my mouth and drank the entire glass of water that Stefan offered me. I leaned against a section of counter that didn't have a server working in front of it and took a deep breath. Stefan moved in front of me.

"Maybe I should go." I said. "I just threw up everywhere, the entire place is in Technicolor, and I really just want to lie down and take a nap.

"I'll see what I can do about that," Stefan said, sliding away from me. I closed my eyes and breathed deeply.

When he returned, I reached out and took his arm. "Could you take me home?" I didn't want to give up on my mission, but what choice did I have? I couldn't function.

He held up a key in front of me and said, "I'll do even better. I got a key to a room where you can sleep it off. All the rooms in the house are locked because of the party. It took all my mad persuasive skills, but I managed it." He grinned broadly.

He directed me there, and I gingerly lay on the bed, closing my eyes. I felt Stefan lie down next to me. What was he doing? I needed to make sure he understood me.

"FYI. If you thought this might be a good opportunity to seduce the wasted girl, you'll be sadly disappointed. I'm concentrating really hard on not throwing up again."

"And what exactly gave you the idea that I might be that kind of guy?"

"Uh, it might be the fact that you asked me to play a round of beer pong, you followed me outside when I was puking, and you lay beside me just now."

"Oh, those little things gave me away?" He chuckled.

"Uh huh. I don't want to lead you on in anyway." I wasn't naïve, I knew in Prague that the drinking age was only fourteen and since pretty much everyone drank, it didn't automatically mean he was a player, but I couldn't risk it.

"Well, would it shatter your image of me if I stayed a while and protected you from other scoundrels that might not understand you in the way I do now?" His accent made me smile. Was he from Germany?

"That would be nice, actually," I said.

"And don't worry, I won't tell anyone."

"Tell anyone what?" I asked, keeping my eyes shut.

"That you can't hold your liquor."

I sighed. Before slipping away into my dreams, I felt his lips on my forehead, his five-o-clock shadow lightly scraping my skin.

Chapter Twenty-Three

I startled awake. Unsure exactly where I was, I sat up and pushed my back up against the backboard of the bed in one fluid motion. After blinking away the sleep and straining to make out the tiniest of details in the room, it came to me. I was at Sophia's. I had fallen asleep…with a boy. I reached out, feeling for Stefan. He was gone. Whew! I wondered when he had left. I also worried I'd embarrassed myself as I slept. And I thought of Reese and how, despite Stefan's attractiveness, I would so much rather have had him at my side. At least Stefan had been a gentleman. I hadn't been expecting that from one of Sophia's friends.

My throat felt dry and sticky at the same time, so I stood and went for the door. Just as I reached it, I remembered that I was supposed to be doing reconnaissance. I pulled out my phone. Three a.m. I quickly texted Cory, in code of course, that I was all right. I was sure they'd been sweating it, wondering what had happened to me as they watched all the other guests leave.

The music had stopped, and I couldn't hear anything stir outside of my room. Would the cameras in my necklace and watch work in the dark? It seemed impossible, but I'd try use them anyway. I'd blown it.

Or had I? Maybe I'd have a better chance at seeing what I wanted to see now that everyone was in bed. I used my hands to get a drink from the sink in the bathroom off my room, and headed into the hall. I would act as if I was just looking for the kitchen to get a drink if someone caught me, or if I tripped an alarm. This was a good time to take risks.

I made my way around the house without a sound, taking real pictures as well as taking my own mental pictures. The full moon shining through all the massive windows and the many floor lights, gave off just enough light to prevent me from running into everything. I got to use the silent reconnaissance tricks Cory had taught me last week. My heart pounded in my ears, preventing me from really hearing anything.

I got around the whole main floor without detection, and I felt triumphant. I tried the door to the study where Fernando had taken my picture, but it was locked. I really needed to master how to pick a lock. I used a bobby pin to try and open it, but it didn't work. Then I noticed the keycard slot next to the door and let out a huge breath. I had just about given myself away. I was sure I would have set off some alarm had I managed to open the door. How would I have explained trying to get into that room? I had no reason to believe it was a kitchen. I couldn't explain that away. I looked for a way to get into the basement but couldn't find one. There were no doors to the basement anywhere.

I started up the stairs, hoping they weren't the creaky sort. I had to stop twice and move my foot to another spot on the stairs when they screeched out. Once on the top, I turned to admire the bloody red, full moon shining through a high picture window. That's when I noticed movement far out in the field. I leaned over the banister attempting to see more clearly, but the extra foot it gave me didn't help.

I hurried down the steps and through the dining room to get a closer look. Bodies moved in a single file in the dark over a rise and then disappeared. Another line of men seemed to be making their way back to the outbuilding the others were leaving. Their movements were militaristic, steady, even, measured. I snapped as many pictures as I could with my necklace and moved in closer to the window. So intent on seeing what they were carrying, I hit my nose on the glass.

I reached up to see if it was bleeding when a heavy hand clamped onto my shoulder. I had to quell the urge to knock whoever it was off their feet. What if it was Sophia or her mom or dad? Besides, even if it were a guard, I couldn't reveal my true ninja self to them. Not yet, anyway. I turned to find the hand attached to a very tall, very solid man in a security uniform.

His other hand clasped my other shoulder hard as I turned, and I saw a bright light issue from his neck area, like a quick camera flash. I shielded my eyes. He said something in Spanish that didn't sound nice. I just stared, letting my eyes go wide. *What would a silly seventeen-year-old who got sidetracked getting a drink of water in a strange house do in this situation?* I kept my eyes wide and let a scream escape my lips. After all, wouldn't that be a seventeen-year-old's reaction to someone grabbing her, snapping a quick picture of her, and then speaking to her in a foreign language? I hoped my delay in reacting wasn't too noticeable. The guard promptly let go of one of my shoulders and clamped his hand over my mouth. Then he said something in broken English, "No Spanish?"

I shook my head, his hand muffled my answer.

"Wait," he said, nodding at me. "Okay."

I let my mouth close as his hand moved away from it.

"Okay," he repeated, apparently listening to someone through his earpiece.

I nodded.

He kept his other hand on my shoulder while he spoke into his radio com. Two more guards arrived and one spoke in English to me. "Who are you?"

"I'm Ari, Sophia's friend."

They all stared at me, and one of the men looked at his tablet screen and nodded. They must've gotten verification of my identity.

"What are you doing out of your room?"

"I just needed a drink," I said, speaking fast, like a freaked out teen. "And then I saw how huge the moon was and wanted to get a closer look. And then suddenly, he was there, grabbing me." I pointed to the man who had a hold of my shoulder.

"A drink?" the English speaker said.

"Yes." I bowed my head.

"Hmm," he said, rubbing his chin. "What did you see when you looked out at the moon?"

"The moon," I said as if the moon were all I had seen out there.

"Okay. Were you able to get that drink you needed?"

"I didn't get the chance, yet." I looked at them with what I hoped were eyes full of shame. The guard who held me let go, and I went into the kitchen and grabbed that drink. They all followed me in there.

After I took a swig, the man said, "Didn't anyone instruct you to stay in your room at night? I suggest you stay in your room when you sleep over, so you can do just that, *sleep* over." He was smiling, but his tone held a hint of warning.

"No problem," I said, taking note that I should make sure to ask about all the armed guards in the morning, because I shouldn't have expected it. I scurried back to my room, turning my head slightly to the side as I walked in hopes of picking up some of the conversation that was still going on between the guards.

I didn't dare chance another sneak peek at the house. If I were caught, I'm sure I'd never be allowed back. And I might not even make it out alive. Scary thought. With any luck at all, I'd recorded some important stuff. The tiny creaks and crackles of a house full of sleeping people lulled me back to sleep.

I woke bright and early to find a coded text from Cory on my phone. Once decoded, it read,

Stay as long as possible. Get more info.

I searched the room for alarms and cameras or other surveillance. It was good practice for Module18.9 from the Academy. I didn't find anything unusual. The windows were wired as expected, and the walls had wires throughout. I had learned to feel the slightest change in temperature through plaster and sheetrock to know where they were.

The home also had a pretty cool intercom system. There was no trigger on the door and nothing in the room was bugged, at least that I could find. I discovered an interesting vent, however. I could hear clanking and clacking through it. I wondered where it led. The lab, maybe? I then headed out the door to the kitchen once my stomach rumbled loud enough for the neighbors to hear. I hoped I'd find Sophia out there already.

I took note of everything around me, making sure to

press the mapping tool on my rings. The dining room came before the kitchen, and I found a woman with luscious black hair and copper skin sitting at the dining room table. It had to be Mrs. Ramirez. She was eating something that looked like a brioche with ham. Steam swirled out of a mug that I assumed held coffee. The room smelled of pastry and salt.

She glanced up at me with a strange expression on her face. "Oh. You startled me. It is proper to announce one's self when one walks into a room." Her eyes appraised me. They were not friendly. I thought of my mom and how differently she would have behaved. I had to repress the sadness that threatened to overtake me.

I straightened up. "Sorry," I said, offering her my hand and saying, "I got sick last night and fell asleep in one of your guest bedrooms."

She did not take my hand. "That's what happens when you drink too much."

I thought about correcting her, but by the look on her face, I figured it would just sound like a lie, and she wouldn't believe me anyway, so I just let it go.

"Sophia let me know you were in the servant's quarters last night before she turned in. I didn't think you'd make it out this early in your condition, however, or I would have made myself presentable."

I wondered what she was worried about. Her hair looked shiny and brushed and her skin, flawless. She wore a strong air of formality and coolness. What was up with that?

"If you are hungry," she said, standing and pushing her chair in. "Just ring this bell and Anje will help you."

As if on cue, my stomach rumbled. Really, the Christy

part of me wanted to say, "That's okay, I was just leaving," but I was not Christy. I was Ari, and I had a mission to complete. I needed to stay.

"Stay as long as you like, just alert Eduardo in the security office if you want to venture outside. If Sophia's not down before noon, I give you permission to wake her. Third door on the left, upstairs." Once she reached the stairs, she said, "Oh, and I called your parents last night to let them know you were staying the night. I think it was only appropriate despite the late hour."

"Thank you," I said. I guess I should have texted them after I lay down in that room, but I hadn't realize I'd sleep so long.

Once she was gone, I picked up a bell on the table and, feeling like a total fool, rang it. It was so loud. I quickly grabbed the bell portion in my hands, muffling anymore ringing, and I looked about wondering who I might have disturbed. A tall, wiry, balding man stepped into the dining room.

"Mademoiselle?" he said, adding several more French words, his thick French accent drawing me in.

"No entiendo," I said, immediately chastising myself for speaking Spanish. Stupid. Stupid.

"Breakfast? Can I make you a crepe suzette?" His words rolled gently off his tongue.

I had no idea what that was, but I said, "Sure," anyway.

After breakfast, which was delicious, I roamed the house, not running into a soul. Where had all the guards gone? Were they only here last night because of the party? Were they watching me on some television screen through cameras placed throughout the house? I looked around, carefully searching for cameras. There were none that I could find. So I set to task searching and searching for the entrance to the basement and the lab. I concluded there must not be an entrance from inside the house.

I sat down to watch TV, tempted to go upstairs and look for Sophia. Now that I knew she knew I was here, I was more at ease. At noon she rumbled down the stairs, opting to enter the kitchen without ringing the bell. I'm sure her hangover thanked her. She emerged a few minutes later with a large green drink in her hands. She started up the stairs, but when her eyes fell on me, she stopped.

"Ari?" she said, turning to come back down the stairs. "Oh, sorry, I forgot you spent the night."

"No big deal. Thanks for finding me."

"My dad made me search the house and make sure no one unlocked any of the doors. He didn't want a bunch of oblivious drunk kids staying the night."

"Why didn't you wake me?"

"You were sound asleep. By the time I found you, I didn't want to bother you."

"Sorry I blew your party."

"That's what you get for drinking too much. At first, I thought you left with Stefan." She raised her eyebrows at me.

"Leave your party for a guy? I don't think so."

"He seemed to have left for you."

"I don't know what you're talking about," I said, turning away from her.

"You both 'disappeared' at the same time. What else was I supposed to conclude?"

"He's the one who helped me into your guest room. He left after that, huh?"

"That must be what happened. After you fell asleep, he must have figured there was no reason to stay." She giggled. Before the party, I would have thought this weird. She didn't do girlie things. But after seeing her let loose at the party, perhaps the alcohol played a part in that, I wasn't surprised. It was like getting a glimpse of who she really was.

"How was it?"

The whole idea of it was absurd to me, and I shook my head. "Go ahead and laugh. Nothing happened even though I'm sure he wanted it to. It's a good thing he didn't try to force me or think me too drunk not to resist."

A dark shadow seemed to cross her face and she said, with stark venom, "He's not that kind of guy, or I wouldn't have allowed him into my house."

"Whatever," I said, shaking my head and wondering where the venom was coming from. What was she hiding?

"I've got some stuff to do in my room. Wanna come?"

Finally, I would get to explore the upstairs. "Sure." I slid my hand along the banister as I swished up the curling staircase, amazed at the warmth of the wood on my hand.

"By the way, Stefan texted me at the break of dawn and asked for your number."

"You didn't give it to him, did you?"

"Of course, I did." She looked back at me and laughed.

I grabbed my phone from my pocket and sure enough, a text from some unknown number stared back at me. Once at the top of the stairs, we took a left. "What's down there?" I asked, pointing down the long hallway to our right.

"That's just my parents' suite and my dad's office."

"I thought you said he had a lab," I commented, following her down the wide hallway and checking out the text.

It's Stefan. Feeling better today?

I rolled my eyes and deleted it.

"Oh, he does, but that's downstairs. I don't know exactly what he has in that office. I just know I'm not allowed in there. Besides, it's always locked."

I took another look back as we passed several closed doors, hoping the scanners in my rings were getting it all. As we walked in, a woman hurried out, wearing gloves and carrying a bucket of cleaning supplies. Sophia acted like she didn't even see her. Sophia's room was huge, and she had soft music playing through her wall speakers.

"Classical?" I asked.

"You have a problem with that?" The edge in her voice warned me to tread lightly.

"I'm just surprised."

"I'm a surprising kind of person." She sat on a chair by her bed and sipped the green drink.

"I'm starting to see that," I said, smiling.

She stared at me hard. "I used to be a concert pianist."

"Did not!" I said, mouth wide. Why was she telling me this?

"Did, too."

"Why'd that change?"

Something dark flickered in her eyes. "I don't want to talk about it." She turned and fiddled with her cell.

"You can't dangle a carrot out there like that and then leave it hanging." I said, sitting in a soft, leather recliner.

"I can, and I am."

"I could force it out of you." I laughed.

"Why did your parents send you to IEA?" Her abrupt change in subject caught me off guard.

"They wanted to make my life miserable."

"Not good enough." Her eyes, firm, locked on mine.

"I was getting bad grades. But you know that already."

Is this why she confided in me about the piano thing? To get me to open up?

"That's just a symptom of the real thing they were trying to get you away from." She didn't flinch. She wasn't talking like the Sophia I knew.

"I don't know what you mean." I really didn't.

"No one comes to IEA without having some problem that parents want to hide from the world. What. Is. Your. Problem?"

I was caught with my pants down. What could I say? Grades were my problem; did I need a more serious one than that? "You tell me yours first," I hedged.

"My house. I get to hear yours first." There was no doubting her belief in that statement.

"How do I know you're not going to go blab it all over the world?" I needed thinking time.

"Why—"

"Sophia," a male voice coming from an intercom in the wall called out. He said more things in Spanish after calling her name.

"Be right there," she said in English into the air and gave me a curious look.

"Who was that?" I asked.

"My mad scientist dad who never talks to me unless absolutely necessary. He wants me downstairs, immediately."

I chuckled. "Someone's in trouble."

She sighed and left the room.

I sent a coded text to Cory to see what my 'problem' should be so he could arrange for the right documentation to back it up. Then I headed to the door and down the hall to see if I could catch a glimpse of Diego Ramirez in real life. Maybe I could overhear something.

Her dad was spouting off a bunch of stuff in Spanish.

"Yes sir," she said. "I did tell you about her spending the night."

They were talking about me. Crap. I'd gotten Sophia in trouble. Crap. Crap. Crap.

"But you didn't tell her about the rules. That was just sloppy," he said, switching to English. "And Diego Ramirez's daughter is not sloppy. She is exact and precise in all things."

She didn't speak, but I could imagine her nodding.

"Repeat that for me, please."

"I am Sophia Ramirez Martín, and I am exact and precise in all things."

"Very good."

"Am I excused?"

"Yes. Go."

Without further pleasantries, she emerged from the kitchen, and I stepped back, hurried back into her room, and jumped on her bed. I checked my phone. Nothing. Great. What could I tell Sophia?

She came back in the room, all attitude. "Thanks a lot, Agave! You just got me yelled at."

"What are you talking about?" I feigned stupidity.

"Your little excursion last night." She forced her head out toward me, eyes wide. "You know, the one where you ran into my dad's goons."

"Oh that! Dude! I thought that guy was going to break me in two. I just wanted some water."

"You can't go traipsing all over my house at night. I told you my dad's a crazy scientist. He's freaked out that someone will steal his inventions, experiments, and even his ideas. It's all he thinks about. Be careful around here.

During the day—you're fine. There's only Eduardo in the house and all the other goons are outside. But at night, my dad has the guards inside because my mom wouldn't let him install any cameras in here. She said she didn't want her privacy 'curtailed' for his silly inventions and that it wasn't 'dignified' to spy on guests." She twisted her nose ring.

"If he's so afraid, why'd he give you a party here?" I asked.

"That's the real question, right? I've thought a lot about it."

I raised my eyebrows at her. Why would she think a lot about it?

"I mean," Sophia continued, "he lets me have a few friends over at a time and stuff, but he's always rented places for my parties. It bugs me because we're just teens, ya know? It's not like anyone I know wants anything to do with any lab, let alone his. His lab has always come first. I'm way down the list. But then, last month, he told me at dinner he thought I should have my senior party here. He picked the date and everything."

"Maybe," I said, lying back on the bed. "He realized he was about to lose you to college, and he wanted to show you he loves you and wanted to do something nice for you."

"Not my dad," she said, a bitter tone to her voice. "He doesn't think about anything else, only creating. He doesn't think about taking care of his daughter or wife. His lab is his life." She sat Indian style on the bed. "My dad is a scientist through and through. There was a reason he suggested I have the party last night. He is exact and precise in all things. I wish I knew what it was."

Her words, *exact* and *precise* left a bad taste in my

mouth. Did this exactness and preciseness mean she never got to go into the lab? I had to find out if she even had access. "Is that why you're so great at science? Do you get to help out in the lab and use it for projects, like our physics' project?"

"No way. He never lets me in there."

"You've never seen his lab?"

"Once. When I was eight, and that ended badly."

"I thought he'd want you in there doing science stuff all the time. It would be awesome to do our project in there. Especially since it's a secret lab."

"It would be, but you can just forget it."

"I bet if you told him—"

"No. Besides, I don't want him looking at me all crazy."

"All crazy?"

"I don't want my dad to know I like science. He looks at me differently, and I don't mean better, just different, like I'm a specimen he wants to alter or collect. He'd love to have me as his mad scientist partner." She changed her voice into her version of a man's and continued. "Hey Henry, meet Sophia, she's my lab partner."

I needed to feel her out on this one. I'd thought she wanted attention from her dad. It sounded like she didn't want to be with him at all. "But at least you'd get to spend time with him."

"I don't want him to spend time with me only because he's getting something out of it. Know what I mean?"

I did, so I nodded. She didn't want to be a commodity for her dad. She wanted him to spend time with her because he loved her just for her. We sat in silence for a few minutes.

"What are you thinking about?" Sophia asked.

I'd sat in thought too long thinking of a way to trick her into showing me the door to the lab.

"Nothing."

"It was obviously something," Sophia leaned closer to me

Then it came to me. "It's stupid, and we can't even do it. So forget it."

"Spill," she said.

"I was just imagining making the most awesome bomb to blow up Ms. Gerty's tires." I had no idea where the idea came from.

"Remind me never to make you mad. Don't let your imagination run away with you. My dad would never allow us to build a bomb to blow up our health teacher's car. It *would* rock, though, and she deserves it for forcing you and me to do those push-ups in front of the class. It's not like we were the only ones talking. She's always doing crap like that." She swore colorfully.

"I told you it was stupid. I warned you. Want to hear the other thing I was thinking about?"

"I don't know if I want to know."

"What about creating a stink bomb like the one on that old show Seinfeld where that guy with B.O. got in the car and the smell wouldn't leave the car or anyone who got in it? We could make the reaction last for two weeks or something." I let that sink in for a second, then quickly added, "Or we could make a hair dye you drink."

Sophia looked at me like I was a bit crazy. Did she have no imagination?

"Why would we do that?"

"Just think of that girl who's been trying to steal your boyfriend. Give her a horrible hair color like bright white, or grey or puke green just by spiking her drink."

"Now you're talking. That would be wicked, Ari.

Totally wicked. So we don't create anything that would hurt anyone, per se. Physically, I mean, but we create some jokes."

"This is all theoretical, you know," I said, making sure she understood I didn't know what I was doing.

"Yeah, but with your brain I'm betting on you." She narrowed her eyes for a tiny second, and then they sparkled. "That would be so fun. You think we could create something like that?"

I had piqued her interest. "In your dad's secret lair? Of course!" I said, knowing it would be way beyond us. I wasn't even sure it was possible, but I wouldn't be around to have to complete it anyway.

"Too bad my dad would never allow it." She sighed and rolled onto her back. "My dad ruins my life."

"You're being a drama queen," I said.

"You think so, huh? Well, check this out. The week before you came, I rigged the senior cotillion so I won queen."

I was shocked. She wanted to be queen? I turned to her. She stared at the ceiling.

"I did it so my dad would come and dance with me. It's pretty lame I had to do that to spend time with him, huh? Anyway, it's the tradition of the school that the father of the queen comes and dances the first dance with his daughter, the queen. I figured he would come because it was tradition, and he would look bad if he didn't show. He said he'd be there, but he never showed. I felt like a royal idiot."

"I'm so sorry, Sophia. That sucks."

We sat in uneasy silence for what seemed forever. I couldn't push her after that admission.

"Maybe," she suddenly said. "Maybe we could figure out a way to break in there, instead."

Her dad had ticked her off, and now she was trying to find a way to piss him off. But did she know about all the security surrounding that lab? I'd better warn her, just in case.

"No offense, Sophia, but if your dad had armed guards and scanned invites for a teen party, I can't imagine what kind of security measures he has for his lab."

"I know. There's no way to go in the front door, but maybe there's another way." She stared off into space. "When I was eight, I got in through a secret entrance. I don't remember there being any security. If it's still there..."

I didn't dare say anything that might interrupt her train of thought. A secret entrance. That was too good to be true. I could feel the danger of her musings. She wanted revenge, and revenge led to bad things. Despite the danger, I was getting excited to complete my mission.

She grabbed her phone and started tapping away.

"What are you doing?" I asked, standing up and moving toward her.

"I thought it would be good if we learned how to pick a lock, just in case."

I sucked in an involuntary breath, and she looked at me.

I turned away. Why hadn't I perfected that yet? It was on my list. I knew how to deactivate wired locks and how to bypass electronic key pads, but no, I hadn't completed the practical for simple lock picking, yet.

"Ari?"

"Huh?" I said, still looking away.

"Do you know how to pick locks?"

"Uhhh..." I said, turning to her.

"You do know how to do it, don't you? I can see it in your eyes." She moved toward me, her face lit up. "That's

251

why you said you liked secret places. You're a heister. I knew you had to have something to hide. Did you get jammed up one too many times or what?"

"Actually, I never got jammed up." I pulled at a spike of my hair. I never intended to get arrested, either.

"So you are a thief!" She laughed loudly. "That totally cracks me up. This I've gotta see. Pick my closet door lock."

"Wait! I'm no thief. I just like to get into places I'm not allowed." I could feel heat pushing into my face.

"Yeah, right. Whatever." She rolled her eyes and tilted her head to the side.

"I'm serious. Anyway, this is a bad idea. Your dad will probably shoot me if we get caught." I sent a quick SOS to Cory on the cell in my pocket. I needed him to call me home so that I could get out of this. It vibrated. I pulled it out to look at it. Stefan. He was persistent. I deleted it.

"Do it. Show me you can." Her eyes were wide, forceful somehow.

I had to think fast. I tried to be smooth, swallowing the hard lump that had developed in my throat. Modules from the Bresen Academy came to mind. All I could see was the miserable failure I'd been at the Academy with the door in the basement. I reached up and pulled two bobby pins from my hair, pretending to know what I was doing. Why hadn't Cory come to my rescue already? "Sometimes bobby pins work. If not, I'll need my kit from home." I had to have an out.

"A lock pick kit?"

"Of course."

I shoved the pins in, concentrating harder than I ever had, heard a click, but no. When I tried the knob, it didn't open. I fiddled with it a bit more, then my phone rang out. I quickly grabbed for the phone and said, "My dad."

"Hi Dad." I sat in silence listening, then said, "I know. But, I got sick last night and didn't even get to enjoy the party. I fell asleep in a guestroom and—" Cory spoke louder, so that Sophia could hear his tinny voice through the cell speaker.

"I know all about it," Cory said, "Mrs. Ramirez called me last night to tell me. You better not have been drinking."

"I wasn't, Dad, I swear. I had a migraine." I rolled my eyes at Sophia, to play up the bad-girl act. Let her believe I'd been drinking—and that I lied to my parents.

"Well, you're better now, and it's time to do your work."

"I know, and I'll still do it. Just please let me—"

"Get your butt home, Ari. Now." Cory spoke loudly.

"Fine!"

"Don't sass me or this lapse of judgment will earn you a grounding."

"Okay. Okay." I made a face.

"See you in a few minutes, then."

I punched the phone off and then said to Sophia, "I have to go. I was supposed to clean my room and bathroom this morning and obviously, I was here, so…"

"I heard the whole conversation. I'll go with you," Sophia said, smiling. "I totally want to get a look at your Night Rod."

"With you there, maybe I won't get yelled at again." I texted Cory again to give him a heads up about her wanting to see my Harley and letting him know they would have to find a way to distract her for my lock-picking lesson.

"Then we can come back to my house and pick some locks." She smiled conspiratorially.

Chapter Twenty-Four

She drove us the short mile to my house on her Harley. When we walked in, Tracey was in the kitchen cooking, and Cory was at the top of the stairs looking down at me.

"Hi guys. Sorry I neglected my work this morning." I said it in an I'm-sorry,-but-I-had-no-choice kind of way.

Luckily, my parents knew just what to do. My mom then said, "Nice of you to join us. And you brought your friend? Don't think she will be allowed to do it for you."

I looked at her, shocked. "Do what?"

"Do what?" Tracey said, "That's what's so fun about you Ari, you're always asking such good questions. Your work. You know that bathroom of yours looks more like a mine field than a bathroom."

"Why don't you just have Rosa, do it?" I was spitballing, making up pieces of a complete life with these people who were supposed to be my parents. I was so glad I had seasoned spies to work with. They never missed a beat.

"We've had this discussion a thousand times, Ari, you need to learn to take care of yourself, and besides, you need some responsibility."

I rolled my eyes at Sophia. I'm sure she never had to lift a finger at her house. I remembered seeing her maid leaving her room as we had entered it earlier that day.

"Come on, Sophia," I said.

We started toward the stairs, and Tracey said, "Uh, I don't think so. You don't get any help on this one."

"Oh, I won't help her, Mrs. Agave." That was a given. She kept her eyes diverted from Tracey. I wondered if she was thinking of her uncle, the meth addict.

"I'd rather you stay down here. Feel free to watch some TV in the family room." She directed Sophia where to go.

Once she was out of sight, I ran up the stairs and met Cory in the spare room next to mine. "That was awesome." I beamed at him.

He scowled.

"We should have worked on lock picking first. It's so rudimentary. How did you miss it?"

I felt stupid, and a hot blush crept up my neck. I wanted to tell him that I'd only been at the Academy a month, but thought it wouldn't help my cause.

"Give me all your gadgets, I'll download what you've recorded from the Ramirez house while you look for the lock that most resembles the one you're trying to break into."

I unloaded all the gadgets and looked toward the bed where he had a ton of different doorknobs lined up. He left the room for a few minutes and when he got back, he said, "Let's get busy. I hope you got a good look at the lock she wants you to open?"

"That one." I pointed to the one that most resembled her closet doorknob.

"Good. That's easy. Old school."

"I'll need to practice on all of them. She's thinking of having me try to break into the lab through some secret entrance, I think." I got another text from Stefan and deleted it.

"We don't have time for that, but let's start with the one we know you have to open." He went through the steps, and I marked them off on my mental diagram as he went. It took me four times to be able to manipulate the lock quickly enough to look like I knew what I was doing. In the forty-five minutes he kept me, he had me try two more locks—the hardest of the bunch. I thought I'd done really well until he said, "Now you just need to practice enough that you do it in at least half the time it took you to do these."

"Have any gadgets I might need if she does have me try and break into the lab tonight?"

He left the room and came back with a tube of Chapstick and all the other gadgets I'd already used. I put them all back on, and he explained that the Chapstick would change color if wiring were present.

"Any idea why they moved a bunch of stuff outside last night?" he asked. "They moved stuff throughout the party and into early morning."

"I was going to tell you about that. Sophia says her dad doesn't do anything without complete precision. Do you think the party was a cover for something else he was doing?"

"Could be. I'll check out your surveillance and see what we discover. Also, you don't need to worry about finger prints. They will come up with nothing unless we want them to come up with something. In that case, we'll make sure they get what we want them to get. Division 57 has complete control of them."

I hurried downstairs, and when I showed Sophia my bike, minus the front wheel, she screeched out like a child full of delight. She ran her right hand up the fork, over the handle bars, across the vivid black gas tank, down the cool leather seat, and off the rear fender as she slowly walked clockwise around the back of it, admiring its physique. "Sickening. You can't ride this sweet thing?" She looked at me with pure sympathy. "It's beautiful. Don't worry, we'll get you back on it. How much longer until you can ride?"

"My parents refuse to be nailed down. They say when I've shown responsibility for my life, they will return it to me. Maybe a few weeks."

"Whatever that means." Sophia said, "Do whatever it takes. And crap! Do your work would ya? It'll soften 'em."

"Says the girl who doesn't even have to make her own breakfast."

"That's all my mom. She loves high society crap. She'd love to be a queen of some country somewhere."

"Is she the one who forced you to be a concert pianist?" I snorted.

"No one forced me. You can't stand not knowing something, can you?"

I laughed. "You'll tell me when you're ready. I'm not worried." I wiggled my eyebrows at her.

We walked back into the kitchen, and I asked Tracey if we could go back to Sophia's to work on our physics project.

"Why can't you work on it here?"

"We could, but we left all our stuff there. Please?"

"Fine, but don't stay too late."

"I won't, Mom. Don't worry." For some strange reason I went up to her and gave her a kiss on the cheek. "You're the best."

When we got back to Sophia's house, her mom was

sitting at the dining table with a bunch of ladies having tea. She was completely made up, prim, proper, and perfect with a huge flowery hat.

We slinked past the society ladies, and up to Sophia's bedroom. She stared at me, then turned her eyes toward the closet expectantly. Now that I felt more confident in my abilities, I smirked at her, ready to show off. I opened it without a single hitch. "It's easy with the right tools," I said, even though now I could do it with a bobby pin, too.

"That's amazing, Ari. Teach me!"

I wondered if it would be wise, but I said, "Sure, come on over."

The tools were thin, delicate, and hard to handle at first. She quickly got bored of trying to do it, even though she got close a few times.

"Screw it!" she said. "Why do I need to be able to do it when I have you?"

I wanted to snap at her that she didn't *have* me, but held my tongue and smiled.

"I saw the coolest thing on the computer yesterday," Sophia said. "You've got to see it."

She took me to her page and pulled up some videos she'd tagged to her site. They were all laugh-out-loud funny. They were videos of pranks people pulled on others or just stupid things people did that were caught on camera by chance. She lost all pretenses while watching these. I liked this girl. My gut ached by the time she closed the page.

"It's four. Let's go see if we can find our way into the lab before the chef starts dinner. It'd be such a kick in the balls for my dad if we were able to get in there. We can't get caught, though. He would kill me, literally. You are good enough, right?"

"I think so. But I don't want to have a hand in your

death—or mine, for that matter." I wondered what the chef starting dinner had to do with finding our way, and I felt a hot rock land in my stomach. I couldn't guarantee we wouldn't be caught. In fact, it was almost certain we would.

"Follow me." She led me to the kitchen and then into the large pantry. A light popped on when we entered, and she shut the door behind us. She started pulling on shelves and tapping the back wall. Finally, she seemed to find what she was looking for. She pried opened a narrow panel in the wall with her fingers to reveal a dark stairwell. "It's still here." She looked around the pantry and grabbed a flashlight, turned it on, and started down the stairs. "Come on."

"Okay," I said. Now I was scared. This was real, and we were on our way to break into her dad's lab. This could go very wrong.

Chapter Twenty-Five

After shutting the false wall behind me, I stayed close to Sophia and held tight to the handrails in hopes I wouldn't fall down the steep, dark stairway. The air was stale and humid. The dankness of it made me breathe through my mouth. Spider webs hit me in the face over and over again. I hoped I didn't have spiders in my hair or on my clothes now. Relief flickered through me when we made it to the bottom. We were in a narrow hallway that had one tall, narrow door. I practiced some quick visualization exercises to edge away my claustrophobia.

She brought me to the door. "This is it." She touched the doorknob, dust flying into the air. No one had been in here in a long time.

"Wait," I said, touching her arm. "What if your dad wired it or something?"

"How can we tell?"

"Just let me look it over. Give me the flashlight."

She handed it to me, and I pulled out the Chapstick. I only had to wave it in front of the area I wanted to check to see if electricity was present. I opened the cap and, using the light from the flashlight, noticed that the color had changed from pink to green. I pretended to apply it to my lips. After replacing the Chapstick in my pocket, I said,

"It's definitely wired." That's when I saw the keypad hidden in the wall, barely visible.

"There's a keypad. Any ideas what the code might be?"

"None."

"I'll have to bypass it then." I took out my lock picking kit and set to work. Good thing I'd brought the full kit that included wire cutters and screwdrivers. I took the pad off the wall. Sophia held the flashlight for me. I looked at the wires and knew from Module 22.14 exactly which wires to cut and splice. My hands still shook a bit even though I'd done this very thing many times in my practical. That was practice, though. This was real. It meant life or death.

With that disabled, I ran my fingers along the wall, feeling for any other trip wires or booby traps. I found none. I was able to use my lock picking kit to open the door. It opened up into the back of a small, tall broom closet. Behind a mass of brooms, mops, and buckets lay a vented door, which I assumed led into the top-secret lab. I looked back at Sophia, squishing my eyebrows together. She pushed the cleaning implements aside and pulled me in with her. "Let's look through the vent and see who's out there." I slipped the kit back into my waistband under my shirt.

"Wait," I said, climbing out of the closet. "Let me put this all back in order, just in case someone comes down this way." I made it all appear to be the same as it was before I disabled it, minus the dust. We then squished together inside the closet, and peered through the vent.

Déjà vu hit me like a punch. The memory of the bathroom in DC crashed in on me. I felt a bit faint imagining, not the senator's aide, but Sophia and me dead through that vent. Then my eyes focused, and I saw no one. No one was in the lab. Sophia must have noticed at the same time, and she pushed the door open, hard. The door rebounded toward us, and I put my hand out to block it from slamming into Sophia. She stormed out.

"What is this?" Her hands flew above her head.

I shook my head in awe; it was as if the place had just been cleaned out of everything. The counters were devoid of anything but empty scales and burners, the beakers were sparkling clean, and the glass cabinets empty. No sign of use, only the smells of heavy cleaning lingered. The shining silver and glass sparkled as if new. The cavernous room was huge and our voices echoed over the bareness.

"This is the super-secret lab?" I whispered, won-dering what it could mean. The people in the backyard filled my mind. Had they cleared this out only last night, and I had missed my opportunity to gather any information? Were we too late? My heart raced as I wandered about the lab, trying to look aimless and attempting to locate signs of security measures. I couldn't even find a camera. An uneasy feeling crept over me.

"It's crap. That's what it is," Sophia raged. "Where is everything, everybody? Where are all my dad's secrets?"

I looked all around again. The only thing that caught my attention was a small, open brown box. The only possible clue I could get. I walked around, running my fingers over the ultra-clean surfaces, slowly making my way to the box. Sophia followed me in silence. My fingers slid across something wet. I pulled my fingers to my nose, a strong astringent smell stung my eyes and nose. This place had been recently disinfected. They *had* abandoned this site last night. I reached the box. Then the worst happened. The doors to our left swung open.

Eight guards with guns pointed right at us advanced in

a quick, SWAT-like swarm. They surrounded us, my hand sat still on the counter next to the box. Whatever was in there, I had to get it.

"Wait! Wait! I'm Sophia, Dr. Ramirez' daughter. Please. I'm sorry." Sophia said, turning in a circle. The doors swung open a second time, and the man I'd seen in photos and knew to be Sophia's dad, strode in. He looked more ominous than in his pictures. He wasn't only tall, he was ultra tall. Although his skin had a dark undertone, years of hiding out underground had given him a white, phantom-like appearance. I shrunk in his presence. A terrible, awful darkness filled my chest. I found it hard to breathe.

His eyes were fixed on his daughter. The soft, yet insistent swish of his feet hitting the floor, over and over again echoed around the room. I noticed Sophia's arrogant shoulders slump, but only a fraction. Then she lifted her head like she was forcing herself to. He had reached us and stood only inches from Sophia, whose face titled up toward her father's. She looked a shade lighter than normal, and I saw her hands shake before she clasped them together. Acid burned my stomach. It was horrible to see a father have this effect on his child. I wanted to run away and hide rather than witness this.

"Sophia Ramirez Martín. What is the significance of this?" Her father said, in Spanish, staring with a menacing gleam in his eye.

"We have a physics project and thought we could use your lab." She spoke in English. For my benefit?

He did not, however. "Por forzando la puerta?"

"The door was open," she lied. "Wasn't it, Ari?" She turned to me.

I could not hesitate. I nodded and thanked my lucky

stars I had put everything back the way I'd found it—
except, of course, the wiring. I could feel a burn up my
neck. I was not a good liar. I hoped he wouldn't search me.
He would find the lock pick kit without any effort, and
then he'd kill me for sure.

He sent the guards away with a flick of his wrist.
Something inside me kept yelling for me to get the box.
The box. I needed to get whatever was in it. My chest
burned. I had to get that box. I hesitated. After last night's
fiasco with the cup, I was afraid to use my illusionist skills.
I would have to be perfect. I could be perfect. I had to be
perfect or not do it. And right in front of her dad. I had to
get something out of this. I couldn't leave empty handed.
But what if I got the contents of the box and then he
searched me? Then again, what if the contents of that box
held the key to all this madness? Sweat ran down the back
of my neck and a surge of fear ran up my spine. This man
would not hesitate killing me if he saw me go for it.

Once the guards were gone, her dad filled the silence
with a horrible rant. He was focused on her and only her. It
was my chance, I could not waste it. The counter was bit
too high for a natural swipe. I watched father and daughter,
waiting for my moment. Dr. Ramirez was advancing on his
daughter, his face growing redder and spittle flying from
his mouth. They were practically nose to nose, and Sophia
turned her head to avoid his wrath. He grabbed her chin in
his hand and roughly turned her face back to his.

In that second, I swiped, dart-like, inserting my hand
into the box and getting hold of two plastic baggies that I
smoothly slid into my waistband. I had missed something
though, my fingernail had caught on a thick piece of paper,
but it remained in the box. I wanted it. I ignored Sophia's
cry of pain as her father's hand moved from her chin to her
upper arm. He gripped her harshly, and he still ranted in

Spanish. I reached again, but my fingers fumbled when Sophia dropped to her knees, her father twisting her arm behind her. The box dropped to the floor.

I leaned back onto the counter, giving the impression that I'd been recoiling from his actions to cover my mistake. His eyes, like lightning, flashed to the box, my eyes followed his gaze.

"Oh, I'm so sorry, I didn't mean to," I stuttered, reaching for the box and catching a glance of a picture of a German Shepherd dog before he snatched it away. It had been a picture that my fingers had grazed earlier.

"Was this your idea, Ari?" He spit this at me in English.

He knew my name? "Sir, I—"

"Dad!" Sophia cried out, standing back up. "I told you. I told Ari you had this cool lab, and that we should use it. Please." A tear slid down her cheek unchecked. The plea in her voice tore at me, and I noticed the red bruises on her arm from his grasp. I wondered if this mission was worth this.

His voice held steaming venom.

"This lab is off limits as it has always been. It was a mistake not to get rid of that exit ten years ago when you found it. I need you two to leave this minute." Sophia headed straight to the broom closet, and as I followed, I felt strangely soft, big hands grasp my upper arm with extreme force. "It would be wise of you to forget what you saw here today."

His lips barely moved as he threatened me, and I screeched out, "Yes, sir." The burn in my arm lingered clear until we reached her room where it started to throb.

With her face contorted in anger, fists balled at her sides, she said through her teeth, "This is your fault." She even stamped her foot.

I nodded and did what was natural for Christy to do. I

opened my arms wide and walked toward her. The anger in her face and eyes melted as she mouthed, without any sound, *I'm sorry*, and she flung herself onto the bed and sobbed.

I wasn't sure what I should do. A deep ache spread from my heart through my chest, and it created what felt like a ball of wax in my throat.

Her father held all the cards. He held back all affection from her, the only thing she longed for. This was the Sophia that looked out from the picture taken two years ago that I'd seen in her file, expectant, full of life, and hope. I didn't know how she would react, but I knew what I would want if I were her.

I lay beside her and wrapped my arms around her, hugging her tightly. She curled into me, accepting my solace. A deep warmth and pity filled me, thinking about this girl, just like me. All she wanted was to be loved. I wanted to take her pain away.

This girl needed someone. She needed me. And maybe I needed her. I stayed with her, not speaking, until the sobbing stopped and her breathing evened out. She was asleep. Wasn't she more important than the mission? I couldn't add to whatever sorrow she held, hidden in her past.

My first instinct was to stay, to be there when she woke to comfort her, but then I got this feeling that it wasn't the best thing for Sophia. She would need time to think about what had happened, how she'd reacted and how I'd reacted to her, as well as how she wished she had reacted. I wrote her a simple note,

I'm so sorry for everything. It was all my fault. I should have listened to you. Call me and we'll go to the gym. You can use me as a punching bag. -Ari

Chapter Twenty-Six

I poked my head into the security office by the front door and said, "I'm leaving, bye," and without waiting for a reply or a chance for him to fingerprint me, I flew out the front door. Even though we were neighbors, it was a good mile to get home, and after the front gate opened for me, I decided to run the distance. My shoes pinched at my feet, but I needed to get away, clear my head. If I'd had shorts and a tee on, I would have just kept running as fast and far as I could, to get rid of the regret, the pain, and the sadness that pressed on me.

Once home, not even winded, I met with Cory and Tracey at the kitchen table.

"The lab is gone," I said. "And we were caught. But, I was able to get this." I grabbed the two baggies from my waistband and threw them onto the table.

They both watched the baggies land and then said, "What?"

"Whatever they were doing in the lab is gone. It's been cleaned and sterilized. No workers, no experiments. I was too late. I'll bet they were using that party last night as cover to abandon the lab."

"I can't imagine how we tipped them off," Tracey said, picking up one of the small baggies and scrutinizing the contents.

"I don't think we did," I said. "Sophia said her dad actually planned the party last month. It's more likely he knew he'd be done with whatever he was working on and hitched the move onto the party. Chaos to hide his dirty deeds. Now we have nothing." I went to the sink and got a drink.

"It doesn't look like we have nothing," Tracey said, picking up the second baggie. "These look like something."

"The lab had been sterilized except for one brown box. Those were in that box, but I doubt it has anything to do with what we were looking for because at the bottom of the box was a picture of a German Shepherd."

"Interesting."

"Let's go downstairs and analyze this stuff," Tracey said. "This one looks like some sort of transmitter and receiver."

"Wait," I said. "What made Sophia turn into a bully, all mean and nasty?"

"Huh?" Cory said. "What are you talking about?"

"In Sophia's file, there were two pictures. Two years ago, she looked like a normal kid, but then she got all dark and angry. What happened?"

"We weren't briefed on that, so it must not be important," Tracey said.

"Not important? I just saw her dad grab her so hard a bruise formed almost immediately. Once we made it to her room, she was inconsolable. Sure, it must have been upsetting to have her dad treat her so terribly, but I got this feeling there was more to it." I didn't want to get into the fact that I felt it was my fault she got in trouble. I wanted to help her.

"That's not important to our mission. Forget about it. I will caution you now not to get too personally attached to Sophia or any other mark." Cory said. "What is important is what happened in the lab. You said you were caught. Tell us about it."

"We weren't in the lab two minutes before an army of guards descended on us, followed by her extremely angry dad. I'm going to ask Claire about what happened to Sophia," I said, standing and pulling out my cell. "It will help me accomplish my mission." Certainly my handler would know about Sophia's past.

I pushed in her number but got no answer. I left her a message to call, then, per protocol, I erased her number from the dialed list.

"Let it go, Ari," Tracey said. "You're getting too invested in Sophia's life. It's making you forget about the task at hand. We need to find out what the contents of these baggies are."

Both Cory and Tracey headed down the stairs to the basement lab. I thought it interesting that both our lab and the Ramirez lab were buried in the earth. A great place for secrets. I followed them down, wanting to learn from them.

By the time they pulled out the microscopes and Petri-dishes, I got a text from Sophia, *I'm coming to pick you up. I'm going to kick your sorry butt.*

I went upstairs to wait for her, leaving the spies to their toys.

She didn't mention what had happened the whole way into town. Once inside the gym, I let her get the better of me, although I made sure she didn't inflict too much damage. It was one of the best workouts I'd had since arriving in Prague, and we both taught each other something. After we finished pummeling each other, we shuffled exhausted to the locker rooms. I lingered a little long under the cold, stinging water, letting it prick my skin. The sensation distracted me and helped me avoid thoughts of all that had happened that day, especially the horrible image of Dr. Ramirez's hand on his daughter's arm.

Sophia drove me home, but instead of just dropping me off, she parked and looked down at the bike's wheel, suddenly shy. She seemed so vulnerable, so not like the Sophia I had known the past few weeks. I couldn't abandon her, so I invited her in.

Both Cory and Tracey were still in the abyss of the lab when we got to my house. When the alarm system alerted them that we had arrived, they texted me, letting me know they knew we were both there. After this day, I was exhausted and ready for bed.

"Do you think I might be able to spend the night?"

"Let me text my parents and ask."

My phone soon chimed with their response. "They said, yes." It was already midnight anyway.

She pulled out her phone, and I figured she was texting her mom.

"You want some pjs?"

"That'd be great. Why don't you just text him back?"

"Who back?"

"Stefan, of course," she said. "If you're not interested, in which case, you're crazy, then tell him. You should thank him, too."

"Fine," I said. "I will. And I'm not interested."

I texted him,

Thanks so much for taking care of me. I hope you didn't get the wrong idea. I'm really not looking for a relationship, but thanks for being so sweet. I'm happy to be your friend, though.

We didn't bring up the lab or what had happened with

her dad, and the funny thing was it wasn't awkward being with her. Besides Melanie, I'd never had a real friend. I wondered if this was what I'd missed out on my whole life.

Sunday morning came and went. I tried to wake Sophia around eight, but she didn't budge at first. When she finally sat up, I convinced her to run with me. On the counter lay a note from my parents saying they had to go into town and would be back at lunch. Tracey ended the note with a heart, the word love and then "Mom and Dad." I wondered if I'd ever again have the opportunity to have a note from my real parents. Would I ever be able to contact them?

While out running, we came upon a small, local church with stained-glass windows and a stone exterior. A few people trickled inside as we passed. I was itching to attend church, so I stopped and said, "We are about to go on an adventure."

She stopped. "I thought we already were." She grunted and gave me a dirty look before turning to run again.

I grabbed her arm before she could get far and said, "Let's go to church." I flicked my head toward the church we'd passed.

"No freaking way." She shrugged her arm out of my grasp.

"It'll be fun. Have you ever been to church here? In Prague I mean?"

"The last time I went to church was when my cousin Nila took communion. Church and I don't get along."

"Let's do it, just to say we did. Come on."

"You go right ahead. I'll wait for you out here."

"You're not afraid of a little church are you?"

"Of course not, but it's not for me. Like I said, go ahead. I'll wait."

"We'll only go in for ten minutes and then we'll

scram." I took her hand in mine and shook it saying, "Please. Please. Please. Just this once."

When she rolled her eyes, I knew I had her.

It ended up being a Protestant church with typical European styling. It loomed above us, the high, gray stone walls seemed to never end. The spire was tipped with a lacey, black, metal spiral. The carpet-free interior echoed with the sounds of the organ and we sat on one of the many empty wooden pews. It was the complete opposite of warm, inviting churches I'd attended growing up. Church obviously wasn't a priority here. I opened my mind up to discover new and exciting truths even though I couldn't understand what was being said. We stayed the whole hour, and Sophia never complained. She told me she was Catholic, but only attended Mass and the occasional special event. It turned out to be fun to compare the differences. It was a nice relief from yesterday—a time for peaceful reflection.

When we got back to my house, she asked me to go back to her house with her. I could tell she was a bit afraid of going home alone. Cory was in the kitchen making a sandwich when I went to ask him permission.

"Do you have any homework?" he asked me when I asked if I could go.

"Just some physics, but that won't take me long."

"Be back at four to do it, then."

"Okay."

When we got to Sophia's house, we hung out in her room, listening to music and flipping through magazines. Spring break was the hot theme. Our spring break started this coming Friday. We laughed about the short shorts and skirts all the models sported and mimicked girlie girls.

"Where are you going for spring break?" she asked.

"Nowhere as far as I know."

"I have to go to Spain."

"Spain sounds awesome! You act like it's punishment or something."

"Spain is great, but it's really only a work trip for my dad. He tries to disguise it as a family trip, but he'll be working at the ranch the whole time, and my mom will go to 'important' parties and meet with 'important' people and preen as much as possible...and leave me very much alone."

Sweet butterflies kissed my insides, but I forced out the obvious question, "What ranch?"

"My dad's first inventions were prosthetics for humans. He made the transmitters and receivers for the brain. You know, to make them smooth and completely on the down-low.

He got tired of that and turned the ranch into some nonprofit thing. Now he does prosthetics for animals. I hate it there. At least he only makes me go a couple times a year so he can check on stuff. He wants to continue to be the best. He's the bomb in the world of prosthetics. People from all over the world bring their animals to get fixed up by my dad's team. He even won a bunch of science awards and grants. Personally, I don't get it. Why spend all that money on a dog or cat? I mean I love 'em and all, but they are totally replaceable."

Something burned in my chest. This was important. "You could take me," I said, laughing. "I've never been to Spain." I needed to get to this ranch. My inner feelings urged me to make it happen.

She stared at me with a faraway look for a few seconds and then looked me straight on and said, "Would your parents let you go?"

"I think so. My dad said he was sorry we couldn't go anywhere this year. He has to work through spring break, and I think he feels guilty about it." Man, I was getting good at coming up with stuff. She got this huge grin on her face. "No guarantees, but I'll ask. They have to say yes, though. They've gotta see that if you come I won't constantly bug them about being bored."

The alarm on my phone went off. "Can you take me home?" It was four.

"Sure," she said. "We'll have so much fun together if this works out."

Chapter Twenty-Seven

Cory and Tracey seemed to be pacing in the kitchen when I got back. I raised my eyebrows, "What's up? You've worn a path in the wood in here."

"You'll never believe what those baggies you got from that box contained, Ari."

"What?" I said, taking a seat on a barstool.

Tracey hunched over the counter across from me and said, "Like I'd thought, there was a transmitter and a receiver in one. Tiny little buggers. They have an amazing range, too."

"Those little vials in the other bag were full of extremely powerful explosives," Cory said. "We had to break into the university's lab and use their equipment to figure it out."

"What?" I asked

"Exactly," Tracey said. "What are transmitters, receivers, and explosives doing in a box with a picture of a dog?"

"I think," I said, "the transmitters and receivers are for the prosthetics her dad uses at their ranch in Spain. As far as the explosives go, I can only guess, and I don't like where my guess leads me." I shuddered to think these animals carried explosives inside their bodies to be detonated at Diego's whim.

I told them everything I knew about the ranch and that Sophia was going to ask her parents if I could go with them when they went.

"Maybe he moved his lab there. It would make sense. He already has a facility there and it would be easy to conceal behind all his 'do-good' work."

"Great, Ari. We'll get hold of Claire to get more information on the ranch and hope you secure an invitation, then get a plan in place. We'll just have to hope Ramirez doesn't put two and two together and figure out that you took something from the lab. As always, be careful."

That night I dreamt of animals with hideous overly huge prosthetics being blown to bits. Finally, at four, I got up and worked out hard in our sparring room. My clothes dripped with sweat by the time I stopped at six. The fierce workout seemed to lessen the stiffness I felt after yesterday's workout with Sophia.

I got to school early to meet up with Sophia, but she didn't show for first period. I didn't have classes with her until after lunch. Raw pain shot through me. Would her dad hurt her worse? Had he discovered I'd taken the baggies? He was exact. I fretted until I found her at lunch, waiting for me by the cafeteria doors. When she ambled into physics, she looked haggard and tired.

"You getting sick?" I asked.

"Maybe. My body aches, but I'm not sure if it's because of our workout or if I'm coming down with something. I didn't want to miss the physics test today, I'd forget everything over spring break. And I wanted to fill you in on what my parents said about you going to the ranch with me."

"Why didn't you just text me?"

"My dad took my phone away."

"I'm so sorry," I said, knowing how vital her phone was to her life. We walked into the cafeteria as she continued to talk. No one else was around, yet she spoke in a whisper.

"They weren't so excited about it at first, but then I kept bringing it up, telling them how nice it would be not to be bored and stuff. I think they like the idea of being completely free of me while we're there." She tried to sound nonchalant as she said this, but I could hear the pain in her voice. "My dad said he'd check you out and if all was well, he'd let you come." She squealed.

I frowned.

"What is it?" Sophia said. "You're going to be able to come."

"He'll never let me go. He'll find out I have a record and won't let me near you."

"I hadn't thought of that. Maybe he won't find anything."

"If he runs a background check on me, he'll find it," I said, grimly.

"Let's hope he doesn't, then," she said, as Sven walked up to us. She instantly switched to the girl her crew called their leader: mean with a lack of self-control.

I quickly sent a text to Cory to ensure my background check wouldn't reveal anything it shouldn't.

Cory, Tracey, and I almost held our breaths over the next two days that it took for Sophia to tell me I had passed the background check.

Divison 57 (1) - Diego Ramirez (0)
Our scoreboard looked great. My team was winning.

I could feel the excitement in Sophia's texts. Right after I got them, she roared up on her Harley. I ran down the stairs, caught up in the thrill of it all, and opened the front door. At that same moment, Sophia rang the doorbell.

She squealed when she saw me and we hugged, jumping up and down in a circle. When we finally stopped, she said, "We're going to have so much fun!"

Tracey seemed to appear out of nowhere, just on cue. "Going to have so much fun doing what?"

"Mom," I said. "You totally have to let me go."

"Go where?"

"Sophia's family is going to Spain for a week, and they've invited me." I clasped my hands in front of my chest and said, "Please. Please. Please."

"I don't know," Tracey said. "That's a long way from here."

"We'd fly, Mom. And her parents will be with us the whole time. Please. I've always wanted to go there and you know it."

"I'll have to talk to your dad when he gets home."

"Are you for or against?" I said, moving closer to her.

"You will not be pitting us against each other, Ari. I'll also need to talk to your parents, Sophia."

"No problem," Sophia said.

"Can you call her now, Mom? Please?"

She called and got all the details, playing her part as concerned parent really well.

When she hung up, I yelled out, "So, can I, Mom, can I?"

"I told you I needed to talk to your father. Now that I have all the details, he shouldn't have any questions I can't answer."

"Thanks, Mom," I said, and Sophia and I ran, full of anticipation, up the stairs to my room. Of course, I knew what the outcome would be.

Claire, Tracey, Cory, and I had forty-eight hours to plan the op.

We talked over secure video cam. "It appears," Claire said, "that Dr. Ramirez has been operating a dark, dirty business behind his do-good-not-for-profit prosthetic ranch. He's been carrying out hits using the animals. We don't know at this point whether his research on DNA targeting has anything to do with it. Nonetheless, we must stop him from using those animals to hurt others. He could be using the animals to test his experiments with the DNA targeting. We just don't know."

"Your mission, Ari, will be to find the server, download its contents and get those contents safely to us. You will be extracted upon delivery. Cory and Tracey will go over the finer details of the mission. Do you have any questions for me?"

"Yes. About Sophia, what happened when she was younger that made her go all dark?"

"That's nothing you should worry about. It's not a necessary tidbit of information for this mission."

"But…"

"No buts. Stay on task."

It must have been bad if they didn't want to tell me. Cory, Tracey, and I spent the next day and a half going over our coding system for messages, where the extraction point would be, how to use the designated drop off points as well as other things I might need to know while there. Even though I felt a bit unprepared, I felt a thrill go through me thinking of the mission ahead of me.

Chapter Twenty-Eight

My world was getting bigger. I stood in the room Sophia and I would be sharing for the week, looking out the window to the vast expanse of land behind the Ramirez' modest ranch house in Spain, while Sophia unpacked her plethora of clothes and shoes.

Outbuildings surrounded a huge inner, grassy courtyard that was sectioned off into smaller, yet still large corrals and cages, containing a different kind of animal in each: horses, cows, dogs, foxes, wolves, and even elephants. They could charge admission and be the world's best petting zoo.

My mind wandered to the contents of the brown box in the lab in Prague, and a shiver snaked up my spine. Did every one of those animals have something besides the relay and prosthetic implanted? Were they all ticking time bombs?

Just as I'd discovered several guards with large guns strapped to their arms, roaming the compound, Sophia tapped my shoulder, and I jumped, making her jump.

"A little high strung, Ari?" She moved to the window and looked out, too.

"All those animals out there have prosthetics?"

"Yep."

"But they aren't limping or walking weird or anything."

"The animals out here are close to going home. They've been through rehab already. All those buildings out there house animals in different stages of recovery. The first building on your left is the hospital where the surgeries are performed. As the animals improve, they're moved through the other nineteen outbuildings. My dad's goal is to have each animal leave better than they've ever been. His human technology is amazing, too. He won this world-wide award for his work. After he won that award is when I started to notice a big difference in him. Nothing mattered but his next invention or discovery."

I couldn't believe she was bringing up her mad scientist dad again.

"I was so proud of him when he turned this into a nonprofit organization. If I didn't know he had that kind of goodness in him, I'd have to hate him." Sophia seemed to be looking in one spot, far off in the distance.

We stood in silence, looking out at the masses of animals for several beats. I figured it was probably best if I didn't say anything about her dad and bring us back to the animals.

"I didn't know prosthetics for animals even existed."

"Yeah. It's kinda one of those things that you don't take notice of unless you need it."

We made our way downstairs, with Sophia calling out the particulars of the house. Four rooms upstairs: ours, a large master suite where her parents slept, a bathroom, and a study. The main floor held a large family and dining area with an extra-long table. I ran my fingers along four of the twenty wooden chairs surrounding it. I tried to imagine Sophia's mom feeding the ranch hands three times a day, but couldn't manage it. A man stocked the refrigerator and it surprised me to find Anje, the family's personal chef, at the huge, industrial stove, filling the room with amazing smells.

"My mom refuses to come here without Anje. She hates it here. My dad always bribes her with cool stuff to come. I, on the other hand, get nothing."

I could imagine that her mother hated it because it was a clear reminder of where she'd came from. The simplicity and downright plainness of the house shocked and surprised me. Why hadn't they ever updated it? It was so unlike their new home in Prague. Sophia explained that they had moved right after winning the prize into a beautiful home on the ocean. We would be heading over there once her dad was finished with his work here. I decided this portion of the vacation was basically camping for the rich. The house remained empty while they were away, and it held an odd musty smell that someone had tried to cover up with a sweet floral scent.

"Can we play with the animals?" I asked, wanting to get a closer look.

"Sure. I could probably even finagle us into one of the surgeries they'll be doing this week if you want."

"Sounds good," I said, not really wanting to watch a surgery, but at the same time knowing it would get me into the building I guessed held all the files for the animals. My new mission was fourfold. I was to find the records for the animals, who their owners were, what implants were used in each animal, and who ordered the hit, if anyone did. I hoped the records were all on a central database in the surgery unit.

Sophia bounded out of the room, down the stairs and out of the house. She went straight for the pen full of dogs.

I was immediately drawn to a friendly, snow white, great Pyrenees. It was a regal looking creature that didn't seem to judge me. It acted like a puppy, bounding around. I looked him over and couldn't discover where his implant was. He seemed completely normal. His tag read *Indie*, and he responded to the name readily.

Sophia went straight to a mutt of some sort that cowered in the corner of the corral. I brought Indie over. His kind, playful disposition got the mutt to play around.

We stayed with them until Sophia got a text telling her to get ready for dinner.

Once upstairs, she headed for the bathroom. "I get to shower first," she announced.

"I thought it was time to eat."

"We have to 'get ready' for dinner when we're here. My mom likes us to dress up like we're at dinner with royalty. It's nuts, but it makes her happy, and according to my dad, I don't have a choice." She went to her closet and pulled out a pink dress with a hoop. I raised my eyebrows unable to imagine rough and tumble Sophia in that dress.

"I didn't bring a fancy dress, Sophia." Who would have ever guessed I'd need one?

"No problem, just pick one from my closet. There's a ton."

I shuffled through the dresses and picked a light blue one. I snorted. The idea of dressing up in a place like this was absurd. I wondered what I would look like, hair spiked, heavily pierced, in a ball gown.

Once she was done showering, I jumped in. We finished getting ready in no time, and we looked remarkable. My dark, spiked hair and piercings really made for a striking appearance. She picked me some tall, amazing shoes. We slid down the wooden staircase like only princesses being introduced at a ball could. Her dad, straight backed and stern looking and her mom, eyes shining, were already seated at the table and stared at us the whole way down, like we were the real thing, and not biker chicks masquerading as princesses. Classical music played softly in the background. I had to resist the urge to laugh.

Dinner was quite the production, and her dad sighed heavily several times during it. I thought their family chef would be serving us, but he didn't. Four waiters in stiffly starched white uniforms hustled about making sure we received all seven courses in a timely manner. No one thanked them or even acknowledged their presence. Her mom talked reverently about a woman's society in the neighborhood and about a few classic novels she'd read lately. Her dad made sounds of acknowledgement but didn't contribute much to the conversation. He was not enjoying this. Sophia only spoke when her mother asked her a direct question.

I watched out the window as the animals were gathered up and presumably taken back to their kennels inside. Once we were excused, we went straight up to her room. I needed to get a layout of the area surrounding the ranch and physically locate my extraction point. I knew exactly where it was on the map, but I needed to see what it took to get there.

"Want to go for a run?" I asked. I pulled out my workout clothes and started to exchange them for my princess dress.

"Really? We're on vacation, and you want to run?" Sophia complained.

"I can feel that rich food sticking to my thighs already. Come on. It'll be fun."

"Fine! But I get to choose what we do next."
"No problem," I said.

Before running through the front gate, we had to check in with the guard on duty. He pretty much waved us past without much of a glance. Then we put our iPods in. The coastal plain of northern Spain was forested but in a different way than Florida or Belgium. The ground was sandy and most trees were not pine, but tall, sparse, leafy ones. We had to avoid the scraggly juniper bushes that speckled the forest floor, which wasn't hard at the pace we were running. I took my time so that I could memorize the topography.

I kept Sophia running longer than she wanted to in hopes she wouldn't want to come with me again. That way, I could explore on my own and find possible hiding places as well as various routes. Sophia was so competitive she didn't want to be the one to say to go back even though I could tell she was past her limit. After pushing it hard for forty-five minutes, I just turned and headed back. I could tell she was relieved because she sighed.

Sophia's choice for our next activity? A guitar game. She kicked my butt.

"Now we're even. You kicked my butt on the run, and I kicked yours with that game. Which is actually cool," she said, smugly.

After a big bowl of ice cream, we chatted and laughed until neither one of us could keep our eyes open. We'd never know who fell asleep first. When I woke at five, I pushed on her arm and asked if she wanted to run with me.

"What time is it, four in the morning?" She slung out a list of curse words.

"No, five."

"Forget it. You're on your own." *Perfect!*

I thought the ranch would be silent and empty like it was last night when we left, but it was already bustling with activity. Some of the animals were corralled outside, and workers were everywhere, cleaning corrals, bringing in hay and straw and other things. I checked out at the guard shack and took off at full speed.

The spy watch Ms. Mackley had given me acted as a GPS for the two miles to the extraction point, and I tried to follow the directions straight there. It was impossible, and I had to weave around all sorts of forest vegetation. It felt great to run up and down the hills in the area. After making it to the little valley where the helicopter was supposed to be waiting for me when it was time to be extracted, I searched the area, memorizing everything I saw.

I made my way back slowly, taking in all the fresh, clean air and looking for hiding places as well as locating a drop off spot at the base of a tree about half-way through the trek.

When I got back at seven, the guard patted me down. I tried not to feel violated. There would be no smuggling things in after a run. Sophia was still in bed, and I wished I'd stayed out longer. The dogs were already outside in the corral, so I went to play with Indie. Sophia joined me about nine asking if I was hungry and telling me there was a surgery at eleven we could watch.

Breakfast was served without ceremony. Mrs. Ramirez was already gone for the day to an early tea with some wealthy locals.

Sophia took me on a tour of the grounds. We went backwards, starting at Building 20 and moving up to the biggest building, Building 1, the surgical center. Each of the twenty buildings had an identical lobby, complete with two uncomfortable chairs for visitors, a desk with a receptionist and two doors leading away from the lobby. Pictures of cute, furry animals hung tastefully on the walls, and the brown tile floors made the room feel clinical. I took note of the camera, which was trained on the doors that led to whatever lay beyond the lobby. The doors were all double secure, requiring a card and a pass code.

"I'll take you into the back rooms later if you want," Sophia said. "We just don't have time right now. Not if we want to watch the operation."

When we arrived at Building 1, we had to grab white lab coats from a rack just inside the lobby. A free-standing coat rack was nestled in the corner with colored lab coats hanging on its racks and rubber boots sitting around it on the ground. I watched carefully as the receptionist swiped her card, and then keyed in her code to let us in one of two doors that led out of the lobby and into the back rooms. We went through the one on the right. Directly after entering, we went up a skinny flight of stairs that led to a balcony where we could watch the surgery below.

I watched, trying to hide my disgust as they put a prosthetic eye into a golden retriever. I had to concentrate hard not to puke. When I thought of prosthetics, I thought of the limbs of animals and humans, not eyes.

When done, the eye moved all around as the man at the computer typed in different commands. It looked eerily real.

When the surgery was over and we'd descended the stairs, I asked her to take me through the rest of the place. We walked down the wide hallway, eight doors led to operation rooms and then the hallway ended.

Back in the lobby, I asked about the door to the left.

Sophia said, "You don't want to go in there. There's

nothing to see. It's just the records room, right, Mattie?" She addressed the receptionist.

"You got it, Sophia," she said. "Nothing to see but files and more files."

That was exactly what I wanted to see, but I didn't dare ask. I'd have to break in and see for myself. I'd been amazed that no cameras seemed to be anywhere, but as I exited the door, I saw two, sitting above it, one pointed at the door on the right, and one at the door on the left. It would be a challenge to get in there. I had worn my picture taking necklace, and at the last moment before exiting the room, I turned and snapped a picture of the view toward the door on the left.

We had just enough time to visit four of the buildings' back rooms before having to head in to get ready for our second royal dinner at the ranch.

Chapter Twenty-Nine

Later that night, we played the guitar game again and sang a bit of terrible karaoke before heading up to the room.

"Did you have a boyfriend back home?" Sophia asked.

I almost said yes, but then thought better of it. Something in my gut told me it would be better if I pretended to never have had a boyfriend.

"No," I laughed a bit. "Boys and I have never really mixed."

"I don't know why not," Sophia said, twisting her hair around her finger.

"How did you snag Sven?" I asked. "He seems like the nicest guy at the school."

"Actually," she said, "when I got to this school two years ago, he was the hottest guy around. All the girls were talking about him. I decided I wanted to own him, so they couldn't."

"That's cold, Sophia," I said. "You don't care about him at all?"

"I didn't say that," she said. "I do care about him. Probably not like he cares about me, but, oh well."

"Can I tell you a secret?" I felt all fuzzy inside, wondering if I was doing the right thing.

289

"Of course."

"Never mind," I said, unable to work up the courage.

"Go ahead. I'll never tell a soul. I promise."

"Promise?"

"I just said I did."

"I used to be a nerdy-geek. That's why I've never had a boyfriend."

She raised her eyebrows. "And..."

I slugged her. "I'm telling you something painful and you're not taking me seriously."

She rubbed her arm and then said, "I just meant, big deal. Everyone was a nerd once."

"No I was *the* nerd of the school. The girl that got teased and taunted and put into lockers and tripped and all that. That's why I'm at the Academy. It had nothing to do with my breaking and entering hobby."

"My parents put me in all kinds of martial arts classes," I continued, "and bought me that Harley to try and toughen me up. I just started tanking in school because I didn't want to be there anymore. I had enough credits to graduate last year, so I just decided to make them look bad. I was really good at it, too."

"I could tell you were smart that first day. That's one of the reasons I wanted you to be a part of my crew," Sophia said.

"I used to have long beautiful hair and perfect skin and perfect grades, so I gave them the opposite." I was hoping Sophia had experienced this same thing. So far, I hadn't seen that reaction in her. Maybe I was dead wrong about her.

"You go girl!" Sophia playfully punched me. I couldn't stop now.

"I finally let the bullies have it. I didn't even know who

I was anymore, and I didn't care. I had turned into the people I hated. Deep down I'm really a good girl, but I've found being a good girl makes others see you as weak and they prey on you. I will not be preyed on. At least as a tough girl, everyone left me alone. That didn't happen here. It brought *you* running to me."

"Hah!" Sophia said. "You were running away from the very thing I wanted you to be a part of. I guess I saw something of me in you."

It had worked to a degree. At least I'd brought out the soft side of her. I wanted more. "I think I saw me in you, too."

She smiled.

From different types of bullies to science geeks, cheerleaders to jocks, we talked about all of them and how they affected us. We laughed a lot about it even though the pain was still so raw.

She massaged her wrists when we hit a quiet moment.

"Did you hurt yourself?" I asked. "Too much piano?"

She moved them behind her back. "You could say that." She said it sharply, a sour note to the tone.

"Let me see." I thought of the scars I'd seen that first day.

"No."

"Fine. I won't pry."

She then inexplicably held them out to me. I couldn't pretend I didn't see the raised white scars on her wrists. She then said, "You weren't supposed to notice. It's a past I've forgotten, buried. A time when my mom loved me because I wore frilly dresses and displayed perfect behavior. Now she despises me. I embarrass her. I'll never be like that. I'm going to be a rocking mother and grandma."

I was surprised to hear her talk like that. She wanted to have children and grandchildren. I nodded. "Me, too. My kids will love me. I'll be their friend." Maybe it was hard to believe because she had had no good examples in her life. I guess it was her innate desire. I'd never entertained the thought of her being a mom or having such an aspiration.

"I agree," Sophia said. "You have to be able to tell your mom everything. I can't tell my mom anything. Not anything real, anyway."

"I don't understand why you quit. Piano, I mean." I couldn't very well ask her why she turned into a mean, Goth bully. "It sounds like a wonderful world." Right after saying it, I wanted to take it back. I'm sure I sounded stupid.

"My mom hooked me up with a duet partner. He trashed me."

I brushed my fingers over the raised scars from cuts meant to end her life. "Is that why you cut yourself? Over him?" I knew she wasn't a cutter, but I thought making it sound like I hadn't immediately jumped to suicide would win me some points.

She yanked her hands away. "I'm not a cutter." Her face flushed. I could see a deep hurt in her eyes.

"I'm sorry, but I don't get it. Suicide? You don't seem the type."

"Is there a type?"

All the information in my brain's file cabinets on suicide popped to the front of my mind. "Well, actually—"

"Look, I had my reasons."

This was important. I had to find out why. I didn't want to ever bring it up again. But she was obviously already back to that time, in a type of trance, like the seconds I hesitated gave her the opportunity to relive whatever horror happened to her.

"I didn't mean to hurt him," she said, "but my parents wigged out anyway when we had to go to court. It was so bad. After I got out of juvie, I thought I'd much rather not be around. I hated how my parents looked at me.

"You know what the worst part of that is? He deserved every last burn, cut, and torture I put him through. The first couple of weeks after it happened, I felt that I somehow deserved what he did to me, that it was my fault. I was so stupid."

Oh my gosh, was she raped?

"And then, I saw him, in town, laughing with his friends and something broke inside me. It wasn't right that I was all torn up, and he was laughing. Laughing. There was no way I would allow that. I had to make him pay."

"Why didn't he end up in jail?"

"I never told anyone what happened."

"Why didn't you just—no judging here, I mean I've never been a rape victim before. I just don't understand why you didn't go to the hospital—" I was hoping she'd correct me and tell me she wasn't raped, but she cut me off instead.

"Get a rape kit done? I'd just been raped. I didn't want to be raped again. And if you haven't noticed, I'm a bit of a tough girl inside. It didn't even cross my mind. Of course, I know now I should have.

"Even after doing what I did to him, there was no peace. Maybe sending him to jail would have been better, but his family was wealthy. He probably would have found a way out of it somehow. There is no justice for what he did to me anyway. Maybe if I'd allowed them to test me," she said, as if in a dream. "I wonder sometimes how I'd feel if I'd only killed him. Would I feel better now? I wanted him to suffer—a life with a mangled face and body, but…"

"Maybe he does suffer," I offered. "People who hurt others tend to. Maybe you just can't see his suffering."

"Yeah," she said, as if she hadn't heard me. "Maybe if I'd killed the freak, I'd feel differently, because while torturing him gave me quite the satisfaction at the time, it was short lived. Maybe having him stuck in jail would have been more satisfying."

"I'm so sorry." I truly felt for her, and here I was ready to take down her father—ruin him, the effects of which would trickle, no gush, down to her. What would it do to her to know her father created things that killed people?

"I don't know why I'm telling you all this. I've never told a soul. Not even my mom."

"That's simple," I said, trying to play it down. "It's because you know I'll keep my mouth shut, and I won't judge."

She nodded, little short, quick nods.

I was glad I'd shared a secret with her even if a great deal of it was made up. It got her to open up to me. Perhaps it would help her heal a little.

Chapter Thirty

After my morning run, I talked Sophia into sparring with me. She showed me some moves, and I showed her some. I was faster than she was, stronger and smarter, so I dumbed it all down quite a bit. Point, Ari.

I asked her to show me some easy Latin dances. I couldn't keep up with her. She was amazing. Point, Sophia.

We played with the animals after lunch until we were called in for dinner. We watched a few movies and then made our way up to our room, exhausted. We talked for a while about what makes a great guy and who would make the perfect man to marry. All I could think of was Reese. It was hard not to tell her about him. Then she got a text from her mom telling her to be ready at ten to go into town to shop in the morning. The conversation changed to shopping at that point.

"I thought you'd hate shopping," I said.

"Every hot-blooded female loves to shop. We just don't like to shop at the same places." She went on to tell me about the cool shops she hoped we could go to in the morning.

I woke at five, like usual. I ran fast. It felt good to stretch my lungs and muscles to their limit. Once I got to the drop-off location, I bent to act like I needed to tie my shoe just in case I'd been followed. Quick as lightning, I tucked the necklace and a note in a hole of the tree near the ground for Claire. The naked eye would never have caught the sly movement. In the note, I informed her that I would be in Bilbao and needed some hardware that would allow me to break into the building where they operated on the animals. The necklace would give her the information she needed to know what would work best to accomplish that.

When I got back from the run, Sophia was up and showered. "How was your run?"

"Great. How long until we leave?"

She consulted her watch and then said, "About a half hour."

"I'll hurry and shower then."

It took two hours to drive to Bilboa. We visited the Guggenheim Museum, which was amazing and then the old town, Casco Viejo. It smacked of cramped medieval times. I needed some air. Finally, we headed for lunch in the newer, posh area of Bilboa, El Ensanche, where both her mom and Sophia were excited to go shopping.

I got a text marked *urgent* and was to meet up with Claire around lunch. I texted her once I knew which restaurant we'd be eating at. Just as we sat down at our table, my phone rang. It was Claire. "Excuse me, it's my dad." I got up from the table and went outside. As per her instructions, I met up with her just around the corner of the restaurant.

"You have a new directive," she said, shoving a small shopping bag into my hands. "We have intel that an important buy is going down in two days. That means you must retrieve the information Thursday, not Saturday."

That was two days early. Did I know everything I needed to know to accomplish it?

"The bracelet in the bag is a second jump drive.

Download a second copy if possible. Under the jewelry box is an electronic device, a looper, that you can hook to the camera and it will cause it to loop until you remove it. Whatever the camera sees the second you attach it will be what is fixed on the screen security. It will be blind to you. There is also a jammer in there. It will prevent security from knowing when you open doors. Just clip it on your clothes somewhere. It has to be close to the lock to work."

I'd read about these devices and was excited to use them.

"Your extraction will be at five-twenty a.m. Thursday morning."

"I thought I was just going to drop the information off. I don't want to just disappear on Sophia."

"What are you talking about?" She grabbed her glasses between her thumb and forefinger, tipping them down and looking at me over them.

"If I disappear, she'll know I was up to no good. I can't abandon her. She can never know I did this."

"It will be too dangerous for you to stay. They will discover the security breach the next day. You must be extracted." She pushed the glasses back onto her nose.

"But she's my friend." I shifted my weight from one leg to the other.

"She's your mark, nothing more. You can't truly befriend anyone in this business, Ari. She'll find someone else. Sympathy makes you sloppy. You don't want to be sloppy, do you?"

"What if I do the drop and then later that morning Cory calls and tells me I have to get home for whatever reason and I leave then?"

"What is wrong with you? You must fulfill your mission. You can't befriend your mark."

"You told me to."

"That was spy talk. You weren't supposed to create a true bond with her."

I knew this, but it just happened.

"She needs me."

"And you need her for two more days and then you are done. Let it go."

My mind reeled. "I will not be extracted. She has had such a hard life. I—"

"You will be extracted at five-twenty, or you won't be extracted at all."

"But I—"

"Get back." She cut me off and turned to go.

I put the phone back up to my ear and walked back to the front of the restaurant and paced for a few more minutes, fighting back the tears I felt pricking my eyes thinking about how hurt Sophia was going to be when she learned of my betrayal. How could I openly betray her? She'd ended up being such a good friend.

After we ate, we shopped until our feet ached. Posh, modern stores lined the streets in this section of town. I tried and tried to come up with a solution to my problem. How could I disappear after stealing all her dad's information and not hurt her? We both slept in the car on the way home.

Even though my mind kept returning to a plan to spare Sophia's feelings, I was able to finalize the plans for my reconnaissance mission into the surgical center as I lay in bed waiting for two o'clock to roll around.

If the computer was there, I intended to complete the mission then and there. That way I could stay an extra day and set up a ruse for me to leave early the next day without hurting Sophia. I would cover my tracks by going to Building 12 to try and visit Indie. I made sure the cameras would pick me up, and I even pulled on the door, knowing it was locked. Then I wandered around all the buildings whistling and dancing a bit. When I got to Building 1, I went to the side and sat on a bench.

I carefully skirted the cameras and hid in the shadows to get to the front door, manipulated the lock and keypad, and attached the looper to the camera before entering. I checked to make sure the jammer was still attached to me. Then I rewired the keypad to open the inside door for me and slipped inside the room. A room full of TV monitors with images on them and filing cabinets looked back at me. I was shocked at what I saw. I whipped around in a circle, making sure I hadn't entered the security center of the ranch.

Once certain I was in the right place, I ran to the files, looking for Indie's name. Only medical information was located in these files. No owners' names and no information on the implanted devices besides identifying numbers. A dead end.

I took a quick look at the monitors. Some of the pictures showed blank walls, some carpets, bars, peoples' faces and other crazy things at crazy angles. Some of the monitors showed movement. Others were static. I went back to the one with bars. Was that the inside of the kennels? I moved along, looking at each monitor. Did the animals have cameras in their eyes? The gravity of the situation sunk deep. Not only were prosthetics being put into these animals, they were being used for surveillance. This way they could easily target exactly what or who they wanted with these animals.

I stared hard at the pictures before me and suddenly,

one picture seemed to explode on one of the monitors. I shrieked. I couldn't help myself. A dog was with his owner and the owner was petting it. Then the picture shook like an earthquake, stuff flew all over and then a blank screen. It all happened in a single second. I clamped my hands over my mouth. Disgust filled me, and fury, too. I thought about all the hundreds of animals in the corrals. Were they all ticking time bombs? Had that many people hired Diego to do terrible things to others? I stood there in shock for a very long time.

Those poor people who loved their pets so much they sent them to get prosthetics at a huge cost and what did they get? They end up being watched by these guys and perhaps even blown up. Complete violation. And I hated to think it, but it made sense that Diego would have orchestrated the injury to the animals so that they ended up needing the prosthetic in the first place.

What was I doing in here still? There were no computers anywhere, only files that gave us nothing and video feeds that gave us some things, but no way to transfer them to the drives. Where would the mainframe be? I had to stop this man.

I slinked out of the room, careful to keep everything the way I'd found it. I took a deep breath once in the lobby. I headed for the front door. I heard someone whistling outside and froze. The doorknob jiggled slightly. I had to hide. The desk was out—what if the person wanted to sit in it? The only place possible, and it was a terrible hiding place, was behind the coat rack. I slid in behind it, pushing the rubber boots in front of my feet and tugging on the lab coats to cover me as much as possible. Just as the door swung open, one of the lab coats I'd pulled to cover me, fell to the floor at my feet. I couldn't help it. I sucked in a breath and shifted more into the corner.

The man walked past me to the room I'd just left. I heard the door click open and after a short pause, I felt the lab coat that pooled at my feet being picked up and hung, right in front of me. I refused to let my body breathe. I kept my mouth closed. This guy had been so close to me. Most of me was still covered by hanging lab coats and boots, but still. He'd almost touched me. Was he just tired or preoccupied? Attention to detail, this guy. But then the door to the files and monitors clicked shut. I stayed still, listening for signs of movement within the room.

When satisfied I was alone, I crawled on the floor. Once I reached the door, I stood, grabbed the looper from the camera and opened the door, skirting around to the side of the building and sitting down on the bench there, relieved to be out. I sank down. I should have been rejoicing, but instead, I put my head between my knees and my hands over the back of my head and breathed deeply. The animals were being used as weapons. My Indie was most likely being used as a weapon, and he didn't have a chance. He was scheduled to go home next week. I wanted to scream out as the horror of it gripped me.

Cold hands grabbed mine and yanked me up. A man spoke to me in loud Spanish. A guard. His camo uniform was freshly starched and ironed and his thin curly mustache moved freely when he spoke. His tanned skin made the whites of his eyes and teeth seem to glow in the dark.

"No entiendo. No entiendo," I cried out, the bones in my wrists knocking against each other as he gripped them.

He dragged me into the guard shack by the main gate. He spoke to the man who sat monitoring the many TV screens all over the walls, who in turn, spoke into a com. Ten minutes later, none other than Diego Ramirez walked into the shack, dressed as if he'd never gone to bed.

"Once again, Ari Agave." His eyes pierced into me, and the temperature dropped at least ten degrees. His look was rabid. "What am I to do with you? You can't seem to stay where you're supposed to. Always snooping around."

"Sir," I said, knowing I was in deep trouble. "I couldn't sleep and thought I'd go visit Indie and keep her company."

"Indie?"

"The Great Pyrenees. She's so sweet."

He shook his head. "What are you talking about? Are you telling me you came out here to play with a dog at two a.m.?"

"Yes sir." I hung my head.

"I don't believe you. Sit." He motioned to a chair behind me.

I didn't hesitate. I sat.

He spoke in Spanish with the guards, and they all looked at monitors. The guard pulled up various pictures of me walking the grounds.

"How did you know where they kept him?" Diego said.

"I saw them take him into Building 6 last night at dinner. I guess I didn't think you'd lock the doors at night."

Luckily, the tapes showed me going there. "The door was locked, and I thought I'd just sit on that bench instead of going back in."

"Were you trying to break in?"

"No sir."

"Your history tells me you like to break into places."

I figured I better act like someone who liked to do that since he was expecting that.

"I won't lie. I totally wanted to, but I thought better of

it. I didn't want to get into trouble."

"Good choice." Diego said.

"We had so much fun together. I don't know. I guess I was being stupid to think you wouldn't lock it."

His eyes still held suspicion, but the anger seemed to have dissipated somewhat. He must be resigning himself to the fact that I was just a stupid girl who wanted to play with a stupid dog because she couldn't sleep.

"Just go back to the house," Diego said. "Don't leave it at night. Don't you know how dangerous it is here? Thieves, villains, and murderers are all about us."

I couldn't help but think that all of those things stood directly in front of me. "Maybe he could stay in my room. I could give him lots of love." I added, thinking it helped my cover.

"No. It cannot stay with you. It's a patient here."

Had Diego just called Indie an *it*?

Any normal person might need to do that to separate himself from the horrors of what he was doing, but not Diego. He truly thought of them as things. Things he could easily destroy with no remorse whatsoever. I decided he was pure evil.

"I expect you to forget it was here," he continued. "A lot of high profile people have animals here. They expect discretion. No blabbing to everyone about it." He said a few more things to the guards in Spanish and ushered me back to the house.

The President of the U.S. popped into my mind as we walked. He had just gotten a dog before I left the States. The token White House dog. Certainly there wasn't a bomb or disease or camera in that dog already. They had made a big deal of the fact that they picked the dog from a local shelter. There was no way they could have known which dog the President was going to choose. *Was there?*

"Because you are with my daughter, I will let you off the hook this one time," he said as we entered the house. "This is a research facility and I can't have you messing stuff up. I must insist you stay with my daughter while at the ranch. *Entiendes?*"

"Sí," I said, gulping and acting compliant.

I sent a coded message to Tracey and Cory the second I got into the bedroom to see if they had any ideas where the computer mainframe would be.

They texted back within five minutes telling me they were getting a huge power reading from upstairs in the parents' room and to check it out. Yeah, sure, I'd just go check it out. I decided it must be in there. Tomorrow night I would get the information Division 57 needed.

Chapter Thirty-One

Sophia and I went hiking early the next morning. Anje packed us a lunch, and Sophia found us some packs full of gear we might need. We laughed and talked the whole time, not a minute passed in awkward silence. We returned before dinner, but her mom and dad were not there, so Anje made us pizza. We popped popcorn and watched sappy romantic movies until we couldn't take it any longer and jumped into bed.

Sophia fell asleep at about midnight. I waited until two and then slipped into the hall bathroom and pulled on what I called my sneak-suit. It was all black, hugged my body and had a hood and footies. With my almost bare feet, I'd best be able to tell if there was a weakness in the floor that might squeak and give me away. I put the necklace and bracelet on and then the barrettes that went together to create a jump drive in my hair. I slipped my lock picking kit down the front of my outfit.

I stood outside the door to Sophia's parents' room for what seemed like ages. So many things could go wrong. What if the jammer didn't work? How could I explain myself? I couldn't. What if they woke up when I was in their room? I would be a dead duck. I couldn't fail. That was all there was to it. I had to be flawless.

305

It was now or never. I slowly, carefully, calculatingly turned the knob on one of the French doors leading into her parents' room. I pushed the door into the room, inch by inch, with not a sound. It was no time to rush. When no one stirred and it appeared the jammer had worked, I took a silent step into the room. I pushed the door, inch by inch until it almost shut. I could hear the breathing of two separate people, and I wanted to take a deep breath, too but knew I couldn't.

I slinked on tiptoe along the wall, coming to a closet door. Could this be it? I listened for a hum. There was none, so I passed it up to check the next door. It was open slightly. The bathroom. After passing it, I came upon another door in the room. I heard a barely audible hum coming from it. It looked like Diego's closet. It was filled with men's clothes and shoes. I shifted the clothes to the side, revealing a large area behind them. On a table sat what must have been the ranch's mainframe. It was large and had a lot of blinking lights and slots of varying sizes. Missing were the keyboard and monitor. I didn't need that, however. These jump drives were programmed to force the mainframe to give up its contents.

I moved toward it, knelt down, and felt for the spot that would entertain the jump drives. Finding it, I quickly put the bracelet drive into the machine. The encoded drive set the machine in motion, dumping all its contents onto the drive. Even with its express dumping coding, it took one hour.

I was tired, but sleep never overtook me. I was too scared. The second dump only took forty-five minutes. Relieved to have it done, I stood and stretched. Division 57 expected me at the extraction point at five a.m. I planned to leave under the guise of running for exercise, like I had the last two days we'd been there. It seemed like the perfect plan and so far everything was moving along as smooth as butter. It was only two miles to the extraction point. I could easily make that in a quarter of an hour. With these thoughts on my mind, after replacing the barrettes and bracelet, and wiping the area down of my fingerprints, which Cory told me didn't matter because they'd never find who the prints belonged to, I pushed the door open. I didn't bother to completely close it when I left. It wasn't worth the risk. I slinked along the wall until I bumped into a wall hanging. It swished to the side.

My hand flew up to the painting and held it still, my heart pounding. The Ramirezes stirred in the bed. I hoped my suit camouflaged me against the wall. I thought I felt eyes search the room. I could see the outline of one of the two sit up and look around.

Please don't turn on the light. Please. I did not breathe, and yet I didn't seem to miss the air. I was too panicked. I heard, more than saw, the person lie back down and snuggle into the covers. I stood there, unmoving for a good fifteen minutes. My arm screamed from holding the picture, and I had opened my mouth to let air in and out without a sound. After another fifteen minutes, I heard a second set of even breaths.

I carefully turned my body and faced the wall so I could fix the picture. I pulled out on the picture so it wouldn't scrape against the wall and made it hang straight. I made my way, like a cat, silently, to the door and, glad I hadn't shut it, slipped out. Inch by inch, I pulled the door shut. Turning around, the big grin on my face disappeared in a flash. I looked into Sophia's big black, questioning eyes. She was near the stairs. What had she seen? Had she seen me shut the door so carefully? Then I realized it didn't matter. I had the black cat suit on. It was obvious I was up to no good.

She moved toward me, brows pulled together, sleep no longer lingering in her face.

I stood, frozen, caught. Every muscle in my body tensed.

"What are you doing?" she asked, still questioning, but a hint of anger lacing her words.

I had nothing. She was still coming at me, and I was frozen. I couldn't explain my way out of this. Nothing came to me. Nothing. I armed myself with the truth. I would tell her about her dad. Surely she'd forgive me and possibly join me against her dad, help me.

"What were you doing in my parents' room, Ari?" Her voice was hard, insistent and loud, now. Her eyes held a fierce look of betrayal and anger.

I didn't have time to explain. She was only ten feet from me, and she yelled out, "Guards. Guards," as she picked up speed to reach me. I ran too, straight at her. It was the only choice I had. I had to silence her. I could not reason with her at the moment. My escape route was through her. I couldn't go back. I chided myself for not having multiple exit strategies. Module 12.2 specifically told me to, and I hadn't bothered.

I barreled into her chest with my shoulder, knocking her down. She cried out as she flew back, hitting her head on the banister. She didn't move, and several things happened at once. I heard feet running, pounding in my direction. I heard her parents' door click open, and I heard a quiet buzz turn into a loud insistent buzz. The house lit up. And I took off for Sophia's room.

I had to make it to the fence before it was electrified. I

pushed my way through the screen on the window in Sophia's room and after grabbing the edge of the roof and hanging, I let myself drop. The fact that only a thin layer of polyester fabric came between me and the rugged terrain was not a happy discovery. I had been overconfident. I should have thought about shoes. I should have thought about emergency exit strategies. I'd have to make it work. I made it to the fence before the outdoor lights lit everything up, but I didn't beat the electrification of the fence. I heard the almost imperceptible low buzz as I neared it. I would have to short it out or find a way over, and fast.

The outside lights flashed on, illuminating almost every nook and cranny of the ranch. Looking up, I noticed several trees that might act as adequate jumping platforms. I didn't have the time to consider them more than this. My heart pounded hard on my ribs. I ran to the first one and climbed faster than I ever had before to the highest, sturdiest branch I could get to. Once up there, it seemed the tree branch I stood on was too far away to allow me to jump the fence. Yelling and screaming voices filled the air.

Then I heard the dogs. Lots of them, barking like crazy. Were they sending out dogs? I couldn't let my fear overtake me. I had to believe I would make it across. If it was too far, I had to have faith, that whatever higher power brought this life to me would help me succeed. I would be saving a lot of lives if I succeeded today. I took a leaping jump, eyes wide, believing. My height made the jump successful. It seemed the barks of the dogs had reached me as I touched ground, tucked, and rolled. The rolling part didn't go very well, and I hit my shoulder hard into a stump. When I stood, it seared with pain. I couldn't focus on it, though, and I didn't glance back to see if they had reached the fence. I just ran with my arm tucked tight to my chest.

I made it to the trees and headed for the extraction point. Some of my strength had been sapped by fear, but I pushed hard, telling myself this was life or death. I checked the time. I was an hour early. I hit the emergency extraction button on my watch, wondering if they would be able to extract me early—hoping they could. I barreled through the trees, ignoring the things poking at and cutting my feet.

The barking dogs seemed to be closing in on me. They must have opened the gate. I ran all the harder, knowing I still had a mile and a half to reach the extraction point. I pushed the fear that I would never make it deep down and focused on being positive. I needed all good things to come my way. I was comforted by the thought that trucks could not traverse this thickly forested area and yet, I still had to outrun or outwit the dogs. If I didn't, I would surely fail my mission, and worse, be mauled to death by the dogs.

I thought of Melanie and Reese and seeing them again. Melanie as President and Reese sitting in the swing on the porch of our home. The future, the life I had imagined for myself was at stake. I also thought of my parents having to mourn for me once again. I ran harder.

I thought I heard the light hum of a vehicle. No. Impossible. No car or truck could make it to me, the trees were too close together, but then I realized the sound was not of cars or trucks, but of four wheelers. On those, they could catch me. Would it be the dogs or the motorized vehicles that got to me first? I thought about DC and killing that man and how the fear of his death made me run harder and faster.

I could hear the dogs' feet now.

I was in trouble. I'd made it to the half mile mark. I still had a mile to go. I had failed. I would die. I grabbed a low tree branch and hoisted myself up, ignoring the pain in my shoulder. As I did, one of the dogs snagged the torn black body suit footie, scraping my leg and foot as he did. I held onto the branch for dear life and cried out. Luckily, the fabric tore under the strain of his sharp teeth, and I clambered higher.

I had been treed, just like a raccoon. When the men arrived on the ATVs, they would shoot me, and I would fall to the ground dead, just like the raccoon. The dogs' barks, insistent and menacing, filled the air. I couldn't hear the rumble of ATVs over the din. I counted the dogs. Eight surrounded the tree, hackles lifted, teeth bared, saliva dripping to the ground.

Then a dog yelped and fell. I was so shocked, I slipped and fell from the branch I was on and hung there, dangling. Another and then another did the same thing. Each of the eight fell to the ground after yelping or crying out and did not move.

I scanned the area and noticed slight movement about 100 yards ahead of me. Behind me, the insistent hum of ATVs grew. The movement ahead of me intensified, more bodies seemed to move forward, rifles in their hands, pointed toward me. I could see four ATVs as well as their riders now, their eyes focused on me in the tree. I knew the ATV men were enemies, but who were these men who had shot the dogs and had their guns trained on me? They must be friends. Division 57. I didn't have time to jump down and join them before Diego's men would be on top of me.

I looked back, and the men on the ATVs started falling, too. The men advancing on me had not been pointing the guns at me, but at the men on the ATVs. Just like the dogs—they fell to the ground, silent. Once the ATVs lost their riders, they halted. An almost-silence filled the forest. Somewhere in the far distance I could hear the hum of motors. More ATVs? The noise got louder. I could hear men yelling and the hum of wheels turning increased.

Several men with rifles waved me to them. They had to be Division 57. They had killed the dogs and the men who came after me. I climbed down and ran in their direction, holding my hurt arm close to my chest, wondering if my extraction team had acted on my need for an emergency extraction. Where would I find Claire? One of the men pointed for me to go up a hill behind him. Once on top, a parked camo SUV came into view just as shots rang out once again. The door to the SUV opened and an arm waved me in.

Chapter Thirty-Two

This was all wrong. I was supposed to be extracted in something that flew out of here. How did they expect to get me out of here in a truck? How did they get here? The sounds of firing intensified, and a shot grazed my arm. It pushed me toward the open door of the car. I slipped inside. The door shut behind me, and the car started to move. Relief eluded me. As the SUV bounced over the rugged terrain, a silent scream of panic rose in my chest. John sat in the front passenger seat. Alex sat next to me, and his mom was driving. Alex reached across me and secured my seatbelt.

"What's going on?" I whispered, feeling I'd been transported to another dimension, my cut stinging terribly.

Alex moved close to me. "We were sent to get the jump drive from you."

"*You* were sent?" I asked. Acid filled my lungs. They were Division 57? No way.

"My parents have been training me. They are free assets now. Contract labor if you will."

Something wasn't right. This whole thing wasn't right. I knew it in my soul. Claire would have contacted me if the plans had changed. But I didn't have my phone for her to contact me. It would have been nice to have Bresen

Academy's 'watch' right now.

As if reading my mind, he said, "Claire wasn't able to get the message to you."

They knew Claire?

"They discovered that what this Ramirez guy was doing was more complicated and dangerous than they'd initially thought and wanted to make sure they got all the intel," Alex said.

"What are you saying? That Claire didn't believe I could do it?"

"No. They believed you could, but things happen on missions. Things like getting treed." He smiled at me, and I glared at him.

We hit a huge bump, and I cried out as the seatbelt tugged on my hurt arm.

His dad was booting up a laptop as we spoke.

"My dad is the back-up plan. If for some reason you weren't able to get the intel, he was to go in and retrieve it."

"I did get it, though," I said.

"Awesome," he said. "I knew you could. Where is it? My dad will load it up to verify it's there and then you can take it to your extraction point." He wrapped his arms around me as the car drove behind an area of dense trees. His scruff brushed my cheek. "I've missed you," he whispered. I pulled away.

None of this made any sense. Why would his dad bring him on an assignment I was on and what was he doing on a mission? The only reason I could think of was that his dad thought it would be the only way to get me to comply. Heat rose in my chest. This was not right.

John turned to me, his laptop completely booted up. "Give me the jump drive." His hand moved toward me, palm up.

What if he was sent by Ramirez to retrieve his information? What if he was sent to destroy it? What if he was taking this information to someone even more evil than Ramirez?

"I can either take it from you, which might cause a scene, or you can willingly give it to me." Could I compromise one of the jump drives and be okay? The bracelet was the more obvious of the two. Was I about to fail my mission?

I didn't move.

"It's okay Christy. It's just my dad." Alex squeezed me tight, trying to reassure me, I'm sure. My arm ached. A terrible dark fog filled me.

"Look, Christy," John said. "I just need to see if you really got the information. That's it. I will give it back to you once I've checked. We're supposed to deliver you to the extraction point in about thirty minutes."

That gave me some comfort. But was he just saying that to get the drive, and he wouldn't follow through? My chest seized as I handed him the bracelet. Even if he did destroy it, I had a back-up copy. How could I refuse him and get away with it? The heavy feeling lingered. The car stopped, but Alex's mom kept the engine running.

Alex opened the car door and helped me out. I kept one eye on his dad.

"How much do you know about this mission, Alex?" I asked, pulling him into the bushes away from the truck.

"Everything, I think." His smile was still so gorgeous.

"Did you read the mission papers, then?"

"No. But my dad told me everything. He really likes being on his own. He likes not having to answer to anybody."

I bet he did. "He does, however, have to answer to the

people who hire him, doesn't he?"

"Of course," he said, grazing his lips over mine.

"Don't, Alex." I needed to think. "Did you see anything that told you who hired him?"

"Sure. But it won't mean anything to you, just like it meant nothing to me. It's just a name. Mack M."

I tossed the name about in my mind. Who was Mack M?

Alex pulled me into a hug, and I resisted and said, "Ouch." I cradled my arm.

He squinted his eyes. "I'm sorry. Is your arm hurt?"

"Look Alex, I'm all stinky and dirty, and I'm in a foul mood." I wanted to tell him I was over him, and we would never be together, but I needed him a little longer to be able to get the information I needed.

"No worries, I think you smell amazing. You don't look dirty to me, and I know exactly what you need to change that mood of yours." He pulled on me again and put a juicy kiss on my lips. A hungry kiss. I tried not to be completely repulsed. I pulled back. I did not want this. He had no idea what had happened since I saw him last.

Then I heard his dad, as if it were a whisper on the wind, say to his mom, "I found it. Deleting it now."

What was he deleting? He wasn't supposed to delete anything.

"Marie won't have anything to worry about now and we are free. We owe her nothing."

Marie. Mack Marie? Marie Mack? Suddenly it came together—Marie Mackley. The coordinator of the Bresen Academy had reason to erase something from that drive? What business had she conducted with Diego Ramirez that caused her to go after this information and get rid of it? I thought of the clips in my hair that were doubling as a jump drive, glad I'd made a copy. We would find out soon enough what she was trying to hide.

"Done," he said. "She was smart to get them to send Christy on this mission. She is too naïve to think Alex would be a part of a cover-up. Or us for that matter." How had I heard him? Had Alex heard, too? He didn't appear to have.

My blood turned to fire. I wanted to scratch his eyes out and sock him in the mouth. How dare he underestimate me? I would contain myself and get the last laugh.

"Did you hear that?"

"Hear what?" he asked.

John climbed out of the car. Only then did I let Alex kiss me. It would serve two purposes. Number one, give the impression that we were busy and not listening in on their conversation, and number two, irritate John.

His footsteps neared, and I kissed Alex more urgently.

"Alright," John said.

We turned and looked at him, and he handed Alex the bracelet. Alex grabbed one of my hands and put the bracelet jump drive back on my wrist, rubbing my skin softly when he finished.

"You better get going," John said. "You have a meeting with a chopper in about ten minutes. Run this direction, and you'll have no problem making it." He pointed. "My men have cleared the area for you. It should be safe." His lip twitched when he said it. What was up with that?

I turned my back to him and whispered into Alex's ear that I had missed him and would be thinking about him every moment—a total lie—but I needed a ruse to check the GPS on my watch. The path to the extraction point sat on the screen. John really thought I was stupid. He had me running in the exact wrong direction. Did he want me to die? Because that is exactly what would happen if I headed back to the ranch.

Alex couldn't know about his evil dad. The way he held me, his soft, tender words and kisses proved his loyalty to me. Better yet, there was no betrayal in his eyes. He was a pawn in his dad's hands. John did tell me he'd kill me if I didn't reject Alex when I saw him again. Now I had accepted him with open arms twice. Once in Florida and now, here, in Spain.

"Okay," I said pulling away from Alex getting ready to run. But he pulled me back to him. "Can we have a minute of privacy?" He said to his dad.

His dad went back to the SUV. Alex's eyes searched mine. "I love you, Christy," he said. "And I want you to know that I have been completely faithful to you." Then he kissed me like only Alex could and if I'd been the old Christy, I'd have had to focus not to faint. He wrapped me into another comforting hug and then pulled back. "Give me your cell number."

I gave it to him before I could think better of it. I thought about Reese and the future I planned to have with him, glad that no connection resurfaced with Alex. I whispered in Alex's ear, "Be careful Alex. Watch your dad. He's a slippery one."

I waved to him, noting the stunned look on his face as I jogged in the direction John had told me to go. He turned to look at his dad before I was out of sight.

Once up over the rise, I turned and circled around to run the other direction. I heard the SUV take off, away from me. Bark flew into my face. Someone was shooting at me. They must be using a silencer. Instinctively, I ducked and started zigzagging through the trees trying to be an unhittable target. From the pauses between shots, I could tell it was one man shooting at me. A sniper of some sort. John had set me up to die. This couldn't be simply because I embraced his son, could it? Or were his instructions from Ms. Mackley to take me out after he copied and then altered the file?

I tore at the watch, removing it from my wrist and throwing it to the ground. If she was tracking me, it had to end now.

I had half a mile to go, and my shoulder and feet were burning. I should have asked John for a pair of shoes. When I reached the quarter mile mark, the shots zinging past me and into trees picked up. Did someone else join this sniper? Was it John?

My running became more erratic. I ducked, zigged, zagged and moved from tree to tree. Suddenly, searing pain raged through my leg. I'd never been shot before, but I knew instantly that's what had happened. Fire raced up my calf and into my thigh. I fell. Shots zinged all around me, so I rolled behind a tree, propping myself up. I prayed a fervent prayer. My leg was bleeding like crazy so I tore the arm of my black suit and tied it tightly around my wound, biting my shoulder to stifle the cry I wanted so badly to let out. I heard a twig crack, and I froze.

Whoever was after me was close. I took a deep breath in and prepared to strike. If that twig hadn't snapped, I never would have known anyone was there. Pain clouded my senses. I pulled into myself, feeling outside of me, feeling for another presence, blocking out anything but that. I honed into it and waited. He was not far. I was ready.

I sensed the barrel of the gun inching around the trunk of the tree. I pictured it in my mind and when it showed itself, I grabbed it, jamming it into the ground and using it to help me springboard into a kick to the assassin's Adam's apple. He flew back into a tree, let go of the rifle and grabbed at his neck, gasping for air. My other leg screamed out in pain as I fell to the ground, but I gritted my teeth and stood once more, grabbing the rifle and jamming the butt into his temple. He slumped to the side and a bullet grazed my neck, lodging in the tree beside me.

Then I heard regular shots ring out. A lot of them. I just needed to get to the valley to the chopper. I couldn't escape this many people shooting at me. Not injured like I was. I lay flat on the ground and pulled leaves up over me, hoping to hide. I was growing foggy with the loss of blood, the panic and fear. I didn't hear or sense anyone approaching, but all of a sudden someone grabbed me under my arms and pulled me in the direction of safety, his lips brushing my ear as he said, "You hang in there, Christy. Don't die on me now."

Chapter Thirty-Three

I cried out, my shoulder killing me. I dug my foot in the ground. "Stop. Please."

He pulled me behind a tree and sat me up. I lunged for him, ignoring the pain in my arm and pulling him to me with all I had. "Jeremy! You're here!"

He winked. "We made a connection, you and I, and I'm not about to let that disappear." He leaned his forehead on mine and said, "Now, we've got to go. Someone is serious about this being your last day."

"Can you help me walk? I think I broke my arm or something, and I was shot in my leg."

"That's my girl," he said, pulling me to my feet, careful not to touch my hurt arm. He wrapped one arm around my waist, and I put my good one around his shoulder. I hopped, while he ran, dragging me along. The pain was outrageous, but with Jeremy there, I could do it. How many people were sent for this little extraction? Shots rang around us, none of them aimed at us, but at the sniper, giving us cover long enough to get into the military chopper and have it lift off.

Jeremy put headphones over my ears after getting me safely in the chopper and donned some himself.

"She needs you, Rocky," Jeremy called into the com.

A tall, thin man in army fatigues hurried over to me.

"Possible broken arm and shot in the calf."

I assumed this man, Rocky, was a doctor. Then I heard Claire's voice, loud and clear through the headset. "Could you grab the jump drives from her, Jeremy?"

"Sure thing, Claire," he said.

"Claire," I said, huffing from the pain, "John was here." I took a breath and undid the bracelet to give to him. After he handed that over, I motioned for him to grab the drives from my hair.

"You want me to get the other one, too?"

"Please."

The doctor was examining my arm.

"John who?" Claire asked.

"John, my trainer John."

"What was he doing here?" she asked. I could see her inserting the bracelet drive into her lap top.

"He took that drive you just put in the computer from me and then erased some files."

"Why would he do that?"

"Your arm's just dislocated, not broken," Dr. Rocky said. "Take a deep breath. This is going to hurt."

"Okay," I said, bracing for the pain. He used his knee on my chest and executed a steady, sharp pull. I screamed. It popped. There was a moment of intense pain and then immediately after the pop, utter relief.

I filled them in on everything that happened with John, while the doc cleaned my leg wound.

"I did hear that they left the FBI, but this? Going against what's humane and good?"

"I wonder why John owed her. He sure sounded happy to be out of Ms. Mackley's debt."

The pinches of the needle filling my calf with anesthetic were annoying. Rocky pulled the bullet out. After sound disinfecting, he bandaged it up and smiled at me. He then tended to my cut feet.

"Well, let's see if you're right, Ari. I'm uploading the second file now. Let's see what he removed from the first one."

"Maybe search for Mack M."

Rocky finished bandaging my feet. "As good as new," he said.

I didn't feel a thing, so he was spot on. I nodded and smiled. "You're the best, Rocky. Amazing. Thank you."

I pushed up against the chopper's inside wall. Jeremy put a pillow behind my back.

"Thanks, Jeremy."

"Oh my, oh my, Ms. Mackley, you have been one busy bee," Claire said, staring intently at the computer screen.

I moved over to her. "Can I see?" I felt Jeremy move right behind me.

"It appears Ms. Mackley has been using Diego Ramirez' services for a while now. She ordered three hits. One of which was her predecessor. Remember how his car blew up when he was taking his parrot to the vet?" she said to the other agents. "Apparently, that bird had a fake eye from the ranch. Diego's handiwork. Apparently, he also inserted a bomb."

Shock hit me like a lightning strike. How could Ms. Mackley betray me like this? The feeling of betrayal was quickly washed away as a sense of triumph at getting the information from Diego and being successful on the mission overtook me. He would now fall.

"What's going to happen to Sophia and her parents?" I asked.

"Does it matter, Ari?" Claire asked.

"Of course it does." I threw my hands in the air.

"I can't say for certain, but I'm assuming Diego is long gone after having given his goons orders to do damage control by getting rid of all the evidence. And his wife and child are there wondering what happened and where he's gone. Unless we were lucky enough to snag him.

"The ground crew leaders just got a copy of what's on these drives in order to collect any other evidence they can find as well as destroy all the dangerous materials there."

"What will happen to the animals?"

"Any that are deemed safe will go under the knife to remove the chemical tubes inserted into them. Others will have to be disposed of."

I shuddered. The animals had been violated. They would never be the same.

"What about Sophia?"

"She will not lead the life she has been living. We will confiscate all the funds we can get our hands on," Claire continued.

"But she's innocent. She doesn't deserve to lose it all."

"Innocent? Innocent? Are you sure about that? Did she stick up for you when you were fleeing for your life? Your friend. The one you were willing to give your life up for by not going to the extraction point?"

I twisted the stud in my eyebrow, thinking about how Sophia had exposed me.

"I didn't think so. When we started to see the scope of this thing, we thought it might be good to track you since this was your first mission. That jammer you wore was also a tracker. It turned out to be a good thing we did since you didn't get out with your phone. It helped keep you safe and the information safe."

"You should have seen the look of betrayal on her face when Ms. Mackley saw me."

"Get used to it. In this business you are forced to get close to people. Sometimes, you end up not only having to betray them, but also maybe even having to kill them. I tried to make it easier for you not to get attached to Sophia by not clueing you or Cory and Tracey about her rape and attempted suicide, but you found it out anyway. Are you sure you're cut out for this?"

Jeremy looked at me thoughtfully, and that warm feeling I'd felt when I'd decided to become a spy fell over me and filled me once again.

"Yes," I said. "I'm sure." I would do everything in my power not to kill, but if it was for the greater good or to save myself or another person, I could kill and feel justified.

"What about their house in Prague?" I asked.

"Agents are there right now, cleaning it," Jeremy said.

"Too bad we can't stick around to see the explosion from the air," the pilot said.

"Explosion?"

"As soon as all the chemicals and viable animals are cleaned out, there will be an explosion."

"You're blowing the place up?" I said. Every dark emotion I'd ever felt surfaced. My whole body trembled.

"The place is evil," Jeremy said. "We need to rid the world of it."

It was true, but it still seemed crazy.

"You do realize you'll be the youngest spy of Division 57, ever," Claire said. "No seventeen-year-old has ever gotten near us. I have to say, you impressed me in so many different ways. I know you thought you failed on some

things, but I'm here to tell you, you shined. I for one am
happy to have you on board. Welcome to Division 57."

"You can be on my team anytime. You're a fast thinker
and capable of way more than I had imagined," Rocky
said.

Jeremy held out his hand to me to join him in the back
seats. I started to slide on my rump and he jumped over to
me, picked me up in his arms and set me down in the seat.

"Are you going to tell me what you're doing here,
now?" I looked him square in the eyes.

"When I heard you were put on this mission, I had to
come back," Jeremy said.

"First of all, how did you hear I was put on this mission
and secondly, what do you mean, come back?"

"Part of my job as an asset of Division 57 is that I
double as an FBI agent," Jeremy admitted.

"You're a double agent?"

"Yes," he said. "The FBI has no idea I'm a Division 57
asset."

"How? Aren't both government agencies?" I said.

"Yes, but the two don't talk. This is the way Division
57 keeps up on the FBI. I'm sorry about what happened to
you. Ms. Mackley never should have sent you. She was
just using you. I don't know what I would have done had
you died out there."

"I chose this, Jeremy. I want to be a spy."

"Really? Are you sure, Christy? It's a hard life. You
can still back out."

I thought about the new me, the one I'd created, choice
by choice with a little help from above. Comfort washed
over me. Even though I didn't have all the skills I wanted
to have to be the best ever, I knew someone would be
cheering me on, making up for what I lacked because I was

doing what I knew I should. "I'm sure. It's the right thing for me."

"I want to send you on a plane back home now that the danger has passed with the terrorists, but my instincts tell me you're right. The spy world needs you." He gave a pressed smile.

I smiled back and laid my head on his shoulder. My desires, my thoughts, they were powerful. I was me now because I had the desire to be more than I was. All because almost three years ago I voiced a prayer to be more than I was.

"I brought you something."

"What?"

He handed me a manila envelope. I opened it. Inside was a recent picture of my family, minus me, and a picture of my family with me in it. At the bottom were pieces of notebook paper that turned out to be letters from each member of my family.

The tears came freely. I buried my face in his shirt.

"I wanted you to have these to help remember who you are. This life can get confusing. I don't want you to get lost."

After a good cry, I asked, "So will I get to work with you?"

He chuckled. "Actually, I'm your handler. Someone's gotta keep you safe." He winked.

"Serious?"

"Serious!"

"How did you arrange this?"

"I've got connections."

"I'm glad, because there is no one that makes me feel safer or more secure than you."

Excitement pounded in my temples.

"What if you hate me as your handler?"

"Never." I pulled out the letters and read each one several times. "This is the best gift I've ever been given."

"And don't you forget it."

We laughed and talked until I couldn't keep my eyes open any longer. I'm not sure when, but I fell asleep.

I woke when we touched down at Division 57's European headquarters. I limped out onto the roof of the building, ready to conquer my future. A woman met me there and gave me some crutches. I didn't get to look around before we went through a door and down some steps to an elevator. Using stairs on crutches is not easy. Jeremy put a key into the keypad, and the elevator moved swiftly down. When it stopped, we got out and took a long corridor that seemed to be a dead end until Jeremy slid a panel to the side and punched some numbers into a keypad. After a retinal scan, the wall opened up to reveal a glass door.

Claire put her hand on a scanner, and the glass door opened up. She walked into the room and lifted her arms in the air and stood with her feet shoulder width apart. A body scan? Nothing appeared to happen, but a few seconds later, the glass door on the opposite side opened up and she walked out, turned to the right and disappeared down the hall.

Jeremy then punched something into the keypad and looked through the glass. An older gentleman with closely cropped, gray hair and a stern looking face punched in some code on that side of the walkway, then Jeremy put in another code on our side. The door opened, and Jeremy told me to go into the middle of the room and stand like Claire had. The door closed behind me. A few seconds later, the other door opened, and I walked toward the man on the other side. He held out his hand to me, and I took it.

"Welcome to Division 57. I'm Director Hughes." By the time he'd introduced himself, Jeremy was through the body scan and the door whooshed open behind me. There was only one way to go and that was right. I followed them down a hall and into a cavernous room filled with cubicles and people sitting at desks inside them working on computers. People were bustling about, giving and taking papers and files.

We continued through the ordered chaos to a large meeting room with a large shiny wooden rectangular table in the middle. Computers had been placed at three spots, one of which Claire already occupied. Jeremy sat next to Claire, and I sat next to him in the soft leather chair. Director Hughes stood at one end in front of a big screen. An aerial view of the Ramirez ranch played on it. I thought it might just be a still shot, but it wasn't. Looking closely, I could see people moving about like little ants going from the buildings to the several semis parked where the corrals and containers used to be. Director Hughes used a remote to zoom in, and I noticed they were sorting the animals and moving them into the semi-trailers.

"Thanks to you, Christy, most of these animals will be saved. The intel you provided Claire, which she uploaded to our computer, indicates that Ramirez' use of animals as assassins was escalating. He had perfected his antidote for the DNA-targeting biological weapon and had also created way of using the animals to disperse it. Unlike the bombs, this method of assassination would not be traceable because the animal would not be hurt when the poison was delivered. Good work, Christy." His voice was one that you thought should be heard on a radio, deep and interesting.

"Claire, any word on how Ms. Mackley was tracking Christy?"

"No sir. We—"

"I think I know the answer to that," I interrupted. "My watch. Ms. Mackley gave me a watch with a GPS function when I left."

"Where is this watch now?" the director asked.

"I threw it to the ground in the forest in Spain after I figured out she was tracking me. I got rid of it right after I met with John."

"Claire, we need that watch. Send a message to the clean-up crew to find it," Director Hughes said.

"No problem, Sir," Claire said. "Consider it done."

"On another note," he continued. "Jeremy, I'm sending you to collect Ms. Mackley this evening. We need to take her in custody as soon as possible. Get her once she's at her home on the grounds. Two a.m. seems like a fitting time. Discretion on this one. We don't want the students to know what happened. Once you have her, inform Eric. He'll take care of everything."

"Is there anyway Christy could be a part of the removal team? It seems only fair after what Ms. Mackley put her through." Jeremy tapped his finger on the table.

My heart raced at the idea. Would I actually be allowed to go back to Bresen and face her?

"You're the lead. That decision is yours."

"Thank you, Sir."

"Sir," I spoke up. "Sophia. Is there any way we can help her and her mom? It seems unfair that they be punished for Diego's crimes."

"I know you made a connection with Sophia, and she is an innocent in all of this. I'll see what we can work out. Maybe if she helps us find her dad we'll be able to do something with Witness Protection. Please don't 'connect' in the future."

"Thank you!" I said, wanting to pop up and hug him. "Will psychological help be available for her, too?"

"That can be arranged, if she'll accept it."

"Thanks, again," I said.

Jeremy nudged me under the table. I looked at him. He mouthed, Sir!"

I blurted, "Sir," just a bit too late.

"We are excited to have you as a part of our team, Christy. I realize this will be quite the adjustment for you, but we do need you to be up to speed as quickly as possible."

"Yes, sir," I said.

"Jeremy can show you a place to clean up and rest up before the op tonight."

I nodded.

"Get to work."

With that, we all stood, and I grabbed my crutches and hobbled behind everyone as we left the conference room. Jeremy took me to a small room with what looked like a comfy couch and a bathroom with a shower. Jeremy left to finish the final touches on arresting Ms. Mackley. I eagerly showered, removed all my facial jewelry and earrings and brushed my hair down on my head. I didn't want the spikes anymore. It was a pixie style for me.

As I tried to fall asleep, I couldn't get Sophia out of my mind. I was worried sick about her. I had to find a way to apologize. I looked at the phone Jeremy left for me. I thought about texting her, but that didn't seem right. I would call her. I knew I shouldn't, but I had to. Just as I expected, she didn't answer, but I left a message. I hope she'd listen to it.

"Sophia." Just saying her name made me choke up. "It's me, Ari." I squeezed out of my ever narrowing windpipe. I closed my eyes to help me not cry. I took a deep breath in. "I'm so sorry. I never knew I'd connect with you like I did. I miss you already." I took in a fast jagged crying breath. "You probably hate my guts, and I don't blame you. Why'd you have to be so cool? I wish things had been different. You were a true friend. I don't have many of those." I wiped my nose on my sleeve. I started to sob. I hoped I could get out the rest. "I wish we had found each other under other circumstances because I'm sure we would be life-long friends. Please forgive me." I pushed *end* and cried myself to sleep, my only consolation found in the director's promise to help her and her mom.

Chapter Thirty-Four

We landed on the helipad at the Academy at two a.m. sharp. I clasped my hands together the second my feet hit the ground. I took several deep breaths as I hobbled out from under the chopper's wind-stirring blades with my crutches. Jeremy grabbed my hand with his and said, "You can do this. You are powerful and in control." I nodded. He let go of my hand, and I let it drop to my side, following closely behind the eight heavily armed agents who entered the home first.

When I entered the room, two agents held her arms, and her hands were cuffed behind her. I was surprised to see her in a pastel colored muumuu. Her face was unreadable. She hadn't spoken the whole time. I walked up to her and stood only a foot away, looking into her goose-eyes.

"I just want you to know, Mackley, that I'm not naïve, and I'm not stupid. I beat you. As you can see, I'm not dead. You don't control me or my future. You were right about one thing. I will be the most amazing spy ever. Enjoy lock-up." I turned and went outside. Relief and triumph filled me. I sat on a bench under a tree in the open field, staring at the Academy.

I felt someone approach from behind. "Thinking of Rick?" It was Jeremy. He walked to the side of me, looked me in the face and then looked at the Academy, too.

"Yep. He's so close." I said, unable to hide the longing in my voice.

"Would you like to see him?"

I pressed my lips together and nodded, knowing it was an impossibility.

"I might be able to bring him out."

"Don't tease me like that, Jeremy!"

"No teasing. Give me a few minutes. But just so you know. If I am able to bring him out, you'll only have ten minutes tops with him. Do you think it would be worth it?"

I smiled. One minute would be worth it. I nodded eagerly.

"I'll see what I can do." He walked toward the front of the building, headed for the lobby.

I paced, limping nervously for several minutes, I brushed my hand over my smooth, short hair and slipped my fingers across my now metal-less face. He'd said he liked the jewelry. Why had I removed it? I turned away from the main building and looked out over the dark grounds.

In my mind I reasoned it would hurt less if Jeremy was unable to get Reese, or rather, Rick if I didn't watch. I didn't have to call him Reese anymore and he could call me Christy. It seemed like hours had passed when I turned back around, unable to handle the suspense any longer. I watched Jeremy come out a back door of the Academy. Rick was on his heels. Without a second passing, I ran to him, as fast as I could with my crutches. He ran, too. Out of the corner of my eye, I saw Jeremy hold up ten fingers. We had ten minutes.

When we reached each other, I dropped the crutches and fell into his arms. He spun me around, and we laughed.

I didn't care that my leg hurt. Then I cried. I touched his face, breathed him in. We pressed our bodies closer still. When my feet touched the ground, his fingers found my tears and brushed them away.

"Don't cry," he whispered. "Don't cry."

"I just can't believe I'm here with you." The impact of everything that had happened in the last few months hit me hard.

"I guess the mission was successful?" he said.

"I guess. It was horrible and exhilarating at the same time. I wish I could tell you all about it."

He raised my chin with his hand. "I'm so glad you're safe. I've been working hard, Christy. Working hard to get back to you as soon as I can. Extra studying, working out—"

I put my fingers on his lips. They were soft and giving. I moved my fingers down his neck. He kissed me. It was a toe curling, heart-stopping, mind-blowing kiss. I melted into him.

Too soon, I heard a whistle. We looked in the direction it came. Jeremy stood at the edge of the building.

There was another sweet, soft kiss and a lingering embrace.

"I'll be waiting for you, Rick, for as long as it takes."

As I pulled away, Rick said, "It doesn't count."

"What doesn't count?" I asked, cocking my head to the side and moving backwards, step by step.

"This. Right now. It doesn't count as our monthly contact."

I smiled and blew him a kiss. "Of course, it doesn't." I climbed into the chopper, my hair blowing all over, and I felt refreshed, alive. My heart burned with joy. I was lucky to have a guy like Rick rooting for me and loving me. And

I was doubly lucky to be doing what I loved and was good at: spying.

I was a spy.

Acknowledgments

MANY THANKS
To my in-person critique group, Jenny, Susan, Angela, and Cindy, for the hours and hours you spend on my behalf. You are amazing.

To my online critique group, Kathleen, Karyn, and Shelly, for pressing through the second edit and coming out brilliantly.

To my fantastic betas, Donna, Kathleen, Liz, Nicole, Michelle, Elizabeth, and Amanda who found what I missed.

To Heather Justesen for her quick formatting.

To my editor, Charity West, whose piercing eye doesn't miss a thing and knows just what the story needs.

And to my husband for enduring the last year without his wife and my children for working hard for their absent mom. Only one to go.

Big hugs!

Visit Cindy on her blog:
cindymhogan.blogspot.com

For Watched series trivia, sneak peeks, events in your area, contests, and fun fan interaction, like the official Watched series Facebook page:
Watched-the book

Follow Cindy M. Hogan on Twitter:
Watched1

Pick up book one and two in the Watched series:

Watched
Protected

About the Author

Cindy M. Hogan is the bestselling author of *Watched* and *Protected*. She graduated in secondary education at BYU and enjoys spending time with unpredictable teenagers. More than anything, she loves the time she has with her own teenager daughters and wishes she could freeze them at this fun age. If she's not reading or writing, you'll find her snuggled up to the love of her life watching a great movie or planning their next party. To learn more about the author and other books she has written, visit her at cindymhogan@blogspot.com.